PENGUIN BOOKS

RECONNAISSANCE

Kapka Kassabova was born in Sofia, Bulgaria, in 1973. Kapka and her family moved to England when she was 16 — and two years later they settled in New Zealand where she is now a full-time writer. Her first book of poetry, *All roads lead to the sea*, won the 1998 Montana Award for Best First Book of Poetry, and she has recently published a second volume of poetry. She lives in Wellington.

I wish to thank Boris Popoff, Liliana Guermanoff, Diana Kassabova, Nikolay Tchervenakov, Vladimir Lubenov, Laurence Fearnley and Nick Ascroft.

All characters and events are purely fictional. Place names do not always correspond to geographical reality. However, the political events set in Bulgaria are true.

RECONNAISSANCE

~

Kapka Kassabova

PENGUIN BOOKS

PENGUIN BOOKS

Penguin Books (NZ) Ltd, cnr Airborne and Rosedale Roads, Albany,
Auckland 1310, New Zealand
Penguin Books Ltd, 27 Wrights Lane, London W8 5TZ, England
Penguin USA, 375 Hudson Street, New York, NY 10014, United States
Penguin Books Australia Ltd, 487 Maroondah Highway, Ringwood, Australia 3134
Penguin Books Canada Ltd, 10 Alcorn Avenue, Toronto, Ontario, Canada M4V 3B2
Penguin Books (South Africa) Pty Ltd, 4 Pallinghurst Road, Parktown,
Johannesburg 2193, South Africa

Penguin Books Ltd, Registered Offices: Harmondsworth, Middlesex, England

First published by Penguin Books (NZ) Ltd, 1999

5 7 9 10 8 6 4

The assistance of Creative New Zealand towards the publication of this book
is gratefully acknowledged by the publisher.

Designed by Seven
Typeset by Mary Egan of Egan Reid Ltd
Printed in Australia by Australian Print Group, Maryborough

*This book is dedicated to those
who know exile.*

Forgetting is one of the symptoms of death. Without memory we cease to be human beings.

Ivan Klíma, *Waiting for the dark, waiting for the light*

The more we are dispossessed, the more intense our appetites and our illusions become . . . I even discern some relation between misfortune and megalomania.

E.M. Cioran, *The Advantages of Exile*

PART ONE

CHAPTER ONE

It is on this side of town, on this side of the Black Sea, on this side of the Equator, on this side of time.

The Penguin of Balchik

It is on this side of town, on this side of the Black Sea, on this side of the Equator, on this side of time.

Nadejda, hair cropped and streaked with sun-struck copper, limbs brown and boyish, sits on top of a lime hill. She is practising a perfect series of marble ball knocks. They are attached to strings with two small hooks for the fingers, index and middle finger usually, and they are the latest in entertainment, after the Rubik cube. The sound is satisfyingly loud and crisp, the way all sounds should be. Nadejda hopes it can be heard and appreciated from the large veranda on the opposite hill where her mother sits, reading. She can almost see her. Her father has gone swimming to Neptune's Bay, which means that they may never see him again, or at least not before dinner time, because his swimming is like his work — he disappears off to a strange, semi-dark space, strictly his, and if he doesn't return by dinner time they have no means of searching for him because only he can go there. Her mother has given up waiting. That is because she doesn't love him as much as she used to.

On top of her hill, Nadejda remembers the summer when she was the size of her mother's leg. The three of them were at the beach; her father had gone swimming. She looked up from the muddy hole she was digging in an attempt to probe the innermost core of the earth, and saw her mother's semi-naked, towering figure turned towards the sea, delicately shaken by silent sobs as she wiped her cheeks, her rings flashing in the sun. Nadejda ran up to her and glued her cheek against her mother's thigh. Wrapped around her mother's leg, her head pressed by her mother's warm hand, they stood for an eternity, the two of them, lost and fatherless amid the bustle of the beach, and Nadejda knew she was going to look after her mother and love her more than her father did. In fact, not loving her mother enough was the reason why he was now swallowed by the big gluttonous sea. That was his punishment: Nadejda knew it. But her father returned, to upset the harmony of the moment, and Nadejda, disappointed, continued exploring the damp viscera of the earth while her parents fought for the rest of the afternoon. You don't know what it's like to lose someone, to wave goodbye and never see them again, her mother said in a voice Nadejda had never heard before. Every time you go swimming, I have the same fear that it's the last time I'm waving to you. I can't bear it any more. Her father stared at the horizon for a long time, stabbing the sand with his

8

big toe. Then he lay down, and her mother lay on his outstretched arm.
    A mad neighing startles her out of rhythmic near-perfection. The
two balls hang limply from her fingers. She looks down and sees a giant
white horse throwing itself around. A bare-chested man runs after the
horse, yelling abuse, the folds of his stomach shaking. Nadejda is too
fascinated to be scared. Can she get down without being mauled by the
beast or the many-folded man? After what seems like hours, Nadejda
manages to escape, puffed and throbbing from the danger. The white
marbles rattle invitingly in her pocket. She crosses the bungalow mini-
town where she and her parents are staying, ducking under her mother's
veranda. She is headed for the Queen's Gardens where she can practise
some more, undisturbed by rabid horses and flabby bare-chested men.
The Gardens are an inexhaustible labyrinth of shady paths, menacing
waterfalls, giant, indecent water-lilies that remind her of something she
can't quite name, death-cold stone thrones where the Queen would sit
and where now Nadejda sits with royal casualness and seeks the blue
patch through a wall of leaves. Once the recalcitrant blue triangle is
spotted, she must run down, as if pulling a thread from a small tear to
unweave the whole gardens and reveal the blue wound of the sea. A
wound full of salt, it hurts. Nadejda runs for the sea, to soothe its pain.
    Once standing by the white stone wall, a boundary of the gardens
and a threshold between sea and non-sea, Nadejda sees the strange
penguin down at the end of the sandbar. Like the day before, and the
one before that, she stands, rocking for a long time, trying to determine
the nature of this penguin. She has never seen another penguin, and
therefore this must be a real one — her first penguin has to be real. She
can't reach it, it's too far down the sandbar, looking out to the sea;
besides, she doesn't really want to touch a penguin that much — what
for? But even when finally she diverts her gaze and looks around to see
if anyone else is watching the penguin, she keeps it in the corner of her
eye, in case it moves behind her back. She can't afford to miss any
miracles.
    There are real penguins in New Zealand, said her mother the
other day, when she got a letter with funny-looking stamps from
Nadejda's uncle and grandfather. She showed Nadejda a picture of real
penguins — they looked exactly the same as Nadejda's penguin here.
She was impressed, but what preoccupied her more was the need to know   9

where Zealand was, and whether it resembled New Zealand. Her
mother laughed, and kissed Nadejda on the head and then, as she
consulted the letter on the subject, for some reason there were tears in
her eyes. Nadejda didn't ask about Zealand again, but she has been
studying the world atlas since then. Perhaps Zealand was an island once,
but it fell apart or just floated away to where no one could find it, and
in remembrance of this island the islands of New Zealand were given
this name.

It was the plaintive moans of the Swedish girl in the bed across that
shocked Nadejda out of her slumber (because you wouldn't call that
throbbing semi-consciousness sleep). Or perhaps it was the eerie
Nadejda-a-a of her mother's voice calling from some veranda,
somewhere in her head. Or the caffeine kicking in. Or the pugnacious
sun, having nested under her skin for two days, now erupting in
vicious subdermal mini-volcanoes.

She sits up in bed, her head feeling abnormally large and
wobbly. What is it, what is it that makes her sick in the heart again?
Searching the slow marsh of her mind, she only finds an incongruous
penguin perched up at the far end of a sandbar. Who is that penguin,
who? The Swedish girl utters a long groan. Earlier, Nadejda enquired
about her crutches, making the gross mistake of saying, flippantly,
'Did you break your leg while travelling?' to which the impassive
blonde virgin replied, 'No, I have always been like this.' Nadejda
couldn't think of anything intelligent to say. Nadejda is not very good
with the physically impaired. But the physically potent repel her. Her
bed is rocking now, like a nauseating sun-swing in the musty darkness of the room. Below her, the Korean woman rips the silence
with a mighty snore, unbelievable in such a child-like physique. And
another one. And another one. They are not just going to be
incidental, no — they are forming a regular pattern of sleep-
shattering vociferation. Nadejda jumps off her bed ineptly and falls
to the floor with a thud. Apart from the compulsive moan of the
suffering Swedish girl, none of the other eight women is disturbed.
She stumbles out of the room, the door clunks behind her.

She stands in the laundry-smelling hallway, her head
enormous, hot and balancing precariously on her neck, nasty shivers

tugging at her body. The penguin is crumbling at the end of the sandbar. There is the chatter of two marble balls knocked together at regular intervals, ripping the silence of an afternoon. What else? The smell of the sea, slow with algae, pungent with rot. Later, up on the lime hill bared like a skull's permanent grin, a white mare runs loose, dark froth at her mouth, tossing her mane like the great flag of pain (if pain were a country). And further down? Down in the gardens hanging flimsy like summer's fishing nets, a penguin stands motionless and chipped at the end of the sandbar. Sea-froth in Nadejda's cupped hands. Is the penguin real? Where is Nadejda?

Balchik — that's where the penguin is. She leans against the wall. The Queen's Gardens of Balchik, where the Romanian queen once spent her summers with assorted lovers. The black rose for which Nadejda searched the Gardens in vain. The penguin of Balchik, a concrete creature fighting an uneven battle with the elements and finally destroyed by them, stripped down to the wire of its skeleton. Giant earthen jars in one of which Nadejda fell once, and discovered it was full of slimy water with dead matter floating on top.

Nadejda sits with her back to the wall, facing through a glass door the pale, boring head of the moon that always turns away and leaves us with its bald nape.

Balchik. Famous for its shore that slips towards the sea, imperceptibly dragging the houses down, splitting the asphalt road and revealing the hot gore of the earth. They predict it will take twenty years for the road to disappear, at this rate of erosion, but twenty years have already passed and the slipping continues. What next? The whole country is progressively drawn to the Blackness of the Sea, in an impulse of self-annihilation — road by road, house by house, horse by horse, mother by child, they will all have wanted it, as her father said. The smell of thick boza fills the avid nostrils. When the road is gone and the boza is replaced by Coke, and this summer is slaughtered and thrown into a common grave with all the empty bottles and ice-cream pots — where is Nadejda going to be then?

Here, right here and right now. On this side of the Equator, on this side of all things. But isn't here there? Isn't now then?

Where *is* here? Where *is* now? Nadejda is less sure than ever. Why can't it be simple, this here-and-now business? Here and now is

11

this hallway in this backpackers in a place whose name she forgets in an island in the peaceful ocean. The island contains her tearful mother. Her bloated uncle. The ashes of her veterinarian grandfather (or did they bury him, in the good traditional way, respecting the worm? Only there were no ample-chested wailing matrons pulling their hair out by the marble tomb, not here) and her once beautiful grandmother (her once beautiful body flown from Hong Kong to be cremated here). Yes, that's all. Here, on an island.

The Balchik penguin at the end of time goes *Pi pi pi pi pi*, then it goes quiet. The penguin seems vexed, floats away on a piece of sandbar, and Nadejda will never know if it's real or not.

Balchik has been trampled under the rabid hooves of a galloping time.

The moon turns sideways, like a restless sleeper turning on a pillow, showing its mournful old profile — nose down, forehead gloomy but devoid of thought, eyes closed. Nadejda could throw up but decides against it, seeing that the floor is too unstable to risk walking to the bathroom. She sits here, trying not to breathe too much, vaguely aware of the danger of sitting in the hallway of a building full of potential male nocturnal wanderers driven from their beds by a hormonal yearning.

Sometimes, in the most inoffensive backpackers in the most beautiful of islands, at three in the morning, we are struck by a sudden, uninvited realisation of the absurdity of being there. The shock of this realisation runs through Nadejda, as if electrocuting her. Just what is she doing here, in this hallway, in this town whose name she can't remember, in this island at the end of all islands, breathing raspingly in this sparse night like the last human on earth?

Why did she land back here? Why smile at the crippled Swedish girl, at the dim, happy Australians, at the guttural, eager Germans, at the self-loving French, at the Kiwis who smile no matter what as if she is peeling them an egg, as the saying goes. Smile as if there is no yesterday, smile as if she has never seen that twitchy pensioner, probably once a teacher, rummage in the rubbish bins right in the centre of Sofia, extracting triumphantly a mouldy quarter stick of bread and an old shoe. As if she has never waved goodbye, I'll see you one day but won't recognise you, to her father whose tears froze in his grey beard. Smile as if she has a reason to be here, as if she chose to be here: ambitious traveller in these exotic lands perhaps, a wide-eyed European amid the lush, elemental beauty of this last paradise on earth. Surrounded by British couples, the men quietly ogling her, the women smiling vaguely at her. Why can't she do like them — have her cornflakes and Earl Grey so that, at eight in the morning, she can seat herself by the window and breakfast sensibly before setting off on her muscular calves for some peak where, clutching one's partner/spouse/elderly but energetic mother/ incidental friend/last night's one-night stand, one contemplates the breath-taking beauty of the country and deplores the rarity of paradise? Oh, but she contemplated — clutching the straps of her pack digging into the flesh of her shoulders, she contemplated. Her breath was taken. She never regained her breath; in fact, she has been gasping for air ever since. Too much altitude. Too much something.

Nadejda sits, her body rocking in a giddy sun-swing, her head resting against the cold wall, and hums a tuneless, wordless song. Nadejda is perhaps asleep.

Chapter One

*There is a place where a
population of semi-blind,
disfigured humanoids scuttle
around on grotesque hands and
legs, doing nobody knows exactly
what, but evidently doing it to
remedy some unspeakable crime
in the vicinity of pure evil.*

Punishments

There is a place where a population of semi-blind, disfigured humanoids scuttle around on grotesque hands and legs, doing nobody knows exactly what, but evidently doing it to remedy some unspeakable crime in the vicinity of pure evil. They may be pushing a rock up a hill perhaps, or stirring cement with bare hands, or trying to put out huge fires by blowing on them. In the process they become terribly maimed. But as Nadejda looks closer, she realises they are doing this in order to expiate their disgrace. One of them, a sensitive Quasimodo with no hope of ever knowing Esmeralda, turns to the observer and says, with his twisted, sad mouth, 'Like a d . . .'. She isn't sure if he says 'dog' or 'donkey'. But she realises, in speechless terror, that their state of disgrace is actually caused by the punishing strain — they weren't like this to begin with. The ugliness comes from the excessive pain. It is impossible. It is so ignominious that just by watching them Nadejda feels herself begin to mutate, perhaps outwardly, perhaps on the inside, at the same time as beginning to feel a diffuse sense of shame trickle into her bloodstream. She cannot take her eyes off this inexplicable tragedy; she must solve the problem of this pain without reason. But the more she looks, the more she becomes part of it and soon she will begin to find it natural, she will join the ghastly creatures in their absurd tasks, as if she has never been beautiful or free before. But where, where is this place, this country of pain, so that she can tell the world about it? She can't take it alone. The world must know what's going on. She wants to wave a flag but there is no one to spot her. Hey someone, someone . . .

In the night, Nadejda walks to the kitchen where she urinates into a small open rubbish bin; she roams around the main building of the dorms, plucking out grass here and there, and in the morning finds herself back on her bunk, uncovered, leaden-headed and still unable to remember properly the name of the town. As she walks into the kitchen, the young, squash-faced reception guy and an English visitor are discussing the toilet habits of stray cats.

'Yes, there was a cat hanging around the place the other week, but I thought it was gone.'

'A bit funny, really, to piss in the bucket when it could do it outside,' points out the ruddy-faced Brit.

15

Chapter Two

Nadejda understands: she has done it again. Once every couple of years she sleep-pees in unorthodox places at night. Sometimes she is seen. She prays she wasn't this time. What the hell, anyway — she'll never see these people again. They're all passing through. Passing through as urine is passed through the body. Passing through, like her. She pours hot water over her instant coffee. As she does this, she notices dirt under her nails and a greenish tinge on her fingertips.

'Actually,' says a Dutch woman in the customary American accent, 'I heard some noise late last night outside the dorm, I couldn't sleep, you know — too much walking, too much fresh air. I had such an exciting day yesterday you know. Anyway, I'm sure it was a cat or some animal like that. It could be an opossum — do they come near?'

'Yeah, could be,' says Squash-face, holding the bin and heading for the door, and after a few more Mmms everybody goes back to their morning routine. Nadejda sits outside on the porch, sipping the scorching coffee, and thinks about punishment.

She gets away with everything, from everything. She gets away with pissing in the bin, with lying and stealing. She got away from *there*, once and now this second time. But it is only the getting away itself that brings a foretaste of happiness, a promise of something to come that never does.

Her father asked her whether she was happy — a typical question he would ask when sophistication failed him, in his desperate attempt to simplify her back to childhood when such questions made sense, and she would say in a chimey, reciting voice (as they taught them at school), *da*. She looked at him, at his grey beard which wasn't grey only three years ago, at his old-fashioned father-like rimmed glasses, at his achingly precious, father-like fingers nervously tugging at dry skin, at his Pierre Cardin shirt that she carefully stole for him a year ago (if only he knew), thinking of what colours suited him — and now she established with satisfaction that she'd made the right choice. Happy. She wanted to give him all the mindless affirmations that would make him feel less forsaken in this godforsaken country of theirs, lots of *da*-s, *da* to everything, to her life in the country of seasickness, of sky that yawns like a giant mouth

16

with no lips, of pink dishevelled blossoms and beaches with an anxious nothing on the horizon, of pale, freckled people who look as if they shouldn't be there, of dark, mountainous women with cracked soles who sail down the street amid a fleet of children and shake with laughter. Of crying with more eyes than she has in the corners of brand-new, ocean-carpeted days, for the world they inhabited once, all three of them — mother, father and Nadejda. Now her father lives in a city of rubble, alone like a mad bedouin in a tattered tent.

'Well,' she began, but seeing that he was reaching for another cigarette, must be the tenth that morning, she said, 'I guess so.'

They could no longer be honest with each other. Honesty, in this time of strife, was indecently decadent. He struck his lighter and tried to still his shaking hand by cupping his other hand over it, but they were both trembling, and he only just managed to light the end.

'Of course I'm happy,' she magnified the lie, to break the oppressive post-lie silence, but then gave up: 'I wish you'd come, Dad.'

He shook his head with mocking bitterness and let out a cloud of smoke. 'Nadejda,' he said wearily. The same conversation they'd had numberless times on the phone, and in letters. He was stubborn.

'You speak the language, and you speak French of course. I mean, you're a bloody professor, you'll find a good job, you'll come and live with us, it'll be great, it's possible, it's still possible!' She blurted it out in one breath, afraid to pause; a pause is a crack in the edifice of possibility. But there was no one living in the edifice except her. Like Flaubert's ivory tower, her father's favourite — '. . . but a sea of shit beats against it and threatens to undermine it,' he had quoted to her years ago and she hadn't understood.

He shook his head and looked out the window to the construction site across the road where a bulldozer was punishing the frozen earth. No, he believes in fate and his fate is to remain here. Important things are taking place, we may be on the brink of a revolution. Besides, all is finished between him and 'your mother', as he refers to her. Why, why does it have to be all finished, asks Nadejda, her hands spread out on the kitchen table as if awaiting a butcher to chop off her fingers one by one. Only because he has decided it is finished, the stubborn mule that he is. An overloaded bus roars by, 17 spitting clouds of black smoke. Perhaps, on the other hand, remaining in the wretched unhappiness of the familiar is the real heroism. He has no hope for a better life here, and he rejects a better life elsewhere. She tries to think of an effective way to tell him this, and much more, much more: she wants to tell him about the unbearable brightness of that strange place where she is living and where her mother doesn't sleep any more; of the emptiness of her new life, of the big fracture caused by his absence.

'Comme la vie est lente,' life is so slow, she said in a flash of inspiration, and shaking off the ash in the direction of the ashtray he completed the verse pensively, slowly, as if he'd expected her to say precisely this line: 'Et comme l'Espérance est violente,' And Hope is so violent.

They looked at each other and an abortive effort to smile passed over their faces like the shadow of a fearful bird. This summed up the futility of her coming here, a voyage she dreamed about for four years. The futility of it was framed in her father's fast-ageing face, this one window remaining amid the rubble of their previous world. She sat carefully — like a wounded animal trying not to move too much, in the hope that the wounds might heal from the rest.

He insisted on calling her Nadejda, at the cost of conflicts with both his and her mother's family, as she was supposed to take one of her grandmothers' names. Nadejda, Hope. But for whom? She is angry at her father. Nadejda will exit the tattered borders of her country free, Nadejda-free.

We are living in a punished country, you see, said her father later as they took the cable-lift to the snow-white Mount Black. Everybody is punished here — from the pensioners rummaging in rubbish bins, to Nadejda's violin teacher Monica, who is a walking chimney, to the students carrying banners: 'The Country is Agonising and We are Here to Say it.' But what kind of punishment is this? It has no meaning, it serves no justice, it follows no crime. A nation is punished for some monstrosity committed by a handful of killer-puppets. The ventriloquist has vanished in the thick curtains of history. The crime becomes ancient, and the more Nadejda tries to trace it, the more she loses sight of all except the immediate, ubiquitous, palpable pain. Does pain have to be a punishment? No, but there is comfort in punishment — just as there was comfort in believing that her father had drowned because he didn't love her mother enough. There is a certain glow of reconciliation about punishment. Pain, on the other hand, is stark and unyielding to decoration, pain fills the world to the hilt, bursting its edges in an unseemly way; pain doesn't admit anything else — it usurps all the space available.

Her father believes in punishment, and that's why he can bear to watch what Nadejda sees as a Theatre of Cruelty, like the one she saw with him at the theatre, and whose author wrote, at the age of seventeen (exactly Nadejda's age at the time), 'I will kill everybody and then I'll go away.' Kill everybody and go away. Or just go away — that's the only way to deal with the pain of others. But something had to be killed.

As they descended through thick snow, in the fast air whipped up by skiers flashing by, Sofia spread below, veiled by a fine smog and lit by a single ray of winter sun — Nadejda's only city. But she was merely visiting. She remembered she had to go back soon. Then why did it feel as if she had returned already? What came after the return?

Nadejda's crunching steps were synchronised with her father's, and she thought how this was the one and only moment of unspoken accordance between them, before the next and decisive wrenching.

When she went to visit her grandparents in Plovdiv, in the course of the conversation Nadejda said 'bloody', bloody communists. Her grandfather was shocked. Not because of the reference to the communists — he was tortured by the communist government as an Agrarian Party member even before the time when yet-unconceived uncle and other grandfather were crossing the Yugoslavian border — but because of the swearing. You know, in my time, he began . . . Yes, in his time, when he was a dirty-mouthed youth and swore at a woman who was passing by, his father tied him up to a tree in the town square where every passer-by had to spit on his face. And he didn't budge. He accepted this deserved punishment — he even recounted it with pride. It's a pleasure to accept punishment when you can believe in your crime. The communist police broke his jaw and he had to eat through a straw for months — that was punishment

19

too, but for a non-existent crime. The communist police strangled one of his Agrarian comrades with a wire. But he never talked about communist punishment, because he sensed that it was gratuitous, uncensored pain in disguise, and he liked punishment to be purposeful. Everything else was unbearable.

Punishment was embodied in the student Blindmen procession she saw the other day: a long column of blindfolded students, every ten being led by a seeing one carrying a torch. A variation on the infamous Tsar Samuel soldiers who, upon trying to invade neighbouring Byzantium, were defeated by the Byzantine emperor, later known by the sonorous name of Basil the Bulgar-slayer: the surviving 20,000 captive soldiers were all blinded. No, not all: every hundred blinded men were given a one-eyed guide to take them home. Seeing this sorry procession, Samuel died on the spot of a broken heart. Here is a procession of blind men and women. But who is the Bulgar-slayer this time, ten centuries later? There are no slayers in sight, because they are conferring in the Parliament building. Nadejda was proud of this insight, and shared it with Anton, her childhood friend, current lover and full-time protester. She watched him being beaten in front of the Parliament by a shapeless cop who screamed, 'Here, take this! We'll show you how our Minister will rule!' His flesh shook like jelly as he kicked the fallen Anton and hit him on the head with his baton. Two hundred people lay punished in the hospitals of Sofia with bandaged heads and broken ribs. 'We had our own Tiananmen Square,' said Anton with badly concealed pride as Nadejda sat by his hospital bed, disbelieving that the worst was finally happening.

Nadejda queued up outside the First Private bank, which was on the brink of bankruptcy, to withdraw all her money, and watched the shivering, angry strangers who spoke the same language as her. The students, who would have been Nadejda's colleagues, friends and lovers had she stayed here, where she hatefully belonged, marched to the Parliament with suitcases, chanting 'You leave or we leave.' A crowd followed up, flooding the square and continuously flowing in from every street. A scruffy, unshaven man mutely held a sign on a string around his neck: 'I bow to the students who protest for their country.' A large, stooped woman in the queue

20

RECONNAISSANCE

carrying a single frozen loaf of bread in a string bag began to sob.

'The future will show,' said her father lamely, 'where this country will end up.'

'Which future? Whose future?' Nadejda protested furiously. 'Always the future, like a distant prosperous relative in America that nobody has seen for twenty years, and who will shower us with gold — one day! The utmost patience and humility are required in the interim. A life of quiet deprivation is required if we are to receive, eventually, the graces of this relative. But does anybody ask whose relative he is? Is he like you, like me? Let him show his face, this proverbial American relative, this cliché of Balkan hope. And like a rich relative in America, the future never shows, the postponing continues, although the suspicion is never voiced — relatives in America are sacred, everybody knows that. The future, Dad, will show nothing more than your white beard.'

Morose men and long-haired women queued outside the German Embassy, the Italian Embassy, the British Embassy, the French, Belgian, American, Canadian, Greek and Algerian Embassies. The irritated clerks nodded unpromisingly behind the glass. Visa, this magic word, haunted the air with its menacing resonance. Transit visa — everybody needed it. Black list — they were all on it, all nine million. But how could they get transit or any other visas, when they were on the European black list? It was a trap. Nadejda didn't need visas any more: she had a foreign passport with neat stamps in it, for which some of these freezing men and women, if nobody were looking, would toss her body in the ditch and run. Snow began to fall again.

An old gypsy wearing a Russian fur hat and the man with the sign, still hanging on his neck, were found frozen stiff overnight, one inside a public toilet and the other on a bench in the Park of Liberty, now renamed back to Tsar Boris' Gardens. The man's petrified eyes were inhumanly blue, like the quintessence of cold: a violent fusion between man and frost had miraculously taken place overnight.

Snow will cover everything and then it will go away. From under the snow, nobody leaves, nobody gets away.

Except Nadejda.

Chapter Two

CHAPTER THREE

A trim white coffin, the plane
sinks into the frozen sky, with
Nadejda inside.

Waving

A trim white coffin, the plane sinks into the frozen sky, with Nadejda inside. There goes his child. He waves and feels as if he is throwing handfuls of soil. The first time, four years ago, it was just a plane that was taking them away for a vague reason, so he waved vaguely and drove home in a haze. Only months later did he begin to realise what had happened: they were not coming back. He raged, pondered, threatened Nadejda's mother across the Pacific, pleaded with Nadejda, had support from friends and colleagues, and finally understood. But never forgave. Now he knows very well what is happening and, stripped of all illusions, he waves to her for a long time, to his only child, and then to the coffin, and then to its furry tail in the crisp winter sky.

He takes the bus home from the airport (the car won't start) and every movement he makes in the bus — perforating his ticket, giving his seat to a woman carrying a child and a shopping bag, looking blankly at the bleak winter suburbia and the two ambulances and police surrounding the site of a heavy road accident detouring the traffic, rubbing his hands and blowing on them — feels like a grotesque pantomime. What next? A bowl of hot soup perhaps? Preparing tomorrow's lecture? But there are no lectures. There is a strike; the students and staff are protesting. There are no lectures tomorrow. There are no lectures tomorrow, he repeats to himself — an incantation which fails to comfort him. There are no lectures tomorrow. He will go in front of the Parliament this afternoon and join in the protest.

In New Zealand it is summer. In New Zealand it is altogether a different time. Nadejda will soon be making her way down that elongated piece of land, through lush rain forests, lakes, sunlit provinces, chatting with carefree tourists. ('Oh, so you come from Bulgaria' — how differently they'll treat her there, where everybody is free and she, the European, is free, where they believe that the rest of the world is like that too. 'What's the climate like in Bulgaria?' And Nadejda, always obliging, will describe the fucking continental climate of Bulgaria, and they'll nod pleasantly: 'So! Lovely hot summers, cooooold winters.') His lips twist in a way which could lead either to an intermediary sour semi-smile masking an onslaught of sobs, or directly to full-blown sobs. He managed to put on a brave

23

face for her, though. That's the main thing — whom could she rely on for strength if not her father? Her mother obviously doesn't have the strength. She made a move that was beyond her capacity: you don't take your child to the other side of this fucking spinning globe unless you are sure you can do it! And leaving everyone behind. Now Nadejda is paying the full emotional fare of this eccentric trip to see the family, or what remains of it — an uncle who is a finished man, a typical neurotic of the family, and the principal cause for this mayhem. Her grandfather died before she even met him, her grandmother too. How many must suffer because of what her uncle did? Still, the fault wasn't his, no. It was the red vermin. Nadejda is paying the price for the red vermin's sins, as is everyone in this Armageddon, though hers is a different price. But you can't un-scramble scrambled eggs, no use ruminating over it, no use wearing a hood after the rain, as the saying goes. He knew full well the risks of this marriage, the inevitability of this flight to join 'the family', this wrenching, this wreckage, this writhing of the survivors. But it was all too distant, the Wall cast its hideous protective shadow over his family — such bitter irony. Go with them? Nadejda is only twenty (or is she twenty-one already?), she can't conceive of the madness of it: you don't change languages, countries, friends, professions and futures when you are going on fifty. You can't. Some try, and fail. Ana did, and failed. Her mother tried, and died trying — the ultimate failure. The lesson is there, only the blind won't see it.

He gets off the bus and heads home, to the ten-floor bulk of apartment building number 181, to a cold apartment. There, his little Nadejda's elapsed presence still lingers like the pulp of a pain he cannot bear to name, and which makes the roots of his hair hurt on his head. You know what the Comte d'Argental retorted to a man who insisted, 'Mais il faut quand-même qu'on vive d'une façon ou d'une autre' (But life must go on, somehow)? 'Je n'en vois pas la nécessité,' he said. I don't see such a need.

Nadejda's father suddenly doesn't see such a need, and his comprehensive knowledge of what the Count said, or what anyone said for that matter, all that knowledge freezes into stalactites in the grotto of his being. He walks through the apartment, acknowledging various objects: Nadejda's half-full cup of black coffee (she drinks too much coffee), Nadejda's unmade bed in her room (what used to be her room and is now his wretched study), Nadejda's orange comb in the bathroom (he knew she'd leave something behind), Nadejda's framed photograph taken just before they left, which he keeps over his desk — an eighteen-year-old Nadejda, semi-smiling, sunken cheeks, dark eyes full of implication, a dimple in her left cheek (it's good that she has put on some weight, that's a sign of well-being). And that's all. Only two hours ago she was here, real and belonging, and now he is collecting memorabilia, like after a funeral. He sits by the kitchen window and lights a cigarette. Outside, the bulldozer has finally stopped trying to break the frozen earth and sits petrified and deformed like a sad Frankenstein monster.

He feels regret. Regret that he ever learned anything at all; regret that he couldn't be asleep and ignorant about the unmendable; regret that he ever loved Ana; that he is here, that it is now, that he is surrounded by the vulgar beauty or fetid ugliness of all those who lacked the courage or the intelligence to see, six years ago, that red has always been and always will be, the colour of blood. It was because of their choice that Ana and Nadejda were driven out of the country. It was because of their stupidity that Nadejda is now flying back to that place where she is not really happy, despite what she said. And he? He will persevere in making soup, in marching up and down the streets with flags and banners and lips blue from the cold, marching until something happens, until someone fires and someone dies. He will keep letting the cyclonic wind sail him down the random, violent torrents of his days, sail him together with the plastic wraps, cigarette butts, pages from yesterday's papers, the obituaries that have come off bus-stop huts, viscous walls and cracked doors, with the ice-cream pots, used condoms, dust-coated lollies in the summer, dirty slush in the winter, and the stench of suspect cooking emanating from the dismal forest of apartment buildings. How does he move from now on? What does he say and to whom? He has so much to say about everything else, but now that the one thing he has always feared has happened, he has nothing to say. 'It's nobody's fault,' he must say, but really it is. It is the fault of those who slide past him in the unswept streets either in frightened silence or in belated realisation, those in embalmed restaurants, nuptial beds, swimming

25

Chapter Three

pools, and museum-like houses — the obscene executioners of this country where Nadejda belonged but no longer does. It is the fault of those honest citizens who believed in the cause, in the Bright Future of Stalin, of Lenin, and who now have a life of misery with no hope for improvement, but latch onto life, stunted and doomed. Those who live in paranoid, melancholy provinces and drink cups of unsweetened tea because they have no money for sugar, or because there is no sugar in the shops, hating the capital, knowing nothing, and waiting for something to change. Those who add to the bulk of crowds at city road-lights, and move along from light to light, in one massive, perfectly co-ordinated swoop, like manure shifted by a spade.

Those in the freedom and prosperity of the mature West who suffer from broken manicure, lack of unconditional love, lack of understanding, excessive body hair, failed relationships, paranoia, fatty thighs, ennui and children — they hate us, our misery, our darkness, our East, he knows it. Those who have never done anything good or bad. Those who are giftless. Those who are grateful to God for some huge, unspecified favour he has bestowed upon them. Everyone, everyone on both sides of the fucking Equator, and on both sides of the fucking blood-soaked Curtain, and on both sides of the Pacific, and on both sides of the family, is guilty of this second, this inconceivable, this ugly departure of his Nadejda. He stubs out his cigarette, puts on his hat again, buttons up his coat, and runs down the stairs to the bus stop, to join the four o'clock protest in town. But all his movements from now on will be vestiges of that senseless waving.

*Nadejda leaves her key at the
reception with Squash-face, and
stooping under her pack, heads
for the door.*

Waiting: the donkey

Nadejda leaves her key at the reception with Squash-face, and stooping under her pack, heads for the door. A pleasant, compact Japanese man holds the door open for her and flashes his white rodent's teeth at her.

And she leaves the town whose name she has no way of remembering and no way of finding out except by asking someone, but that would be embarrassing since she has already spent the night here, and half a day. She looks for her map but can't find it, and finds instead that the box of made-in-Plovdiv walnut lokum she bought the other day has opened, and has been quietly shedding its powdered sugar among her clothes and books. She pulls out a piece and puts it in her sour mouth, sucking the heart-warming sweetness from it with a vague expectation of a miraculous transformation — sprouting wings, perhaps, or acquiring teleportation abilities. But where would she teleport herself? She knows where she would teleport herself from, but where to? Where, in this vast and unlike-Nadejda world, would she go merrily? The world is getting smaller, apparently. But not for Nadejda. For her, the world is becoming sparser, as the people who wait for her become unhappier. The familiarity of the world is the sum of those who wait for us wherever we go, she concludes, and has another piece of lokum. Let's see: how many people are waiting for her?

A mother who has nothing else to wait for: 'No one has or will love you more than I love you, Nadejda, don't forget that.' And she cried, as usual.

A father: 'Don't forget, Nadejda: whenever you decide you want to come back, there will be a home for you here, with me, in your homeland, for as long as I live. Don't forget that.'

Tony, Tony of the ashen hair, smooth chest and vague ideas, who loves her impotently through a haze of dope and who is probably smoking himself senseless during her absence. But what else can he do in that flat-hearted town? 'Christchurch will be a desert without you.'

An uncle who doesn't really count, since he has given up all because he has nothing left to wait for, and is living in a state of permanent lapse, like a drugged fat bumblebee: 'Don't be fooled, Nadejda, they don't want us there, our motherland is infanticidal, don't forget what they did to the family.' Well, how could she forget! And Anton. 'Remember: I will always love you.' Typically melodramatic. He can't wait for her though, because she has returned to New Zealand. When she leaves for a place like New Zealand, nobody in Sofia can wait for her. No one can follow, no one can understand, no one can wait. They just say goodbye.

And the old-time friends scattered to the five continents like ashes — they don't wait, they need someone to wait for *them*.

Nadejda has reached the local supermarket, where she takes a packet of apricot biscuits and some milk for tonight; she takes a piece of camembert too, on impulse. On her way out, as she strolls past the checkout girls, she notices their badges and pauses briefly to read: Megan. Favourite sport: touch-rugby. Tracy. Hobby: socialising. She rushes outside, forgetting to look relaxed lest she arouse suspicion. She is anxious to get on the bus which will take her far away from here. It doesn't matter where to.

She waits for the bus. The bus arrives and she queues up together with the Dutch woman from the backpackers, a rotund Scandinavian couple, a matter-of-fact French Canadian with her gaunt American lesbian lover, three grinning Japanese girls, and some others. She puts her Walkman on so she doesn't have to talk to anyone and proceeds to a window seat. The Dutch woman comes last and after a quick predatory inspection of the layout of passengers, takes the seat in front of Nadejda, glancing at her in a way that promises hours of chatting. Nadejda curses her Walkman's flat batteries and her ability to attract the most boring northern Europeans in the southern hemisphere.

Off to the kingdom of smell, then. She tries to perk up by stressing to herself the ridiculousness of her situation. Those vapours will be good for her: exorcise the inner stench through external therapy. She glances across to the other aisle and sees a couple of tanned, sandal-clad Vikings looking at her brightly. She waits for them to make that small friendly gesture of the civilised, aware young man, designed to reassure and remove all sexual significance from the incidental eye contact. But the Vikings just grin, unashamedly,

29

and she smiles back noncommittally, vaguely noticing the dazzling denture of the one by the window and the grotesque pink of the other's singlet. Now she wishes she didn't have her Walkman on. To remove it would be too eager; to leave it on would be to miss an opportunity to charm a couple of gullible, well-fed, appreciative representatives of a privileged European race. Or perhaps talk with the headphones on, and thus dangerously expose herself to a later assault from the alert Dutch woman who is still occupied by the novelty of her seat and the view (but she may be feigning it, for all Nadejda knows).

It's too late now, anyway. White-teeth is asking her a question: 'Where are you from?' They're Germans, judging by his accent.

'The Balkans,' she says, waiting for the customary blank, 'Ah.' But Pink-singlet knows his geography: 'Which country?'

She searches for the right intonation. Indifferent? Defiant? Matter-of-fact? 'Bulgaria.' It comes out rushed and somehow harsh.

'Ah, Bulgaria.' The 'a' is pronounced as in 'danke'. They both nod, suddenly serious. 'We know Bulgaria.'

Nadejda has always been bemused by the way some people say 'we', when talking in the first person and having no indication from the others that they agree. But they are both nodding, that's an indication.

'It's like Czechoslovakia, no? Very poor.'

'No. It's much poorer than Czechoslovakia.'

They are obviously from West Germany. Nadejda regrets having smiled at them at all.

'Ah.' Indeed, she thinks, Ah.

'Are you on holiday here?' Pink-singlet gets away with his pink singlet only because he is manly to the point of vulgarity, she notes. His muscles twitch under the smooth skin like creatures buried alive.

'Yeah,' says Nadejda, deciding not to grace them with the truth.

'We haven't met any Bulgarians.'

Again, the strange 'we' — how does he know that White-teeth hasn't met any Bulgarians? He may even have met them carnally, in a clandestine nocturnal arrangement unknown to Pink-singlet unsuspectingly snoring in his bunk.

'And I have met a lot of Germans,' Nadejda says, sure of their inability to grasp the irony in her voice.

'Ah yes,' they laugh.

Why do they laugh? They aren't even surprised that she guessed their nationality. It is pleasant to look at these dazzling teeth, though, designed solely for laughing.

'And . . . do you travel alone?'

Aha, she thinks, now *we* come to the point. 'Yes.'

To the discerning traveller her situation should appear increasingly bizarre — a lone girl from the Balkans leisurely touring the Pacific while there is the aftermath of war there, plus crime, poverty, national protests and general chaos. But these two are not discerning, she notes, and as the standard exchange is completed and the next stage of eliciting delicate personal information announces itself, Pink-singlet and White-teeth turn to each other, sharing a joke in their abrasive German consonants. Nadejda puts her legs up and looks out the window, but instead of the view she sees the reflection of the Dutch woman in front, also looking out, her aquiline nose creating a bird-of-prey profile which fascinates Nadejda momentarily.

Dutch . . . That boy, in the recesses of her seaside childhood, was Dutch. She fancied him, although he was unattractive — but he was blond, had blue eyes, a tall body and spoke English. He was at least thirteen, an essential asset — she didn't bother with 'retards' her age. They looked at each other from their respective beach towels. Nadejda felt outrageously sexual, wearing her first top ever. She waited for him to come up to her and say something in English, something terribly personal. All they said to each other, while standing in the ice-cream line on top of the Dunes Beach was:

He: Do you know the time?

She: It is four hours without twenty minutes.

Later she realised the dreadful mistake, which was obviously the reason why he didn't speak to her again. Back in the bungalow, she lay listening resentfully to her parents' snoring in the other bed and tasted the hot salt of her tears, as the boy's departure for his plentiful foreign country was approaching and the end of summer was looming. And with it — the only chance Nadejda had that year

31

to meet, touch and talk to a blond foreign boy. She spent the rest of the year waiting for the summer, for the blue stripe of the sea to dispel the dreary sealessness of the land where she lived and the sound of foreign languages to tantalise her into better worlds where she could have as many kinds of chewing-gum as she could imagine, instead of the one boring mint-flavoured type she was stuck with.

But the next summer it happened, or almost happened, after the summer started off dismally. She was supposed to spend a month on a school camp in the mountains, but her friendship-encouraging, activities-driven camp was disrupted by an incident involving her room-mates. She was put in a big room with five other girls, none of whom she liked. There was the vicious gossip Veneta, envious of everyone; the teachers' pet Monica, whose father was a big fish in a government department; the vivacious, blonde and everybody's favourite Denitza; Temenujka of the foul breath and rude jokes; and the self-conscious, stinking Svetla who shook like bad jelly when she ran (and she ran a lot, always catching up with the others), much to Nadejda's fascination and disgust. They were all from different classes, because the organisers thought it important to try to 'encourage new friendships'. But Nadejda did not want new friendships. She wanted to run on a wild beach in a sexy see-through dress, chased by a blond boy from a rich country.

Each morning they were woken by the zealous, piercing sound of a horn, and rushed out to line up in neat rows for the ceremonial red flag to be raised by the Pioneer Battalion Leader, a senior student. Before the flag went up, all the Pioneer Division Leaders, the division being a group of three or four classes, marched up to the Battalion Leader to salute her with the customary lifting of the straightened hand to the forehead and yell bellicosely, 'Comrade Battalion Leader, Seventh Division is present!' Nadejda had been elected a Pioneer Leader of her class that year, as well as a Leader of a division at the camp — a rare honour — and performed her duties from day one. 'Comrade Leader, Second Division is present!' Marching up in front of several hundred eyes first thing in the morning and getting the intonation right — bright yet serious — made her nauseous, and standing before the crowd through the tedium of reports, salutations and counting, followed by compulsory morning exercise and cruel breakfast, made the horn at seven in the morning the most dreaded sound ever. At night she liked to stay up late, long after the nine o'clock curfew. It was in the second week that she 'split' from the others, a favourite incriminating term in the Pioneer vocabulary, and while they sang 'It's such fun to be on vacation' around the camp fire, she sat in bed and wrote in her diary a few essential words about her room-mates and the whole camp experience. She kept her diary at the bottom of her suitcase under her bed. She didn't manage to put it away in time, and was caught in the act by Veneta, Denitza and Temenujka who arrived, flushed and bubbling with excitement. 'Ah, here you are!' Nadejda said she had a headache and then, leaving the diary on her bed and negligently throwing a tracksuit top over it, headed for the showers. She couldn't really open her suitcase and hide it inside — that would be an invitation for the prying eye; on the other hand, she had to have a shower. She just prayed they wouldn't notice. But they noticed.

When she returned, she found an ugly sight: all five girls were sitting on their beds, all with a facial expression familiar to Nadejda — the mouth and nose pressed together in an idiotic contortion. This was Nadejda's tic for which she was mocked from time to time. They sat there, grimacing, serious and sinister. They'd got hold of her diary. The fear of unpopularity crept up in the Division Leader, but then she thought that at least they knew the truth about themselves now. And the truth was, she was put in a room with four malignant wasps and a chunk of walking jelly, and as for the camp on the whole, the boys' rooms were too far down the corridor, she hated the morning horn and the toilets smelled, as a result of which she had constipation for the fourth day in a row. There was nothing more to say or do, really, and she settled on her bed, drying her hair and ignoring the five grimacing beasts, while tears welled up in her eyes. She lay in bed, facing the wall, and thought of a golden beach where she frolicked until sunset with an ash-blond foreigner; they drank lemonade, chewed strawberry-flavoured gum and smoked cigarettes, and when the sun set they reclined on the waterline, their feet buried in wet sand, their bottoms wet, and kissed; the kissing part was rather vague, because Nadejda couldn't picture what exactly kissing might involve.

The next day she was summoned by the teacher in charge and

33

the Battalion Leader, a spotty, ingratiating girl. They explained to her that the privilege of being a Pioneer Leader had been bestowed on her, that her comrades trusted her and that she should not betray their trust. Nadejda nodded in agreement, not sure how serious this was going to be. If she found that her room-mates were unsuitable, she could be shifted to another room — that could be arranged, she was a Pioneer Leader *and* a Division Leader after all. Would she like to be shifted to another room? No, she wouldn't. She was okay in her room. The teacher in charge smiled her beautiful horse smile and said, 'Good girl.' Nadejda wasn't sure what that meant.

She went to her room where nobody was talking to her. Which one was the foul informer? Veneta, as usual. Shaking and light-headed, Nadejda went up to her and said, 'Malignant wasp!' Veneta blinked several times and, unsuccessful in her efforts to think of something similar to say, pulled the face she had by now mastered to perfection. Nadejda rushed out of the room, determined to find a telephone and call her parents; they would come and take her away. But the only telephone in the area was in the reception-room next to the kitchen and the laundry, where the Division Leaders gathered occasionally and listened to the teacher in charge or the Battalion Leader, or any of the other teachers, talk about nondescript matters. There were two teachers in the room: Vasilev and Georgieva, who were snogging.

'Comrade Vasilev,' said Nadejda in a shaky voice, horrified by the inopportuneness of the moment, 'could I please use the phone to call my parents?'

Comrade Vasilev, a Phys Ed teacher, was athletic, deep-voiced and half-adored, half-abhorred by the girls. He terrorised them by making them run more than the boys because they were 'fat slobs'. He was popular with all the female teachers, and now Nadejda witnessed the degree of his popularity.

'Ssssure,' said Comrade Vasilev, and flicked his fringe like a nervous girl.

'Why do you need to call them?' Comrade Georgieva interrupted, having collected herself and adjusted her chignon.

Nadejda sensed the danger of failing to sound convincing, 'I have to tell them something. I am feeling sick.'

'Okay then.' Comrade Georgieva was in a good mood, thanks to Comrade Vasilev. Nadejda mentally thanked Comrade Vasilev for his input.

As soon as she heard her mother's voice, Nadejda burst into such violent sobs that she couldn't say a word.

'Nade, love?' Her mother's voice was a sudden oasis in an alien desert of rising flags, trumpets, hissing vipers of room-mates, smelly laundry, boys who liked Denitza because of her blonde hair, and absolutely no sea.

'Nadejda, are you okay?'

No, she wasn't. Comrades Georgieva and Vasilev looked on in surprise. 'Mummy, can you and Dad come? I have a headache.'

She didn't want to divulge any more in front of the teachers but at the same time didn't want to sound like a wimp. 'Can you come, please Mum?'

They could. They arrived the next day in their new white Lada, picked her up and took her away. The camp, including the teachers, watched the Pioneer Leader of Class J and now former Division Leader of Second Division crawl into the white Lada while her father put her suitcase in the boot, and disappear in a cloud of dust. Normally, such occurrences were scandalous. But somehow, not least through the power of his smile, which seemed to work with Nadejda's teacher in charge, her father managed to convince her that Nadejda needed time away from her comrades and that they were taking her to the seaside, where she was going to recuperate and gather strength for the next year when new responsibilities were awaiting her.

On the way to the sea, Nadejda sang 'It's such fun to be on vacation' and told her parents how she'd been promoted to a Division Leader, even if only for a week. Her parents were pleased and said, 'Well done,' and after that Nadejda forgot about being a Division Leader. She was now waiting for the blue note of the sea to chime in the distant heat, announcing the blond presence of boys with veins that showed through the skin of their hands, vanilla ice-cream, sleeping until ten in the morning and suntanning in risqué positions near the white, red or black beach flag (depending on the degree of safety or danger for swimmers) where handsome lifeguards dwelt attractively behind sunglasses and girlfriends.

35

Chapter Four

That was a voyage towards the sea. Such a voyage made sense, if nothing else did. But what sort of a voyage is she on now, ten years on? Because clearly, she is going somewhere.

Why a voyage anyway? Why does everything worth mentioning always have to be in the form of a voyage? Why is life supposed to be a voyage, a trite, contrived movement from one point to another, like some stunted game of join-the-dots? The figure is only apparent towards the end. Nadejda is back from her trip. This means she is drawing towards the end of her voyage, and what appears in her mind is a donkey carrying a misshapen figure with a large head, the forehead weighing it down, the eyes bulging and demented, the mouth twisted into a semblance of a smile directed at Germans, Dutch, English, New Zealanders and Americans alike, as if its ends have been cut right across the cheeks — a big, bloody smile, a heavy, agreeable nod of the sick head, and a mobile body that suits all seasons and all climates.

What happened to this figure, what has been done to it? Adaptation, as they say. A stranger in the depths of Balkan strangeness, a scarecrow carried through white villages lingering on the verge of memory extinction, eclipsed by giant, quiescent mountains, where bare-bottomed children and pigs wallow in the dust of cobbled streets and women shake their heads — that's what Nadejda's voyage shapes up to, in the end. Here or there, Balkans or the New World, she is the stranger on the donkey, the scarecrow that scares itself. Wherever she passes, there is desolation.

She could hardly call that an Odyssey, and she wants nothing less than an Odyssey. But this is the opposite of an Odyssey: beginning at a foreign place, she goes home, and gradually returns to the foreign place. New World, Balkans, New World. No, Odyssey or nothing, that's Nadejda's desire: she refuses to be content with anything less than a grandiose voyage; anything less would be a sign of servility, of mere survival. She would survive, oh yes, like her nation which survived five centuries of the brutal Turkish yatagan and half a Stalinist century of waving red scarves and singing 'Lead us, oh Mother Party, lead us to the bright future!', half a century of broken lives like those of her mother's family. Survival is necessary. But survival can be adaptability taken to its abject extreme. She is not going merely to survive.

The two Germans are sleeping.

It occurs to Nadejda that the point of a voyage is to counteract waiting, to speed up the waiting. A voyage is a state of constant getting away — the opposite of waiting, surely. So the donkey trots along, carrying the scarecrow on its back, and a bag with a quarter of a loaf, an onion, white salty cheese, and a goat horn for self-defence. Defence against whom though? What does the scarecrow need a horn for — to prod the donkey? But the donkey doesn't need to be reminded. It does the only thing it knows, the wily animal — because the scarecrow is deceived, the poor scarecrow still wants to believe that a voyage is the opposite of waiting.

Chapter Four

CHAPTER FIVE

The two Germans are sleeping.

Gnomes, mince, chewing-gum

The two Germans are sleeping. If Pink-singlet could comment, he would say, 'We are sleeping.' White-teeth is dribbling. Nadejda watches the bird-profile of the Dutch woman in front. Suddenly she turns round, sticking her head through the narrow gap between her seat and the window, brandishing a map. 'Excuse me, do you know what town is this?' Nadejda doesn't. They are driving past a butcher's shop displaying a large sign: 'Mince: $3.40'. The beak yaps: 'I was just wondering because you know, I like to know the names of all the towns which I see, and follow on the map.' Nadejda nods and tries hard not to smile her compulsive, insincere smile, knowing the dire consequences of smiling at bus neighbours she doesn't want to befriend. The bird-reflection returns to the window. Before they exit the somnolent town, they pass a sign saying, 'Gnomes for sale', but there are no gnomes in sight. Nadejda wonders what the gnomes look like and what one does with them. It strikes her that she could get off and purchase some gnomes right now, if she felt like it — an inconceivable decadence in the eyes of her earlier self, who never saw real dollars, only francs, when her father returned from a conference. Even francs were sacred then. Her father's professor salary is $20, and she could buy at least five gnomes for that price (depending on the size, of course), whereas he could buy six kilograms of mince, for example. How would she explain this gnome-mince phenomenon to the Dutch woman, or to the two napping giants, or to the Polynesian bouncer in Auckland who was surprised to learn of her nationality: 'Shit man, you look so normal!' Fortunately, she doesn't have to explain anything to anyone — they all know about the war in Yugoslavia, about the orphans in Romania who were so fashionable a few years ago, about the Kurds in Turkey and so on: the whole merry bunch. The particularities of Balkan misery are of no interest to the civilised world, as her father said, bitterly. That's understandable, Nadejda concedes, and is gripped by an irrational desire to pinch Pink-singlet's pink arm and make him squeal. She refrains of course, and wonders what she has against these people except that they have never known misery — something which can't be classified as a crime against humanity, however Nadejda looks at it.

She watches the plain where a forest has been devastated either by a hurricane or by some senseless tree-cutting rage. Such violent elements in so tidy a country! She tries to remember a place similar to this. She can't. It is terribly unsettling when things remind her of nothing else. Everything should remind us of something, if we are well-read enough — her father's theory. It's a bullshit theory, and Nadejda let him know this. But everything should remind us of something if we are to sleep at night. That's why Nadejda's mother doesn't sleep at night — because nothing here reminds her of anything she knows. It has taken Nadejda four years to realise this and now finally, on this bus heading to Hell's Hole in the Paradise of the Pacific, she discovers, proud of her discovery and shocked at its incurable nature, that being reminded is essential, reminded of anything, anything at all. Likeness is the only mould that can contain the shapeless mass of previous life. Nadejda has a lot of previous life, twenty-one years of it. One jerk of this smooth-running bus, and it will spill. It will spill, something will spill. There is a crunch under her foot, as she leans forward in an attempt to ease her nausea induced by the sun — the delicate and unmistakable crunch of her sunglasses. Damn! She picks up the frail, insect-like object, and searches the seat pocket for a paper bag. But the whole idea of messy vomiting is so off-putting that she leans back instead and tries to drift off into a nausea-free unconsciousness. Some sea is gurgling and bubbling in the narrow sea beds of her temples.

'The Black Sea reminds me of the Peaceful Ocean,' said Moni the Australian, the summer of the camp, the summer when it happened. Nadejda was flattered, as if the similarity between her sea and such a foreign, majestic notion as the Pacific, was a compliment to her.

Nadejda and her parents went to Nessebur, in the new white Lada (which was grey by the time they got there), where they stayed at a coquettish little bungalow complex from her mother's work. Her colleagues with their kids stayed in neighbouring bungalows, but Nadejda didn't get on with the kids, except with Anton whom she tolerated because he adored her and did everything she said. (Her body still aches from the finished pleasure with that same Anton, only days ago. It's over and he is now marching down the street with thousands of students, he is blowing a whistle or shouting 'We are the students, we're not afraid!') His father was Russian and very funny, and his mother was a colleague of Nadejda's mother. But Nadejda wasn't interested in him — he was only a year older, very thin and had that stupid mania of Bulgarian boys at the time to collect Western chewing-gum wrappers with cars on them. It was a whole industry of exchange and of precious, elaborate knowledge of different makes, nonsense for which Nadejda had no time. She collected Western chewing-gum wrappers with pictures from *Star Wars*, a much more sensible pastime. Anton once offered to give her his entire collection of car wrappers, the most valuable thing he had — for nothing, so that she could exchange them for *Star Wars* ones. She refused, magnanimously.

Nessebur, town of churches, ruins (Byzantine or Roman, young Nadejda could never remember who had invaded her country, when and in what order) and narrow cobbled streets at whose top the blue, unbreakable window of the sea waited to be opened. She climbed, followed by the puppy Anton, towards that window, past lurching houses under which black-kerchiefed women sat and knitted endless socks for ungrateful grandchildren in the city. Nadejda knew something was going to happen, at last.

She met Moni at a shooting gallery near the wharves, where she ventured because there were only boys there, ineptly holding guns pointed at the targets indicated by the fat, gum-chewing, pink nail-polished woman behind the counter. Moni stood out because of his Western clothes, but otherwise he was dark, like the other boys, and unlike Anton whose Russian father had generously endowed him with a decent degree of fairness. The foreign-clothed boy didn't seem to know anyone, he just stood there, absorbed in the shooting. While the woman was recharging the guns for the next three boys, he looked away and his eyes met Nadejda's. She stared at him. He looked Bulgarian, but he wasn't. Anton was talking to a boy from their complex, the moment was good for the foreigner to make a move — but he didn't, although they kept staring at each other. Minutes passed; Nadejda despaired. It was his turn to shoot. He took the gun the flabby arm held out to him, and said in perfect Bulgarian, 'Blagodaria,' thank you. Nadejda had a jolt of disappointment, but simultaneously sensed there was something wrong — it

41

was unheard of to say thank you to the woman in the shooting gallery, or to anyone for that matter. You did not say please and thank you, you just demanded and took. And ran. What strange place did the boy come from? He was a hopeless shot anyway, like most of them. He managed to score some pathetic chewing-gum, but nothing major like a key-holder or a Kiddies egg. She turned to him, determined to find out: 'What's in your chewing-gum?'

'Excuse me?' Now that was beyond unusual, that was just ridiculous. A 'What?' was still acceptable, or most likely a 'Huh?', but 'Excuse me' was beyond the pale.

'What's in your chewing-gum?'

'Ah.' He understood the question now. 'Wait.' And he proceeded to unwrap the gum, which revealed a *Star Wars* picture. '*Star Wars*,' he said in perfect English and was given away.

'*Star Wars*? I collect these wrappers,' said Nadejda, cunningly sustaining the conversation. Anton was watching them, the little jerk, pretending to look through his own stack of wrappers.

'Excuse me?' said the boy again. It was becoming annoying.

'Where are you from?' said Nadejda, sending her sophistication to hell, and suddenly realising with trepidation that she should talk to him in English.

'Me?'

'Yes.' She still couldn't gather enough courage to attempt a few English words.

'I am from . . . Australia.'

Nadejda knew Australia's exact whereabouts on the map — it was the large continent, larger than Europe, which squashed New Zealand into the corner of the map, but she decided to show off her knowledge later. 'Then how come you speak Bulgarian?' she continued, unassumingly.

'My mother is from Bulgarian.'

Nadejda puffed with laughter at this hilarious mistake, but then had the sobering thought that her nationalities in English weren't so great either. 'Aha.' She hoped she hadn't offended him.

'My mother was born in Bulgaria, but her parents immigrated to Australia when she was six.' He switched to English, without consulting her. She was taken by surprise and indignant.

'Pardon?' she said in English, and her cheeks went hot. Anton was now watching them openly, mouth agape.

'My mother,' began the boy in Bulgarian, 'is born in, in Bulgaria.' He said it correctly this time.

Nadejda told him, after a brief mental consultation with her mother about the safety of divulging this information ('Don't tell strangers about uncle and grandfather'), that her own uncle and grandfather lived in New Zealand. 'Why?' said the boy, and this struck her as a very sensible question. But she didn't know why. Not that it hadn't been explained to her, but when suddenly she had to explain it, it lost all meaning. But one thing was clear to her: her uncle whom she'd never met and her grandfather whom she'd never met, just had to live there, in that island of real penguins and Maoris, in that town with an unpronounceable name, just as she, Nadejda, and her parents, had to live in Sofia. It was natural, even if she couldn't explain why.

Moni also seemed to find it quite natural. He was named after the Bulgarian king Simeon, now living in exile in Spain, he explained to her proudly. 'What king?' said Nadejda, who didn't know there was a real, living Bulgarian king. Funny they hadn't mentioned that at school. 'Are you sure that's the Bulgarian king, not the Spanish one?' Simeon was sure, and dismissed her question with a royal, condescending nod. They parted at the shooting gallery, Nadejda's white dress aflutter with excitement, and Anton scuttling after her in helpless anger.

They met by the wharf the next day, as both happened to be buying fish and chips at the same stall. Anton didn't follow her, having gone for a moody walk on the beach. They sat in an empty boat called *Albena* (all boats had women's names) and ate out of the greasy paper bags. Moni gave her some strawberry-flavoured chewing-gum from Australia, and their love was thus sealed. Nadejda took him to her favourite place in return: the derelict white-washed house on the rocks, behind the fishermen's tavern. It overlooked Neptune's Bay. The house was basically a ruin — two walls were missing. Grass grew through the cracked floor and lizards moved their flat heads once every two hours. It had been deserted for years and there was a belief that it was haunted, but Nadejda never saw anything. She liked to sit among the obscene wall drawings and the

43

graffiti, facing the direction of the sea which she couldn't see unless she looked out the large window holes, or just stepped out of the house. She knew the graffiti by heart; they were pretty standard. Stoyan + Veneta = VL, VL standing for Vechna Ljubov, eternal love. Or simple dirty words, a delight for the delinquent hands of bored kids from the city: cock, cunt, etc, with corresponding drawings of each item. Nadejda was embarrassed and hoped Moni wouldn't understand those words and, what was more important, wouldn't ask what they meant but content himself with the descriptive drawings. They leaned out the large window holes, one to each, and looked down to the warm, turgid sea.

'You know, the Black Sea is not actually black,' said Nadejda.

Moni didn't reply.

'They call it black because in the winter there are huge storms.'

'Yes?' Moni was intrigued. He looked at her as they were both leaning out, so that their heads communicated in mid-air, two dark-haired, sun-tanned heads against the whitewash, their arms dangling out.

'Yep.' Nadejda felt confident about her story. 'So huge that the waves crash on top of houses along the waterfront.'

'Yes?' Didn't he know the word 'really'? She forgave him, though, because at least he was impressed, which was the main thing. Moreover, he now drew closer to her side of his window, turning his body towards her, his left elbow resting on the former windowsill, his striped T-shirted shoulder slightly poking out in her direction. Nadejda felt the main thing was to keep talking, as if she wasn't affected by this shift.

'Yes. And there are dead animals all over the beach after the storm. I once saw this dead donkey, and then I saw this dolphin. It stank.'

'Dolphin?' he repeated with difficulty.

'Yes.'

'Like in the Peaceful Ocean.'

'Like what?'

'The Peaceful Ocean?' His voice rose strangely, as if it was him asking the question. He smiled tentatively.

Nadejda laughed. 'The Pacific Ocean you mean.'

44

'Ah! The Pacific Ocean, yes.' And he repeated, as if to learn the words, 'Pacific Ocean.' Nadejda found this charming. She found Moni quite charming. A real Westerner *and* kind of Bulgarian. And he was at least a year and a half older than her. Not very tall but at least he had those protruding veins on his arms which signalled real manliness. His lips were chapped, he kept looking at her, and Nadejda was faint with the proximity of her dream. She wanted to prolong the sensual delectation, fearing that all this may turn out to be some ghastly misunderstanding. So they stood, framed in white, their loins hot and tingling, their dizzy heads exchanging the same thought, while gulls squealed and circled above the house and the distant roar of the crowd punctuated excitingly the adult-like intimacy of their situation. But nothing more happened; they were perched on the edge of unbearable yearning, but to make a move would have meant to fall out, crashing messily on the rocks below.

They had no way of knowing that their fugitive families too, had shared a moment of bleaker intimacy, thirty-three years ago, in a refugee camp in Northern Greece. Nadejda's youthful uncle and grandfather slept in the same over-crowded hall as Simeon's grandparents and toddler-mother, as well as fifty other motley escapees from this side of the Iron Curtain. They breathed the same air scented with a cocktail of the multinational misery of those referred to by the authorities back home as traitors, deserters and enemies of the people. It was a very specific kind of air, which none of them were to forget. The intimacy between Nadejda's and Simeon's families took place when Simeon's grandfather witnessed the beating of Nadejda's uncle by a Greek guard, after he complained, with the same young verbal recklessness that catapulted him out of his fatherland, about the mouldy bread and suspect meat they were being fed. The guard knocked out her uncle and kicked him in the stomach and loins repeatedly, screaming, 'Shut up, shut up, shut up, shut up.'

The onlookers, a colourful crowd of Poles, Czechoslovaks, Bulgarians, Albanians, Romanians and one Russian, stood in depressed silence. Only Simeon's grandfather, otherwise an unassuming man, stepped in and shouted in dodgy Greek, 'That's enough! You'll kill him.' This unleashed a torrent of eloquent, barely comprehensible sociopolitical comment on the importance of Slav immigrants to the well-being of Greece that went something like this:

'Shut up, you Bulgar swine! Shut your fucking mouth, vermin, scum, parasites, living off our backs, you beggars, thieves, liars, filth, we should've shot you as soon as you crossed the border, that's what you deserve, that's what you deserve, not to be fed and treated like kings, you should be manure for the great Greek land, you . . . you . . . go to hell!'

The last exclamation was what Nadejda's uncle, through the haze of his pain, and Simeon's grandfather, helplessly clasping his fists, understood beyond doubt. They simultaneously thought that to go to hell was impossible in the given circumstances, because they were already there. Two days later, the volatile guard was discreetly moved to another part of the camp. Vassil was threatened with incarceration on the island of Crete, and he didn't complain about the food any more. A month later, Nadejda's and Simeon's predecessors split, the first to go to another Greek camp, the second to a more fortunate destination — Australia. They never saw or remembered each other again.

Nadejda spent that week in a state of febrile agitation. She didn't tell her parents (her mother always got upset when uncle and grandfather were mentioned, and Australia was pretty close). She didn't need to tell Anton — he knew that the first inept shot of that Bulgarian-Australian impostor sent him flying to the far side of Nadejda's attention. He was becoming more withdrawn and snappy every day; but he never mentioned Moni. He made a pathetic attempt at demonstrating interest in Irina, a pretty redhead, whom Nadejda couldn't even compare with — she had long shiny hair, green eyes and some breasts. But she could see that he wasn't really interested in Irina, and felt sorry for him, in the rare moments when she had time to feel anything for him.

She saw Moni every day at the beach or by the wharf, and in the evenings, when she went out on the town with her parents (and Anton with his parents who were more fun than Anton) she usually saw him in a tavern or by the waterfront where the tourists strolled to the sound of live music, showing off their toasted flesh. They talked, looked at each other furtively, and kissed once, at dusk, in a boat called *Antonia*. Nadejda was too surprised by the sensation to know whether she liked his ice-cream wet mouth, and if it hadn't been the last night before Moni's departure, they would no doubt have kissed more, much more, and longer. Who knows what else could have happened? Moni, it turned out, was thirteen — an unattainable age of sophistication and sexual knowhow which Nadejda unfortunately had no time to explore beyond that somewhat panic-stricken kiss and the occasional brush of his hips against hers.

The remaining week of their holiday was the saddest in Nadejda's history of seaside holidays to date. She lay in the small stuffy bungalow, aware of her sleeping parents' embrace and feeling with her whole body, like a terrible, crippling illness, the distance that separated her from Australia. Why, why did Moni have to live there? That was not natural. Nothing was natural, in fact: being in Nessebur was unnatural, going back to Sofia was unnatural, having no one to kiss in the boat *Antonia*, or any other boat for that matter, was unnatural. Soaking her pillow with heavy hot tears, Nadejda knew that she would never ever love another.

The last night of the holidays, long after everyone had gone to bed, Anton, whose parents hadn't returned from their night promenade, was sitting outside by the mini rose-garden across from Nadejda's bungalow. He was hoping she would come out after her parents had gone to sleep, and had a jolt of happy surprise as he saw her emerge from behind the roses. She was wearing nothing except her undies and a singlet. Anton thought he was dreaming. But she walked straight ahead, not taking any notice of him. She was playing games with him, clearly. He followed her, not sure what kind of game it was and whether he should be happy yet. Fortunately there was no one around, or they would have seen a strange sight. Nadejda walked, at an even pace, right through the comatose complex, and kept walking past the Goldfish camping ground, where a merry party was still going around a dying fire, and fish smell hung in the air: the party was too drunk to notice anything odd about the two children. One man yelled out, 'Hey kids, don't get too carried away!' — a

Chapter Five

remark everyone found so funny that one laughing man nearly fell into the fire.

By the time they reached the arching ruins of the St Archangel Church, at the top of the large stone steps, Anton had realised it was no ordinary game, and was scared. He tried talking to her. 'Nadejda? Nadejda?' She gave a grunt, while still walking straight ahead. He didn't try to stop her, from fear she might do or say something truly horrific. They reached the old whitewashed house where Anton knew she liked to go by herself. She walked in, lay on the ground in one corner, huddled, and closed her eyes. Anton wanted to bawl. The moon, thoughtfully framed by one of the windows, cast a special pale copper beam onto the floor. He didn't dare get too close. He crouched, shaking, and watched her attentively. She was sleeping, and it was as simple as that. But was she sleeping before? Could you sleep with your eyes open? Anton knew about somnambules, but they were generally strange people who walked on roofs at night. He moved closer, reassured that she wasn't a somnambule. He saw that under her transparent yellow singlet the imaginary beginnings of breasts he had desired under her beach bra didn't in fact exist. Her skinny arms twitched slightly.

Anton was faced with the biggest dilemma of his life. If she was going to sleep here, she would find herself with no clothes in the morning — that would be terrible. If he were to go and fetch her clothes now, she might wander off in the meantime, and God knows where — that would be even more terrible. If, on the other hand, he was to stay with her ... In fact, that was what he did, heroically ignoring the danger of his parents in the morning. Both pairs of parents kept insisting they 'played' together anyway. Here's playing! He removed his T-shirt and covered her bare shoulders, although there was only a faint, warm breeze. He lay next to her on the warm stone floor, his heart pounding madly like a mad gong under his naked skin, his shaky hand laid out next to hers, barely touching it.

The sea darkly and turbulently dreamed below them. He watched in the moonlight the shadow of her eyelashes, the fine moss over her top lip, the minute dilation of her breathing nostrils, the peeling skin of her arms. And Anton knew that he would never ever love another.

48

Nadejda awoke at dawn, and so did Anton. She was surprised to find herself there, and at first thought it was the middle of the afternoon. She wasn't surprised to find Anton next to her. 'It's happened before,' she said. Anton believed her, although he wasn't exactly sure what that meant. They lay a while longer, their arms around each other, the first fishing boats invisible by the rocks below. Anton had a piece of mint-flavoured chewing-gum, the boring, ordinary type, and they shared it. It was the best ten minutes of Anton's life so far. In those ten minutes Anton also caught a glimpse of what he was to encounter in women for many years to come and what he years later formulated, in a bout of melancholic frustration, as 'the Nadejda syndrome': Nadejda basked lazily in Anton's caring presence. It was years later that she coined the term 'Anton's over-availability syndrome'.

Then Anton went down to get her clothes. Nadejda leaned out of her window and looked at the translucent sea, unable to cry any more at the thought of the Peaceful Ocean. She had the conviction, sudden and profound, that one day she would lean out of a window like this to look at the Pacific Ocean, while someone fetched her clothes — and she wouldn't feel scared.

A quarter of an hour later, while she put on her shorts and T-shirt (fortunately her parents were still asleep), Anton, happy like a thief who had got away, found a piece of dirty green chalk. Putting in brackets the graffiti she had scribbled earlier in the week, Nadejda + Moni = VL, he wrote directly above it, Nadejda + Anton = IVL.

'What does that mean?' Nadejda enquired. 'Istinska Vechna Ljubov.' The chalk flew out the window. True Eternal Love.

Nadejda smells the sulphurous vapours already. So do the two Germans because they stir in their sleep and soon open their eyes, crumpled and disoriented, forced into wakefulness by the offensive smell. Nadejda turns back to the window, seeing no point in making further contact with them. She tries to block the smell by only breathing out — it doesn't work. She takes a deep breath. The smell reminds her of nothing except the future memory of itself, in a future place where there is no smell like this.

49

Chapter Five

CHAPTER SIX

Before Nadejda's father went to
France, his first trip to the West, a
colleague at Sofia University, a
sharp-tongued, balding cynic who
had recently and unofficially
developed an interest in the
Decadents from the end of the
nineteenth century . . .

Warnings

Before Nadejda's father went to France, his first trip to the West, a colleague at Sofia University, a sharp-tongued, balding cynic who had recently and unofficially developed an interest in the Decadents from the end of the nineteenth century, casually whispered to him in the university cafeteria: 'Don't go, Mladen.' Nadejda's father looked at him in anxious surprise — not because of what he said, but because of his enigmatic smile: he smiled in that way whenever he had something serious and tricky to say. He was a pain in the large, vain, vigilant bureaucratic arse, and never got promoted to dozent, associate professor, because of his long-standing failure to kiss that arse.

'What do you mean?' said Mladen.

'I mean, my friend, that you'll go, you'll come back and you'll grieve for the rest of your life.' The colleague's face suddenly fell back into its natural expression, one of melancholic derision. He said no more.

Mladen thought about it. The colleague had an unrealistic history of sojourns in the West, which ended with his and his wife's deportation back to the motherland when they were handed over by the Turkish authorities. What saved them was his wife's father, who carried the most useful title of 'Active fighter in the struggle against Fascism and Capitalism' and was able to intercede for them. Ten years after those escapades, he knew he would never be promoted and had to be thankful to have a good job and a dead father-in-law whose beneficial aura illuminated his dissident life even from the grave.

Nadejda's father respected his colleague precisely because of this. Sitting in the cafeteria, aware of the nearby presence of one of his students, an intense young woman in a fur coat who was staring at him provocatively, he thought about what his colleague had just said. Suddenly, in a most unusual swerve of thought, he thought of his brother-in-law.

His brother-in-law was in a situation diametrically opposed to his own: exile in the land of the free, whereas he, Mladen, was in the home of the unfree. It was ironic, and because he was on the verge of venturing out and rather excited about it, he smiled at this irony.

51

The balding, cynical colleague was right. Mladen, naturally ignoring his warning, went to the West, came back and was sad for a long time. But he was not entirely right — because Nadejda's uncle, heeding a warning about his safety, went, never came back and grieved for the rest of his life.

Indolent smells, indolent people: sulphur induces a strange sense of relaxed well-being after the initial shock.

The spine

Indolent smells, indolent people: sulphur induces a strange sense of relaxed well-being after the initial shock. The locals stroll, large and confident in their undisguised idleness. Nadejda understands them. Crushed under the weight of her pack, she heads for the backpackers where she finds Dutch Birdie, cheerfully chatting to the lively receptionist in her gaudy American accent: 'Yah, yah.' She should have known. There is no getting rid of her now — they'll probably be in the same room.

They are. Two others come later in the day, a Korean (Nadejda prays that she doesn't snore) and an American. As the two of them unload upstairs in the minimal room with a view to some bright buildings across the road and the brooding, envapoured mountains in the distance, Birdie stretches her long neck and smiles at her room-mate. Nadejda smiles back.

'So, you are from Bulgaria.'

'Yes.'

'And I am from Holland, you probably have guessed.'

'Yeah,' nods Nadejda, smiling.

Again, and again, and again, hundreds of smiles, or rather the same one smile, cut out on her unsmiling face, the mouth cut all the way to the ears. 'The Laughing Woman', perhaps, as opposed to 'The Laughing Man'? But she must free herself from her father's useless, compulsive French references. He is a fool, her father has always been a fool with his French obsessions. The laughing man's story: he was captured by some gypsy as a child, and they cut his mouth's ends into a huge, ineffaceable smile for the purposes of their travelling circus-show. Nadejda knows that the gypsies would in fact do that sort of thing for a foreign visa or for something foreign; but worse yet, they would capture Nadejda the pale, frail child and tear out her paua-shell earrings (a present from uncle), then drag her by the ankles into their caravans and put an iron collar on her neck, like a dancing bear, and take her around, naked, to collect money from her bruised beauty, from her shame. The gypsies were a common child-threat: 'Go to bed now or the old gypsy will come and snatch you away.' Nadejda was advised by the wild-eyed mother of a schoolmate not to wear paua-shell earrings because the gypsy slums were too close to their suburb and you never knew . . . The last bus stop of the *Nadejda* suburb was a border zone, beyond which spread the shabby, desolate camps, of the tsigani. You never knew. Nadejda took off her earrings immediately and put them back in their dark blue box. She would take them out sometimes at night and watch them glow faintly in the dark, and swear to herself never to let the gypsies have these drops of the Pacific Ocean.

Smile, smile. Someone must have told Birdie in that backpackers yesterday, 'She's from Bulgaria.' The mild gent from Yorkshire perhaps, or the Australian pair of thirty-somethings who exuded niceness like some cheap talc-scent from a chemist's shop.

'And are you here on holiday?'

'No.' Nadejda forgets to lie.

'You live here?'

'Yeah.'

'Permanently?'

'Not really. Just for a while.'

'Aha.' Birdie seems content. Birdie seems like a contented person altogether. Nadejda feels lousy, as if in the aftermath of an ignoble lie. Who did she lie to this time? Or is the feeling the same after an ignoble truth? Because there is nothing noble about telling the truth, really.

Downstairs, Nadejda looks at postcards and rings the bell for service. It's lunchtime, there is nobody around, it's ridiculously easy to just pick a few cards and walk out, but Nadejda is particular about small things like this. Pettiness is ugly. She picks up a few leaflets describing various sightseeing tours in the Valleys of Hell, and steps out into the lascivious stink of the midday sun. She has no sunglasses to put on and this makes purposeful the itch she feels coming on. She must book a tour for tomorrow, but at present she is itching.

It has been a long time, days of flying there and back, hours of waiting at airports. She didn't feel at all tempted at the airports, for some reason — everything seemed so bland there, so well-shelved and impersonal that she didn't even consider it. It's funny: it isn't her hands that itch the most, it is an itch inside her chest, a well-defined, burning hollow which must be soothed somehow. There is a busker at the corner of the pharmacy where she is headed — a handsome Maori guy, playing a mediocre guitar and singing some country song. The incongruity of it all, Nadejda vaguely senses as she looks for a coin in her wallet. The multiple, unending incongruity, to which we just get accustomed, whether or not we see it: there's her, a virtually orphaned child of the poorest provinces of Europe, giving money to this Pacific Islander who gets five times more from his weekly bum's benefit than her professor father gets a month, this pretty boy who is playing the tune of his invaders, the same boy who waves a fist outside some council in some drowsy dreamtown on Waitangi Day or some other decisive day, shouting obscurely his anger at something, but only because everyone else is shouting. She watches herself drop a fifty-cent coin in his incongruous cowboy hat, and watches him smile at her. She watches the pharmacist align some cans of hairspray in the window, and walks inside.

Nadejda is having fun at the sunglasses stand trying on various styles. But the white-clad figure is always there to ruin her fun. If she is to gain her trust and be left alone, she must talk, ask for help and then sensibly decide to 'browse' some more before making up her mind. Above all, never appear anti-social or nervous. So she talks, and accepts the help (which consists of indifferent agreement with whatever pair she tries on, 'These look lovely on you'), eventually boring the woman to the point where she says, 'Well, I'll leave you to have a browse,' and attends to another needy customer, an obese American tourist whose matching wife momentarily obscures the doorway as she comes in. Nadejda snatches the glasses of her choice and slips them discreetly inside her top, so that one thin, light insectile limb barely shows on the light fabric, and is further enmeshed with her two pendants. She turns to the pharmacist who cracks her foundation with a careful smile, the fan buzzes, Nadejda says 'Thank you' with the polite smile of an unsatisfied customer, and walks out. Sad Nadejda has new sunglasses to the value of $75.95.

There is nothing like the sensation of a newly acquired object, the moment she steps out of a store. It's a post-traumatic jubilation; it is a cooling balm to the aching hollow in Nadejda's chest. The sunglasses are not as good as she thought — too dark and yellowish, so that the world is a sepia-coloured film, some amateurish footage from somebody else's life, somebody else's trip. She is being shown this film without having asked for it. She wants to stop it, not because she doesn't like it, but because it is somebody else's and she feels uneasy watching it.

Faces squint against the sun; sunburnt tourists stroll, carried forward by their cameras propped up on bellies; multiple bubbling geysers beckon from the sulphuric valley like raised fingers. But Nadejda no longer smells the gas, she only feels the indolence. The indolence of a world that would have been just as indolent without her, indolence unaffected by her, only affecting her.

A rust-coloured cat leaps out from somewhere, in slow feline motion, and lands at her feet, wrapping her body around Nadejda's ankle. She starts walking again, refusing to stroke this hot furry body which would have solicited someone else's affection if she wasn't here. But the cat walks after her, and as Nadejda stops the cat stops too, lifting her grey, knowing eyes in imploration. Nadejda squats and strokes her half-heartedly. The contact of her hand with the soft palpitating body makes her ache dully with pleasure, an ache similar to that of Anton's hand travelling in one perfect sweep from her hip to her breast. Whose pleasure is it? Whose ache? The cat purrs, the only way it has of showing enjoyment. Nadejda gets up and as the cat continues to fawn on her she gives it a kick, not a serious one, just enough to discourage further bonding. Why did she do that? The cat will find another leg, and another hand to comfort her. Nadejda walks on, her heart full of aching and badness.

She spends the rest of the afternoon soaking in a spa, a book lying open on the border of the pool, untouched. It's a gift from her father — Simone de Beauvoir's *The Second Sex*, in translation. Nadejda has no interest in the second sex. Right now, she is lying under clouds of humid warmth, her body rocking with the ripple of therapeutic water, her hands sliding into the bare surface, merging with it, flesh feeding translucence, water feeding flesh. Right now she can only be here where no voice, in no language, can reach her and teach her anything. All there is to learn is here.

A man floats up to her, his bug's eyes bulging intensely. 'Hi.'
'Hi.'

Chapter Seven

'You look a bit lonely.'

'Do I?'

'You would like some company?' Even if it weren't for the stressing of the 'y', the familiar gallant arrogance betrays the French. None of the desexualised friendliness of the New Age New Zealander or Australian.

'Maybe.'

He is quite attractive, although the water conceals the beginnings of a premature late-twenties belly, a landmark of the early sensualist. His bulging green eyes have a cat-slant and a twinkle of narcissistic humour. It is a pleasure to be dealing with an expert, thinks Nadejda, even if he is a prat.

'I was feeling a little lonely,' Narcissus confesses in an attempt at disarming self-revelation. Nadejda says nothing, unresponsiveness being the best stimulation for the ambitious male. She stirs the surface with wrinkly fingers. Narcissus is now leaning against the ceramic wall, revealing toned, long biceps. His head is cocked in the classic pose of undisguised seductive intention. He sees the book and grasps the opportunity.

'Are you reading this?'

'Yes.'

'I am French you know, but euh, I haven't read this, in fact, I haven't read any Beauvoir. But I know she is excellent.'

'I haven't read any Beauvoir either.'

'You aren't English, I mean euh, New Zealander?'

'No.' Nadejda already savours the inadequacy of his suppositions.

'Can I guess from where you come?' He leans on his right elbow which touches hers. She doesn't move. He shades his eyes against the sun as he scrutinises her. 'Euh . . . Spain?'

'No.' She is sick of telling the truth, but she is too well disposed to lie.

'Czechoslovakia?'

'You mean the Czech Republic.' Her voice is stern, but it won't ruffle his ego, she thinks. His ego is so big it would need a real hurricane of disapproval to ruffle it.

'Pardon? Ah, yes, the Czech Republic. No?'

'No.'

'I don't know, euh.'

But of course he doesn't know, he's French, he doesn't know about the rest of Europe, how could he know, she reflects bitterly. To a Bulgarian? Over my dead body! Nadejda sees the bitter colour of her father's humiliation as the wine glasses sway in the soft evening light in the hand of the French bastard in Nice. Nice time he had in Nice! She will never read a word in French, or speak French to a Frenchman, no matter how fine a jawline he has and how well-built he is. Jamais de la vie, over her dead body! Or so she thought.

She puts him out of his miserable speculation. 'Really? Ah bon.' He is so surprised he almost breaks into French. But she is firm in her mute refusal to join him. Never again will she speak this language, she vowed to herself that night in the enraged silence of her small room, staring wildly at her bookshelf where the spines of French books, given to her by her father, were pressed together in a sneering crowd. She tore their spines out and wept as she did it. Now her eyes are dry, and her throat is dry, and she can't tell whether it's with desire for Narcissus or with resentment.

'And do you live here?'

She knows the question-answer programme, and wishes she could lie better. 'Yes.'

'I live here too. Temporarily.'

'Me too. Temporarily.'

'And you travel by yourself?'

'Yes.'

'Where are you staying?'

He too is staying at the backpackers, what a coincidence! He twitches with delightful anticipation. Nadejda's throat is dry. They stay in the pool for another hour talking about New Zealand, France and Bulgaria. Narcissus is doing a PhD. In what? Botany. Of course.

'I 'ave heard that Bulgaria is a beautiful country.'

No he hasn't, thinks Nadejda, he is just trying to bed her. But has she heard that France is a beautiful country? Of course she has. And New Zealand, what does he think about it?

'Ah, New Zealand, it is beautiful, but they don't like the French.'

59

'Really? Why?'

'Oh, I don't know, because they euh, because of the *Rainbow Warrior* I suppose, and in general, you know. They don't see how nice we are,' he laughs heartily.

Nadejda sways between contempt for what he is saying and attraction to his sonorous laugh. How nice are you? she thinks.

'Are you from Nice?' she says, without thinking. She knows that even if he says yes, she couldn't hate him half as much as she vowed to, that night by the broken window, by the broken sparrow.

He doesn't get the bad pun. Just as well, thinks Nadejda. He is from Tours, where the best French is spoken according to her father. 'I've heard that the best French is spoken in Tours,' she says.

'That's correct.' His English suddenly sounds impeccable.

'So you speak the best French?'

'Euh, I don't know. Maybe.' He is flattered.

The temptation becomes too great. Here he is, in all his simple manhood. He calls out for her touch. Narcissus is a man incapable of resisting the faintest promise of languor. Nadejda, feeling languorous like a crowd of semi-naked, loose-haired Echoes in a sweltering pool, wants to repeat his stray call coming from the sepia-coloured sulphurous woods. As soon as she does, he will come to her.

They walk to the backpackers together. He has an attractive, feline walk and glances at her sideways. Does the vow against speaking the language include abstention from sleeping with its speakers? Did she ever envisage such a clause? Anyway, there are three women in her room, and probably three men in his, and that should solve the problem. As they part, he squeezes her elbow and one corner of his lip curls into a smile which is not really a smile. They both know what it is. 'See you later then,' he says. 'Yeah, I'll see you later.' says Nadejda, and in that meaningless, automatic phrase is the germ of her forgiveness.

But as she stands under the shower five minutes later, she evokes, half-heartedly but inevitably, that evening, ten years ago. Her father came back from the conference in Nice. Tired-faced and tense, he gave Nadejda and her mother presents from glamorous, distant France (books for Nadejda, as always — *The Little Prince*, *Les Misérables*, and some detective novels by Georges Simenon, by request, which her father considered trash but bought conscientiously). He told them in a vague, abstract way about the good time he'd had and the places he'd seen. Later, her ear glued to her door — a device which enabled her to access the information that truly mattered and that shaped clandestinely her view of her parents and life — Nadejda overheard the following exchange:

He: We were standing there, Dupont was talking to this woman from Poland, I think, and I was kind of stuck with this other guy. I'd seen him before — he's a critic, so we started a conversation. He was a nice guy, you know, cordial, he asks me what my main interests are, and I tell him, trying to explain that I don't actually *teach* those authors because they can't be part of the curriculum for such and such reasons, and he listens politely although I can tell he doesn't quite understand, and then . . .

She: You can't expect them to understand, they live in a different world, they can't even conceive of this! It's, I don't know . . .

He: Anyway, he says 'Actually, my wife specialises in the Romantics too,' and I say . . .

She: Do you want some more Scotch?

He: Yes. So I say, 'Oh, you must introduce me to her then,' you know, a perfectly normal thing to say.

She: Was she there, his wife?

He: I don't know, I don't think so, but that's beside the point, because then he says, you know what he says to me?

She: Mmm.

He: He says, 'Quoi? Introduce her à un Bulgare? stressing Bulgare. Jamais de la vie.' What? To a Bulgarian? Over my dead body. And he just sipped his wine as though it was the most natural thing to say, you know, totally nonchalant.

There was silence after that. Then Nadejda's mother said in a flat voice: 'Well, I suppose they've always seen us as the poor relations. What do you expect?'

He: What do I expect? What do I expect? I expect a bit of respect, nothing more, just to be treated like an equal, not like some . . . His voice breaks. He gulps his whisky. She doesn't say anything.

He: Because I *am* their equal, you know, and they know it, it's just that . . .

61

Chapter Seven

She: Yes, I know. I'm sure they're not all like that, I'm sure they realise.

He: No, no, they're not. In fact Dupont caught the last bit of what that idiot said and came over to us. I think he felt kind of uneasy.

She: Did he say anything later?

He: No.

They talked about something else, after a brief sipping silence. Nadejda sat at her desk and looked blankly at her French books. She had always known they were the poor relatives. But she had never hated being the poor relation so much. She hated it so much that she didn't know whom to hate more — her parents for being in this dismal poor relation position, or the rich French who hadn't really deserved to be the rich relation, not as far as she could tell. In a flash of vindictiveness, she grabbed her French books and, one by one, tore their slender spines out. She cried at the butchery of it, the ugliness of it. She had loved those books and still loved them. But they didn't love her; so they perished. Her father had been a sad fool.

Nadejda slipped outside, in her slippers. She didn't know where she was going — there was nowhere to go, but she had to. She ran down the six floors. Most lights were out; there was a broken window. On the third floor she saw a small dark flutter in the corner by the jagged window. She looked closely — a sparrow. It was hurt; its leg was hanging lamely. It palpitated like a feathery heart. Nadejda was at the age when at the sight of hurt birds and animals girls overflow with intense pity verging on sensuality; but being unlike most girls her age, she was mainly overflowing with a sense of intense loneliness. Like her, this sparrow was completely alone, but she couldn't feel any love for it. She had no love to give to a sparrow. She had no love. She slumped down on the grimy floor, her eyes getting accustomed to the semi-darkness, and stared out the window.

Outside thousands of lights decorated the concrete slabs, like austere decorations lighting up a badly misconceived pine forest. Each light meant at least one life, but most probably four or five (allowing for the grandparent). The last buses growled past. Nadejda heard a faint noise somewhere downstairs. The sparrow had stopped twitching, probably dead. She wished she could cry. But her throat ·

was dry. She moved down the stairs on tiptoe. Everybody knew that venturing out in the dark foyer of the building was foolish, especially for a girl. But she felt foolish that night.

It got darker and creepier as she descended towards the ground-floor lobby, the concrete stairs exuding a deadly coldness. There was someone in the corner. Peeking from the top of the stairs, she could see a dark heap below the clinical glow of forty metal letterboxes covering one wall. The heap was producing an ugly, fascinating noise, a mixture of hoarse moans and grunts which Nadejda had never heard before but whose nature she guessed immediately. They didn't notice her, or rather what was a woman-like creature didn't notice her, since the man-like creature had his back to her and was covering the woman's face.

She came down a few more steps. Her heart was thrashing about in its cage like a hurt sparrow. She didn't know why she was trying to get closer; but there had to be something more to see or know. She could hear the generator ticking gently in the opposite corner. Faint cigarette smoke rose up to her face, making her eyes water and threatening to unleash a fatal sneeze. For a moment she concentrated very hard on not sneezing. When the danger had passed, she took a few more steps down and stopped at the junction with the top of the last flight of stairs, almost losing the heaving heap from sight.

Then she saw, in a flash of disbelief, the two men standing opposite, at the bottom of the stairs. One of them she recognised with certainty, as he inhaled from his cigarette. She would have recognised him anyway, just from the outline of his hair and leather jacket. They were watching and smoking in silence. In another hideous flash they saw her. Or rather, Dimo saw her and the cigarette dropped from his mouth. He stubbed it out. She stood there, unable to move, petrified and fascinated. The other one also looked at her and made a movement as if to leap up the stairs and grab her. 'Hold it,' said Dimo. 'Hold it. Leave her alone, she's my friend.'

The girl was now whimpering, reminding Nadejda of the stray puppies that infested the *Nadejda* suburb. She knew why the puppies whimpered, but why was the girl whimpering? Maybe she knew that girl, and maybe even the guy who pressed her against the wall. She

63

knew Dimo, after all. Dimo took the ten steps in two gigantic strides and crouched next to Nadejda, instantly enveloping her with a warm cloud of real man smell — tobacco, leather and something else that she couldn't name but wanted to sniff for a long, long time. He was so big that when he crouched she could face him comfortably, although he was looking up; she liked that. Dimo was looking up at her. He said, 'Nade, you mustn't go out like this in the dark. I want you to go home now. You will go home, won't you? Don't mind us, we're just having a bit of fun. Don't take the lift, go up the stairs. Batko Dimo will come with you some of the way, okay?'

Suddenly, Nadejda's teeth were chattering, she didn't know why. Her head was spinning, her eyes were watering.

'Batko Dimo will come with you, okay?' She nodded, but it was as though somebody else's head nodded. 'Okay?'

His large palm pushed her back gently towards the steps. She walked up and looked back. He was still crouching, his patched leather elbows propped on his strong, square, jeaned knees. 'Go on,' he said, indicating with his hand how she should go on. He was serious, she'd never seen him so serious. The noise had stopped, but she was too preoccupied following Dimo's instructions to dare look down to the lobby. She kept climbing the stairs, her legs wobbly and strangely long, so long she couldn't feel her toes touching the concrete. When she reached the top of the flight, Dimo got up and whispered, 'Don't tell your parents, okay? For my sake.' He winked at her.

The head nodded. She wanted to stand there and look at him standing at the bottom of the steps, one leg lifted as if to follow her, his long fringe over one eye, his face in darkness but so handsome, turned up towards her in the total, frightening intimacy of the strange night. But he said, 'Go on, Nadejda. Home.' And she went home.

Past the broken windows, past the dead sparrow which lay with its legs pointing up towards the ceiling as if somebody had tied a thread around the tiny legs and had pulled them up as a sick joke. Past the apartment doors behind which she could smell strange smells, hear strange sounds, and match them with the familiar strange faces: the giant crane-driver Ljubov, Love, and her forger-husband

Dimitar who constantly knocked on people's doors in the evening with a bottle of rakia and wanted to talk crap to the sound of the TV, over gherkins with salty cheese; the divorced teacher Vera with her nerdy overweight son; the physicist Damyan and his beautiful, neurotic blue-eyed wife Violeta and two beautiful, annoying daughters Irina and Malinna, whom Nadejda got mixed up; the little crumpled woman in black whose son committed suicide last week, and whose other son was in prison; the Greek-born, white-haired director of some factory or other and his crippled wife and delinquent son; the quiet young couple — the man a PhD student and the woman grotesquely pregnant; and the others, all the others on the next floors. Dimo lived on the top tenth floor with his parents. His father was an officer in the army, his mother was a secretary in some office or other and his brother was in the navy. Dimo was Nadejda's batko, her big brother, her flame, her impossible love, six years older than her. He protected her from the gameni, the thugs in the neighbourhood, and even saved her once from the aggressive come-ons of the red-haired fifteen-year-old who was constantly after her. Dimo pushed him against an iron fence and said, 'You touch her and I'll bash your head inside your neck.' She thought he loved her then.

She rang the doorbell and her mother opened the door, her face drawn and eerie in the dim light of the corridor. 'Where have you been, Nadejda?' The full name, rather than the usual diminutive, signalled a foul mood.

Nadejda's throat was all shrunk. She couldn't speak, which created the impression that she was in some kind of shock, when in fact she was fine. Only she couldn't say anything to that effect. She walked in. Her mother slammed the door. Nadejda was unharmed and therefore dismissed.

She wondered, as she lay on top of her bed, if Dimo was taking his turn now. She tried to imagine what it felt like for that girl, but she couldn't get very far beyond the kissing part. Was it the same as kissing Moni? As she imagined kissing Dimo, the hot, unbearable tingling in her stomach spread up, reaching her throat and blossoming into a huge, loud sob. Dimo didn't love her. But she wouldn't tear his spine out.

That night Nadejda had a nightmare.

In a bright room with low, humming chandeliers, her father, dressed in a sack, stands in the middle of a mocking circle of French gentlemen. They drink a toast to 'nos collegues de l'Est', our colleagues from the East. 'They have come a long way, on a donkey! The donkey is waiting outside, we presume?' exclaims one critic and everybody shakes with joy. Their glasses tinkle, the chandeliers rock, and the sound of the collective tinkle is in fact a deafening crash of tonnes of glass onto her father's back. Underneath the magnified sound of shattering crystal, Nadejda hears the crushing of her father's spine, and is devastated to see that under the shapeless sack he is a heap of mushed bones, a body of pain. He stands upright because he wants to be treated with respect, but underneath he sags horrifically. Nadejda cries her heart out, and at that point batko Dimo flies in through a broken window — a great black angel with leather wings. He winks at her, then proceeds to bash every French head inside its neck, while the bodies still hold their wineglasses. But it is too late — her father sags under his sack. It is too late.

Early in the morning, Nadejda's father woke up to find the white ghost of Nadejda bent uncomfortably in the narrow space between him and the edge of the bed, her feet on the floor, her nightie pulled up at the front and crumpled into a knot, her cold hand with white knuckles and bluish nails clutching his pyjama sleeve, her shallow-breathing face resting on a darkened, drenched patch of sheet. He covered her and stroked her hair, thinking how he could bear anything in this world but to lose her.

Nadejda steps out of the shower. Her fingers are even more wrinkled now. It is dinnertime. She looks in the mirror. Her nose is brown, her chest and shoulders are slightly burnt and the whites of her eyes flash more whitely than ever. She knows that Narcissus is waiting for her in the lounge, leafing through inane magazines and lifting his eyes every time someone comes through the door. Narcissus waits for her to lie rippling underneath him like water, so he can see and adore himself in her. She is not going to. She is going to do something else, she isn't sure what yet, but she knows that she has stepped out of the anaesthetising pool and her strong, blind legs are carrying her towards the sepia-coloured woods. She can do nothing about it. With morosely gritted teeth, Nadejda steps into the lounge where Narcissus is leafing through some inane magazines and lifts his gaze towards her. What the hell, thinks Nadejda as she smiles at him. French, Bulgarian, New Zealand, circumcised or hairless, whatever — once naked, they are stripped of language or national vices.

He offers to take her out to dinner. She accepts. What else would she do — write smiley cards to friends? Which friends — the desperate ones of the old world who get beaten by the police or the wide-eyed, humanist ones from the new world, who think that poverty and anarchy are romantic? She doesn't know what to say to either. Write to her mother who doesn't know she is back? 'I'll be home soon, Mum.' Will she be home soon? Write to her father to whom she has failed and will still fail to say everything there is to say? 'I'm having a really good time travelling here' or 'I had a really good time with you' — both would be dishonest. Talk the small tourist talk with the homely tourists already buzzing diligently in the kitchen over steaming pots and sizzling onion pans?

No. As she looks around, Nadejda has to admit that there is only one Narcissus presently lingering among the international crowd of scuttling gnomes and awkward giants. So she puts on a tight T-shirt and goes to dinner.

They have seafood and white wine. Nadejda, already drugged by sun and vapours, calls him Narcissus in passing. Jean-Luc is charmed and worried by his strange new acquaintance. Soon he resigns himself to the fact that this girl with the unpronounceable name is strange and probably lying about a thing or two. They lean towards each other with increasing symmetry, if not grace. On the way to the backpackers, he rubs her back gently, as if showing her the way. This way, his palm says to her back, this way, please, for my sake.

He shares a room with one other, who is currently out. They collapse on his single bed and undress messily. After a fitful foreplay, Nadejda sits on top of him and hastily rolls a condom over his erect penis. He watches her, and a shadow of worry passes over his face. She remains in this position until the last spasm, her left hand tucked underneath him, her fingers pressed against his fleshy back. She refuses to lie next to him and when he disengages himself and

67

turns over to lie on his stomach she remains in this position, sitting on his lower back.

With a tanned finger she travels down the ranges of the botanist's ribbed spine. 'Ma foi,' he exhales. Well, well.

The world is good and intact again.

CHAPTER EIGHT

Once I only read about

pineapples.

Pineapple

Once I only read about pineapples. Pineapple was the ultimate dream crystallising into fruit. Impossible by definition, unlike bananas which we could buy sometimes on New Year's Eve after long hours of queuing. But your uncle wrote about the bananas *there*, how they were freely available, the pineapples which you could just go and buy as you please. It was like talking to him through time, not simply through space — he was somewhere ahead of us. To talk to him, I had to look at the luminous patch of his letters, a window to the new future. I was blinded by the unearthly light of that quasi-real country, a drop of heaven in the fiction of the Pacific Ocean. Now I look at the pineapple — the thorny body of my dream — and I have no use for it; somehow it remains a prisoner of its own myth.

You used to respect me for imagining too much. Now you blame me for accepting too much. Now you blame me for everything, for that which is too much, for that which is not enough. My only one, hard-headed, merciless, unhappy one. The sky is blue today, but there is a deep ripe bruise arching over the valley, though I didn't notice any rain. When you see a rainbow, you want it for yourself, you don't know what for — perhaps to wrap it around your shivering body, or to stuff it into your drawer and take a peek at night, or to make sure nobody else touches it with dirty hands. When you see a double rainbow, you want to know which one is false, and you blame me for not knowing. But I had the most terrible knowledge, the minute we landed among the palm trees in the livid Pacific dawn. You were busy having to believe this was a temporary arrangement, an exotic voyage to see the long-lost family, you were busy being eighteen, but I knew. You blame me for pretending there is some kind of order in things, beginnings and endings. But I knew.

I wish I didn't. When I pretend to sleep, I dream of you, and in my so-called dream I gallop madly around the world, froth at my mouth, looking for you. On what balcony edge are you balancing your precarious weight, in which garden are you crouching, what greedy, hairy hands are reaching out to grab you and cover you in mire because the best apples are eaten by the pigs, as the old saying has it? What railway are you crossing in the pitch darkness, oblivious of passing trains and stray beasts, where are your hips and collarbones rattling in the Balkan wind, my skinny one?

I cut up a pineapple today. As the knife dug into the spiky carapace, I knew I was committing an act of butchery. You will frown with scorn — I dramatise, you'll say. But Nadejda, this pineapple didn't belong to me. I hacked it in two without wanting to eat it, I couldn't think of anything else to do with it. I watched its clear aromatic juice run down my arms and it was blood, the blood of severed halves which are no longer halves because they can't be joined back together. What are they then? I stood in the middle of the kitchen, knife in hand, the seeds of my mind spilling out, the surface darkening, the sickly sweet smell corrupting the afternoon, and nothing left to butcher. You cringe. You blame me for cutting the pineapple, but then you blame me for crying over it, my dry-eyed, my fruit-devouring Nadejda.

You say there is a gulf between us. I can swim, but you wouldn't let me. You sit on the other side, looking straight into the sun, refusing sunglasses, refusing to divert your gaze, because you know that the world is only a figment of the sun, and you want nothing less than the source, the essence, the ripest fruit, the most dazzling seas. I was like you once. The sun burned my retina, dried my skin to shreds, and I saw nothing, and I put on my sunglasses. Sometimes you cross the gulf with awkward strokes, and you bring back from the beach of your bitter youth grains of sand in the mouth, salt in the hair, exhaltation in the skin. I lie in the middle of a night without a middle, facing the slow, gigantic waves of mud rising on the blurry horizon. Are you seeing the same waves?

Don't stay, Nadejda, my angel, run. They'll hit you in the face, they'll fill your mouth, they'll blind your eyes, they'll turn you into themselves, they're coming to wash you out, not to teach you surfing, my brave one, my burning one, don't watch.

Chapter Eight

CHAPTER NINE

Ana and Vassil are sitting at the
kitchen table.

Worms

Ana and Vassil are sitting at the kitchen table. Ana is chain-smoking, Vassil is playing irritably with his coffee spoon. This is what they are saying:

'You can't undo the past, bate.'

'You always tell me the obvious.'

'Don't be ratty with me, Vasko, I'm trying to be helpful.'

'I don't need help.'

'I know, I know.' She sighs, stirring the ashes in the ashtray with her cigarette butt. He stirs his empty coffee cup with a spoon, then digs into the layer of residual sugary blackness. 'But you can't stay away forever, when you know you want to go there.'

'I *will* go.'

'You've been saying this for years. I have the feeling you'll never go.'

'Why do you want me to go so much? It isn't as though hordes of cheery relatives will greet me at the airport with pita bread and white cheese, or anyone will recognise me.'

'I want you to go because I know that's what you care about. Because I know that's what you want.'

'You know everything!'

'Not if you ask Nadejda I don't.'

'Nadejda doesn't know anything, Ani. She is, how old is she now? Twenty-two?'

'Twenty-one.'

'Twenty-one! She doesn't know anything!'

'You were nineteen when you left. You knew what was wrong then, when most didn't.'

'Everybody knew what was wrong, everybody knew the system was rotten to the core; they were just smart enough not to say it. I was young and I only spoke my mind.'

'Nadejda speaks her mind too.'

'You listen to her too much. You've lost your grip on her, she doesn't respect anyone. She isn't doing well at all in her studies, and you don't push her.'

'I can't push her. She does what she can.'

'Minimalism. You're being a minimalist. You've always been a minimalist, Ani.' He smiles without amusement.

73

'And you? You ran away from it all and had the choice. I had no choice but to be a minimalist if you call it that. I call it survival!' Her voice rises in a sudden outburst of despair, her hands cut the air, dividing it and pushing outwards in the direction of those who ran away from it all.

'Let's not start this.' His voice is conciliatory, as if dealing carefully with a lunatic. 'I'm sorry.'

'I know, I know.'

'You know this is not what I really think. You *know* what I really think.'

Actually, she doesn't any more. Too many thoughts have bustled in her own mind, too many thoughts have been thrown backwards and forwards between them, for forty years. The gist has been lost somewhere. But she is in no mood to find out now. Perhaps there is nothing to find out. She is in no mood for pondering the past either. She looks out the window towards the Lego-like, green, tidy town feasting on sunshine below. If she could draw a picture of her heart at that moment, it would be the exact opposite of this view. She would have liked to draw a picture like that. He could probably do it for her anyway, he is a dissector of the human heart, after all. But he can't see into his own heart.

'Sometimes we just have to go with our feelings,' she says, wondering if she actually agrees with this. Sometimes she says things just to test them out.

He sneers, his nostrils flaring to reveal a forest of black hairs. 'That's what I tell some of my patients, the intelligent neurotics. "Sometimes you should go with your feelings." Stop rationalising, let go, let your feelings lead you. But that's a lie. I don't want to "go with my feelings". To go with my feelings would mean to contort in a clumsy, sick dance, like one of those chained "dancing" bears. You know the ones? Do they still have them?'

'Yes.'

'In the centre of Sofia?'

'Yes, right next to the Sheraton.'

'Christ!'

'So ...'

'So, to go with my feelings is an eccentricity I've learnt to unlearn, if you see what I mean. I went with my feelings when I married Pat. When I said to Mum, "Come." And above all, when I spoke then, in front of people I couldn't trust and who betrayed me, I followed my feelings then.' He opens his palms towards her, his strong fingers pointing at her, thumbs outstretched, as if he is offering his feelings on the trays of his palms.

'But you're not saying you regret all those decisions?'

'They weren't decisions. They were leaps of faith disguised as decisions. Leaps of feeling rather.'

'But are you saying that you regret them?'

'No, I don't, I don't regret them, but . . .' He regrets nothing, and they both know it. But it isn't so simple. All the things, all the blows. Marriage: his wife wanting the impossible from him all along. His mother: he persuaded her to fly over and stay with them, after so many years and with a weak heart. And saying those things then, at Sofia University. He had to — he couldn't have lived in humiliated silence for the next forty-four years, half a century of abject muteness with the family. No separations, no deaths, no tearing of the heart — this soft lokum with an unsavoury flavour — and total humiliation. Everything follows those words he said then, at nineteen: his father, his mother, his marriage and divorce, Ana and Nadejda here, in this flat-hearted town on the edge of oblivion with no resemblance to Sofia. No regrets. Only anger. Anger has fed insidiously on the lifeblood of his reasoning like a tapeworm: eyeless, sluggish, so deeply rooted and so monstrous that he is terrified at the thought of seeing it come out. The tapeworm grows, weighing him down. He is bloated on the inside. To state his anger would be to invite the tapeworm's ghastly head to come out of his mouth. But not all the way, no — just a peek, before it plunges back in, where it belongs. He shudders. If he is pushed, he will imply the existence of the tapeworm, by denying it repeatedly. No, there is no tapeworm inside him, none.

'No, of course I don't regret them. But I don't trust my feelings.'

She is not so much leaning against the edge of the table as gripping it with great force. 'I don't know. I think you're wrong, bate. You must be wrong.'

'I must be.' He leans back in his chair and smiles his ironic,

Chapter Nine

brooding half-smile, the left side of his mouth tugging upwards and revealing smoker's teeth, the same as hers, though he has never smoked in his life. His thick greyish eyebrows pucker in the middle of his forehead for a second and are then smoothed out.

As he leaves, she gives him a large piece of the spanachena banitza, spinach and cheese pastry they had for lunch, wrapped in foil. They kiss on the cheek and smile. He drives off in his new silver BMW.

She is sad for him. He knows it and resents it. She thinks she is sad for him because he is in exile, because he never saw his mother again, because his marriage failed. But all this wouldn't have been enough to make her quite so sad, if he had children of his own. He senses the nature of this sadness, and says as often as he can without sounding defensive, 'Patricia and I wanted different things.' And she acquiesces, her sadness undiminished. She resents Patricia, whom she hasn't met and never will because Patricia lives in a small Canadian town now, with her second husband and three kids. Patricia got what she wanted. Vassil didn't. But what *does* he want?

He didn't ask if she'd heard from Nadejda. He knows that she hasn't and didn't want to stir her by making her say it. But she says it to herself all the time, in a dissonance of freakish voices: *Nadejda hasn't written* — she doesn't have time to write, fair enough, fair enough. She calls instead. *Nadejda hasn't called either* — she always calls, why, why, it's been a week, she called only once. Is something terrible happening? *Nadejda is fine* — she is a grown-up girl, she doesn't need to report to her mother every second day. She hasn't seen her father for three years, she is torn between them, it's so tough on her. *Nadejda will be flying home soon* — home? What is here for her? Is her mother enough of a home? Can she be her moving house, or is it too late for that? Nadejda is so distant these days, but she is the sole reason for this enormous undertaking. She is the one who keeps her mother's floating house from falling into splinters and drifting off to Antarctica where everything drifts off. And again, *Nadejda hasn't called.* Why, why?

She can't call *his* place, their place in another life — the only way to contact Nadejda. If she calls and *he* answers, it's unimaginable. He doesn't speak to her. She can't speak to a mute man. She can't just say 'Hi, it's me. Can I speak to Nadejda?' It would be absurd to beg for a favour after everything he has denied her. She can wait. Nadejda will call. It's been only a week since her first call. It's been a whole week since her first call.

She can't sleep. She used just to be a bad sleeper; now she is a full-blown insomniac. This is what happens: in the moments when she is closest to falling asleep, she has a recurrent vision. Giant waves of mud rise in the distance, in a stupendous, horizon-altering wall (the horizon is far, she says to herself), spattering the sky which flinches as far back as it can and flattens out its swellings, gathers the folds of its flesh and retreats heavily like a surprised eunuch in a Turkish bath. The horizon is far, she says to herself, but it travels at the speed of my fear — my fear makes it move and I can't help it. If I could be unafraid, this ochre mountain of bubbling mud would stop. But she is afraid, she is struck by an immemorial terror, and the waves roar nearer and nearer. On the beach where giant birds of prey are casting ragged shadows, stands a lone figure. She is surprised that she can see the figure — is it her or is it someone else? It is both. Then she suddenly sees and is shattered: the figure is also Nadejda, her long hair fingered by the wind, unaware of the danger, watching the organic mountain charge towards her, as if invulnerable. She screams, trying to warn Nadejda, but her screams are choked by the blunt, concussive thunder of the muddy mass. Nadejda has her back to her. It is too late. Soon the crest of the monstrous yellow wall curls high above the little head which looks up, unafraid, and then ... Then she sits up in bed, breathless and shaking, forever awake, and lies in the bright patch of the bedside lamp, stunned by a numbing grief. Only her mother would have understood this. Only mothers do.

She looks at the phone long and hard. Finally, it rings, a shrill, piercing sound. She bolts out of the armchair as if given an electric shock. She grabs the receiver and drops it, then picks it up again, and shouts 'Da?' But it isn't Nadejda. Once again, telepathy hasn't worked. It is an unctuous voice doing a survey on ... She hangs up and swaying, leans against the wall, knocking down a small oil-painting of Old Plovdiv.

*

Chapter Nine

Vassil, driving down the hill, looks at his watch. He has no commitments today, being Saturday. Why did he look at his watch then? Because he is thinking of a place which has a ten-hour time-difference from this car and this town. Ten hours and forty-four years' difference from this self. It is midnight in Sofia. He thinks of the only person in that city who recognises him — Nadejda, strange Nadejda. She is somewhere out on the town probably, trying out the new bars with her friends, or whatever it is they do. Or at home, talking to her intransigent father. Or sleeping, though apparently she is an agitated sleeper — it runs in the family. But certainly not reading; she is not a great reader — an odd thing, almost an oversight, considering her parents are both scholars. In any case, she has reason to be there. He would have no reason, and being in a place that reminds you of the loss of a reason that was once there is a dangerous experience. He lived with this for many years, in this quaint town of silences, clean roofs, and absolutely no resemblance to Sofia. 'I know it's what you want,' Ana said. To leap headlong into the buried city of his youth, to dig out of the peaceful ashes of houses, faces, parks, autumnal rusty leaf-falls on Vitosha mountain. To find blocks of flats where delinquency thrives, mud-flats without rivers, armed neckless idiots in Mercedes, pornographic pictures strewn over the streets at bookstalls, their old building with the chestnut trees near St Sophia Church forty-four years older and stripped of its yellow paint. 'Sofia raste, no ne staree.' Sofia grows but never ages, the slogan of the capital. Though ancient, it fits perfectly the communist lack of regard for the natural order of things, the denial of the immutable gradation and degradation of reality, in their monumentally clownish bid for . . . For what? For glory. The perverse glory of minimalism, where everybody is equally poor. But only the honest were equally poor. The others devoured, and still devour the last crumbs of that luscious carnival bride that was Bulgaria. Bride that turns into scarecrow, her ribs sticking out through the rags, birds of prey picking at the last scraps. The poor get poorer, and the rest of Europe looks on and shakes its head at these distasteful Eastern laggards. And Vassil too, shakes his head because he is now the rest of the world.

Is that what he wants? He looks at his watch again. The time difference is still the same. Forty-four years, more than half a life. A cat crosses the road in jerky jumps: he breaks to avoid it and the car behind, with a horrible screech and crash, sticks its pointy muzzle into Vassil's new rear. 'Shit!' says Vassil as his chin hits the wheel.

The woman in the Honda crawls out and, instead of an explanation or an attack, bursts into tears. Vassil feels very tired. He wants to look away, but the event persists, the crushed steel must be straightened somehow, people gather to watch and must be dispersed, a church bell chimes in the distance, the sky is packing up. Vassil feels a warm liquid trickle down his mouth and chin. 'Oh my God, you're bleeding,' says the woman, stopping mid-sob, momentarily entranced by the sight of blood. She is vaguely attractive, Vassil notes, in a worn-out, pallid sort of way. The thought, absurd and uninvited, of bedding her shocks Vassil and then fills him with a queasy fatigue.

Mladen looks at Nadejda's photograph above his desk. Nadejda looks at him unsmilingly, but a post-smile dimple in her cheek reminds him of her lost laughter. He looks at the photo long and hard, but Nadejda doesn't come to life, nor does she wink or smile. He has just returned from the protest outside the Parliament building. His colleagues and students were there, and he shouted with them 'Communists — out!' He really meant that two hours ago, but now he feels indifferent, now he can't honestly say that's what he wants. The TV babbles in the lounge (which is also his bedroom): 'Communists — out!' It's news time. It's always news time here. He can't tear his eyes from the photograph. What happened, Heavens empty of gods? Why didn't he go with them in the first place to bloody New Zealand? There must have been a reason. There must be a reason still. Of course there is, only he can't remember it. He searches Nadejda's post-smiling, dated face. Nadejda has forgotten his reason too.

From three lone, vertiginous balloons of hot air which they can't navigate properly (because the balloons are faulty), three highly educated and toughened adults circle in space looking for a spot to land. But what they see below isn't looking good.

Ana sees a swollen ocean of mud with no intelligent life in it. She calls 'Nadejda-a-a-a', but there's no reply. The waves grow on the horizon, and suddenly they are here, towering above her head. Or is it Nadejda's head? At the foot of these waves, she is so alone that she almost can't feel herself at all.

Vassil sees two lonely specks of sea-locked land. Time after time he draws closer, recognising the velvety ranges, the violently jagged coast, the lakes perfect like the unblinking blue eyes of Cyclops struck dead by lightning, the naked roads, like languid worms travelling across the hills. So alluring, this land of freedom, so accommodating, so unlike him.

Mladen sees a jungle. A jungle at the fringe of civilisation, full of starving, disease-stricken savages who employ their last drop of strength to damage each other. Hungry blind worms squirming in the empty, punctured belly of his ancient country. A belly of darkness that, after being violated countless times, has learnt to violate itself. Ah, he can't bear to watch.

They have nowhere to land, they are tired to the point of hallucination. They wish at least they could spot Nadejda down there, so she could wave and smile, and tell them where it's safe to land.

They can't land because they are not flying in hot-air balloons. They have never been above the dreaded ground. Stranded at the very spot where they would be terrified to land, they hallucinate, willingly.

And Nadejda? Unarmed, stranded in the middle of summer's desert, Nadejda is fighting her own worms.

CHAPTER TEN

*At one in the morning, in the
backpackers' lounge, a young
Korean man is diligently copying
some new English words into a
notebook, his bilingual manual
open in front of him under the
bright white lights.*

Wonderland: boiling mud

At one in the morning, in the backpackers' lounge, a young Korean man is diligently copying some new English words into a notebook, his bilingual manual open in front of him under the bright white lights. The fridges hum in a cheerful harmony. He is so absorbed and confident of his total privacy that when he sees the semi-naked figure moving noiselessly towards him, he gives a squeak of fright. The long-haired girl is wearing only a long yellow T-shirt. She has one sock on. He watches her stroll leisurely around the lounge, then go into the kitchen, then come back to his table and sit down, facing him. Her hair is messed up on one side and her eyes don't seem to focus on anything. He saw her earlier, in the kitchen, while he stirred his noodles. She didn't hang around for dinner. She talked only to the handsome guy she went out with.

He waits for her to say something. His head is buzzing from the coffee he drank earlier, which is why he is staying up so late. Now, in the white humming light, surrounded by exotic nocturnal insects that fly into the open French door attracted by the light, in the sudden company of this dishevelled girl, he feels decidedly strange. The following exchange takes place:

'Kolko e chassa?'

'Excuse me?'

'Kolko e chassa? Chassa', she points at her wrist.

'Excuse me?'

'Oh, English. Have you got the time?'

'Oh, time!' He is distressed at his failure to recognise English. He must be very tired. He looks at his watch and thinks for a few seconds. 'Ten minutes past one.'

'Thank you.'

She looks at him, but doesn't seem to see him. He doesn't like this.

'You are from Japan, yeah?'

'Korea.'

'South Korea?'

'Yes, South Korea, yah,' he nods, reassured by the fact they are both making sense now.

'South Korea,' she repeats dreamily, and suddenly shivers.

He adjusts his glasses, feeling very uneasy once again.

82

'Do you have a sea in South Korea?'

'Sea?'

'A sea. Do you have a sea or an ocean in South Korea?'

'Sea.'

'Sea. We have the Black Sea. The Black Sea is not really black, you know. I haven't seen it being black.'

The Korean man nods, completely lost.

'They call it Black because in the winter there are huge storms. So huge that the waves crash on top of houses along the waterfront.'

The Korean man nods again, desperately trying to follow.

'And there are dead animals all over the beach after the storm. I've seen them.'

The Korean man gives up nodding. He just listens, realising she is not expecting or wanting him to respond. She needs to tell him about something and that's all. Maybe she's very lonely.

'Various animals. I don't know which animals I like. But there are no animals strong enough to stand up to the waves. Or people. I saw something terrible you know. Just now, I saw something terrible. I can't . . . it's just . . .' Her face screws up as if she is about to cry or give in to pain.

The man gives up trying to follow and just watches her speak, her eyes wandering in his direction, but never looking him in the eye for longer than a second, her hands tucked between her bare thighs, her shoulders pointing up as if in a perpetual shrug of bafflement.

'There are huge waves of mud coming from the horizon and all the animals on the beach are waiting to be swept off, swept out, away.' She makes a large sweeping gesture towards the door. 'I am there too. Maybe I'm an animal, doesn't matter. But I can't move, just can't move. I'm too fascinated, you know. The waves are like alive, like someone is coming, not just a tsunami of mud, but someone, someone . . .'

She lays her head on the table and makes a feeble plaintive noise. The man feels he should comfort her, although he doesn't know why she needs comforting. After a brief deliberation, he says carefully:

'Are you all right?'

She closes her eyes and mumbles.

83

Chapter Ten

'Excuse me?' He bends over to look at her face.

She doesn't open her eyes. She could be asleep, so he decides not to disturb her; besides, he's safer like this, he doesn't have to worry about what she is saying. Her face is partially covered by long locks, her hands are laid out symmetrically on both sides of her head, the fingers spread out. He examines her, uneasy from this prying into a strange girl's sleep but compelled to do it. Her hands are long and strong, naked of jewellery, except for a thin woven macramé bracelet.

After the incomprehensible outburst of this apparition, it is back to the humming of fridges. Disoriented insects fling themselves with suicidal exaltation into the hypnotic light like a crowd of sleepers jumping off a cliff in a dream of flying. The man sits motionless, still gripping his pen, his eyes pinned to the dishevelled head across the table, next to his English book. His girlfriend is sleeping somewhere in one of the rooms down the corridor, with two others, her head under a pillow, her long black hair covering her face, her mind impenetrable just like this strange girl's mind. Except that he can understand what his girlfriend says in the morning. He sits there for a long time, unable to get up or make any other movement, until he begins to drift off. Then, in what seems a supreme effort of will, he gathers his papers, his Walkman and empty cup, and trying to be noiseless, gets up (the chair legs make an unpleasant grating noise on the floor and give him goose-pimples) and heads for his dormitory, leaving the lounge lights on.

There is a place that was the bottom of an ocean once, when in the place of Europe there was an ocean. Once again, Nadejda stands on the cliffs overlooking what once was an ocean bottom and is now the petrified Rocks of Belogradchik, Whitetown. Nadejda believes it is deliberately confusing. Belogradchik never overcame the shock of no longer being an ocean bottom. Belogradchik is a place which continues to conceive of itself as the bottom of a prehistoric ocean, even though long, winding Turkish fortress walls have been built, acrobatically, across the ripples of the hills encircling the Rock sea.

Nadejda starts counting the Rocks, but soon gets confused. That too, is deliberate. There are hundreds of them, gigantically purple, each one towering in isolation, looking away from all the rest — an impossible achievement, since each one is surrounded by the rest. The most famous are particularly recalcitrant, for example the Student, perched up on a rock higher than the others, a girl with a beret and a backpack, headed somewhere, her shoulder-long hair blown by the wind. The Mother with a Child is standing apart too: a powerful woman with a powerful bosom, nursing an undersized lump which is most commonly and becomingly identified as a child. The Old Man could be any old man from the countryside, bearded, stooped and defeated (or in other words wise, sneers Nadejda), venerable (or in other words pitiful). Nadejda knows these well.

These are the official figures, the named wonders. Hundreds of others stand around, slightly more defaced, slightly less well defined, waiting to be found and named. Nadejda is looking out for those, in the anxious certainty of finding something familiar there, someone familiar, thrown in with the others by mistake, lost and mute, unable to signal to the world this terrible chronological mistake. This is what such an unnamed rock somewhere in the vast forest would say: 'Here, this way, me! I don't know what I'm doing here. Please take me out, make me human again, make me speak and explain this to you. Here, this way! But I can't, I can't, I can't . . .'

Nadejda stands at the very edge of the cliffs, aware of that presence trapped somewhere in the petrified sea. But she can't move forward unless she jumps — she has to inspect the Rocks from this point. And naturally, the official figures are the closest, while the rest recede, untraceable and stooped from grief, into the languid ochre sky. For a second she is aware of the necessity to ask herself what she is doing here, but she quickly flicks that thought away like an annoying fly; if she is here, there must be a reason for it, it's as simple as that.

She starts walking away from the cliff, in the hope of finding a path that runs around the shallow valley. There must be such a path. She walks faster and faster, eventually running. Soon she is running along the top of endless fortress walls that enclose an austere old castle. From here she can see, to the left, the ragged mauve sea frozen under a sepia-coloured sky which at once begins to shed rust. That's odd. She keeps running, as the wall leads towards the valley. Someone needs saving. She runs (or is it the wall that runs?), passing enormous rocks

85

in the shape of nuclear mushrooms, or misshapen phalluses, bending towards her despite their inflexible stone nature. That's odd too.

Finally, puffed but victorious, she reaches the edge and comes down the wall steps. She has reached the opposite end of the platform, higher up than the starting point. Again, she looks down. No student, mother or old man. She examines the new giants and there, amid the ugly, indistinct ones, she recognises the three figures of the Pieta. The Grandmother sits, hands on her wide lap, looking straight ahead and over the hills but seeing nothing, dead, as if struck by the lightning of some irreversible truth (but is it the truth or merely its lightning that struck her dead?). Kneeling by her side is the Hanged Man — his hands tied behind his back, his head flopping on his chest, his neck broken by the cord that now hangs around it. The Donkey — or is it a wild goat? — bearded, its front legs propped up on the back of the Hanged Man, is looking up. Nadejda too looks up. The sky, at a closer inspection, turns out to be a pool of clay, or orange mud, bubbling and gurgling obscenely, spattering here and there the petrified Rocks.

But why Pieta? she wonders. Who is lamenting whom? They stand, close together on the fringe of the frozen sea, as if off the stage of official lamentation, patiently waiting to be seen, to be acknowledged in their silenced stonedom. The Hanged Man is very familiar, not his face — for he hasn't got one — but the concept of him, kneeling in this way, broken. The Grandmother is Nadejda's grandmother. She must have been here for twenty-one years — she flew to that Pacific island twenty-one years ago. She never landed, and now her stone will never take off; it makes sense to Nadejda. But what are twenty-one years compared to the eternity for which she must pose? And the Hanged Man? — there are no indications as to how long he's been here.

Nadejda knows they are waiting for her to find them out, sphinxes that she must decipher in order to save them, sprinkled with rust-flakes, spattered with mud — she must wipe them from the oblivion of the world, give them their names back, and wake them from this spell. She always ends up here, at this last step of the Turkish fortress wall, not knowing what to do next. The only way back is the wall, but she knows, from previous experience, that the wall should be used only to lead her here, not to go back. The wall runs only one way, and accepting this is the very condition for coming here.

86

She sits on the last step which ends exactly where the cliff ends, and dangles her legs in the gaping precipice. There's nothing to hold on to, but despite the vertigo she must solve the riddle. In her pocket, she finds a pair of marble balls attached to strings on her index and middle finger. Naturally, she starts knocking them. In a quick crescendo, their bang reaches an eardrum-bursting pitch, but Nadejda must endure the pain. The Rocks below begin to crumble, as if made of mouldy cheese. It is their way of sighing. Only the Pieta stands intact.

Once again, Nadejda has failed. She can't stay, and she can't go back.

Nadejda's alarm goes off at eight, and wakes the other two first. Birdie's feathery head pokes out from under the cover and grunts, the slits of her eyes still glued. The Korean girl violently tosses over on her other side, like a mermaid out of water. Nadejda comes to life slowly, extracting herself limb by limb from sleep, her head coming out last (she must be upside down, it's hard to tell which way her legs go as opposed to her head). A faint sulphur smell greets her at the doorstep of wakefulness. The tour begins at nine. She doesn't want to go on the tour. She wants to stay in this feverishly warm bed, rest her lead-filled head in the pillow now shaped only for her head, in the sticky marshland back wherever she was before. She strains to remember. Stones against an odd sky, an uneasy feeling. Something to find out, something odd and unsettling. Rust rain. Rain rusting. She sits up. Her head spins. She looks for her shoes, and puts on her other sock and her shorts. Is it okay to wear shorts? What do you wear in a volcanic valley? Something protective? But it's warm. She changes into a vest. Her shorts' zipper is a bit tight, in fact her stomach doesn't feel so good, it is bloated and tense, as if . . . She looks under the cover, and there it is — a spot of bright blood on the sheet. At last, the precious, belated bleeding. As she feels with relish the onset of tentative cramps, she takes two pills — however celebratory the pain, she needs to be pain-free for the boiling mud. She wants to face the Inferno Crater in the Waimangu Volcanic Valley at least lucid, even if bloated and bleeding.

Birdie's head is safely under the cover. She changes her blood-

Chapter Ten

soaked underpants and heads for the bathroom. She looks in a mirror above the sink. Two thoughts occur at once, and their collision results in a short-circuit which means that Nadejda walks out of the bathroom thought-free and nauseous, but craving coffee. These are the thoughts that meet in her head.

One: she has bluish circles around her eyes, and her nose is peeling, just like Narcissus's. She hopes she won't see him today, or any other day for that matter. He has left no trace on her anyway — no love-bites, no inflamed skin, no bruises, just her own blood, her own fever, her own peeling nose. How she hates sexual utilitarianism! Everybody using everyone. Pretending that sex is just fun. Except Anton. When they made love Anton looked as though he was a hero in a tragedy entitled *Anton and Nadejda*, he looked more pained than pleasured — because he loved her. And Tony? He has no sense of tragedy, but his expressions too verge on pain, wasteful and small like everything in his life. She supposes that he loves her too. Where is Tony now? Killing the time he can't share with her, living for the day of her return from that romantic, dangerous country! What if she was never to see him again? Never to go back to that moribund town where people scuttle around under a stone sky, where her mother is burying her head like an ostrich? That would be fine with her. It's bad enough sleeping with Tony, but how could she do it with Narcissus, this stuck up sleaze who couldn't even pronounce her name? The cramps are launching another offensive. The welcome novelty of her period is beginning to wear off.

Two: Grandmother broke all the mirrors she encountered, because she was so beautiful. No, despite her beauty. She was so beautiful that Vladimir the Master, the great interpreter of the Bulgarian face, after seeing her walk past his open window where he sat white-bearded and angular, observing the chromatic people of Sofia through chestnut foliage, asked if she would have her portrait painted by him. She had just given birth to Ana. She had long black plaits. She declined politely, supposing him to be some kind of gentle weirdo. And she forgot about the incident. Ten years later, she saw a big obituary in the paper, taking up an entire page, with his photo: 'The greatest Bulgarian portraitist of the century has passed away.'

In the kitchen, Nadejda is approached by a Japanese-looking guy with glasses, who says: 'Are you feeling better?'

She looks at him blankly. Better than what?

'I'm sorry?' she says.

'You . . . you . . . during night . . .' It is a difficult thing to put into words, let alone English words. He regrets having started at all.

'You came to kitchen,' he braves.

'Sorry?' She begins to gather what has happened, but prefers not to show it.

She keeps her bemused look. The guy is easily discouraged anyway. She smiles naïvely, he mumbles an apology and goes about his breakfast business. But suddenly she is curious to know what actually did occur; he may be able to illuminate her about things she said which she has no way of remembering. Perhaps she was talking about her dream . . .

'Excuse me.' She approaches him this time as he pours unfamiliar-looking flakes out of a packet.

'Yes.' He turns to her with ready politeness.

A few others are scuttling about, with sleep-compressed heads, so she lowers her voice.

'Last night . . . hum . . . what happened? Was I walking around?' It is difficult to put this into words.

'Last night I sitting here.' He waves vaguely in the direction of the table. 'You come in. You sit down. And talk.'

'I talked? What did I say?'

'Err . . . I don't understand a lot. You not feeling well.'

'All right.'

'You ask where I from.' He is happy to provide information, although he finds it strange that she doesn't remember. It's as though last night he talked to someone else. She really is a strange girl. But at least she's more convivial now. That's backpackers for you. Just as well they are leaving tonight — he doesn't want to face her again in the night.

'Oh.' A dull question to ask while sleeping, she notes with annoyance. But what else? She must've said something else.

'You think I Japanese.'

'Really?' She isn't surprised at all, and for a second she is embarrassed that she still thinks so. After all, it is hard to tell with Asians ...

'So I asked you where you come from?'

'Yes.' He nods, and she can see that's the only thing in their nocturnal conversation he is likely to have remembered, because it concerned him.

'Okay. Sorry about that,' she says neutrally, and the guy nods neutrally.

She yawns and holds her coffee glass under the kitchen boiler (she uses glasses because the cups are too small). As she pours hot water, the cool glass cracks down its entire length, and a trickle of hot water oozes through the crack. At this point she becomes aware that someone is standing behind her. She turns and catches a fresh whiff of mint toothpaste.

Narcissus is clearly a morning person. And he is a nice guy too, it seems. He beams at her: 'Good morning, Esperanza.' There we go, Nadejda thinks, already irritated beyond measure, she must have told him the meaning of her name! Last Frenchman, last one-night stand. She smiles, thinking of her coffee. He takes a glance at her cracked coffee glass, then at her face and hair, then at her upper body, thinking of last night and already going through possible future scenarios of repeated carnality. She reads this on his nice face, and prays he isn't on her tour.

He isn't. But Birdie is. Nadejda can't believe this. They board the Kiwi Tours minibus together, Birdie smiling and Nadejda smiling as if there is nothing they want more than to be reunited after the breakfast separation. They are bound by a misconceived, suffocating European allegiance: one from the poorest region in Europe, the other from the richest. But Nadejda is beyond such things, she tells herself. Gone are the Iron Curtain times when Monica, her violin teacher, on a tour to Holland, was greeted by a Dutch choreographer with: 'Bulgarian! Really! But you look normal. We thought all people from there dressed in some kind of brown uniform and didn't smile.'

Monica, a sharp-tongued and animated artiste, replied, 'Actually, it's slightly more complicated: we do smile, but only when we wear our brown uniforms.'

90

No matter, no matter, thinks Nadejda as she glances at Birdie's badly groomed head two seats in front and smoothes her own hair which doesn't need smoothing. That's history now.

Rodney the driver's talk is a well-aimed machine-gun. In Nadejda's torpid mind his highly instructive talk about Rotorua's origins and current volcanic activity blends into an indistinct anticipation of vaguely menacing, overflowing sulphuric matter. They drive around town, passing tidy but lacklustre living areas and numberless tourist havens, stopping at several points to pick up the remaining members of the tour: a heavy-boned, humourless middle-aged German couple munching some biscuits; a sprightly British man with a comic moustache and a sophisticated video camera, who immediately locates the single young woman and elegantly slips beside her; an extravagant couple of unidentified origins; and a small, compact hairy man of obscure nationality, who climbs up the bus steps as if ascending a scaffold before hundreds of gloating eyes.

Enter now the gardens. Nadejda is terminally bored by gardens, though she has to admit that these geysers and this vegetation remind her of the Queen's Gardens with the penguin. Except there is no castle here, no stone thrones, but a large, former bath-house. 'The Maoris call this area Whangapiro,' drawls Rodney, 'which means evil-smelling place.'

'Indeed, indeed,' says Nadejda's neighbour quietly, bowing slightly towards her.

She smiles and glances at him — always a tricky initiative, because of the uncomfortable proximity. He smiles at her too. Sulphur explodes here and there with a stench, behind impeccable rose beds. 'Thank God no children,' he says with a sigh.

'Sorry?'

'We're lucky there are no screaming children on this tour,' he elaborates.

They both smile. He is the classic British traveller: perhaps old-fashioned and twee, but with incisive, ironic erudition. Nadejda takes an instant, ironic liking to him. Fortunately, Nadejda's pills are working: the cramps have subsided.

The road is straight. Rodney speeds on. Everybody is silent, except the Brit, who tells Nadejda about his gruelling, hilarious trip to Eastern Europe. She nods, smiling in his direction, and looks at the steaming wild greenery that unravels at a reptilian pace like a Jurassic Park film into which she has inadvertently fallen. A time traveller in a prehistoric loophole, she is still watching through a window. But as soon as she sets foot on the real crater, on the real rock, what will she crush, what infernal butterfly, what fictional insect? Whose history will be fatally altered thereafter? These are thoughts she can't share with Cameraman who is having a great time relating his experience in Romania (one anecdote per country).

'So I get to Bucharest. Full of beggars, the misery is unlike anything I've seen in the rest of the Balkans.'

'Have you been to Albania?' Nadejda knows the futility of frank exchanges with Westerners who have no idea about these things, but can't help correcting him.

'Albania? No, I never intended to go to Albania. Too obscure, really. I thought I'd see the rest of the Balkans that time. Besides, I heard Albania was unsafe. Mind you, Romania wasn't exactly a fun fair either.'

Obscure? Nadejda doesn't know much about Albania, except that it is the poorest country in Europe, but is somehow vexed by this adjective. Obscure — what does that mean? Obscure to bright English Cameramen. Obscure because it wasn't colonised by them. But she can't help liking this British amateur of obscurity.

'I mean hordes of gypsy kids running after you, well they look gypsy but it's hard to tell if they are just Romanians, asking for money, cigarettes, and what not. And those huge deserted squares in the city centre . . . It was desolate. And people stare at you as if they've never seen a Westerner. In Sofia it's different — people go about their business. Obviously they've had more contact with the outside world since the coup. But then the Bulgarians, being more worldly, aren't as friendly as the Romanians.'

Nadejda wants to point out that Bucharest is not the same as Romania, nor Sofia as Bulgaria, but in the meantime they arrive in the Volcanic Valley.

The group walks down the wooden platform that eases the delicate tourist into the rough tracks of the valley. The platform is lined with maps, signs, drawings and pictures of the places they are about to see, as well as those they are already seeing. Nadejda yawns and shakes her head, feeling her hair whirl about. Cameraman, walking behind her, yawns too, as if in solidarity. Birdie is walking ahead; she hasn't made any attempts at interacting with her room-mate, but that makes the moment of tête-à-tête even more imminent. She has a backpack on her long, hunched back, and absurd large-framed sunglasses which give her the appearance of a tsetse fly.

Rodney switches himself on again, and launches into another narrative about volcanic formation, citing years of eruptions, destructions and numbers of victims. 'The valley as you see it today was formed as a result of the Mt Tarawera eruption. In June 1886, the northern peak of Mt Tarawera erupted. The roar was heard as far away as Christchurch. At least 153 people died. Debris and ash were scattered over at least 16,000 square kilometres. It's interesting that prior to the eruption, there was no record of thermal activity in the area.'

'Very interesting indeed,' whispers Cameraman to Nadejda, almost brushing her cheek with his moustache.

'In 1903, four people were killed by a sudden explosion in the Waimangu Geyser cauldron. Their bodies were swept down the valley, and recovered later.'

They descend, in an unnecessarily tidy line, towards some gorge, some crater in the pit of the valley. There is so much monstrously thick, humid growth that Nadejda wonders if the sulphur hasn't caused some mutation in the flora over the centuries. Humans must be susceptible to some kind of mutation too — but not necessarily excessive body hair. Body size perhaps, like the young generation of Bulgaria — Anton told her in his typically apocalyptic vocabulary — who are growing abnormally tall (and cynical), as a long-lasting effect of Chernobyl radiation. But this is nature's effluvium — it can only be good. 'Nature's goodness.' She inhales nature's goodness and her head spins.

Walking down Vitosha Mountain, steps muffled by a shed forest of autumnal gold and rust, short-haired Nadejda sang tramping songs with her parents, both terrible singers but excellent trampers. 'Eho, eho, bezkraina shir I dluj . . .', Echo, echo, far and wide, endlessly . . . Her father in front, carrying the big battered backpack, her mother behind

93

him carrying everybody's jackets, and Nadejda at the tail, holding a
luminous bunch of jagged dry leaves.

    So far down Vitosha Mountain has she walked, all the way
through the centre of the Earth where time accelerates, and come out
the other end, in the pit of this Echo Crater. Alone. She has lost everyone
on the way. Her parents have tripped over some insignificant stone and
tumbled down the Vitosha slopes, blankets, thermos, jackets, transistor
and sandwiches flung in the autumn air above Sofia, never to be seen
again. She has come out at this end, long-haired, bleeding and speaking
another language, a language that none of them understood only a
moment ago, while marching down to the sound of their own false
voices. 'Echo, echo, far and wide, endlessly . . .'

    They arrive at the yellowish blue lake of Echo Crater. 'The
Echo Crater was blasted out in the 1886 eruption. In April 1917, the
crater had the most violent eruption since 1886, in a blast which
swept across the valley, tearing off the roof of the hotel and killing a
woman and a child.'

    Nadejda expects some obscure monster to emerge from the
vapours, rustling with its impure sulphurous scales, rolling its yellow
eyes in their direction and then, in one huge, palaeolithic sweep, arch
across the lake and put a playful tentacle around Rodney. And he'll
be gone. Nadejda is drawn to the steaming water, but naturally there
is a fence a metre away from the water's edge to keep the impulsive
tourist away from stray monsters. Birdie breathes elaborately, as if
doing relaxation exercises. The German couple are taking photos
furiously, as if their livelihood depends on their photographic
produce. The other couple move about separately from each other,
as if they're not really together but only incidentally share a life. As
if. Nadejda stands by the little fence, as if the monster-feeding water
is an escape route and she can dive in at the drop of a hat,
disappearing into a puff of volcanic possibility. In due time, sick with
worry, her mother would phone Sofia, and have to speak to her father
— both of them she has lied to. Both of them she loves too much to
tell the truth. And the truth is . . . Yes, what is the truth, Nadejda
wonders. That she hates it both here and there. That she left Sofia
with relief and landed in Auckland with resentment, just like the first
time they left for New Zealand. Her mother knows this anyway, but

she always waits to be told the worst. 'It is love's favourite perversion,' her father read aloud from an English book (about Flaubert, it seemed) just before they left Sofia, 'to always want to know the worst.' Or something like that. What would they say to each other on the phone then, after three years of pained silence?

Where is Nadejda?

Isn't she with you?

No, she hasn't been in touch for a week.

She said she was going straight home.

What!

What are you saying? She hasn't gone home yet and she hasn't been in touch with you? There's a mistake . . .

Silence. Then sobbing at one end, crisp clear as if they were in neighbouring houses, consternation at the other end. They haven't spoken for two years.

She must have been kidnapped. Her father is helpless. Her mother calls the New Zealand police. They begin a search. They find her name in two backpackers' lodger books. They trace her stunted journey to its end, here at this lake, in the Echo Crater. The echo . . .

Yes, only the gravestone of Nadejda's disappearance could replace the stone silence of their bitter separation. A mauve stone on a carpet of rusty leaves. Or is it under a sky of flaking clay? She stares at the steaming water. What a wasteful replacement that would be. Nothing, nothing can bring them together, least of all death.

Again, in a tidy line, they tread behind Rodney. Here — walking backwards, to face the brave explorers — he points to the bush on the side of the track, where one finds a plant that causes diarrhoea. The plant looks uninvitingly poisonous, notes Nadejda, but the starving tourist is no doubt capable of foolish acts. Further down, one finds another plant which is called 'bushman's friend'. He giggles, and asks them if they can guess the meaning of its name.

They are approaching the Inferno Crater, announces Rodney. It's invisible, but it throbs warmly in the near distance, like a nest of fantastic plumeless birds. Nadejda can feel her blood leave her body in jerky, warm bursts. This immoderation of growth, this overflowing of subterranean activity, makes her bleed at a desperate pace. She prays that she has enough protection, that the blood won't trickle down the inside of her bare legs for all anonymous voyeurs to see and hold in their memory, in a steaming red neon flash: GIRL BLEEDS AT INFERNO CRATER. She has no way of checking, except glancing casually at her thighs every now and then, as much as it's possible to glance casually at one's own thighs.

Nothing could have prepared them for the infernal splendour of the last and innermost crater of this valley. In a shock of blue for which there is no word in the languages known to Nadejda, the lake flaunts before them its inhuman colour. Pure poison, or jiva voda, the water of life? If you dip your bare foot, will you regain your youth or dissolve in an agony of sizzling?

'The lake overflows every thirty-eight days,' prompts Rodney usefully. 'The last overflow was thirteen days ago.'

'Damn,' thinks Nadejda, and everyone else. They have missed the real spectacle.

They lean gingerly against the wooden rails, fascinated. What would it be like to be dropped into this water, screaming and kicking, and soon frying?

'Charming smell,' says Cameraman to Nadejda.

She nods. She asks him to take a photo of her, handing him her camera. He sets up the backdrop and asks the bulky German couple to move out of the way, which they do with instant obedience. Tormented by the thought of her period breaking through her clothing, Nadejda smiles self-consciously. SNAP.

'Thank you.'

'You're very welcome.'

Rodney loads them on a bus back to the entrance, to save their vital energies for the forthcoming hellish sights of the Thermal Wonderland. Afterwards, they drive for another immeasurable period of time, in which Nadejda keeps her forehead pressed to the cool window in an attempt to counteract the internal bubbling heat of her body. Cameraman leaves her alone this time, and sits in a corner, leafing through a notebook. Birdie talks with the extravagant couple; the German couple brandish a packet of chips and start crunching in silence.

Upon arriving in the visitor centre of Sacred Waters, Wai-O-Tapu, Rodney announces a twenty-minute break and vanishes into the café, followed by the day-dreaming hairy man and Birdie, who seems to Nadejda more gaunt and sexless than ever. Cameraman confides to Nadejda his need to 'investigate the toilets' and disappears gradually, like a cat, his smile the last to go. The Germans unwrap juicy ham sandwiches and bite simultaneously, as if by order. In the toilets Nadejda discovers that her face is drawn and pallid but her bleeding normal. The blood must get diverted somewhere on the way down, like a manic river unfaithful to her distant, obscure sea.

She eats the remainder of the apricot biscuits. Cameraman is fortunately tending to his introspective needs and is scribbling in a notebook at the next table. The sun is in mid-sky. Nadejda sits in the exact centre of a bench, her hair parted in the middle. The summer assaults her body, invades her consciousness. It is only through the Echo Crater that she can swim back to the singing, tramping shuffle in the autumnal glow. All other gates are sealed gates to sealed exits. She is sitting here, next to the ironic Englishman, across from a chirping Japanese group, under an umbrella, clutching a stolen packet of biscuits, about to enter the territory of somebody's Sacred Waters. Nadejda's descent into this hellish wonderland is a search for a door, an exit to let her out of this smouldering summer that she has stepped into by mistake.

Lady Knox is activated by an ebullient Maori who pours a prodigious quantity of washing powder inside her barren-looking hole. The crowd watches through cameras. Cameraman stands behind Nadejda, in full gear. Nadejda hates taking photos. She sides with the ephemeral. The crowd holds its breath as a faint gargling noise comes from the awakened hole. Nadejda feels the onset of more cramps, but ignores them as contemptuously as she can. Water gushes out in a precipitous, fifteen-metre shot, sizzling and spraying the nearby watchers who still don't cede their positions. The crowd gasps and then rumbles, busy capturing the instant; for a few moments only camera clicks can be heard.

'You're not taking a photo?' The Englishman squeezes her elbow from behind. A poor creep, thinks Nadejda, but endearing. 97

Chapter Ten

'I just don't like it. I side with the ephemeral.' She turns to glance at him, provocatively.

'Aah.' He nods with a knowing smile and then points a manicured finger at the sky. 'The ephemeral too sides with us.'

They walk across a vast stepped stretch of metallic grey substance, faintly tinted by rainbow hues. Marsh-like and quietly alive, these Primrose Terraces are the stuff with which the waiting room of the mind's hell is carpeted. A low, narrow wooden walkway takes them to the other shore. Nadejda searches for a pill in her bag with cold, shaky hands, unable to ignore the cramps any more. This would be the worst place to collapse — to roll down these primrose terraces, down the volcanic mire, down these wonders of lace, to roll and roll and roll, and to fall, finally and inextricably, in a pool of boiling mud.

The pills have lost their grip. She may as well be taking lollies. Pain's almighty flood breaks down the doors of medicine. But she must keep on walking, trapped in this trip, in front of someone, behind someone. She is a sick walking sponge soaking up the humours of this thermal inferno. Wonderland or inferno, who is to say? Everything bears names from our human world — Champagne Pool, Bridal Veil Falls, Artist's Palette, Primrose Terraces — but remains inhuman. Rodney informs the stunned group that they've arrived at the Boiling Mud Pools. Nadejda has arrived in Painland.

Nadejda doubles over, then crouches, praying for pain's almighty flood to be reversible. But that would be to ask a jumping jaguar to stop in mid-leap. Nadejda's pain, muscular and conquering, instantly covers the world which now consists entirely of a pool of boiling mud. Nadejda crouches under the scorching sun, vaguely aware of the others, and looks, through the distorted, multiple lenses of pain, at the mud eruptions breaking the surface. Where does the pain come from? From this gurgling mud, surely. That's it: the boiling mud is pain itself. It broke through to her from afar, grew and fed on her as she approached, and erupted obscenely and muddily when she got here. Its way of saying welcome, Nadejda. She stares, an entranced prey of Mudland, of Painland, her hands stone cold on her knees, her teeth chattering. She sits on her bag.

'Are you feeling okay?' Cameraman and Rodney simultaneously bend down.

'You're very pale.'

'Yep, I'm okay. Just a bit dizzy.' Speaking is intolerable. Every word is wrenched out of her body like a tooth.

She just wants to lie in a warm pool of mud, somewhere at the far end of Hell, alone, without sounds, colours, light or future, just breathing and being, rocked in the hideous intimacy of pain and mud. Someone touches her back. Don't touch her back!

'Are you sure you're okay?'

Nadeeeeee, her mother calls. Her mother cries. Something terrible happened to Grandma. In the plane. What happened to Grandma?

Something touches her back. It's the Donkey! The Donkey that carries the Scarecrow — no, the Hanged Man!

She is crouching in a pieta. Boiling mud is flying towards the rusty sky — no, the sky is shedding mud, clay, rust, tears of gold. The Pieta is crouching in the petrified sea of pain.

An eternity passes. Pain is eternal.

Voices collide, bodies float about.

Then her teeth are no longer chattering. The cramps begin to quieten down. Cameraman crouches beside her. A few lenses fall off.

'You're feeling sick,' he knows. It's obvious she is feeling sick. 'What is it?'

'I'm not sure. Probably my heart.'

'Your heart!'

'I have a weak heart.' Where did that come from?

'Seriously? You should've told us, that's no good.'

'Yeah. I'm better now.'

She is better. She can speak, and the current level of pain, which could have been agony for a dilettante of pain, is lessening, and therefore verging on pleasure for Nadejda. The group moves on. Only Cameraman lags behind, his melancholic eyes on the girl with a weak heart.

'I'll join you in a second. Don't wait for me,' she says with her pale lips, still sitting on her bag.

'All right,' Cameraman nods and obligingly turns to follow the others, but then comes back: 'I could carry your bag?'

Old-fashioned gentleman, likeable but a nuisance, especially the moustache. Nadejda declines politely and sends him on his way.

By the pool of boiling mud, Nadejda is recovering. She has a drink of juice from her plastic bottle. Pain tried to kill her and then it went away. Mud-haired pain tries to turn the world into stone with its medusan glare, choke the world in a sea of soft clay, petrify the world in a cast of putrid gold, close down its arteries, arrest its blood and turn it into rust. Nadejda gets up but feels as if she is standing on her hands, looking at an upside down pool of joyful mud which must be the sky. Down below, three giant chunks of stone travel slowly, shaped like clouds. Nadejda follows them.

CHAPTER ELEVEN

Ana pushes a trolley into the
supermarket.

Supermarket dreams

Ana pushes a trolley into the supermarket. Or rather, the trolley pulls her in. She needs the trolley in the supermarket. She needs some protection — nobody should be expected to just go into a great big supermarket unarmed with a body of steel like this.

She is doing the week's shopping. Ha! The week's shopping. For whom? The trolley rolls past the bread section. She picks up a pack of white rolls for Nadejda — she eats only white bread, faithful to the Bulgarian understanding that dark bread is a lesser species. Then she picks up a jar of gherkins — Nadejda's favourite snack. Drumsticks — Nadejda doesn't eat any other meat. Potatoes, for fries. Apple juice, Nadejda's favourite. Flavoured milk. There was strawberry milk in square plastic bags in Sofia, thrown in a big open fridge and most of them leaking; Ana was experienced at spotting the healthy bags in the sea of wounded pink fish. Here, she just has to take a bottle — and if it leaks, she can complain. Here, she can choose from strawberry, chocolate, banana and vanilla. Now soap, detergent, chocolate biscuits, apricot biscuits for Nadejda, bananas, salami, yoghurt for Nadejda ... Everything, she wants to buy everything for Nadejda. Now she can. Even if now Nadejda isn't here, not for another week or so, she can buy everything for her. Nadejda eats well. Ana, once self-consciously endowed with hand-some curves, has lost them in the last three years. She has melted away in this Cornucopia. Dry-mouthed and stomach in a knot, she has smoked herself away from eating, far away. This abundance makes her stomach close down. Once, she would queue up for oranges or freshly baked bread or fish or anything at all really, and she would feel rivers of saliva bathe her palate, a fierce drive to reach that counter, to grab and run, and run, and devour the precious catch.

Once, in a bitter Sofia winter, after an appendectomy, she queued up in a pharmacy full of dirty snow slush and blue-nosed people. She had a fever, and her teeth were chattering so violently that the woman in front turned round to look at her. The woman behind, a thin, pale-eyed thing in a fur coat, leaned forward as if she was going to break, and said to Ana in a cultured voice, 'Excuse me, would you mind terribly if I was to go before you? I've just been released from hospital, I'm about to collapse.'

Ana heard herself say, as if in a dialogue from some dreadful theatre of the absurd, 'Yes, of course, except I've just come out of hospital too.'

The woman looked at her in disbelief. Ana gave the woman her place in the queue, too stunned to prove what she herself would have laughed at if she'd been an observer, if she hadn't been feverish to the point of delirium. When finally she reached the counter, they didn't have the medicine needed for Nadejda's cough, and Ana had to buy an Austrian import at the price of one third of her university salary.

The numbing, pitiless, hilarious reality of that life meant constant queuing, deficits, shopping madness and chance discoveries: shoes for Nadejda, a base and cream for her birthday cake! She carried on, she fought, she survived, like everyone. Absurd survival in an absurd world, but she came out of it, so she could come to this great big Supermarket of Supermarkets today — with no queues, no leakages, no rot, no flies, no rudeness, no deficit, no limits, and shop for Nadejda all that her heart desires, even if Nadejda isn't at home. Where *is* Nadejda?

Ana stands at the top of the cereals aisle, suddenly overcome by a great fatigue. Now what? Where to now? She needs to get some toilet paper, yes — food and toilet paper, the cycle closes . . . The trolley dances on. Ana follows.

Fish, many, too many. An orgy of fish colours, a rainbow of fillets. Cooking fish was always a supreme effort back there. It had to be taken out of its sodden brown wrap, and cleaned, scale by scale, in a smelly sink full of blood and glitter. Every meal an achievement, every purchase a victory, every success a triumph of the imagination combined with physical endurance: queuing, standing in sweaty crowded buses with shopping bags hanging from the arms like weights, then struggling to tame the raw products. Mladen was rarely there to help; always late from work, always preoccupied by work, much like her, only spared from the constant worry about Nadejda's practical needs, because men are spared from the trivia of the humdrum of the everyday of the weekly of the yearly of the centennial of the eternal material where children need to be fed, played with, talked to, given birthday parties, taken to the zoo, the library, swimming and violin lessons in town.

The trolley shakes along by the big freezer. Ice-cream — triple chocolate. Nadejda is big on ice-cream, always has been. When Ana bought her vanilla ice-cream in cones, Nadejda, knowing that she was restricted to only one, would ask if she could at least have three cones, so she could imagine that she was having three ice-creams. Then ice-cream became so expensive that she hardly had any for a while, until they came here, to the land of the hundred ice-creams.

Ana is big on pineapple and bananas, except these days she can't swallow much, and the little she does she can't taste. These days, banana tastes like pineapple tastes like shit. But she enjoys food knowing that Nadejda enjoys it.

Next, she is facing the biscuit wall. Once, in their first year in New Zealand, she started counting how many types of biscuits there were, and before she finished counting burst into tears, right here, by the biscuit section, much to Nadejda's angry embarrassment.

'You've gone nuts Mum, you've lost it completely,' Nadejda hissed, wrenching the trolley from her hands and pushing it violently towards the checkouts, leaving her mother behind, to be approached and touched by benevolent strangers. They thought she was having a breakdown, as so many people do; there are hundreds of reasons for breakdowns. How could those sympathetic strangers know that this well-groomed, red-haired woman with flashing rings was crying because of . . . biscuits? Because there was in her ruffled mind an image of little Nadejda at the table, her sleeves rolled up to her elbows, with a packet of the only biscuits available in Sofia, the hard, white, square 'Ordinary Biscuits', and three types of homemade jam. Nadejda, a greedy child, wanted different-flavoured biscuits, and since there was only the one type, she cunningly asked her mother for as many types of jam as they had. The jam was made in the summer by Nadejda's grandparents in Plovdiv and sent over. Sometimes, Nadejda would have a biscuit and chocolate sandwich, and on one such occasion she asked, 'Mum, why don't they make chocolate biscuits, it's so easy, look — you just stick the chocolate and the biscuit together.' And she demonstrated with her chocolate-smudged fingers.

No, they couldn't know. But if she couldn't explain to the

biscuit-ignoring strangers, she couldn't explain to Nadejda either. And this made the stretch between the biscuit stand and the tills where Nadejda was now queuing like just another stranger, a corridor of draughty alienation. It was neither the first nor the last time Nadejda was ashamed of her mother. When her own child refused to understand, why should strangers understand? Crying by the biscuit wall (people were now tactfully ignoring her), Ana felt like an autistic child rocking alone in the corner of a strange midnight hospital.

She had told Nadejda everything — about her grandmother, her grandfather, her uncle, the escape, the deportation to that godforsaken place . . . but Nadejda lived in the present only. She had no time to look back. She had no time for her mother any more.

There is a moment — gaping among the rough stitches of time like a wound that won't close — when under a wolfish yellow moon little Ana and her mother are shoved into a cattle wagon, together with a crowd of others, to be deported far away from their home in central Sofia. There is another moment, when grown-up, motherless Ana is standing before a wall of brightly packaged biscuits. In between, there is a breathless, black ocean of liveable and unliveable matter.

Somewhere above that ocean, Nadejda is flying on her wax wings, this way and that, headphones over her stubborn ears, latent dimples in her unsmiling cheeks. Somewhere above that ocean Ana's mother is flying in a Lufthansa plane, dead and still dreaming of the Pacific where her son and husband, aged beyond recognition, have been waiting for her since the cattle wagon. Ana too, is flying above that ocean, in a shopping trolley, gripping its barred walls, ducking under shapeless cloud. Three women make this aerial triangle of loneliness. Three women have gone missing: you will not find them.

The trolley rolls into the cereals aisle, and gets stuck behind three others. Ana has extremely low tolerance towards even the mildest trolley jams. A small boy with short hair on top and a lock of long hair at the back tries to squeeze under her trolley. His tattooed teenage mother follows on insect legs behind a trolley full of cans. She stops behind Ana and calls out, 'Mike, come back here!' The little troll turns round and does a little wriggling dance in between trolleys.

Ana looks at the boy. She is paralysed. She stands, waiting. The needle of her heart begins to dart about like that of a crazed compass. She can move neither forward nor back. So she lets go of the warm steel handle and turns back, ploughing her way through the motley shoppers. 'Excuse me, excuse me. Sorry.' She reaches the end of the cereal aisle. Her heart reaches her throat and stops. She needs that monster of a trolley to protect her; it's her transport and reason for being here. She turns back — the aisle has cleared up, and her half-empty trolley is drifting along slowly. She takes hold of it and manoeuvres it around, feeling decidedly queasy. A flash of another, ancient queasiness darts through her body: she is sitting pressed against her mother inside the dark cattle wagon, clutching a bundle, and her head spins as if they are being driven round and round in a railway circle.

'Mum, I'm feeling sick.'

'Lie on Mummy's lap and you'll feel better.'

'Mum, I want a piece of lokum.'

'We don't have any, sweetie. Just lie on my lap.'

'Where are we going?'

'To a new house.'

'Why are we leaving Sofia?'

'Because we have to, like all these people.'

'Why are they leaving?'

'Because somebody has taken their houses and they must look for new ones now.'

'Has someone taken our house too?'

'Yes.'

'But we didn't want to go.'

'No, but we must.'

'Is that because of batko and Daddy?'

'Yes, that's right.'

'Are we going to see them then?'

'No we're not, Ani, not now. But try to sleep now.'

She fell asleep, her head on her mother's lap, soothed by her mother's warm hand. But one question was tossed around in her confused mind: why were they going away when they weren't even going to see her father and batko?

The trolley takes Ana back to the freezer. She looks over a smug sea of frozen food, leisurely strollers pregnant with trolleys, the tills ticking dutifully down at the far end. She becomes achingly aware of the smoked meat at the counters behind her, the shelves of dairy products to the right, the crackers to the left, the canned food further to the side, and everything begins pressing towards her. The shelves begin to draw closer and closer, forming an almighty food embrace around her, not to comfort but to threaten her; the floor begins to swivel, the trolley is gaping at her like a mouth to be filled, and strangers flock and disperse in infinitely slow motion, like a damaged kaleidoscope. She is alone in her wagon, in her trolley, rattling down the railway, no hand to soothe her, not knowing where she is going. White lights descend from the ceiling, freezing clouds invade the air, mussels tremble under a trickle of water in an aquarium, the silence is complete for a second.

'*Mama a a*' cries a girl's plaintive voice from under the ice cream boxes in the freezer of Ana's heart. She feels, in a moment of extraordinary, unaccountable physical terror, her hair stand on end.

She lets go of the trolley which nudges another one near by, and half-walks, half-runs, to the tills where she squeezes herself between some people, some trolleys, some uniforms, and runs for the exit as if chased by the most elaborate monster of her sickest dream. She runs to the car, unlocks the passenger door by mistake and gets inside. She doesn't move over to the driver's seat. Why? Because she has nowhere to go.

The past slams its heavy iron gate behind her, the future stretches ahead — a vast, empty province of rainy days that begin and end seemingly for no one, like the worst one-act play ever written by a demented hand and replayed ad infinitum in private, for some octogenarian despot who sits in the murky shadows of a mausoleum. The trolley drifts like a deserted boat stacked with provisions. In the seat of death, in her motionless car, Ana is falling through the hole of her life, like Alice falling in the well. But unlike Alice, her fall does not lead to Wonderland. Nobody can tell just where it leads.

*

Chapter Eleven

There is one thing Vassil can't cope with in life: the supermarket on a Saturday. He has coped with a number of things in his life: the 'Stalinist gang', Greek camps, heavy labour, exile, death, sterility, divorce, loneliness, guilt, grief and despair. But the supermarket on a Saturday is something he cannot face. When he was with Patricia, she did the shopping; she enjoyed it, although her idea of marital harmony featured, among other things like children, doing the shopping together — this requirement too, Vassil thoroughly failed to fulfil. The truth is, it isn't only on Saturday that he can't cope with the supermarket — otherwise he could have gone on Sunday for example, or late on a week evening. He hates the supermarket at all times, and Saturday is simply more treacherous because he has time to absorb the spirit-crushing banality of the shopping experience; but essentially, Saturday is no different from any other day. So Vassil plunges in with pinched nostrils and a repelled heart, as usual. He has to eat, after all. He engages in a mental conversation with himself — it is a coping technique he has engineered for himself, with all the deftness of a professional psychologist.

'And once again, the unclean daze of the shopping world!'

'Shopping fatigue accumulates with the years.'

'Everything accumulates with the years.'

'Yes, except wisdom.'

'There's only the supermarket left now. What type of cheese to have this week, that sort of thing.'

'There's no need to be sarcastic. I did what I could, the best I could.'

'Did. That's right, you only did things in the past. Now you just are.'

'Let's not get existential. Anyway, it could have been worse. I could be dead. Shot, hanged, tortured to death. I was a hair's breadth away from it.'

'Now Mum and Dad are dead instead.'

'Parents die, it's natural.'

'Ha, natural! Not the way Mum died!'

He picks up a packet of peanuts. He likes snacking, especially with his red wine.

'Peanuts have a high percentage of oil.'

'Peanut oil: it's good for you.'

'It's bad for you.'

He throws the peanuts in the trolley with a gesture of defiance. Internal dialogues are tiring. For a dialogue to exist, there has to be conflict. He is tired of conflicts, the weekend should be a conflict-free zone.

'When you were young, you thrived on conflict. You feared nothing. Now everything frightens you.'

He refuses to reply and heads towards the checkouts with half a trolley of products. He doesn't need much, although he spends a lot of money on food. He is a bon viveur, everybody agrees. They don't know that he is in fact a desperate viveur. Does he live well? Yes. Does he enjoy it? He supposes so. But he has no choice: he's run for his life, he's worked like mad, now he has to reap the harvest of his success. He has to live well and enjoy it. Otherwise, what a nonsense.

'And you've become defeatist. Because you have nothing to fight.'

'Everybody's gone. I have only myself to fight.'

'And Nadejda.'

'She's a funny girl.'

'She's a sad girl.'

'Yes.'

'She has no boyfriend.'

'She might have.'

'She doesn't think much of her uncle.'

'How do you mean?'

'She thinks you're a bit of a pathetic fat old man.'

'She doesn't have respect for anyone — including her mother, who has bent over backwards to provide her with a better life.'

'Nadejda is unhappy in this better life. She misses her father.'

'She misses more than that.'

Vassil — both of them — can understand why she isn't happy in New Zealand. This much at least he understands his niece. This is what the West has to offer to an anarchic post-communist youth with excessive expectations: an army of biscuits, a slaughter-field of meats, a forest of deodorants, a townful of English roofs under which

109

a population of hothouse plants is drowsing. Like him, in fact. Christ-church: the most English city outside England. The Cathedral City. The Garden City of the plains. Supermarket thrills. Thank-yous. Normality. Animal rights. Vassil sneers at the fallacy of things like animal rights. Progressive, caring New Zealanders campaigning for the rights of chained dancing bears in Turkey, when there are journalists and writers rotting in dismal jails.

'They are very cruel to the bears!' said the thick-limbed girl collecting money the other day. 'They pierce their noses with a ring and stuff, which tears the flesh. They starve them and stuff.' Of course they do, they do the same to people — but that's a little too much for you to comprehend, Vassil thinks.

'There are also people in Turkey who suffer greatly,' he said. 'And in Turkey's neighbouring countries.'

'Oh,' she said but then picked herself up: 'That's not surprising really, is it.'

No, thought Vassil, there is no surprise in this at all. He smiled, made a donation, and went his way.

The smelly gypsy who takes the bear around, who puts his tattered hat on the pavement and tortures his cracked fiddle, a broken expression on his dark unshaven face, is just as wretched as his wretched beast — he makes his wretched living out of this. Free the bear, dig the gypsy's grave. It's like the bloody anti-abortion fanatics. Kill the doctor who performed an abortion and killed a non-existent human being. But Vassil hates the gypsies too (thieves and parasites) — he is arguing for the sake of fairness, not in defence of gypsies. He hates the Turks too, to be precise. He is definitely not arguing in favour of any Turk, writer in jail or not. In fact, he is not arguing at all. Just noting in passing. He is too tired to argue.

This is the new world where Nadejda has been planted and, like a sick cactus, kicks against the generous, moist soil. She has been through too much already. A revolution. Her father beaten by the militia during the Ekoglasnost protest before the coup. The euphoria of incomprehensible, brand-new freedom — then the bleakness of shortages, no electricity, no water. Then, at the last moment, her father staying behind. Her father's ultimatums, her mother's devastation. Nadejda has lived in a time and place too large for a

110

child. For anyone. Now she is squeezed into a pot too small for her. She needs another forty years, like him, to sink in, to take root, to stop sleepwalking, to stop fighting those hideous, real ghosts ...

He unloads his trolley into the car boot and pushes it to a trolley stand in one corner of the parking lot.

He sits in the car and pulls out the seat-belt. A regular, middle-class family of four is busy around an overflowing trolley. Further down, a malnourished young mother is violently shaking a little blonde monster with short hair on top and a long lock at the back. A large mother emerges from the exit, surrounded by three chubby, thin-haired blonde girls, all four in Lycra leggings and all four industriously sucking ice-creams.

'Oh God, reproduction doesn't bring improvement, just more of the same!'

'Somewhere, in a province of ice, Pat is doing the shopping with her three kids and husband.'

'Good for her.'

'Good for them all.'

Good for this procreated humanity. Impregnating itself. Pregnant with itself. Procreating more of itself. Gushing and crooning in clusters around new-borns, unborns, ugly-borns, borns-in-vain. 'I want a baby,' sobbed Patricia in the pillow. Vassil wanted a baby too — for her sake. Sometimes we want things despite ourselves. He wanted Patricia, not a baby. She wanted him so she could have a baby. She got what she wanted. He lost what he wanted. But it could have been worse.

He drives the shopping home, carefully, as if it is a sleeping child.

Mladen needs to go shopping, but the local supermarket is closed because of the protests. Before the protests began, Mladen hadn't been paid for two months. Now payment is out of the question, since there are no lectures. The university's old rusty mechanism has ground to a halt. No money to pay the staff, no money for research, no money for heating — it's the same old story. Now there are no students either, they're all at the protest. He can't go to the protest

111

because the car wouldn't start in this stone-cracking cold, and the buses are unpredictable in the massive transport paralysis in the city, with everybody on strike. Because 'the glass of patience overflowed long ago, but now it's starvation that's pushing people out on the street,' said the long-haired student protester on the news. Mladen gets a ride to town with a neighbour — a researcher at BAN, the Bulgarian Academy of Sciences, who hasn't been paid his salary of $US15 for three months. Dimitar has no petrol so they make a difficult transfusion between his and Mladen's reservoir.

In town, students are dancing around large tape-recorders, there are hot-drink stands. Clouds of human breath freeze in the air and drift away slowly. In the Batenberg Square, a crowd of students wearing pyjamas under large military-style overcoats, and holding alarm clocks, is progressing towards the Parliament building, followed by an endless stream of demonstrators, mostly young. There are hundreds of bystanders. When the crowd reaches Parliament, their alarms go off all at once, in a strident orchestra of mechanical garble. This is their message to the Socialist government: 'Wake up! Wake up you hibernating minotaurs! Look how you've fucked up the country!'

Mladen's stomach is rumbling — he hasn't eaten today. Gaunt Dimitar next to him probably hasn't eaten for longer than that. If she were paid, his wife, a senior research associate in BAN, would get the same salary as him, and together the family would have roughly 75,000 lev or $US30 a month, to live on. For this money, they would be able to buy two kilograms of cheese and pay the power bill for the one-bedroom flat. But as it is, with the crisis at the Academy, they are spending their last savings, once a reasonable sum but increasingly less reasonable as the lev shot up from 78 to the dollar to 2500 in the space of a year. Mladen has nothing to moan about, really, in this relative world where the only absolute is near-starvation or near-hypothermia; not quite death, just extreme affliction.

He looks around and sees the same thing on every face — the awareness of that absolute, the dizzying closeness of each individual to the nightmare of this absolute. When driven to the dire extremes of pain, even a crowd of senior researchers would gladly murder a Marie Antoinette. There are many Marie Antoinettes in this country, with ties and good teeth. There is pain crouching behind each rubbish bin of Sofia, round the corner of each trendy shop along Vitosha Street. In every shop there are unbuyable goodies. In every eye there is a madness. In every second pocket there is a gun. In every chest there is a broken heart.

Seeing a few familiar faces in the ever-growing crowd, Mladen joins in, light-headed, with numbness in his feet. It all started with a handful of them protesting for freedom in the Kristal Garden, some nine years ago; the rest of Sofia looked from behind drawn curtains, in tacit agreement. They were beaten, some died. Mladen was left with broken ribs and a punctured lung. Later, the Cities of Truth protested against the newly reborn communists who had just reclaimed their power. Mladen slept in tents, together with colleagues and students. The euphoria of the just cause, the readiness for self-sacrifice, the bravery, excessive like a feast after a prolonged starvation . . . They could have been crushed if the army had gone along with the wish of that thug in the Parliament — 'The best thing to do is let the tanks come' — but the army was made up of young men who didn't raise a hand.

Now, after years of misery, of power cuts, water crises, food shortages the likes of which only war-survivors can boast, of terror by the 'insurance' Mafia, the whole country is rising in one massive movement of roaring, hoarse, uncontrollable fury. Because they are hungry. This time they are protesting for food. Not for freedom or democracy, but for bread and meat. Supermarket protest, to the death.

Nadejda chooses a packet of the best regular pads. With wings on, 'for extra protection and adhesion.' She puts them in her basket. She looks around — a few indistinct looking shoppers gaze at shelves. She picks up a herb shampoo and negligently slips it into her shoulder bag.

Red Riding Hood assembles a few goodies in her little basket and pays for them at the tills, feeling that she deserves praise. But nobody seems to acknowledge her staggering law-abidance (with a touch of fresh herbs). It's a waste of goodwill. Next time she'll go

113

back to being the wolf again. A girl turns wolf turns girl — what is that? The donkey nods its long-eared head. The donkey knows the nature of Nadejda. Where is the donkey, though?

The donkey is quietly grazing on the bank of a smooth lake now. Faint hills lie supine in the haze. The afternoon displays its pastoral possibilities. The sky is so mirror-like that a breath would leave a smear on it — but the sky doesn't reflect anything. The donkey has arrived before Nadejda. Soon, Nadejda will be in a boat. The boat will be in the lake. The lake is island-locked. The island is ocean-locked. Nadejda has passed over, once, twice, thrice. The ocean has rippled through her each time, like through thousands of outspread fingers, their tips stuffed with nerve endings. Nadejda's hands will tighten into fists, small and perfectly smooth like stumps. The stumps will be in her jean pockets. The jeans are New Zealand-made.

"*And I will always*
love you . . ."

Wondrous bridges

'And I will always love you . . .' Whitney Houston unfolds her divine throat in the midst of engine roar. Nadejda's Walkman has no batteries, but she still keeps the headphones on, to block off the radio pollution and in case someone wants to talk to her.

On the same road, in a dark blue Honda, a middle-aged man is listening to a tape of Pink Floyd. He drives slowly, because he is behind a bus. He knows Nadejda is inside, but can't see her. He wants to see her. A mellow wave of resigned longing washes over him. Of course she wouldn't accept an offer for a ride from a virtual stranger! There is no point in following the bus now. They have already said goodbye. They are going their separate ways, as they should. He presses on the accelerator, but a large truck is heaving his way. He slows down. These empty New Zealand roads can be treacherous.

Nadejda spent the previous evening at the backpackers, watching the news ('Barricades have been erected in Sofia and other towns, a national strike still paralyses the country. In neighbouring Belgrade, the protests continue peacefully.') and then some tepid American film about adultery and betrayal. Later, she sat in bed dressed, trying to think of what to do with the rest of her life, whether to call her mother and tell her where she is, put her out of her misery, or her father — to see if he is all right. Instead, she kept catching herself staring at her new room-mate — a beautiful Israeli girl with mournful puppy eyes stuff her face with some mud-coloured cake and read a thick novel. Strangely hypnotised by the sight of this girl, she gradually drifted off. When she woke up in the middle of the night, sweating and confused as to which end of the bed was closest to her head, she found a blanket covering her. A single moon-ray divided the bare floor in two. The Israeli girl on the other side of the ray was asleep, gripping an old, battered teddy bear. Nadejda threw the blanket off. Her stomach was throbbing. A stray remark popped into her head: 'And watch out for those umbrellas!'

A silly laugh, a flash of moustache, a painful stab in the leg, and a sombre man with a felt hat and a sharp umbrella speeds up past her. 'I'm sorry,' the man mutters. The Thames flashes its impure tale somewhere below. Cars roar up and down the bridge. Pain spreads through her body, she begins to sweat. She spins and falls through the bridge, or does the bridge fall in the middle, thunderously, pouring its traffic into the polluted water. The entire city slides down both sides of the descending bridge in one massive sweep of vertigo.

Nadejda sank into unconsciousness again, with a whimper.

Cameraman offered to drop her off on his way south: he had a rental car. She declined. He was probably going to include her colourful character in his next book, because Cameraman is a writer. She didn't understand exactly what kind of writer though — he was gathering material for a travel book, but he also wrote novels and had been a journalist. 'What kind of journalist?' asked Nadejda. Political, came the answer. What other journalists are there, she wondered, but didn't want to sound unsophisticated.

'Way back, for instance, when I was just starting up, I wrote on the case of the Bulgarian umbrella in London.'

'The murder of the writer Georgi Markov, you mean?'

'That's right.'

'Where was he stabbed?'

'In the leg. It's the most deadly poison.'

'You still remember all this?' Nadejda felt odd not knowing half of what this foreigner knew about her country's unofficial history.

'Of course I do. It's one of the more memorable things I have come across. Since then, the Bulgarian umbrella has been rather famous. It doesn't make for a great national image of course,' he smiled indulgently.

'But that was politics. That has nothing to do with the nation.'

'Yes, you're absolutely right, but these things get rather mixed up in the eyes of the public. Even journalists. In fact, journalists perpetuate the tacky myths. So there's this enduring idea of the Bulgarian umbrella murder, even if the Bulgarian people had nothing to do with it.'

He smiled his ironic smile.

As they parted, Cameraman squeezed her shoulder gently, his   117 hand lingering there for a long moment. 'When you travel alone, you meet silly people . . .'

'Thanks a lot!' She feigned insult and laughed.

'Like me,' he added, serious and melancholic, his hand still on her shoulder.

'All the best,' she said, finding nothing else for this conclusive moment.

'Have a great . . . rest of your life.'

'Thank you. It was nice to meet you.'

'And watch out for those umbrellas.'

He squeezed her shoulder again and headed for the bus door, his camera sadly dangling from his neck like a flaccid penis. Nadejda was suddenly afflicted by a pang of loss.

Yes, she has met silly people, and sad people, over the last few weeks, here and in Sofia. She meets them, then never sees them again. Each fleeting encounter afflicts her somehow. She looks out the window. A blue Honda is overtaking the bus. She could have been in a car like this, listening to Cameraman bragging about his books, or his obscure travels in Eastern Europe and God knows where else. But she is better off here, high above the road, alone in her double seat. She closes her eyes, trying to block out the crescendo of 'And I will always love you'. She'd rather not think about what afflicts her, but it's too late.

The last time they made love, a week or so ago, Anton said, 'Remember: I will always love you.' She would remember. Outside his window the swollen, low sky was shedding rags of snow. His clear blue eyes, his fading black eye complemented by an eyebrow scar still raw from the police baton two weeks ago, his angular shoulders, his inexplicable passion after four years of separation and very little correspondence, made Nadejda think, quite absurdly, that one day he would commit suicide. She could have cried but she had a rule never to cry in front of others. She is a rare and restrained crier. They sat naked under his duvet, backs against the wall, her legs draped over his. He buried his face in her neck and breathed in the scent of her hair.

118

'I want to remember this forever.'

Two weeks earlier, after their first night together, they were sitting in exactly the same position, and Anton said to her, 'You should come with us, this afternoon, in front of the Parliament.'

'Mmm. Yeah, I don't know . . .'

'Why not?'

'I've been away too long. I'm not up to date with what's been happening here.'

'Yes, you are. Do you want to get rid of the Red scum?'

'Yes.'

'Do you think Bulgaria deserves better?'

'Oh yes!'

'Are you still Bulgarian?'

'Yeah, I guess I am.'

'Then you're up-to-date. This is still your country and you have the right to do something for it.'

This is still her country. She has the right. But march shoulder to shoulder with this boy she hasn't seen for years, chatter together their teeth in the minus ten degrees cold while the rest of the world ignores them, while soft-spined Tony back in New Zealand is smoking dope on a sunny porch? What badge would she wear, what banner would she carry? She would have to suffer somebody else's suffering — the ultimate venal paradox. She would no longer be accepted by the others, by Anton's fellow students, by those who had nothing to lose except their teeth and their eyes when they faced the forest of police batons — because there were going to be such forests, she could tell. 'We are the students, we're not afraid!' they chanted. They marched with suitcases. But her suitcase was real — how could she take part in that march? 'You leave or we leave!' they chanted. But she was leaving anyway.

'Yeah okay, I'll come.'

He leaned on her, sealing her lips with a kiss and pushing her slowly down onto the bed. They made love quickly, as if time was running out. Anton was a quick comer and didn't leave her enough time to finish. She pressed his heavy breathing face against her neck, forgivingly if unhappily, and they lay still but quivering, as if trying to bury their passion in some thin crack of the majestic new edifice

Chapter Twelve

called 'Operation National Salvation'. A few minutes later, he took a large thermos of coffee from the kitchen, and his Bulgarian flag. His parents were still sleeping. Nadejda called home — her father was unsurprised by her absence during the night, having already guessed the resuming of the play with her old friend — and arranged to meet in town later. The two old friends had jam on bread and thin coffee.

'Too bad there'll be none for Mum and Dad,' he said. 'They'll have black tea instead.'

They kissed in the lobby, his hands squeezing the skin of her back through her jersey. 'You haven't changed at all. The perfect face, the sulky smile, the gorgeous long hair, they're still the same,' he whispered as he brushed away a long lock of hair from her face.

'And you have.' She instantly regretted saying this. Changing implies ageing, and at twenty-one ageing implies a hard life.

'How?'

'You've . . . well your hair's longer for one thing, and you're kind of thinner.'

'Yeah, it's those prices. Great for the waistline.'

They went down the stairs. He was carrying the flag and wearing the badge of the philosophy faculty: 'I think therefore I protest.' The students of Sofia University were going to announce their strike officially today. She would never have suspected such patriotic consciousness in this once weedy blond boy who followed her like a shadow. Now she was following *him* down the musty, creaking staircase, out into the sunlit winter street lined with bare trees petrified into frosty poses, littered with banners, paper ribbons and wrappers. Good morning, Sofia. Nadejda was a shadow seeping out of her own past. Anton, a denizen of the archaic present of Sofia, began to pump blood into that shadow.

Forty hours later, in the early morning debacle in front of the Parliament, Nadejda watched two cops beat Anton about the head with batons. As she hurled herself to his rescue, a short young cop spread his arms to bar her way and shouted without a touch of humour 'And where are *you* going, beautiful?' The next moment she was in his arms and he was pushing her back. 'Anton!' she yelled, trying to see over the cop's shoulder. The cop gripped her elbows as

120

she kept trying to disengage herself from his embrace. He was holding a baton but did not use it on her. In the struggle, she saw Anton's body stretched inert on the ground and his two attackers run away. 'Let go of me!' she hissed at the cop as tears spilled out of her eyes uncontrollably. Whistles ripped the frozen air, uniforms fired rubber bullets at the backs of dishevelled runners, women and men screamed, bodies were falling to the ground, shoes and odd objects picked up from the ruins inside Parliament rained on their heads. In the meantime, the last socialist MPs crawled out of the building and straight into their cars, back to their hotel rooms with windows broken by demonstrators, where they would get their few hours' sleep.

Eventually, the cop let go of Nadejda, brusquely shoving her away. She slumped down by Anton's body, shaking all over, her teeth chattering, her stomach turned inside out. Things didn't seem to be the right way up. As she bent over Anton, he appeared to be hanging above her, and she to be reaching up to him, like the previous morning when they made love. His eyes were closed, his face and hair were bloodied; in the yellow light of the square he looked dead. She lifted his head. A trail of blood marked the wet yellow pavement below but in the mess of his hair she couldn't see the wound. She looked around for help; a great, indistinct bustle surrounded her, moaning bodies were scattered around the square, uniforms ran about brandishing pieces of broken Parliament furniture, police jeeps took off with a violent screech, spotlights looked on with clinical eyes, sirens wailed from afar. She checked Anton's pulse but couldn't find it. Nadejda pressed the heavy torso to her chest, and started rocking gently, as if to soothe him. She didn't know if he was alive; on the other hand, death seemed quite absurd, so she decided that he couldn't be dead. A couple of battered students from her father's faculty ran in her direction shouting 'Nadejda!' but before they got to her they were grabbed by energetic policemen and beaten senseless.

'These filthy bastards, criminals, they'll pay for it!' someone shouted, limping past them and spitting out blood and teeth, and repeated, turning to a group of cops. 'You'll pay for it, criminals, Red scum!' They jumped on him and beat him. Someone else tried to pull Anton away from Nadejda, to make sure he was okay. It was his

Chapter Twelve

ex-girlfriend, who had been spared except for her bleeding nose. So far, she hadn't been particularly warm towards Nadejda but now there was the fraternity of disaster. She was sobbing. Nadejda let go of Anton. He was already coming to, with a groan. Ambulances arrived. Anton was dragged onto a stretcher and taken away.

Nadejda remained kneeling on the slushy yellow tiles in the middle of the square, next to Anton's bloody mark, overlooked by the Russian Tsar Osvoboditel, the Liberator, serene and safe high up on his horse. The horse's legs were firmly planted on the platform, which meant the rider died a natural death.

Two frail-looking young army soldiers were helping the ambulance officers with the stretchers. Nadejda felt gorged with something. Her tears had frozen on her face long ago, but for the first time she knew exactly where she was. This glossy pavement was real, this white city was real, this monument to the equivocal Russian liberators was real and, above all, Anton's blood, still trickling out of his cracked head somewhere in a dingy hospital, was real. A transfusion had occurred: blood pumped out of him and into Nadejda's unsure, groping body, so that Nadejda could be here once again. She was seventeen-year-old Nadejda again. Never left her home city, never crossed the Pacific, never lived in a city of neat houses with trim gardens and smiling people, never bent over a quiet boy whispering to her English words of near-love, never mingled with a student crowd in track-suit pants yielding plastic no-leak bottles . . .

Sirens dissolved in the distance. Running steps echoed across the ghostly town and sank into the secrecy of snow. More police streamed out of the Parliament and launched a keen hunt-down of the fugitives. Somewhere in snowy backstreets, they chased students into old buildings, up heavy staircases all the way to the attics, and left them bleeding and broken. There was no one left in the square except some soldiers who paced up and down in confusion, some cops at the Parliament entrance, and Nadejda.

Everybody in the square was beaten, except Nadejda. There was no good reason for this, except that she was perhaps not altogether there, or not as much as all these people. She was leaving soon, they were not. Even the neckless, monosyllabic cops smelled this and left her alone. A great loneliness froze Nadejda's body in the early morning slush. She was so numb she couldn't think or feel. A single, piercing scream rose from the garden behind Parliament. A spotlight suddenly went out. Nadejda could die a white death, if she stayed here much longer. When at three in the morning everyone is unconscious in hospitals without morphine, asleep in apartments without heat, or awake with cruelty serving no cause, while the rest of the world couldn't care less, you die of loneliness, she suspected. White death could simply be death from loneliness. She got up and walked to a taxi stand. Go to Pirogov hospital, where Anton must be? But they wouldn't let her in at this hour. There were small clusters of people standing in front of the university, smoking, and no police in sight. An eerie quiet had replaced the tumult in the space of half an hour.

She got into a smoke-filled Mazda. The beefy driver was leafing through a porn magazine.

'You got away from them, right?' he said good-heartedly.

Nadejda's mouth moved to say 'Yes' but nothing came out.

'So, where to?'

'*Nadejda*,' she managed to mumble.

It sounded like introducing herself. 'Nadejda. How do you do?'

They took off. He turned the radio on. 'And I will always love you,' bawled Whitney Houston. She wouldn't be let into Pirogov at this hour. Anton could be in a coma — they had beaten him on the head, after all.

Nadejda was under the spell of that fascinating, ugly spectacle, as if she had come out of a cinema and must get accustomed to reality. But what *was* reality right now? Going home where her father was probably sick with worry. 'Stick with Anton and the others,' he had warned her earlier that day, resigned to her decision to stay on. 'And try not to get too close to the front, there could be provocateurs there. Watch out for any unrest. If things get heated up, get away, don't hang around. It could get nasty. I'll wait for you at home. Get a taxi, don't use public transport. Or stay at Anton's. In any case, call me.' She stuck with Anton and the others. She didn't get too close to the front. There *were* provocateurs, trying to break into Parliament. 123

It got nastier than her father would have imagined. And she couldn't stay at Anton's. But she got away.

They were driving along the Lions' Bridge. The four lions squatted enigmatically, large and afraid in the darkness. When Nadejda was crossing the bridge earlier with Anton, he had said, 'Look at them carefully. Do you notice anything odd about them?'

She didn't.

'Look harder, look at their heads. Anything missing?'

Nadejda had never looked at a real lion's head very carefully, and these ones seemed normal. 'Well, they look sort of . . . benign. Not very predatory.'

'Yes, you could say that. But why?' And before giving her time for more observation, he added, 'Because they have no tongues.'

Nadejda laughed. It was true.

'When he discovered his omission, the sculptor committed suicide.'

Nadejda laughed. Anton contemplated the lions for a moment. 'Why do you laugh?'

He looked at her sombrely, as if the sculptor was his own father.

'It's just . . . a bit ridiculous really.'

'Well, the guy was committed to his artistic cause. That's no subject for amusement.' But then he shrugged his shoulders as if dismissing the subject and touched her elbow, moving on. He couldn't be cross with her for very long.

'Another interesting fact: the four lions were a tribute to four bookmakers who were hanged just before the Turkish Liberation for distributing a revolutionary songbook. One of them is in the Madame Tussaud's Museum, labelled "Criminals from the Ottoman Empire"! That's the British for you.'

'Where do you learn all these things from?'

'Well, the press.'

He shrugged his shoulders, pleased to have impressed her, at last. She stopped. He stopped. She put her hand on his unshaven cheek, turned his unshaven blond face towards her and kissed him. It was their first grown-up kiss. They were leaning on the bridge stone railing darkened by a hundred years of fumes. Below, the river was

124

thickly frozen. Above, the hardened, colourless sky was almost touching the manes of the lapsed lions. Nadejda and Anton were sandwiched in between, clutching each other, her cheek on his Adam's apple. She felt him swallowing deeply. A black crow brushed their heads, cawing satanically, and vanished into the mist. Traffic was thundering up and down the bridge. A mauve-faced old woman in rags limped past them, mumbling, 'The kids are kissing, and I am freezing. The kids are kissing, and I am freezing.'

The bus turns off the road. Nadejda opens her eyes and the sunlight pierces her temples. They have entered a parking lot, swarming with cars and tourists. She looks around. Her co-travellers are moving in their seats, searching for cameras under layers of spread-out maps and bags. Nadejda searches for her sunglasses but her luggage is a mess: they could be anywhere. The passengers trickle out of the bus, armed with cameras and sunglasses. Nadejda can't find her camera either. She doesn't want to take a break or go sightseeing, but she joins the sheeplike column. Follow the column, clutch the camera, croon in a chorus of admiration, get your money's worth, eat your lunch, converse seriously with some Germans, laugh with some Australians, listen to some startling native birds, rock in the coma of crystalline waters, climb the bus steps again following the sturdy bottom of some Dane, and forget everything else in the easy Pacific sun. There's nothing else. How could there be anything else? Sofia pops like a soap bubble.

Nadejda crosses the parking lot towards the sightseeing spot, a still invisible mass of vociferous water. The bus driver unwraps a sandwich: 'It's one hell of a waterfall,' he says. Nadejda smiles and nods as if they've been talking about this waterfall all day and now finally she gets to see it. Perhaps they have. Perhaps the driver has been telling the attentive passengers all about it, and she missed everything. Waterfall, of course! Of all natural phenomena, Nadejda has a predilection for waterfalls. She catches a glimmer of unnatural blue through the shrubs lining the riverbank. The thump of water muffles all other noise; a dazzling fury of bluish foam fills her senses. She sets foot on a bridge.

Chapter Twelve

As she crosses the deafening chaos of water, Nadejda sways. She sways but doesn't fall. Why doesn't she fall? Perhaps because the bridge is wide. Perhaps because Nadejda never falls except in dreams. In dreams she falls off crumbling cliffs, concrete staircases, chalet roofs, but especially from bicycles on tight-ropes. Why does she sway now, she who can walk along a banister in her sleep? Because she is not really crossing this river — this river is a conspiracy which her mind has suddenly stopped believing. She is crossing an altogether different river. She keeps walking, swaying, her eyes fixed on the luminous froth below. The thumping noise gives away the real identity of the river.

Nadejda walks inside a dark loophole and comes out the other end where *lush greenery mourns beheaded naked bodies whirling about in the river for centuries. Giant arches bend over the dark water that knows too much. There is no protection here, no signs, no guides, no lunch break. If you stand on that giant back of stone, carved to perfection by ancient waters, there are no railings to protect you. There is no bungy jumping here, at Chudnite Mostove, the Wondrous Bridges. There is something else, though. Nadejda is standing high up on the cliffs. The river rages below. On the other side appear horsemen with fezzes and yatagans, static but vicious, overlooking some punishment. Then, in the early morning mist, she distinguishes a long column of women, men and children, moving towards the cliff.*

'Move, move, you dirty giaours!' says one of the horsemen, clearly the chief.

Nadejda zooms up to his face — nasty though imposing green eyes, dark moustache, unusually handsome face with a sensuous mouth. He has raped thirty-eight girls and women since he became governor of this region. As the first man in the convoy reaches the edge of the cliff, the green-eyed horseman shouts, perhaps in Bulgarian, perhaps in Turkish; in any case Nadejda understands: 'Will you convert to the Muslim faith?'

The moustachioed man in rags says in a deep, solemn voice, 'Never.'

Only now does Nadejda notice that his hand is missing. The torn white sleeve is drenched with darkness. One swift metallic flash of a yatagan sends his head flying off. He tumbles down, crashing on the sharp rocks. The river embraces him and, swelling his white shirt into a bubble, sets him asail in the wake of his head.

Next comes a young woman with long dark hair. Her dress is torn at the top, her white bare shoulder catching the sun, she stands proud and unflinching. The horseman asks her, in a slightly altered voice (for he has enjoyed her many times): 'Will you convert to the Muslim faith, Kalinna?'

Kalinna spits in his direction with all the strength of her wrecked body and leaps off the cliff. She falls like a white kite, her dress spreading in mid-air. When she hits the water, her face remains a blur carried by the fast frothy stream. It's a body chasing another body.

Back through the loophole, and now Nadejda is on the other bank of the river. Fine spray tickles the air. Instead of savage horsemen and a human row of pain, there are tourists with cameras and sandwiches on this side, all headed down in the direction of the falls. She has just come out of a cinema and must get accustomed to reality. Chudnite Mostove vanish. But what *is* reality? The Huka Falls, she guesses. A crowd flocking at the railing by the falls, this is reality — tons of mindless crystalline water flowing ad infinitum.

Nadejda leans over and watches the effervescent orgy of water. She thinks how it is so unlike the violence of men. Water takes you when nobody else wants you. Sometimes she takes you by force, before you are ready. Sometimes she comes to you, in big mighty crashing waves. She breaks you, then she soothes you. This is a country of water, surrounded by ocean, punctuated by lakes, waterfalls and rivers. This country is rocked by the latent violence of water.

She stares as if hypnotised by the crashing mass. It pumps more light into her: she is not sure whether she is seeing the real thing, or its luminous imprint inside her closed eyelids. Nadejda is a ghost groping its way across this island — the head of the fish that is this country. Nadejda hasn't quite arrived yet. Then she will leap across the Strait to the other island, the tail of the fish. Then what? If she called her mother now, it would be a ghostly finger dialling the Christchurch number, and a ghostly voice would say 'Mum, I'm back.' Her ghostly voice could lie: 'Mum, I'm not coming back.'

A long-haired girl in flat sandals and tight denim shorts is in   127 the focus of a lean, middle-aged man's camera lens. Could he be filming a ghost? That will become apparent only when he plays it back, later. If no Nadejda appears against the luminous water madness, then we would know that she was not really here. But who is the girl in the focus of the BBC journalist's camera in front of Alexander Nevski Cathedral, marching in a thick, face-painted, cheering column headed by a balding horseman with a blue flag? That too must be Nadejda. Will she show up in the BBC news later? She will, she has. Her uncle watched her on New Zealand television, smiling through what would have been his tears if only he could cry (but real men don't cry, he has been taught by his father). And he rang his sister to tell her to watch, quickly, now . . . by which time Nadejda's smiling face had disappeared in the human sea. Nadejda really was there. Why wouldn't she be here, too, now?

Blood has to be pumped into ghosts before they feel real once again.

She is not going to call her mother. Let her think she is still there, on the merry new barricades, stuck in the vile country where she belongs, not a free-roaming ghost in this one where she speaks nonsense with well-meaning, sunstruck people.

The sun is unrelenting. Her sunglasses hang from a tangled cord on her neck. Ah, that's where they were. She takes the cord off and tries to disentangle it, but her fingers shake inexplicably and the glasses slip out, pirouetting down like a fabulous sun-insect, engulfed by the foam.

'Woops,' says a lumpy woman in leggings with breasts hanging to her waist.

'Mum, Mum, see the glasses!' yells an angelic-looking boy.

'You just dropped your glasses, right?' A young man turns to her with an American drawl. He is from her bus — she remembers him because of his protruding chin and general resemblance to Quentin Tarantino. 'Do you wanna have mine? I have another pair.'

With a deft movement, as if he had been practising especially for such occasions, he takes off his glasses and holds them out to her. 'Here.' Suddenly, something in him shrinks nervously and his real shyness surfaces on his weird face like a corpse's back on murky water.

'Oh, thank you.' Nadejda shades her eyes with a hand and smiles, bemused. 'But I'll be okay. Thanks.'

She isn't sure how to take this. There is something grossly child-like about him, something awkward and embarrassing. She gets the feeling that if she said to him 'Jump!' and pointed at the falls, he would jump.

Her eyes are still watering. Perhaps she should call her mother, tell her the truth about her whereabouts. Or her uncle, just out of general spite. He couldn't care less about her anyway. In any case, she will have to acquire another pair of sunglasses soon, or she'll never stop crying.

Back on the bus, Quentin retires to his seat at the back after letting Nadejda before him. Something in his self-conscious smile melts the crust of Nadejda's heart. Once in her seat, she tosses her hair back, aware of his presence behind her. She puts on her headphones. And the next moment she forgets about him.

But she doesn't forget about the green-eyed horseman and the face staring up at her — how could she forget her own dead face? The Wondrous Bridges were the site of executions by the Turks, once upon a time. No living Bulgarian has any memory of those events. Only the mountains brood there and water gurgles stupidly and peacefully under the arches. And now this untimely scene, this blood gushing out of the past that isn't even Nadejda's past, but some film she must have seen years ago ...

She slumps deeper in her seat. She doesn't want to think of that face floating on the water. Or her mother's and grandmother's harrowing story of survival by Chudnite Mostove, that time they went on a picnic. She is so sick of harrowing stories. Of her strange uncle, of her grandmother's death on the plane, of her chain-smoking father in the sad flat. Of her grandfather in Plovdiv, with his permanently misshapen jaw and tobacco-yellowed fingers. Of the barricades in Sofia. Of the unbearable stark sun of New Zealand.

She wants to think of sex. Sex is an impish creature twitching tirelessly in the jumble of her mind. She could have thought of it in the following way:

Sex with Narcissus, the other night — obviously she enjoyed it but now she can't recall much beyond his hairy thighs, dilated feline eyes, and the pressure of his long-nailed fingers in the small of her back. She didn't even have a thorough look at him. 'You are magnifique!'

Sex with Anton, about a week ago, for the last time. 'I wonder why we didn't have sex earlier, when I was still around,' she said. 'This isn't sex,' he said gravely, 'this is making love.' And in fact, Nadejda's sex-reverie about Anton inevitably clicks out of joint, under the crippling pressure of love. She doesn't know how to distinguish between the two — but she does know there is a sadness about one and not about the other. The day when she went along with him and a few thousand other university students inundating Vitosha Street, they drew hearts with pastel sticks on the windows of trams, making the tough-looking tramdrivers cry. Anton drew a heart and wrote 'Nadejda' underneath, the way they did in high school. The way he did exactly ten years ago, in the white ruins by the sea: 'Nadejda + Anton.'

Sex with Tony, barely distinguishable in the daub of her mind under wet layers of recent sensations. His speechless adoration tinged with drug-heightened mystical terror when he bends over her, his bloodshot eyes, his stubborn silences during sex, his prostration afterwards. And the others, before and after. It is good taste not to entertain the thought of others to come, while she is with someone. But they do come, oh they come, and when she was with Tony and Anton, she thought of them, the next ones, unknown and different, and better, lurching blindly into the margins of her desire.

But she doesn't think in this order. She thinks in no order. The creature jiggles violently, stirring an impenetrable mass of sporadic limbs, moans, bed edges, full moons, pillows in disarray. What to do now? Where to go? Who to go to? She longs to become one with that creature, to inhabit its jungle undisturbed and naked.

There is a song I play in my head
over and over: in the warm fitful
wind the wheat reclines with
autumnal languor.

The voice: nestinarki

There is a song I play in my head over and over: in the warm fitful wind the wheat reclines with autumnal languor. Roses burn in the sultry shimmering distance, little scarlet fires punctuate the Balkan night. The song is dark, drawn and crackling, a family of bodies stretched at a crossroad. The song is the shadow of their blood, it creeps parallel to the vines of their veins like ivy, flaps its wings dissonantly in the heavens, the heavens that spread their mortuary shroud above the land. The song stirs bones, centuries deep. Over there, in the mercurial light, I watch the nestinarki, the fire dancers, smile their copper smiles among so many flames weaving their giant limbs at the borders of the wheatfield.

Somewhere, a donkey chews his cud, dutifully. It is my father's donkey — the one I used to ride with him, when I was little and he was awake. It is always the same donkey, because there is only one donkey. Somewhere, a petrified scarecrow sways in the air currents stirred by passing vultures, in some vague remembrance of decay. Is it a family's decay, their bodies? Yes, but if you ask them, it is always someone else's decay. The moment they state their own decay, they would no longer be themselves, they would become scarecrows.

The nestinarki, women who have passed the age of child-bearing, are the eternal salamanders of pain. They leap across sky-reaching fires, and dance on red coals, their faces devastated with beauty, their lips dark and chapped, their eyes cavernously black, their bodies a harmony of storms, their voices, like scorpions, cut by their own song and bleeding thickly in the empty tunnels of summer. They are in a trance.

One of them is a little girl. Her long hair trembles around her white face as if the night itself is stirred by her. She is exactly my age. By her side, a full-bodied woman with a mask-like face steps over the incandescent coals without a muscle of her face twitching. She is looking straight ahead. The little girl looks up at her every now and then, with serious inquisitiveness, but the woman is staring into the distance. It is hard to say whether she is hypnotising herself or being hypnotised by some invisible, private spectacle taking place before her unblinking eyes. The other nestinarki look vaguely familiar. The red coals breathe and hiss under their hard soles like a creature before slaughter. Where are the men? There is no reason why there should be no men in this song. But I always see the women, only the women. And the two vanishing men. This is how they vanished.

A donkey carrying two men is swallowed by the darkness. Just before they dissolve, one of them, the older one, turns his head. It is hard to say what his expression betrays: his thick dark eyebrows lurch over his clear green eyes, his smoothly shaven face is crossed by pairs of lines: two between his eyebrows, two running down from his nose to the corners of his mouth. Everything that is in his heart is in those four lines; I could even say that his heart is made of these four lines. The lines becomes deeper, as if a frenzied sculptor is chiselling his face this very minute, as he turns towards the fire. This man will never come back. The young man in the front doesn't turn back, because he is nineteen and he thinks he'll be coming back soon. He too will never come back.

In the field, blue men hang for some forgotten crime. My father was one of them. I tug at his foot. His shoe comes off. I don't understand what he is doing so high up. His eyes are open and yet he is not awake. I want to ride the donkey with him. But the men in uniforms took the donkey away. There was only me and my mother left in the world, in the house by the woods. She wore black until the end. Even at night, when she was transformed into a ghost in a white night-dress, I knew she was still wearing black on the inside.

There is a railway at the far end of the field. It is concealed by the high wheat. It can be seen only from above. I can see it now: an iron staple on the warm fur of the earth. A cattle wagon is passing, and another one — a convoy of wagons thunder along, cutting through the dark field. Destination: Deli Orman, the Mad Forest. Inside one of the wagons, the serious girl is sleeping on her mother's ample lap. The mother, stone-faced, is looking straight ahead. Her velvety round eyes are like those of a wounded gazelle too proud to collapse under the rifles. She is crammed together with seven hundred other 'enemies of the people' from Sofia, all to be taken to the Mad Forest, that godforsaken province of the country, for an indefinite period of time. They are all either distinguished families or the remaining parts of families of 'defectors'. They have no possessions — their capitalist belongings have been appropriated by the state.

Next to the mother and daughter is sitting a judge with his family. Their house was looted by the militia, and a greasy-haired government official moved in. The judge's little daughter clutches the only doll she was allowed to keep. His wife, wild-eyed, presses the girl's head against her breast as if to hide the ugliness of this cattle wagon from her. The judge, haggard and middle-aged, squeezes the family bundle between his large knees; his powerful shoulders shiver every now and then, agitated by vast, silent sobs. And so on. Children sleep or whimper. Their expressionless parents stroke the little heads with automatic hands.

The wagon rattles on, passing through deserted landscapes. Goodbye city, goodbye house, goodbye future.

Any one of these refugees could have been the hero of this story, you would think. You would be wrong: out of the seven hundred exiles only little sleeping Ana will find herself in the Land of the Long White Cloud. And so will you, Nadejda, yet unborn. And so will I. Incongruous but somehow necessary: here we are.

Sleepwalking, desperate, brave Nadejda, you are a bundle of contradictions. You are making your way down towards me, though you don't know it yet. Unsuspectingly joining the dots of your destiny down the length of this faraway country. Wanting to know. You will. I am waiting for you, patiently and inexorably, just as death waits for me.

RECONNAISSANCE

CHAPTER FOURTEEN

And there she is.

Barbary

And there she is. In a corner of the vast, evenly rippled lake, the boat is a white dot. Now — a close up. There are seven passengers on the two o'clock cruise. A jovial yacht-master ('Hello folks, I'm Bill') tugs at ropes and levers. His face is so overgrown with grey bristle — up to his eyes — that Nadejda finds it impossible to determine his age. Another sail is erected and flaps in the wind desperately like a bound seagull. This must be a sea, then. Nadejda leans against a railing and looks up at the gull-to-be, waiting for it to tear itself away from this enforced fraternity of sails. The white refraction of sunlight blinds her unprotected eyes and deepens the hue of her arms and legs by the minute. Her body is strangely cold, while her head is like an empty furnace. But it isn't a sea, because this is the centre of the island. Is there an island whose centre is a sea? She guesses there isn't. The centre of this island though is the largest crater-lake in the world. She stretches her legs and accidentally kicks the porcelain-faced Scandinavian woman across from her, who is clutching her Scandinavian man. 'Sorry,' says Nadejda absent-mindedly, not bothering to show concern. The woman smiles with her thin lips and withdraws her thin-boned sandalled feet under the bench.

'*Barbary* was designed in Scandinavia, built and raced in California, and in 1938 Errol Flynn won it in a card game. It came to New Zealand in 1947, and was wrecked in a storm near Auckland.' Hairy-faced Bill knows his lesson by heart after all these years. The Scandinavians nod with polite indifference. A German or maybe Dutch couple listen intensely. Another German watches the lake through his camera. The side of his face and neck are raw with burn scars. The other man, big-chinned and awkward, is Quentin. Nadejda is surprised not to have noticed him until now. She wonders if he has noticed her — because he is looking her way behind his sunglasses without a sign of recognition. Perhaps he is a weirdo, or simply a typical American — hugging you and calling you friend, and then not knowing you the next minute. Perhaps he is dangerous. Nadejda doesn't acknowledge him either, in case he is dangerous.

'I got hold of *Barbary* in 1981 . . .'

Nadejda doesn't care for history — that of people, objects and places. What's the point in recounting events that have no relevance to us? But history haunts us. She sighs. We are blind slugs that crawl out of history's caves to bask in the grubby communal sun; when our time is up, we crawl back in. We *are* history. This is how Nadejda would explain why she hates history.

'. . . and then did it up. I worked on it for two years, until it was fit to sail again, and it's been cruising the lake ever since.'

He laughs unassumingly somewhere in his beard. What is he laughing for, Nadejda thinks irritably, so blinded by the sun she can't even listen properly (why didn't she take those glasses Quentin offered?). It doesn't take much for some people: give him an Errol Flynn yacht and he'll be happy ever after. *Barbary* gathers speed, it is gliding noiselessly on the luminous surface; the lake swells like a giant body floating face down. Nadejda is anxious to see its face, but the body won't turn. She wants to know why the name of this battered vessel is *Barbary*. What meaning lies behind it? It would be easy to ask obliging Bill. Just casually ask — but she can't bring herself to. She has the unpleasant sensation of being sealed off from this blue afternoon in a private, tight bubble. She feels that if she tried to ask, her mouth simply couldn't form the words. The world ripples around her without stroking her as sensuously as one would think by looking at her. Copper jumps from her hair gently lifted and fondled by the wind, her sharp elbows propped up on the railing. Nadejda decorates the boat, and the lake, if you look close enough. And yet she is not exactly here. But if she is not on this lake, under the flapping gulls, she is not anywhere. Nadejda doesn't like the feeling of not being anywhere. She needs something to pull her out of her bubble. Some acute pain or pleasure to wake her up from this sun-drenched dream of somebody else's island. She needs to be naked against a male body, for example, to be called by her name. Nadejda. Nadejda. The accent, the mispronunciation don't matter. But the only voice she hears calling her name is her mother's — distant and insistent — 'Nadejda!' How she hates being called by her mother! How she hates going back to her mother. Of course, she doesn't have to. There is always a choice.

Bill's weatherbeaten assistant with a baseball cap emerges from the interior of the boat carrying a tray of plastic cups. 'Tea, coffee? Biscuit?' Her voice is rasping, like her looks.

Quentin helps himself to the sugar, sprinkling three spoonfuls on his coffee; he shakes his big head every now and then — it must be

Chapter Fourteen

a tic. He glances at Nadejda and her eyes meet his sunglasses for a second. He's definitely a weirdo. The two couples gorge themselves on biscuits. The porcelain doll dips her biscuit in her tea. Her husband mutters something and then chokes, red-facedly, on some crumbs. She pats his back. Everybody except the scorch-faced German man, who has removed the camera from his face and is half-heartedly getting used to seeing the lake with a naked eye, sips the hot drinks with relish.

'Lovely,' says the muscular assistant to Bill for a reason that escapes Nadejda. The dainty word strangely clashes with her muscular calves and not-so-dainty manners. Nadejda wonders what she assists in apart from the coffee and biscuits distribution. Or perhaps Bill just enjoys the company of a young woman on board to whom he can speak and be sure to be understood, among all these foreigners.

'We're approaching the Maori rock carvings,' announces Bill and swerves to the right, causing Nadejda to spill some coffee on Scorched-face's over-sized, bare knee. He twitches and Nadejda says, 'I'm really sorry,' this time with more conviction. She is clumsy today. He is the worst person to spill hot drinks over, but he is also the one with the greatest surface per body on board.

'Are you okay?'

The bubble bursts: she is speaking. This momentary pain felt by someone else but inflicted by her, pops the bubble.

'Yeah, it's okay.' He nods, but doesn't go as far as to smile like the Scandinavian woman. Of course, being kicked lightly on the foot doesn't compare with being scorched. Scorching has to be one of the most painful injuries; being boiled to death has to be worse than hanging, or decapitation. But why is Nadejda having such thoughts? A vague rumination on a vaguely barbarous act is gnawing at her stomach, something between nausea and sensually pleasurable cruelty. Is she cruel? This is yet to be discovered. Is she sensual? Tony in Christchurch and Anton in Sofia think so, but they are not very experienced, and they are both in love with her. Her body demands something, and whatever it is, the demand is single and shrill, rising in pitch by the minute.

138   'Here it is folks!' They draw closer to the steep rocky shore,

and sure enough, the huge carving lurks in the rock indentation, guarded by a carved lizard at its foot. It is a patch of intricate bareness amid the green-yellowish growth. For a second Nadejda falls victim to a ridiculous trompe-l'oeil. The carving looks like a naked backside as well as a face — the face of an orang-utan, it seems. And the backside of something else . . . It must surely be a human face. Those lines descending from the nose to the mouth, and around the outer corner of the eyes, are the traditional tattoos. No pupil either — the look is blank; it doesn't need to see, it knows. Nadejda wants to be like this face: highly stylised, self-contained, eternal, guarded by a tuatara rising out of green translucent water, facing the white curve of the sun without blinking.

Cameras click behind her. She is leaning against the railing at the raised end of the boat, standing above the water, her back turned to the cameras. She has decided not to take any photographs. 'The ephemeral too sides with us,' Cameraman said. Immobilising the flow of the world: that's what photography is about. Cameraman, and all these tourists who sleep with their cameras, are herbalists of plump ripe moments, fairy-catchers, warriors against the ephemeral. Their cause is a lost one. And what should Nadejda do? Be a fairy, the most natural state — but for nobody to catch. Like her grandmother: she lived in the obscurity of Deli Orman with no witnesses except her daughter, and died in midair with no witnesses, no snap-shots, no explanation. She was beautiful once but never got to be painted by Vladimir the Master. Where is she now? In a petrified sea, under a sky shedding rust, waiting. Like this stone face. What is it waiting for? The next eruption, in some five hundred years or so? This face is both dead and alive, animal and human, front and back, perfect and unfinished. Nadejda wants to be that face. She also wishes that if the face could have desires it would want to be her, so that the exchange would be perfect.

In the evening, Nadejda hangs around the spacious, busy Youth Hostel kitchen, trying to improvise a recipe of rice and sausages. She turns to a flushed blonde woman to ask for cooking oil.

'Sure.' The woman obligingly hands her the plastic bottle. She 139 is Nadejda's cooking neighbour at the stove. Fat, sizzling sausages suffer gruesomely in her frying pan.

'And where are you from?' She turns to Nadejda, making her aware of their height difference. Nadejda has to look up as the woman bends down, menacing hands on her large hips.

'Bulgaria.'

'Ah, Bulgaria. I've seen some Bulgarians. What was your capital? Bucharest?'

'No, Sofia.'

'Aha. In Germany, there are many Bulgarians. Like the Turkish, they do the dirty jobs, you know, sweep the streets, cleaners, porters. There are lots of them arriving in our country, they are difficult to control.'

She turns the sausages, now striped with burns. But many of those cleaners have university degrees, Nadejda wants to say, like the foreign taxi-drivers in New Zealand. The woman brushes away her whitish blonde mane with the back of a fork-yielding hand and Nadejda knows there is no point. She reminds Nadejda of a healthy, over-sized mare — big breasts, big hips, big hair, big teeth.

'And you must be very happy here, no? You have many more opportunities here, and a brilliant future. You wouldn't have that in Bulgaria, no?'

'I don't know what future I would've had in Bulgaria,' says Nadejda and is shocked by the sincerity in her voice. 'It could've been brilliant too.'

'*I'd* be extremely happy to live here. It's a beautiful country. In fact, I'm thinking about it. This country is a, what do you call it, Fullhorn. Horn of . . .'

'Horn of Plenty?' Nadejda prompts helpfully.

But the dynamic Mare-woman is already neighing with delight as she stabs the sausages and shakes them off on a plate one by one. Nadejda watches with morbid fascination. When she checks her own rice, it's burnt at the bottom. The Mare-woman trots off to one of the long wooden tables where a few full-cheeked diners are already seated.

Television noises come through from the lounge where a trio of identical, sunburnt British boys are playing pool and warmly hugging jugs of beer. There is a programme on the royal family and they have turned up the volume so that the kitchen populace are fully up to date with every royal adventure.

To avoid the masticating congregation at the table, Nadejda carries her hot plate to the veranda where a few solitary eaters occupy a small table each, except a glamorous young couple with carefully tanned legs and blonde ponytails. The man is particularly dashing, notes Nadejda — his blue eyes look up from his spaghetti mountain (for a second it seems to Nadejda that he has no plate and the steaming heap is dumped straight onto the table) but he doesn't notice Nadejda. His bleached stubble brushes the static hair of his girlfriend who is absorbed in a map examination. Nadejda can't bear to watch them, so she sits at the very front of the veranda, facing the fading lake.

'Hello,' says an ominously familiar voice behind her. She turns around but Birdie is already sitting on the bench beside her, armed with a cup of tea. Nadejda struggles with an unmanageable, greedy first mouthful before she can respond. The shock of this cruel encounter slows down her chewing.

'Hi.' It is her damned fate to cross paths with this dull creature all over the island.

'Nice to see you again, in Taupo.'

'Yeah, you too.' Nadejda wonders if the limpness of her voice betrays her feelings. It doesn't. Birdie sips her tea serenely, her long spindly legs crossed and under-crossed in multiple knots.

'Did you go on a cruise today?' (She has been following her!)

'Yes actually, I did. It was good.'

'Aha. Was it? So did I. Beautiful lake. And the mountains too. In Holland it's all flat. I love mountains.'

'Yes, they are magnificent.' Agreeing with someone is the gentlest way to ease them out of a conversation — it doesn't generate any further discussion. On the other hand, it might be interpreted as a sign of enjoyment and therefore seen as an invitation for more sharing. But they don't share much more. Nadejda keeps her mouth full, first because she is starving; second because a full mouth can act as a conversation inhibitor; third because there is nothing else to do.

Chapter Fourteen

'What do you do here, are you a student?'

'Yes, at university.'

'In Wellington?'

'No, in Christchurch.'

'Christchurch? Where is that?'

'In the South Island.'

'Aha. And what do you study?'

'Well, I changed my major a couple of times. I started off doing philosophy, then I dropped that and changed to history, and now I'm doing computer science as well.'

'Interesting. And why did you drop philosophy?'

'Oh, I just took philosophy without thinking. My uncle did philosophy once at university but he never finished it because he had to leave the country.'

'New Zealand?'

'No no, Bulgaria.'

'Ah, yes.'

Nadejda doesn't like talking about university and what she studies, because she hates it. Saying 'I do computer science' makes her realise just how absurd this pursuit is. But Birdie is a strangely compelling, gentle listener. Why is she interested in her? She must be lesbian; she certainly has those looks. Nadejda doesn't dare stuff her mouth again, and the loaded fork steams suspended halfway between the plate and her face. 'What do you do?' she braves, dreading more questions about her hateful subjects.

'I'm a teacher.'

'What do you teach?'

'Disabled children.'

'Oh.' She would have never thought. This phrase seems to put a natural end to the conversation, though she is not sure why. There is something solemn and prohibitive about disability when it pops into a trivial conversation.

'Mentally disabled.'

'I see.' Nadejda savours the dregs of her plate. Birdie goes inside to make dinner. From the large table the Mare-woman's voice dominates the subdued buzzing of voices and cutlery. Nadejda tunes her ear in.

142

'Asians work hard, you know,' she nails every word in her harsh accent. 'They will eat us if we don't stick together.'

Nadejda goes back inside. A group of Chinese women, silent and hunched, suck noodles at a small table within earshot of the white table. They don't react. Nadejda is embarrassed for her fellow European. Two passive, discomfited young men listen to her while everyone else is engaged in their own private conversations. They nod politely as the Mare-woman elaborates. 'They dominate the world purely with their number. They are like ants. They spread all over Europe, you have them in New Zealand and Australia, they are everywhere . . . They will eat us, you know!'

The two young men sit behind empty plates. They seem unable to leave the table, as if every word the German says staples them back to their seats.

As she returns to the veranda with a cup of coffee, Nadejda notices Quentin, sitting by himself under the large umbrella, sunglasses on, eating soup. He looks up and smiles his irregular, sad smile, staring at her. Nadejda smiles back. He has been here all along.

Later in the night, Nadejda finds herself in Margarita's bar with Quentin. The place is packed with youthful tourists, some of them vaguely familiar but she is not quite sure where she has seen them; she is not particularly interested. Quentin offers to buy her a drink but she refuses — it is her second no. Why does she keep saying no? Is this an instinctive guard or a reaction this type of person elicits from her? His type? Big, with awkward hands, a roughly chiselled face, remotely and unsettlingly reminiscent of a Frankenstein creature — good at heart, but unpredictable because so odd-looking. His eyes, deeply set in bony sockets, his disproportionately large, protruding chin, his slow movements: there is a mournful, almost pathetic quality to his demeanour. He buys a beer, Nadejda buys a cider. They sit at the bar, dangling their legs. She is dying to tell him he looks like Quentin Tarantino, but he might take offence so she refrains.

'Nice place,' says Quentin and takes out a packet of Marlboros. Nadejda acquiesces with a nod because she is in the process of

143

savouring her cider. He puts a cigarette in his mouth and holds the packet towards her:

'You smoke?'

'No, thanks.'

He draws avidly from his cigarette and after what seems minutes, he releases rolls of fog.

'This is an incredible country.'

'Yes,' says Nadejda and burps discreetly.

'It's just incredible. I want to come again.'

'Where are you from?' she asks.

'Boston.' He stubs out his cigarette and lights another one. His eyes disappear in their sockets as he inhales. A familiar grating accent reaches Nadejda: 'No, no, I think . . .' She looks around. There she is, the Mare-woman, arriving in the dwarfish company of the two mute young men. Her space-consuming presence sets off the two men's subservient, minimal movements. Who is a bodyguard to whom, wonders Nadejda, attacking her second cider and increasingly prone to amusement: the dwarfs to the giant or the other way round? The grotesque trio sit behind her. 'My father died and left me too much money. I didn't know what to do with it so I went to Brazil, but it's dangerous for a woman there, you know, if you have an attractive white face.' She laughs whinnyingly and the dwarfs smile feebly.

Nadejda is tempted to turn round and butt in with 'I don't see why you were worried about the danger,' but she can't face the Mare-woman so she listens on.

'I love other cultures, different foods, different drinks.' The Mare-woman laughs again, and this time it's straight into Nadejda's ear. Nadejda shifts her chair forward and in the process bumps into the standing Quentin.

'That woman's from our hostel, right?' He nods in the direction of Mare-woman.

'Yeah.'

'I heard her before, in the hostel. German, yeah? Man, she's loopy!'

'Oh, I don't know. I think she just loves herself.'

'Yeah well, for sure, that's enviable.' He smiles and Nadejda is again struck by his sadness.

There is a great bustle around. In the dim light everybody looks copper-skinned. Quentin is making his way through the Marlboro packet. Nadejda watches him inhale and exhale with fascination. She has never smoked in her life, but she likes watching others smoke and breathing in the noxious smell.

'So, why did you come on holiday here?'

'Oh, I'm just travelling the world really. I'm going *everywhere*. Everywhere I ever wanted to go — Australia, New Zealand, Fiji, Indonesia, the entire Pacific. Until I run out of money.' He shrugs his powerful shoulders. His hands rest on the bar counter uneasily, like agitated ugly creatures dreaming of strange caresses. Eruptions of jerky raucous laughter shake the atmosphere behind Nadejda, but she tries to block it out. She can't stand that woman. If only she wasn't so tall and strong, Nadejda would've loved to punch her big face in.

'Is this the Bulgarian?' a noxious, friendly voice trumpets in Nadejda's ear. She turns round. Nightmare-woman is already lurching towards her, exuding beer-vapours, her upper body spilling over the counter. 'We were just talking with Rob and Lloyd about Germany.'

Rob and Lloyd shrink on their stools. What if they really are mute? thinks Nadejda. Mutes make the best slaves and confidantes — no secrets are divulged, no opinions are voiced.

'They've never been to Germany. And I told them . . .'

Nadejda shifts away towards Quentin who shifts backwards to make room for her. At the same time, a familiar gaunt figure perches up on the counter, next to Quentin.

'I told them that Germany is full of immigrants. It's true — all kinds of refugees, we don't have anywhere to put them. It's impossible.' She slumps off her stool and stands closer to Nadejda, completely turning her back to the two dwarfs. 'You are all the same, Bulgars, Turks, Romanians, Arabs, whatever. You are all barbarians. Germany is not the same any more.'

The dwarfs look at Nadejda blankly. Nadejda looks at them blankly, then looks back at Mare-woman. The silence is stirred by outbursts of buzzing voices backed up by soft music, as if this has never been said. Quentin's mouth is agape. Nadejda can't wake up, as if these words have cast a spell on her.

145

Chapter Fourteen

'What are you on about?' says Quentin, but getting no reply, turns to Nadejda. 'What is she on about?'

Nadejda can't begin to explain, even if she wanted to. She can only shrug her shoulders, but it is more like a shiver.

'You know what I have to say about Germans?'

A familiar voice. It's Birdie speaking, leaning across the bar past Quentin towards Mare-woman who is adjusting a hairclip.

'I have to say that Germans are the most hated nation in Europe, in Holland we hate them, and all of Europe hates them. After what you did to Europe — and you speak about barbarians! Everybody knows who were the real barbarians, I can tell you. So be quiet!'

Mare-woman is quiet; she just shakes her head sideways dismissively. Birdie has spoken calmly but very clearly, nailing each word with the hammer of her fake American accent. The two dwarfs have vanished. Were they grumpy and hungry perhaps? Nadejda smiles to herself, but then feels her eyes fill with untimely tears.

Mare-woman rotates on her stool and finds the two empty seats. The dwarfs surface again though. 'We're off to the hostel,' Hungry smiles to the group, while Grumpy retreats, busy fumbling in his pockets. They are possibly New Zealanders. 'See you later.'

And they leave their Snow White.

Nadejda needs to get out of this cluttered place. 'I'll see you later,' she says to Quentin and Birdie with a fairly convincing smile, and starts walking in the direction of the lake. The night is black and warm and trickles down her chin. The night is liquefied into Nadejda's cider-tasting tears. Are they cider-tears or tears-tears? It is hard to say. She stumbles around the block. The moon casts patches of light on the pavement which seem to form a pattern — irregular, but maybe worth following. Nadejda follows the pattern. The lake is that way. She crosses a lit, empty road and steps on the grass bank. The lake rustles gently in its sleep. She keeps walking alongside, as the bank rises and the lake sinks deeper below. Her feet feel very light, in fact she is barely touching the ground; all her weight has gathered in her chest and crushes her stomach with an iron persistence, as if she has swallowed the anchor. Does *Barbary* have an anchor to put it to sleep at night? Or does it continue to sail the invisible waters in

146

search of rock carvings? She wipes her nose with the back of her hand.

If only she'd had the presence of mind to retort — there is so much she could've said! That Hitler murdered King Boris II when he refused for the hundredth time to deliver Bulgaria's Jews. That it was the Habsburg Empire's greed (she often gets Austria-Hungary mixed up with Germany) that made the history of the Balkans in the twentieth century and precipitated the First World War. And as a result the division of Europe into free land and Gulag-land. The Iron Curtain, the Cold War, the Communist Bloc — the freezing works of the Nazi war. The good, the bad and the dead. Now it's just the sad. Which is why Nadejda is here — because her uncle was forcibly catapulted here with his father, as was her grandmother, as was her mother. But that is not why Mare-woman is here. Mare-woman has chosen to come here, with her attractive white face, while Nadejda, with her attractive white face, is here because . . . because she has to be.

She has to be? No, she doesn't have to be anywhere, damn it! She is free, after all. She doesn't have to end up in that cemetery town again, where her mother and her uncle are entombed with their secrets and pains, as are the white trash with their white trash kids and beer bottles and the petty bourgeoisie with their petty gardens and pets. She doesn't. She can stay here, for example, here in the centre of this island, which is a volcanic crater, watch the lake go nowhere, become still and mystically omniscient like the rock face. She has half of her student loan in her account, enough to live on for months. She'd skip university this year — it depresses her anyway.

'Hey, wait!'

A flashlight hits the ground under her feet. It's Quentin. He has had to use his powerful key-ring torch to find her. 'Where are you going?'

'Just taking a walk.'

'Can I join you?'

'I guess so.'

They walk on.

'Smoke?'

'No thanks.'

He lights a cigarette. Under the trees, they look like shifty midnight dealers on an unclean mission: he tall and gaunt, exaggerated like a flashing, broken question mark in the brief halo of the lighter; she eclipsed by dark copper falls of hair, shivering in her T-shirt from the slight breeze, stubborn and compact like the dot of his question mark.

'It's funny,' he says. 'People come all this way from Europe for a holiday, and they just have to get at each other's throats over trifles.'

'What do you mean, trifles?'

'Well, you know, it's all history. What's the point?'

'It's not all history. In Europe, history is alive. We *are* history. Everything that ever happened matters to us.' She is stunned by her own verve.

'Yes, Europe will always be Europe. I've always hated the States but sometimes Europe doesn't look so hot either.' He looks down at the invisible lake as if it is Europe. Nadejda too looks that way.

They slump down on a timely bench. Quentin sighs with his whole uncomfortable body. Nadejda sits carefully, upright, acutely feeling the anchor's edges catch on her ribcage. She dreads a silence heavy with pre-seduction vibes. In fact she dreads the mere prospect of Quentin behaving seductively; she is not in the mood for sexy interchanges, she wants to forget that he is a man and just be as sad as she wants to be. Suddenly she is aware of the danger of being alone with this stranger, a few hundred metres away from all other human life. Normally she wouldn't wander off like that, but nothing is normal any more. She is not her normal self any more. And it seems that nobody is their normal self. What is Quentin's normal self, for example?

'Do you feel that you're your normal self?' She doesn't even know how she said this.

'What, now?' Quentin is strange. He is not easily surprised.

'Yes. Or recently.'

'I dunno. I don't know if I've ever been my normal self. Not for a long time anyway,' he smiles with his terrible jaw as he blows out a cloud of warmth.

'Why is that?'

He is silent for a while, and Nadejda begins to think he hasn't heard her.

148

'This trip I started. It's like I had to get away. I'm learning to be myself again.'

He takes the last cigarette out of the packet and holds it between his shaking fingers as if waiting for a light. Nadejda's sadness blends into another, less intense shade of itself — a kind of curiosity about Quentin.

'I have, I had a sister, Miranda. She was very sick. She was always in and out of hospitals. My parents died in a car crash when I was eighteen and she was fifteen. My mother died instantly, my father later in hospital. She'd just come out of hospital, Miranda I mean. She was gonna be okay this time. I didn't tell her for a while, but she sensed it, she's an extremely sensitive person, she just knew what'd happened. She relapsed.'

'What did she have?'

She has known all along that there was something chilling about Quentin.

'She was schizophrenic. And depressive. She had a relapse after the accident. I nearly had a nervous breakdown myself, although I didn't really get on with my parents. But I tried very hard for her sake. I was the strong one, you know. I had to stick it out. When she came out of hospital again, we lived by ourselves. My parents left us with a lot of money. I looked after her. It was really working out — until last year. She was an artist. Well, she wanted to make it as an artist.'

Quentin is crushing the cigarette between his fingers. Tobacco is falling out onto his jeaned thigh.

'She was very jealous. When I started seeing this girl, she had a fit — the first one in ages. I was scared but I guess I was in love and it'd been such a long time, I thought she'd get used to me having a girlfriend. But she didn't. She had a relapse instead. I guess I underestimated the situation, I thought she'd recovered. I mean she was still on medication but I thought . . . I didn't realise how serious it was. Otherwise I would've done something. I would've stopped seeing Alicia even. I don't know, fuck! One night when I was at Alicia's, I stayed over for the first time. The first time I stayed at a girlfriend's house since my parents' death six years ago. 'Cause she couldn't stay over at our place. Fuck! I was careless. For once I was careless. I found her in the morning. Took her to hospital. She'd been dead for four hours. Cut her wrists, did a good job too. She was twenty-one.'

He throws the crushed tobacco on the grass and leans forward, elbows on his knees, staring straight ahead. Nadejda is relieved she doesn't have to make eye-contact.

'I can't go back now. I've gotta keep moving.'

'What happened with Alicia?'

'She left me.'

'Didn't she love you?'

'I thought so, but she left straight after Miranda's death. She couldn't handle it. Who knows?'

Nadejda leans forward, elbows on her knees. The anchor has moved on, but her chest is now full of rust. He glances sideways at her tense face.

'She looked like you. You remind me of her.'

'Who, your sister?'

'No, Alicia. She was Bolivian.'

It occurs to Nadejda that Quentin could be a pathological liar. His story is over the top, and the Bolivian connection just tops it off. But why would anyone fabricate such a depressing story? To impress. To provoke pity — some men are like that. To get her into bed. Just for the hell of it. It's why pathological liars lie after all — for the hell of it.

Quentin takes out a photo from his battered wallet: a girl with long copper hair, striking features and startling green eyes that Nadejda can only describe as disturbing. 'Alicia?'

'No, Miranda.'

She can't tear her eyes off those green eyes; nor can Quentin. They stare at the photo for a long moment. Nadejda feels pleasantly paralysed, as if floating in something sticky — until she hears a rustling noise only metres away. They look up, startled. And there it is, some ten metres away, on the very edge of the bank, head cast downwards, ears pointing like antennas at the splashing murmurs of the lake below. 'It's a horse!' says Quentin, startled.

'It's not a horse, it's a donkey!' Nadejda feels as if she has been imperceptibly dragged onto the stage of some theatre of the absurd.

150

The animal is oblivious to them. Nadejda recognises reality's way of playing up — by throwing in a donkey at the most inopportune moment. She also realises that she has been waiting for this donkey to appear ever since she had that image, a few days ago, of a scarecrow on a donkey. And here it is. Suddenly everything is possible.

She walks towards the animal, her feet barely touching the ground, her heart fluttering in her chest like a caged parrot.

'Where are you going? Don't get close. It might be a wild horse.'

'It's a donkey.'

'It's a horse for Christ's sake, you'll see.'

Nadejda reaches the animal. It turns its head towards her, but it's hard to say whether it looks her in the eye or just in her direction. Nadejda is feeling reckless. She reaches out and strokes it between the ears. She has never touched a donkey before (or a horse for that matter). She forgets all about Quentin. The animal is warm and alive under her hand. Its ears twitch pensively.

'Kak se kazvash, a?' she says. What's your name?

The animal either doesn't have a name or doesn't want to share it with her. It moves away from the cliff, facing west. She gets closer, puts one arm around its neck, and climbs onto it more or less successfully. It doesn't protest. She clutches onto it with all her strength, her cheek on its neck, her thighs tightly squeezing its flanks. She feels they are about to take off.

And they do. They go east, and all around the lake, circling it anti-clockwise like a rebellious hand. They cross soft-sanded bays, slippery rocks, raging rivers, impenetrable bush. They move at the speed at which the lake sleeps, which means, mathematically speaking, that they will finish the lake's tour at the exact moment when the lake awakens. The lake won't remember a thing. Nor will Nadejda.

The mountains push against the lake, rising on tiptoe. The lake too rises darkly, and begins to sleepwalk them around itself.

On a bench by the Taupo lake, at two in the morning, Nadejda is sleeping on an American man's lap. He strokes her hair lightly, so

151

lightly he is barely touching it, the way he would stroke his sister's hair when she fell asleep on the sofa next to him in front of the TV: carefully, very carefully, because he doesn't know what is happening in this exquisite head. After an hour, during which he strokes her hair, she gets up, but doesn't wake up. And she tugs at his T-shirt, saying: 'Can I go home now? Can I go home now please.' And she cries heartbreakingly, without a sound. But he doesn't understand because she is speaking in a language which sounds like this: 'Moga li sega da si otida v kushti? Moga li sega da si otida v kushti, molya vi se?'

So he has no way of knowing that these are the exact words his sister would say to him, as she cried heartbreakingly, without a sound.

CHAPTER FIFTEEN

Nadejda, you are the future.

The voice: Deli Orman

Nadejda, you are the future. You don't know this of course. Funny how only I know it: and I am the past. I am nothing but the past. Nobody remembers me. Nobody knows me. I see you sitting in a taxi with a large, awkward boy. You are saying something to the boy, and he nods. He has a good heart but he is confused. Let's see, what are you saying? 'Deli Orman in Turkish, Ludogorie in Bulgarian, Mad Forest in English.'

No wonder he is confused — this doesn't mean anything to him. He doesn't know where Bulgaria is.

Your eyes are open but you are not awake. It is as if you are watching your dream. I watch your dream too. It is a terrible dream.

A family are sitting down to have dinner. It is a late dinner. The father, one girl and one boy are sitting down, while the mother and an older girl are serving: hot white bread fresh from the oven, greasy rich soup, boiled potatoes. Outside it is black, there is no moon tonight. They are not talking. The father breaks the steaming bread and gives out pieces to the children, while the mother dishes out the soup. He is unshaven and of indeterminate age; she is young but her skin and eyes look tired. The older daughter is fifteen but looks at least twenty. She has long black hair pinched on top by a hairclip. The two other children merge in an indistinct background of big black eyes and white teeth.

The roar of a truck engine approaches. The truck is now outside the house. Heavy footsteps and torchlights wake the chickens in the yard — they flee in a flurry of flapping wings and clucking. The door is pushed open.

Three militia men stand in the doorway. The father gets up. The children gape, their full spoons dripping into the soup. One of the militia men steps inside while the other two guard the door. 'Here's an order for you,' he says, handing the father a form. 'You've got to sign it. With your new names, that is.'

He sneers, his outstretched arm still holding the pad. He is neckless. The other two sneer as well. The father is gripping the back of his chair, legs apart, not budging. 'What new names?' he says slowly and his stubbly face frowns.

154

'You haven't heard? All Turks in Bulgaria are to change their names to Bulgarian names. It's a new law. You have to write your family's new *Bulgarian* names *here*.' He says the last word as if stubbing out a cigarette, and stabs the graph with a thick finger.

Suddenly no one is sneering any more. The three servants of the law are deadly serious. An oppressive silence descends on the room. Only the soup's bubbling can be heard from the stove. The mother has forgotten to turn it off.

'We already have names,' says the father, slowly and emphatically, but a trace of uncertainty undermines his voice.

'We know you have names, but they're fucking Turkish names. You've got to have proper names, if you're living in our country. Do you follow me?'

The father is still standing motionless. The mother covers her face with her hands. The older daughter sits very straight and still.

'We have names,' the father says.

Neckless nods to the other two. They rush inside, seize the raven-haired daughter, rip her blouse open and clear some space on the table with a plate-shattering sweep. The mother screams and reaches to cover the girl. The father rushes to her rescue, but one of them points a pistol at him and he freezes. Two more men rush in and grab the father, twisting his arms behind his back as he moans. The truck engine is still hiccuping outside. Torchlights circle the house; heavy boots are kicking the chickens about.

'Check out the mother,' says one of the new arrivals.

They grab the mother by her long hair and drag her onto the floor, lifting her skirt. They unbutton their trousers.

The women are strangely silent. They don't scream, though their faces are horribly contorted with pain. In this ghastly silence, the two children wail behind the table, their fronts covered in soup, snot and tears running down their chins.

'See what happens when you're stubborn?' Neckless is speaking to the father, spitting in his contorted, red face. He grabs his face and turns it towards the raping scenes. 'Pretty, huh?'

The father stares, wild-eyed. He is losing his mind. 'Bastards! Sons of bitches!'

Chapter Fifteen

'What did he say?' Neckless asks with pretend naïvety his colleague who is twisting the father's arms.

'He said "sons of bitches".'

Another man unzips his trousers and jumps on the girl, who is almost unconscious. Neckless punches the father in the stomach. He doubles up. Neckless punches him in the face. Blood drips on the lino floor. 'This is what you did to us, you Muslim dogs, this is what we'll do to you now! You raped our women, we'll rape yours. You changed our names by force, we'll change yours!' shouts Neckless, waving the form in the father's face. 'You'll sign now, son of a bitch?'

The children continue to cry, choking on their tears. The form is signed. The men do their trousers up; the torches go off. The truck drives on to the next house.

Why are you having this terrible dream, Nadejda? You have never known what happened in Deli Orman, you were only ten, and at the seaside when this happened. Nobody knew what was happening at Deli Orman — it all happened at night. Nine hundred thousand people were forced to take new names, while the rest of the nation slept. You were little. You shouldn't have known anyway.

Your friend takes you to your room and opens your door. But you have woken up. Your teeth are chattering. You can't go to bed. You go to the veranda, lean against the railing and look out to the dark blur of the lake. The moon is crippled, and casts feeble broken light onto the neat houses ahead. A cat mews somewhere next door. Your heart pounds against your small rib-cage like a wounded parrot wanting out. Behind you the large, awkward boy sits, smoking, but you have forgotten about him. He too, has forgotten about you. You grip the wooden railing so hard your fingers hurt. You can't bear to think of your dream, but you can't stop thinking about it. There is nothing left in your mind except this dream.

It is not a dream, Nadejda. Nothing is a dream.

CHAPTER SIXTEEN

*Vassil sits at an impeccably
polished table, holding a glass of
red wine and prodding with his
fork a pile of crispy hot potatoes
topped with sour cream.*

A phone call

Vassil sits at an impeccably polished table, holding a glass of red wine and prodding with his fork a pile of crispy hot potatoes topped with sour cream. The bar is slowly filling up with smartly dressed couples, men in ties and wallets. Vassil is waiting for a colleague to turn up so they can go to their weekly poker game. The colleague is due to arrive in half an hour. Vassil is engaged in another of his mental dialogues, in the hope of clearing his head.

'Feeling strange tonight.'

'I know. But you know why that is. You know the date today.'

'Of course I know the date. But there's something else too.'

'You are thinking about Nadejda. Why are you thinking about her tonight?'

'Because she hasn't called for the last two weeks. Because I'm worried about Ana, she's lost her sleep completely. I should really consider calling Sofia, Mladen's flat.'

'Mladen's flat? Are you sure? You've only spoken to Mladen once since Ana and Nadejda arrived, when you tried to convince him to come over. That was three years ago.'

'Yes, yes, I know. I don't really know the man.'

'It seems that his own daughter and wife, or former wife I should say, don't know him any more.'

'Mladen is stubborn. I resent his cowardly selfishness, his pitiful ultimatums. He is a frightened man who has finally under-stood that he has lost everything, and doesn't know how else to deal with it.'

'Calm down, calm down. You've got to understand his circumstances too.'

'Yeah yeah. His circumstances. We all have our circumstances. I don't see why his particular circumstances allowed him to let his own daughter down, his only child, and to continue to do so. Not to mention Ana.'

'Nadejda is very attached to her father. She understands him, she doesn't blame only him.'

'No, she blames her mother too, I know. She always blames her mother. She has no idea what Ana has gone through.'

'Ana chose to come here. She took the risk of separation.'

'She didn't know he was so determined to stay behind. She wasn't prepared for that.'

'Well, we're sometimes unprepared for what happens to us. Were you prepared for the Greek camps? For the years of labour on the railways here? For losing Pat? No. And you came out the other end just fine.'

'That's enough. I get the point.'

Vassil hurriedly swallows a warm potato but it gets stuck in his throat. He can't swallow. He takes a sip of wine to wash it down. But the potato won't travel. Vassil pushes the plate away.

'Going now, are we?'

'He let Ana down. He's never said a kind word to her since their departure, only threats, pleas, and accusations.'

'Well, yes, he did. But there's nothing you can do about it, so stop getting worked up. You've worked through these things already.'

'Not enough. I haven't talked to Nadejda enough.'

'No, you haven't.'

'She's so damn difficult to talk to.'

'You haven't found the right words.'

'There hasn't been the right time.'

'There's never the right time.'

'Now is the right time.' Vassil pushes his chair back and gets up heavily (he just can't seem to shed that weight). The vague outline of an idea appears before him. He takes out his mobile phone and dials a number.

'Peter, hi. Look, I can't meet you, I've got a headache, tough day, you know. I'll have to give it a miss this time.'

Peter, a fellow psychologist, obviously does know, because Vassil laughs quickly and says a few more words before slipping the mobile back into his jacket pocket.

He gets into his silver BMW and drives home in silence, because his decision is beyond discussion. He knows exactly what he is going to do. He'll never have a better chance to talk to Nadejda. And there is so much to say.

At home, he pulls the curtains in the lounge, pours a glass of red wine, produces a small tape recorder from a drawer in his study, puts a blank tape in, dims the standing lamp in the corner and settles on the sofa. He sips the wine and tugs at his beard for a while, the way he longs to do while listening to patients but he has to watch his body language. Then he presses 'record'.

Some time later, the phone rings. 'Uncle?'

'Nade! Where are you?'

'I'm still in Sofia. Look, I can't leave, the airport's shut, there's a strike. I'd like to stay longer anyway. Can you tell Mum that I may not be coming back?'

'What?'

'I'm not coming back yet. I'm staying here.'

'But you can't! We're expecting you back here.' Vassil feels a sudden violent tightness around his heart, like an iron fist. He falls into an armchair. He can't breathe.

'Look, I don't want to come back, okay? I hate it in Christchurch.'

The fist holding Vassil's heart is tightening its grip. He can't speak.

'Can you tell Mum I'll be calling her later? Tell her also not to call Dad's place. I'm not there.'

Where are you, Nadejda, where the hell are you? Vassil wants to shout, but his fingers open despite him and drop the receiver. His entire body hardens in a second, turning into a pillar of concrete. The clear voice chimes from the floor, then stops. He holds his chest with a concrete hand, as if its contents are about to spill out, and collapses on the soft carpet.

The dialling tone is recorded for another twenty minutes, until side B runs out.

CHAPTER SEVENTEEN

*When Nadejda finally goes to bed,
it is four in the morning.*

The best country

When Nadejda finally goes to bed, it is four in the morning. She gropes for her bed and in the dark she touches a head and shrinks back. The head doesn't react. She crawls into the empty bed and instantly falls asleep.

Upon waking, she looks at the time. She has missed her nine o'clock bus. There is hardly anyone around on her floor. In the kitchen, a couple of Koreans are bending over guides and maps. A solitary blonde woman is writing postcards. The radio is on, and a hyperactive voice is announcing the winners of some competition. Nadejda makes a cup of coffee. She feels hung over, although she only remembers drinking two ciders. She calls all the bus lines in town, but there are no other rides to Napier. She can't stay here, it's out of the question: there is nothing left to do here, and she needs to keep moving. Staying in one place makes her anxious. She is not sure why, but she needs to go south.

She goes back to her room to pack up. On her backpack there is a note saying: 'Come to visit me in Amsterdam, I live at the address below. Good luck. Ank.' Ank? Who is Ank? Dutch Ank, which means Birdie. Does this note mean she was sleeping in this room? It is true that Nadejda didn't get to see her room-mates in the dark. The head she groped could have been Birdie's. Ank's, that is. How strange that Birdie has another name. Weird Birdie is not what Nadejda had expected at all, including the name. People have lives beyond their appearances.

As she packs up, she wonders whether Quentin too has left her a note. She spent most of the night with him, after all. He told her his life story, he opened up his heart. They listened to the lake together. He took her home, though she doesn't remember how they got here and when. She has a vague remembrance of something else happening by the lake too, something odd defying reason and understanding, defying memory as well — because all that is left of it is an odd physical sensation. Anyhow, Quentin has vanished — unloaded his heart and vanished.

She goes down the stairs, dragging her pack behind her. In the morning she is always alone. She feels unclean but decides that she has no time for a shower. The lake's colour is ripening as the sun slides towards the middle of the sky. She doesn't know

162

where she is headed. Not that city down south, that much she knows.

When she reaches the waterfront, she still doesn't know where she is going. But the main thing is to keep moving. She walks past a golf course. Two weather-beaten tourists hold their thumbs out. It's the healthy pony-tailed couple from the hostel. The traffic passes them by with discouraging consistency.

Now Nadejda knows that, for the first time, she is hitch-hiking — she has known it all along, without formulating it as a decision. She is hitching south. Wherever the driver is going, she will go too. She stops and drops her pack, holding it with her free hand. Her rivals further up the road squint in her direction; they don't seem pleased and that's understandable, Nadejda grants them this without budging. She has more of a chance than them.

A Mercedes pulls over and backs up towards her. The driver is a small, rugged-faced man with sunglasses on and a grubby linen jacket. She throws her pack in the back and gets in. The driver utters a friendly but serious 'How are you', and it occurs to Nadejda that perhaps she has just set herself up for a gruesome adventure. 'Where are you going?' she asks as they take off with a screech.

'Wellington. Where do you want to go?'

'Wellington.'

'It's your lucky day then.'

She already finds him unpleasant. It's not her lucky day, it's her impromptu day.

'I guess so.'

'Cigarette?' He picks up a packet of Holidays.

'No, thank you.'

He lights up a cigarette and winds down the window. 'So, where are you from?'

'Bulgaria.'

'Ah yeah. I've been there. It's the most dismal place.'

At least she is safe — even if this wretch is obnoxious and insensitive. Nadejda doesn't feel obliged to respond but she does, more out of curiosity. 'Why was it dismal?'

'Oh, you know, you drive through villages, really poor, and women in black stare at you, nobody's smiling, there's gypsies

163

smoking at every corner, everybody looked just . . . dour. I mean it wasn't dangerous or anything, but just hard going.'

'I see. When was that?'

'Oh, let's see. When did I go there? Shit, it's been a long time. Seventy-one? Yeah, seventy-one, something like that.'

'Where did you go?'

'Oh, I can't remember the names of the other places, but we went to Istanbul, Budapest . . . You know, the works.'

'That's Turkey. And Hungary.'

'Yes, yes, that's right, we went to Turkey. Yep.'

'And Budapest is in Hungary.'

'All right. No, we didn't go to Hungary.'

'Do you mean Bucharest?'

'Bucharest? Yeah, that's right, it was Bucharest.'

'That's Romania.'

'Yeah, we went all over.'

'Why did you go there?' Nadejda is trying to be objectively curious.

'I was doing a tour of Europe, for the first time. I thought I'd check out the Soviet bloc as well. Turkey and that.'

Nadejda is already in a bad mood. She wishes she didn't care about such things. After all, why care about nationality? She is who she is. The driver lights another cigarette and as he lets out the first puff of smoke, he glances at Nadejda's lap, but not her face. 'So, you're travelling by yourself?'

'Yes. I live here now.'

'You must be really pleased then.'

Is she pleased? She is not pleased. But she must be. Besides, it's hard to say why she isn't pleased.

'Why?'

'Because we've got the best country in the world! I've seen a bit of the world, you know, Europe. But New Zealand is the best country. We've got . . .'

You do, thinks Nadejda while he explains, you do. Why is it that you have the best country in the world? Do you have to deserve a country like this? No, you don't have to deserve anything — not the punishment, not the wealth. Nadejda's country too has lavish forests with beasts in them, peaks just as high, snow just as deep, lakes just as blue, rivers just as wild. But she doesn't have the best country in the world. Why?

Because of the tramps rummaging in rubbish bins, the police bashing up demonstrators, Anton's ribs sticking out, her father's tears freezing in his beard, her grandfather's misshapen jaw, the eighteen-year-old bank clerk shot right through the heart during a robbery, the woman whose husband got into trouble with the insurance Mafia and found her with a slashed throat, the ten-year-old boy who hanged himself the other day, the woman at the dairy who was tied up by a hungry crowd while they pillaged the food, the kindergartens without milk and sugar, the pensioners who live on $1 a month . . .

She would like to explain all this to the driver from the best country in the world, and explain it in such a way that the cigarette would drop out of his mouth. But she can't because she doesn't know how to put it. She can't, because now he is saying: 'Mack is an engineer, doing really well. John is a lawyer, very successful, he's working in London at the moment. He's the oldest. Larry is into building. Amanda is doing a degree in nursing. And Heidy, my youngest one, has just enrolled at varsity to do a management degree. They're all very different of course. But I wanted them all to have degrees — polytech or varsity. And they all got them.'

Randy bugger, thinks Nadejda. Five of them! And all living in the best country.

'What do you do?'

'I'm a farmer.'

Nadejda looks at him in disbelief: a farmer in a Mercedes. They're passing a few hundred sheep scattered around the green plain like white stones. From a distance they look like stones, and sometimes Nadejda has to stare long and hard to decide just what they are. 'Yeah, I've got a farm out in Plimmerton. I was into estate a few years back, but got sick of it and felt like getting myself a little farm in the country. I did rather well and so . . . Yeah. Not giving up my farm yet!'

He lets out a modest little laugh. Nadejda feels nauseous. She lowers herself in the seat and leans her head on the head-rest.

'And whereabouts in Wellington do you live?' he says.

Chapter Seventeen

'I don't live in Wellington.'

'All right. Where do you live then?'

Nadejda is drifting off to nausea-land, so what she says next is not a product of any deliberation. 'I don't know.'

The driver laughs heartily then glances at her, and his laughter peters out. He becomes quiet and looks straight ahead.

She doesn't know where she lives any more. She knows where her father lives, where her mother and uncle live, where some other people live. But Nadejda's dwelling place is yet to be located — because right now she is not living anywhere. She is travelling, which is the opposite of living somewhere.

She leans back and closes her eyes. On the insides of her lids she sees the mountain that erupted last year and scared away the skiers. Why didn't anybody die — was it a miracle, or was it only natural that nobody should die in a volcanic eruption in the best country in the world? Her grandparents called from Plovdiv, the day after the eruption, at the request of her worried father. Nadejda explained to them that the volcano was in the other island, but they didn't seem to grasp the concept of two islands. They kept asking, 'But are you okay?' Her father would rather have lived in torment and anxiety than risk speaking to her mother. And she flew all that way, naïvely thinking that there was still hope of convincing him! Before that, she spent four years convincing her mother to move out of that grey city they both hate and where only her uncle is keeping them. No, it appears that nobody can be convinced of anything other than their own misery or contentment. Not this farmer. Not her father. Not her mother. Not her uncle — to go to Sofia, now that it's safe for him. Not her grandparents — that there are two big islands and several small ones, all of them constituting New Zealand. The world is selfish both in its happiness and in its suffering. The precarious way of life Nadejda just witnessed in Sofia has taught her nothing except that life can be precarious. But nothing follows from that, because suffering is not more important than happiness. And just as she witnessed somebody else's suffering in winter Sofia, she is a witness to somebody else's happiness here, on this summer road, in this Mercedes, next to this farmer as self-absorbed as Anton.

Nadejda is tired of trying to make sense of this. She is tired of caring, of thinking, of running away from best countries and worst countries, of being neither here nor there.

The farmer turns the radio on and drives in silence, occasionally glancing at her in the way one glances at cripples and freaks in the streets of big cities — with casual friendliness disguising a morbid curiosity.

Nadejda sits, giddily watching the island, this half-country, gallop past her with its clouds, hills and sheep. Something is telling her that a voyage is just a more picturesque form of waiting: for the final destination, for someone to be there that we didn't expect to be there, for something to happen which cannot happen, for the donkey or someone, someone, to stop and speak, and say that all will be well.

Chapter Seventeen

PART TWO

CHAPTER EIGHTEEN

*Sometimes I wonder if you are not
a figment of my imagination,
Nadejda.*

The song: a phone call

Sometimes I wonder if you are not a figment of my imagination, Nadejda. For so long I have awaited our meeting. Twenty-one years, you could say. Nobody told me when you were born, but I felt it. I have felt you ever since. Your mother has never spoken of me, of course. I stopped existing for her as soon as she met Mladen. But I knew her, oh I knew her since she was four and I was four. I knew her for a long time. I knew her better than she would admit now! I knew Mladen too. I knew your grandmother. I tried to know your uncle, but he hung up on me. He didn't believe me or didn't want to believe me when I told him who I was.

And I've never met you, my child. If you are real, it is now only a matter of days before you come. Of course you are real. I have freed myself of the sad malice of guilt, so that I, the past, can meet you — the future.

Right now, when I close my eyes, I see you get out of a car on the highway — a Mercedes. You have your big backpack. You wave to the driver. And you stand on the highway, disoriented for a second, before you stick out your thumb. The afternoon sun teases your eyes; you shade them with your other hand. Your backpack tumbles down. You pick it up and straighten it again. But you don't have enough hands for all this.

Soon a car pulls over, an old one, rusty. You jump in; your pack gets stuck in the door. Your hair gets caught in the straps. You disentangle yourself, while the driver, a young woman, watches you with a smile and says something. You take off with a jerk. Soon, a blue harbour appears silk-lined with tall buildings. It seems to me you have been here before. Your eyes light up. It seems to me you like it. Then I lose you from sight. I shut my eyes and strain to conjure your frail figure moving about in that pretty, self-conscious city, but you elude me for a while. I only catch glimpses of you: Nadejda crossing a supermarket car-park, nearly getting run over; Nadejda walking on the waterfront, hair blown in the wind, the city towering on your left with its tinted windows, like a petrified forest; Nadejda standing on a wooden bridge-platform with intricate carvings, overlooking the harbour, hair blown in the wind; then, from the same bridge, Nadejda looking the other way, towards the city — a clean white square punctuated by extravagant metal palm-trees; a passer-by's backpack brushes against you — the boy turns round

169

Chapter Eighteen

to apologise, you smile but your smile merely brushes your face. You turn around the axle of your shaky self like a boat twirled by the harbour wind. Before you is the picture, behind you is the sound. You want to surprise the sound, but it instantly turns into a picture, and vice versa. Behind you the city rustling with its white wings; before you the harbour rocked by the stooping embrace of the hills. And then behind you the harbour, a blue ball punctured by the shrieks of gulls, deflating with a slow sigh; before you the city shedding its glittering scales in the mellow decay of light.

Your face gathers all the shadows of this city, all the chills of its sea winds at dusk. I sense some painful thickness welling up in you, some dark flower blossoming, something you will do before you understand it.

And here it is: when you appear to me later, you are on the phone, in a corridor. It is night-time, though the sky peeking into the window keeps its purple tinge, a spillage of the sun's private orgy. You are speaking into the receiver, chewing a lock of your hair, then flicking it away nervously. I focus with my whole mind, and I hear your clear voice over the buzz of passing backpackers.

'Uncle?'

'I'm still in Sofia. Look, I can't leave, the airport's shut, there's a strike. I'd like to stay longer anyway. Can you tell Mum that I may not be coming back?

'I'm not coming back yet. I'm staying here.'

'Look, I don't want to come back, okay? I hate it in Christchurch.'

'Can you tell Mum I'll be calling her later? Tell her also not to call Dad's place. I'm not there.

'Uncle? Chicho? Chicho Vasko?'

You put the receiver against your chest, as if listening to your heart. You hang up and chew another lock of hair. You cross your arms and lean against the phone. Three round plastic clocks show the time in London, Tokyo and New York. Your father read to you once from a book: 'In the dark night of the soul, it is always three o'clock in the morning,' or something like this. You didn't understand. Now you understand. It

170

is three o'clock in Sofia, but no clock can show this. It is always three o'clock in the Sofia where you have remained, stranded because the airport is shut. Because the sky is locked. Because the key has been thrown in the Styx of time, guarded by four great lions without tongues.

The shadows have settled on your face. You prod your hatred, your alienation like a tired old donkey. You want it to run faster when it only wants to rest. Now what?

Chapter Eighteen

CHAPTER NINETEEN

*Ana is trying to get hold of her
brother. She rings in the evening,
but the phone is disconnected.*

The philosophy lesson

Ana is trying to get hold of her brother. She rings in the evening, but the phone is disconnected. Sometimes he does this when he reads, although he hasn't for a while. His mobile has the answer-phone on, so she leaves a message. She calls his work the next day.

'Vassil?' says the receptionist. 'He hasn't been in today. We tried to call his place but there's no reply. Do you want to speak to Peter? I think he tried to call him.'

She doesn't. She gets in her car and drives straight to Vassil's place to which she has a key. Her heart is pounding like an impatient fist on a door. She has been waiting for the worst to happen. Although he has never mentioned anything specific, her brother is a desperate man who lost the one thing he loved: his life with Pat. He never recovered from their mother's death, and somehow took it on himself, although they don't talk about it. He treats people with impotence problems, with obsessive-compulsive disorders, with phobias, anxiety neuroses and suicidal tendencies. But somehow Ana always senses the shadow of desperation hanging over her brother's learned, experienced head. Despite his routine existence, he has always been unpredictable to her. She never knows what is on his mind, or in his heart. She never feels close enough to him. He doesn't try to get close to Nadejda either, and yet they are similar in a strange, subtle way.

At the door, she fumbles with the keys. As soon as she steps inside, the silence and the coolness lap at her — she feels as if she has just entered a bone-vault.

'Vassil?'

She walks down the dark corridor, not touching anything, almost certain of her worst fears, and unnaturally serene. She looks in his bedroom — empty, the bed is made, immaculate. She looks in the bathroom — empty. Her stomach is rebelling. The fist of her heartbeat is trying to knock the door down. She has been expecting the worst. But is she prepared for the worst? She looks in the lounge.

After she is told that he has been dead for seventeen hours, and the cause of death was a heart attack, Ana drives back to his place with calm hands and a broken heart. She can't bear to see her brother's

173

body, white and blue, his beard no longer groomed, his eyebrows tufts of overgrowth over his extinguished eyes, his powerful chest caved in like a deflated Michelin. So she goes back to his house, where he was alive until last night. She can't bear to know that he is dead. How to undo knowledge, how to unlearn what she has learned? She swallows the bitter thickness in her throat, a waterfall of tears so heavy they can't even reach her eyes. How to reverse the course of events, so that nobody dies, nobody is lost, nobody disappears, nobody is left listening to the lone sound of their own heart? How to mend the unmendable? How to forget, forget, forget?

Ana presses down on the accelerator, although a car is overtaking her. Speed makes us forget, but speed only lasts a second. She can forget for only a second.

Vassil's house is what's left of him, and it is alive with the freshness of his living self, only seventeen hours ago. It hasn't learned the news yet. It retains his presence, like a pet waiting for its owner. He doesn't like pets, but he loves his house. Loved. The unbearable sneering quality of the past tense. Loved! As if the past tense yelps mockingly to the present: loved, you loser, loved!

Ana walks around the house. She knows it by heart, but now she tries to see everything with Vassil's eyes, as if in a childish attempt to fill in his place, to be him. On the lounge table lies his mobile, unfolded like a begging palm. Ana reaches to fold it back, but shudders, as if by touching something she will break the spell of drowsy silence and the entire house, like a giant organism, will activate its piercing, wailing sirens.

She notices that the receiver is back on its hook. One of the ambulance medics must have put it there, although that isn't their job. Will she ever know what brought about his heart attack? A phone conversation — but with whom? It can't be Nadejda because she'd call her mother first.

She slumps on the couch, stabbed by a hideous thought. What if something has happened to Nadejda and her father was calling Vassil to tell him — because he wouldn't call her. No, that's ridiculous. If something has happened to Nadejda, he'd call her first. On the other hand, it could have been something completely mundane, unrelated to emotional shock of any kind. Heart attack often occurs for no good reason other than a malfunction of the organ itself. The doctor would have explained all this to her if she'd stayed longer at the hospital, but she knows enough about heart attack.

She learned about it twenty years ago, when the news about her mother reached her from New Zealand. It was Vassil who told her on the phone then: 'Mum died on the plane yesterday.' They listened to each other breathe through the wire — two strangers on both sides of the globe, who suddenly had lost the same mother. They listened to each other's invisible life, and they were suddenly four and nineteen again, like they were when they waved each other goodbye in the thick Sofia night. Ana had sent her mother alive, Vassil and their father had received her dead. It was the last time Ana saw her mother, and the first time in twenty-two years that father and son saw her. The fact that they had a common mother had not bound their two disparate lives. But in the space of ten seconds, the time it took to say 'Mum died on the plane yesterday', they were bound by a wordless pain which stayed with them throughout the years. And this bond will outlive them.

Telephones, planes — Ana's life has revolved around them. They bring people to each other. They kill.

On the small coffee table she sees a tape recorder, an empty bottle of red wine, a nearly empty glass. He was drinking. She looks inside the recorder, opens it and turns the tape over to side A, then presses 'Play'.

'Nade, this is your uncle. Your mother and I have been wondering why you're not calling. I know you must have your reasons. You obviously don't want us to call you, and so we won't. You'll call us when you want to.

'Now, I'm speaking in English because I'm tired and it comes to me more naturally. And because I don't want to speak my own language with an accent. I'd rather speak English with an accent. To you it won't make any difference, I believe.

'Today, the fifth of February, is my New Zealand anniversary. Your grandfather and I arrived in Lyttelton precisely forty-two years ago. Long time ago, huh? I was twenty-one, your age. I am not

175

celebrating. There is no one to celebrate with. It's okay, I don't need to celebrate anyway. This year, 1997, is also an anniversary: twenty-two years from Mum, your grandmother's death. I know, it doesn't make sense. But it's an anniversary nonetheless.

'I am talking to you so that I can say certain things I haven't managed to say for one reason or another. I want you to know that there is a home here for you, when you come back from Sofia. Don't doubt this for a second. New Zealand is your home now, and it is a beautiful home. You'll realise just how lucky you are when you return. Dad and I, your grandfather and I, chose New Zealand. Others from the ship stayed in Australia, in fact most did. We wanted to go further: as far away as possible from the torments of that horrible country Greece, and as far away from the Stalinist gang. As if it made any difference whether we were in Australia or New Zealand, distance-wise. But above all, New Zealand seemed like the final Pacific frontier. I don't regret my decision. Your grandfather, too, loved this country for as long as he lived. We had a tough time, I had never done labour in my life, you know I was studying philosophy before we left, and here we were, working at the railway, lifting, pushing, hammering away. And not knowing what had happened to little Ana and your grandmother. That was the hardest thing of all — not the labour, not the poverty, not the struggle with a foreign language. But not knowing what those criminals had done with your mother and your grandmother. We didn't get any mail while we were in Greece, and we didn't know if our mail was reaching them. You can't imagine . . . but anyway. This is not what I want to be telling you. You know all this, don't you.'

There is a long silence, and the sound of sipping.

'You know, I was driving home tonight. I have a new car, a silver BMW. You'll give it a go when you get back, I'm sure you'll like it. Anyway, I noticed something on the road: there is a particular type of driver, or person, I should say — they put their lights on before it's dark. They are anxious to have their lights on before everyone else, they want to be ahead of darkness itself. They can't stand to be caught out. And suddenly, I thought of Dad, your grandfather. Why did I think of him then? He didn't drive. I realised something: this type of person is the same as the one who is in a hurry to see their children leave home, to have their children married off and producing grandchildren, to go into retirement, and so on. Dad was like that. You never knew him of course. He was an unusual man. He went bald rather young, he had the bald look and large hands of men capable of great tenderness and great cruelty. He was both. He was both crude and romantic. He'd say things like, "Just as well I'm a vet, you can be a vet anywhere, animals have the same assholes everywhere." And then he would say things like, "There is only one woman for me in the world, ever — your mother. You and your sister were children of love." And he would cough and cry in clouds of smoke.

'Anyway, he was the type of person I was referring to before: if he'd been a driver, he would've turned his headlights on before seven, in the summer. Not so much out of competitive ambition, but out of . . . impatience. He was impatient to see me get married. And, of course, to have grandchildren. As if he never understood that the sooner these things happen, the older you get. I don't have children, as you know. He couldn't get over that. He wanted a boy in the family, to take his name, and the fortune (that he didn't have any more). You know how it is with boys in the family. He had the conviction that the house in Sofia and everything taken away from us would be restored to us one day. It doesn't happen that way of course. What was taken from us could never be restored. So, yes, he was like that. That's why I thought of him. I, on the other hand, would be quite happy to drive in the dark — well, metaphorically speaking. To grope my way around, you know, but there are always lights to disturb the darkness, like tunnels cutting through it, and I am stuck driving in those tunnels. However . . . I wanted to tell you about what happened in '53. I know you know, but you've never heard it from me. It's strange how I've known you for four years now, but we always talk about other things. Still, we have to deal with the immediate pressures of life. That's why I'm talking to you now. This time there's no trivia. I'll tell you what happened in May 1953, in Sofia, the same Sofia where you are now, waving a flag or a balloon in the young crowd. It's still the most beautiful city, isn't it? They haven't succeeded in wrecking it completely.

'I was in my second year of philosophy at Sofia University.

Chapter Nineteen

When I started, I knew there were limitations to the philosophy we were taught, but I was naïve. I thought that philosophy was all about free discussion, speculation, comparison, relative truth. I thought that despite the Marxist-Leninist dogma professed by our lecturers, we were expected to expand and voice our views. I was an idealist, and too young to realise the repercussions of even a minor action or word against the establishment. I believed that communism was the right way to go, the future of the world. But that's because I hadn't understood the true nature of communism. I was made to understand it. I was taught my most complex lesson of philosophy the day I announced, in a throw-away manner, in front of some classmates: "They're just throwing dust in our eyes, really!" I said. "They're not teaching us any philosophy. I mean the theories of bloody Lenin do *not* constitute philosophy, right? Everybody knows that Lenin was a numbskull. I think we should do something about that or our brains will turn into mush soon. Do they call that philosophy?"

'Nadejda, you can't imagine the silence that fell on the cafeteria. I will never forget the sound of that silence. The terrible vibrations of that silence told me that I'd just made a dreadful mistake. That silence seemed to last a lifetime. I just sat there, looking at my friends' faces turn into stone. They were pale with fear. Not that they didn't agree with me, of course they knew exactly what I was saying, but the fear paralysed them. Everybody in the cafeteria had heard. They started talking among themselves again, but the atmosphere had changed — as though somebody had released a poisonous gas and everybody was gasping for air. Some left straight away. Some of my friends too. Of course, we'd talked about the stupidity, the lack of critical judgement and criteria in the teaching, we'd talked about all that before, in small groups of two or three, but in veiled words, in allusions. Never the way I said it then. I knew it was foolish, but I couldn't help myself. I was full of frustration, two years of frustration bottled up, with no hope of respite. I wanted to learn real philosophy, to know about Hegel not just as a forerunner of dialectical materialism, but as a philosopher in his own right. About Nietzsche, Heidegger, Sartre, you name it. All the big minds of European thought, you know them. And all I got was that halfwit Lenin, and Uncle Marx. Dialectical materialism coming

178

out of our ears. I couldn't stand it. It took two years of listening to bullshit, and a momentary lapse of the self-preservation instinct, to change my life.

'And to this day, Nadejda, I can't say whether I would've done it, had I known the consequences. I was not a revolutionary at heart. I was just a bright kid, and hated pretence. I was naïve. And one naïve act, which in a place like New Zealand wouldn't have made any difference, changed the lives of the whole family. It changed your life too. Sometimes, when I think about it, I feel as though the weight of this single act which only lasted a few seconds, is crushing my body to powder, and I panic, and try to shake it off. But I know it's part of me, it's the hunch on my back, I can't cut it off. We all have our crosses to bear, as they say.'

There is a silence, but no sipping noise this time. Vassil clears his throat as he is beginning to lose his voice.

'From then on, for the next two weeks, I got two letters and several anonymous calls. I was summoned by the Academic Board and the Party Board, verbally lynched, so to speak, and then publicly expelled from university. My party card was taken and torn up for all to see. That was the ultimate disgrace at the time. You knew you were in trouble when your party card was confiscated. I was in trouble. You might wonder who denounced me, which one of the listeners in the cafeteria reported me. That was irrelevant. It could've been any one of them. It could've been no one in particular. Even the walls were red then, so to speak, the walls would've put me on trial if no one else heard. Everything anyone said was known by everyone. Or didn't say, for that matter. Even our thoughts were overheard and discussed behind closed doors.

'One of the letters I got said, "Remember: to a dog, a dog's death." This was the phrase used on Radio Sofia a few years earlier after the execution of Nikola Petkov, the Agrarian Party leader who mounted a campaign against the communist government. He was accused of conspiratorial activities, tried without witnesses before a so-called People's Court, deemed traitor of the people, and hanged. I don't think you know all this. A week later, by the way, the United States officially recognised the Bulgarian communist government. But that's not unusual. We are a small country, we don't count in the eyes of the Great Powers. It's in the order of things. After Petkov's execution, many more were hanged, strangled, tortured to death in interrogation rooms. So, to a dog, a dog's death — that was the official comment of the Worker's Union. And now somebody was promising the same fate to me. Dad was worried sick. We started getting intimidatory phone calls. One voice said, "Don't hang around, you're poisoning the atmosphere." Another voice said, "We'll teach you a lesson soon," another favourite expression in the communist vocabulary of persecution.

'We lived in fear for about two weeks. One night, after dinner, a cousin of Mum's who was in the regional secretariat of the party — a nice guy, well-meaning towards us — came to our house and said to Dad, "Bobby, it's looking very bad. It looks like they're coming for the boy tomorrow night. I overheard last night's meeting. Get him out, Bobby. It's going to get really ugly. If they take the boy, you know what's going to happen."

'Dad knew, and so we packed up, took some food and clothes, threw them in an old leather bag, and waited until midnight. We turned all the lights in the house off so we didn't arouse suspicion, and we sat in the dark kitchen. Mum didn't shed a tear. She was just making sure we had everything. We planned our route with her. Ana was in bed of course. But when we were leaving, Mum woke her up and brought her out into the kitchen to say goodbye. She was half-asleep and grumpy. Dad lifted her up and squeezed her to his chest, kissing the little head with his eyes tightly closed. I kissed her on the cheeks, kissed Mum goodbye. She couldn't speak. She just stood at the door for a few seconds, like a white ghost in the black doorway. Little copper-haired Ana was holding on to her skirt and waving happily. I waved to her too, and smiled.

'Strange how all these years, before you came, this is how I thought of your mother. It's silly, how stubborn the memory of the heart can be, in the face of reality. I knew that she got married, had a child, Nadejda, and that Nadejda had grown into a young woman. I knew that, but somehow, for me she was always the midnight child with copper hair waving at the doorway of our house.'

Vassil chokes. He clears his throat with exaggerated vigour and raises his voice.

'Yes. Anyway. That's how we left. We walked through Sofia. At the time it was a much smaller city, of course. Within two days, we had crossed the Yugoslav border. We decided to go that way, rather than go south and cross the Greek border, which is what they thought we'd do. We had to trick them, you see. We crossed the Yugoslav border illegally of course, at night. Dad knew this local guy, Kosta, a forester at the very border with Yugoslavia, a respected guy, everybody knew him. I think they were old school friends. He knew where it was safe to cross the border, to avoid the land-mines and the guards. I think he'd helped others before. He had a golden heart, that man, considering the huge risk he was taking. Now, he had a donkey cart. He could hang around the border-zone without being hassled by the guards. They all knew him. In the afternoon, he put us in his cart, covered us with timber, and drove the cart to the border, to a safe spot where the forest didn't end suddenly, but petered out gradually, merging into shrubbery. Until the evening, we lay under that timber, catching the occasional glimmer of light. He made himself look busy for a few hours. His boy was "helping" him. When it got dark, he and the boy went home. We'd already discussed our movements. We waited a couple more hours. Our bodies grew numb. Then we got out, making as little noise as possible, and just stepped over the barbed wire. We walked through the low vegetation on the Yugoslavian side, not looking back, expecting any second a voice to shout: "Freeze or I'll shoot!" But no voice came, no guns went off. We had made it.

'Kosta, this simple, weedy man, saved my life. He had a big hairy mole on his nose, and gentle blue eyes. If it weren't for Kosta, we would've been captured by the guards and handed back to the authorities, and I would've been shot within a matter of hours.

'A week later, we crossed the Greek border and were seized by the Greek authorities, who put us in refugee camps together with hundreds of escapees from the Eastern bloc. You know the rest of the story. I don't even want to recall that time. It was pure hell. Greece, this land of sun and myths, is a big lie, it's the . . . But I won't go on.'

He stops abruptly, coughs and drinks in big gulps. He pours wine   181

into the glass. The tape stops. Ana turns it over. Her hand is shaking.
Play. He clears his throat.

'This is a previous life. It is a story which to you sounds absurd. To me too. I am the nineteen-year-old fugitive in that story, but that's me in another life. I am no longer that person. There has been a transition from one self to another. We shed our selves on the way like snake-skins. And yet we retain a certain familiarity with the previous skin, a certain raw feeling. Sometimes I wonder: have I become incomprehensible to myself? In a way, it takes a constant effort of the imagination to remain acquainted with my past selves. You will see, with age it becomes more of an effort.

'Sometimes I look around this grey city, and it seems to me that something is pushing through the façades of stone buildings, something is bending the calm curve of the streets. The sky sags like a sick udder, the smooth faces of people are about to contort. Something is pushing through the skin of this city like a broken bone, never quite puncturing the flesh, but never healing either. Sometimes at night, I lie, peeking through the slit in the curtains, in the vague hope that the succubus of truth will come and violate me, release me from this paralysis, from the constant flooding of memory. Set the broken bones, I don't care about the pain. But she is visiting someone else.

'Of course for you, Nade, it doesn't have to be that way. The world is open to you. For me, the world will never be open, it's always been too vast, because I got lost from my family. Distance in itself doesn't mean anything; there is a greater evil. But you can come and go as you please. You're not exiled. You're not forgotten. You are free wherever you go. You have a choice. You don't have to close the curtains, so to speak.

'I hope you understand. I am talking to you not like your uncle, but like a person who would like to understand you, and hopes that you can listen and think about these things, appreciate what you have and not be afraid of anything.

'You know I have no children. I don't suppose you know why. Not many people know. Your mother does, but she seems to want to believe it's not true, and that I simply didn't want to have children. It's true — I didn't. But I would've had them, if I could. Patricia wanted kids desperately. But that's beside the point. My point is that you are my only heir, so to speak. Now I have this house. I also have . . .'

The phone rings. There is a shuffling noise from one end of the room to the other. He picks up the receiver.

'Nade! Where are you?'

'What?'

'But you can't! We're expecting you back here.'

A voice chimes from the receiver. There is a soft thud. The dialling tone is recorded, until side B runs out.

Listening to the dialling tone, Ana lights a cigarette. She shakes off the ash in the wineglass. It floats on the red surface. She waits diligently for the tape to finish, as though some explanation will be revealed at the end, after the dialling tone. As though Nadejda's cruel, childish voice will speak from the receiver again, undoing what her words have done. She sits on the couch carefully, trying not to speculate, postponing interpretation. Nadejda is somewhere she shouldn't be. Nadejda has said something horrible. Suddenly Ana remembers there is no smoking in Vassil's house and drowns the cigarette in the red puddle of wine.

The tape clicks. In the absolute silence that follows, Ana hears the last knock of her own heart on the door of this day. The door collapses and hot geysers spill out of her eyes. She bites her fist.

Chapter Nineteen

CHAPTER TWENTY

Nadejda is facing a dilemma.

Curtain falls, curtain rises

Nadejda is facing a dilemma. She would like to contact Maria, a girl she knows in town, but is afraid that Maria's parents, who know her mother, might give her away. The family used to live in Christchurch but moved up last year. Maria and Nadejda are not best friends, but Nadejda is used to not having best friends any more and doesn't mind seeing Maria. She doesn't know anyone safer in the capital who would be less likely to become an informer to her mother and uncle. They all know about Vassil — one of the veteran Bulgarian immigrants in the country — even if nobody 'really knows him', as he puts it. To call Maria would mean to make her whereabouts known. But then her mother believes she is still in Sofia, since Vassil is probably telling her about the phone call this very minute. So she won't start calling various acquaintances in the North Island. But if she calls Sofia to find out what's happening with Nadejda, or more likely if she asks Vassil to do it for her, she will quickly find out that the bird has flown. After talking to Mladen, she may think that Nadejda has lied to her father about leaving and stayed on somewhere else in Sofia. Or that she has gone to Plovdiv. Or . . . In any case, Ana wouldn't think of calling Maria's parents.

Standing by the phone, Nadejda hears the muffled sound of the radio news. She makes out a few words: 'Balkans, demonstrations, escalating, nationalism, outbursts . . .' Suddenly, Nadejda is chilled by a flush of shame, as if a tonne of cold water has been poured on her. Here she is, making her pathetic little decision whether to make a phone call, while thousands in Sofia are making decisions that will result in life or death. The consequences of their actions may mean death for thousands, civil war. And the consequences of Nadejda's action? She shivers at the inconsequence of her dilemma, of her entire trip in fact. It strikes her that she should have stayed there, until the end of the unrest, whatever the consequences. 'You must leave, Nade,' her father said in a choked voice, 'before things get out of control here.' Her uncle called once too, obviously a spokesperson for Ana, to say how worried they were, how Nadejda should come back as soon as possible, how the situation was clearly escalating, according to the BBC. She promised. And she left.

Perhaps she would have made an even bigger mistake by staying, with Anton and the others, with her father who didn't even

185

try to hide his immense happiness at her visit, betrayed by the shaking of his hands and the emotion in his otherwise even voice, the way he had of rubbing her back with helpless love, just as he did to comfort her years ago when she would cry after a nightmare, or after falling off her bike. The same helpless remedy for her every distress.

A kettle whistles disconsolate in the kitchen. It is as if the hot steam of that kettle pierces the ice of Nadejda's torpor. She decides to book a flight back to Sofia tomorrow. And not only that, but call Maria too, right now.

'So, how was Bulgaria?' Maria's Bulgarian is impeccable, despite the fact that she has lived abroad for over ten years. Her English too is impeccable, with a soft South African touch. Nadejda finds Maria alien — her tall, forceful figure, her confidence, her artistic ambitions and talent, her new Wellington life, the contentment she exudes.

'It was . . . cold.'

Maria nods with absent-minded attentiveness and sips her cappuccino, glancing around the irregular-shaped café. She seems more interested in the café clientele than in any news from Bulgaria.

'It was weird to go back, you know, especially with what's going on.' Nadejda savours the pleasure of impressing Maria with her tales of heroism and violence. But Maria leans towards her and breathes a coffee whisper in Nadejda's face: 'That guy over there, in the linen jacket, see? He's my arts tutor. He's amazing, and I think he has a crush on me.' She smiles in his direction and does a little charming wave with her white, swan-like hand, flicking her long hair back. 'You were saying.'

'Yes. I was saying about the protests. I actually took part in them.'

'Yeah, I heard about them, Mum and Dad have been like glued to the TV. I saw a news item on Sofia a couple of days ago. It's horrible, what's happening.'

'Well, not really. It had to happen. I mean, people really are starving. I saw it with my own eyes. We've been taking too much shit, listening to promises from the bloody "socialist" government.'

'Gosh, you seem quite up-to-date. I suppose you would be, if you were there these last few weeks. But how's everyone there, anyway?'

Nadejda is stunned at this lack of interest but she finds she is quite desperate to talk to someone, interested or not, about what she's just been through.

'Oh, they're good. I mean my dad's caught up in the events, so he doesn't have time for anything else. Everything's in a state of arrest. There are no lectures, lots of institutions are closed. The city transport is crippled.'

'Right . . . Gosh. So, what did you do there, apart from the protest? Did you go out? Any nice nightspots?'

'Yeah, lots of them. I mainly hung out with Anton, this friend of mine from way back. We went out quite a lot, with his friends. Some excellent places, but very expensive. Anton couldn't afford all that much. I mean, he works part-time.'

'What does he do?'

'He's a philosophy student, second year.'

'Oh really? Philosophy! This guy I'm seeing at the moment is also a philosophy student, he's doing second year. He's very brainy.'

'All right. So how've you been?'

'Oh good, really good. Yeah. I'm doing my last year, and guess what! I'm having an exhibition in July! With a couple of other senior students.'

'That's great!'

'Yeah, I know, isn't it.'

Maria has become positively feather-brained, Nadejda notes sadly, as she stirs her bitter coffee and licks the spoon. Maria waves to another acquaintance walking past. 'You know,' she confides in a discreet whisper, 'this place is known as the fish bowl.'

'Why?'

'Why! Because this is *the* place. This is where you come to be seen. It's very central. I can't come here without being recognised or bumping into someone I know.'

Nadejda is feeling increasingly inadequate. She didn't even get anywhere near telling about the night of the beatings. Her stories of winter protests are out of place here, in this fish bowl, in Maria's worldly presence. In this crowded, aromatic café, so

187

European with its tables out on the summer street and its soft jazz, Sofia with her blood on the snow, her students in pyjamas, her processions with horses, her full-bodied songs 'We're no longer slaves', becomes a fiction. A lesser reality, because of this bigger one. A vast stretch of sand helpless against the tide of reality: when the tide is in, there is no proof that the sand underneath exists, only the memory of it, only the good faith. That's why she must go back, make the tide go out.

Noticing Nadejda's despondency, Maria gracefully changes the topic. 'How long are you staying for?'

'I'm not sure. I'd like to get back to Christchurch,' Nadejda lies. She too has a city where she knows all the cafés and people, even if she hates it more than she hates Maria right now.

'All right. I can't believe I lived in Christchurch for two entire years! God, I hated it even more than Harare. That place stinks. I think you should move up here, you know, enrol at varsity here and just get a perspective on things.'

'Yeah, I don't know. I've got to go back to Mum, she's waiting for me.' The lie resembles the truth too much. Indeed, she has to. A lump in her throat makes her stir her coffee vigorously, as if the lump is in the cup. Get a perspective on things, huh? Get a life, in other words. Like Maria.

Maria is perceptive enough to feel the invisible lump in Nadejda's coffee. 'It's really good to see you, you know. I don't have any Bulgarian friends here. Not that I miss that but, you know, it's nice to catch up. What are you doing tomorrow?'

The lump in Nadejda's coffee grows instead of dissolving, the coffee splashes out of the cup, a glass is broken behind the bar, and Nadejda covers her eyes with her palms, her elbows propped on the table, her fingers digging into her fringe in a childish gesture of despair. She knows that if she speaks, her voice will break. But if she doesn't speak, her voice will break anyway. 'I'm going to Sofia,' she says and her voice remains surprisingly intact. Only her eyes hurt as she presses them with her palms.

It is only when certain things are said out loud that we become aware of their absurdity. If Nadejda hadn't said this aloud, she would have repeated it to herself; in the musty intimacy of semi-articulate thoughts. She would've left the country tomorrow.

'What?' Finally Maria is paying attention. 'But you've only just come back!'

'I know. But I have to go back.'

'What do you mean, you have to? Is there something you're not telling me about Sofia? Nade?'

Maria is probably thinking of some steamy affair. Nadejda takes her hands away from her face. She knows they have left red marks.

'I feel like a coward, leaving in the middle of things there. It feels like running away from my fate, from my country. I can't pretend that nothing is happening there, and just go back to Christchurch or whatever, as if, as if . . .'

A slick-haired man passes behind Maria's chair and squeezes her shoulder. Maria turns her head and smiles, then whispers to Nadejda, 'That's Charlie. He's from London. An okay sculptor, but what a body! Sorry, you were saying about Christchurch?'

Nadejda holds her spoon. Half her coffee is on the saucer, looking cold and unsavoury. It has been stirred to death. 'That's all really. I feel like I'm betraying someone, something. I mean, by comparison, nothing happens here!' Nadejda is raising her voice.

For a moment, she feels that she has made Maria, and the entire café — which seems to go silent for a fraction of a second — see the truth about nothing happening here. For a moment, she feels understood. But then Maria says, 'What's the point of going back? What are you going to change? The change has already happened. I mean, the protests are over. It's over. What more do you want to change?'

'What do you mean, it's over?'

'It's just over. The government resigned, they showed it on the news tonight. You haven't seen the news.'

'What, you mean the communists stepped down?'

'Yes. The guy who was supposed to be the new Prime Minister has resigned, reportedly saying that he didn't want blood on his hands.'

'And that's it?'

'That's it.'

189

'What's going to happen now?'

'I don't know. But Mum and Dad said the president will be a dominant presence, he's very popular. And there's a provisional government before the next elections, or something like that. They showed people dancing in the streets, and crying, the atmosphere is elated, everybody's on a high.'

'Why didn't you tell me before?'

'I thought you knew. I didn't know it was so important to you.'

The lump in Nadejda's throat melts violently, but she remembers her rule about not crying in front of people she doesn't love. And if she cried, she wouldn't know why she was crying — from relief or from regret. From pride or from shame. For Anton or for her father. For her country or for herself. No death at the barricades. No going back to save anyone. No second chance for the deserter.

Maria goes to buy a piece of cheesecake to share, to celebrate the news, but mainly to queue behind her arts tutor in the linen jacket. Alone at the table, Nadejda feels exposed. The tide is out again, the sand is bare and stretches endlessly, beyond the horizon. Nadejda can't see all that way ahead. So much sand, she can't take it. She runs towards the water, seeking the comfort of its concealment again. Running, running.

With Maria back at the table, they stab the cheesy yellow flesh through to the biscuit base and clink their water glasses, each toasting something different.

In the hostel kitchen, Nadejda is waiting for the one o'clock BBC news on TV. There are three other women in her room upstairs; she doesn't feel as if she has a room at all. The kitchen at least is empty. Outside all traffic has stopped, except for the occasional pedestrian. She hears lonely steps outside the window every now and then. Maria invited her to go and stay with their family, but they live in a suburb somewhere, besides Nadejda doesn't want to give herself away completely; she needs to keep some distance.

She sits staring at the rudimentary painting of four giant penguins, in a tableau of friendly wildlife high up on the wall above the cupboards. She isn't booking a flight tomorrow, after all. The night descends thickly like a velvet curtain on a stage. The play of protests is over. The theatre of cruelty is over. Maybe. It's a success, it appears. The actors clap to themselves in the crispy winter air of Sofia, as at a rehearsal. Nadejda is now merely audience, a strange kind of audience — having gone backstage, to this island at the end of all islands, she hears only the faint sounds of the noisy finale. And paradoxically, now that she is offstage, she suddenly feels more involved. She sees the meaning of those protests, the endless possibilities for unhappy endings. She sees beyond the inert body of Anton on the wet yellow pavement. Maybe distance means greater clarity, or at least less blurring. Like these penguins: from where she sits the penguins are clearly delineated, they almost have expressions. She walks towards the wall, bumping her knee painfully into a chair. She limps on, keeping her eyes on the penguins. Yes, the penguins become quite blurred as the distance decreases, quite expressionless, losing their shape and therefore their meaning, until she no longer knows what she is looking at. Just as, faced with her father's familiar gestures, she couldn't see the ridiculous short-sightedness of her pleas: 'Please come, Dad, it'll be great. It's not too late. You don't have to live with Mum if you don't want to. You'll love New Zealand.'

Her father! She must be so wrapped up in herself not to think of calling him straight after she heard the news. She limps to the phones in the corridor and dials the Sofia number. There is no reply. Her father must be out celebrating with the crowd. But listening to the sound of her father's absent voice, it is as though she hears his ultimate refusal, his final no. And not only his. Anton's, everybody's. The protests, the beatings, the elation and now the celebration have been happening without Nadejda. She hangs up.

Her mind rejoices, but her body doesn't. Is it her egotism that prevents her from celebrating a nation's triumph, or is it that celebration is intrinsically a shared rejoicing, a benign mass hysteria which can't be a private madness? It is a question she can't formulate because she is delirious with tiredness. But even if she could, she wouldn't be able to answer it, because she would be too close to the question. It's the penguin syndrome all over.

Sitting at the table again, Nadejda rests her head on her outstretched arm, her other hand winding and unwinding a lock of

Chapter Twenty

long hair. She feels herself decreasing, becoming lighter, occupying less and less space, until she pops like a soap bubble. Then she gets up and skilfully avoiding all obstacles in the kitchen, makes her way to the exit and out onto the desert moonlit street.

An elegant young man emerges from a discreet jazz bar around the corner, jingling his car keys. A dozen metres away he sees a girl walking down the main road, past the small square with a little bench. In a reassuring greeting reflex of the solitary night wanderer — not unlike the greeting truck drivers have on the road or dog-owners at the beach — he glances at her face to make the brief eye contact of reconnaissance. But she doesn't. She looks straight ahead, her face quite expressionless. He is struck by her air of ... something he cannot name. He gets into his red Mitsubishi van and watches her stroll on past him. In a flooding of streetlight, her face looks pale.

As she disappears round the corner, leaving behind the small alley where he is, he starts the van and backs it out onto the empty main road. She continues to walk in an unnaturally straight line. The wine has worn off and his mind feels white and tidy like this midnight city. And like the city, his mind is deserted. The only movement in his consciousness at present is the bizarre, automaton-like movement of this long-haired girl, casually dressed in a white top and low-cut fashionable trousers, walking in total oblivion. She is like a white apparition disguised as a regular city dweller. She is not drunk, but may be on drugs. She may be some kind of freak. She may be about to commit suicide. She may need help. She is pretty. Her lightly tanned arms contrast attractively with her white top; her waist is small; her hair is long and straight, brownish-red, tied in a dishevelled ponytail.

He hesitates. He starts driving very slowly down the wide road, catching up with her and driving alongside her. Too bad if she thinks he's stalking her. She doesn't, because she turns her head in his direction; their eyes don't meet because she is not looking at him at all. It's hard to say what she is looking at. She seems to be registering only the noise. The soft summer wind plays with her hair.

He reaches over to the passenger-seat window and winds it

down. The car is now gliding imperceptibly, almost brushing against the pavement. Holding on to the wheel with one hand, he bends across the empty seat and says to the apparition: 'Excuse me, are you okay?'

The apparition looks his way but again doesn't actually look at him. There is something chilling about this. He should probably just drive home and let her be, whatever she's up to. But the girl steps down from the pavement and reaches out to the car door, not taking notice of its movement. He stops and opens the door. She gets in, smelling faintly of musk. She looks straight ahead. She presses her hands between her legs with a shiver. 'It's cold,' she says in a husky voice.

He feels a cold shiver run down his back, but it's not unpleasant. 'Yes. It gets cool at night doesn't it? Are you going home?'

'Yes,' the husky voice says. She leans back, looking at the roof.

'Where do you live? I mean, I can drop you off if you like. No hassles.'

She doesn't reply.

'Are you all right?'

'I'm all right,' she says in a flat voice which has a strangely disembodied sound.

'Where do you live, then?'

'I don't know,' the voice drawls, now with a touch of plaintiveness. 'Where do you live?'

This sounds more like an echo of his question, rather than a question in its own right, but he has to play the game, whatever it is: 'I live in Auckland, actually. I'm just down here for business.'

Already having lost interest, she slumps towards the door, her head resting at an awkward angle, and closes her eyes. There isn't much he can say that would make sense. He looks around, as if for a suggestion. The parking lot in New World, the road behind and ahead, even the sky, are empty. A ghost city.

He looks at her. She is breathing evenly, still pale. As he looks closer, uncomfortable staring at a strange sleeping woman but unable to resist, he notes that her skin has a warm light-bronze tone. Her nose is small and slightly turned up with charming cheek. The matching chin is small and square rather than round. The

193

cheekbones are high. There is a tense harmony about her face, a stubbornness, as if she wants to keep her secrets tightly shut in the Pandora box of her sleep.

She twitches. He looks away, as if reminded of his intrusion. Looking at her doesn't help him decide on his course of action. Sirens wail in the distance. Someone is being saved somewhere, like in every city.

This is just what he needs: a foreign girl asleep, possibly sick, in his van. He can't dump her on the street now, but leaving her here all night is also out of the question. She may have some ID in her pocket, some indication of where the hell she comes from and who she is. But he can't search her trouser pockets — if she wakes up, it may look as if he is taking advantage of her. In fact, it will look like that anyway, when she wakes up in his car. She might start screaming or God knows what. He can't stay here forever, in the middle of town, with her sleeping it off. But he can't take her home with him either. He was looking for trouble, talking to her. He is feeling tired and irritated by the whole situation, his initial enchanted curiosity cooling down as a result of this discomfort. Then a brilliant idea strikes his mind like a cymbal stick.

In the emergency ward, there is a man with a rough, blood-soaked bandage over his ear and neck, and a large pasty woman by his side. They both stare straight ahead, like dummies. What is this, night of the zombies? He turns to a nurse. 'There's a young woman in my car. She kind of just got inside and then fell asleep or passed out. She might be sick. I think you better have a look at her.'

His words sound hollow and implausible. 'Right,' says the downy-faced nurse, looking at him with suspicion, and thrusts her pudgy hands in her white pockets. Her badge says 'Judy: nurse.'

'What made you think she might be sick?'

'Well, she wasn't very coherent. She didn't know where she lived, that sort of thing. I don't know her, this is the first time I've seen her in my life. I was just worried that . . .'

'We'll get her inside. Where's your car?'

'Just out in the street.'

'Right. Can you wait here?'

He waits while two men with a stretcher fling the doors open and shuffle down to the exit. Judy comes back, this time armed with a pad. 'Can you come over this way please,' she instructs him severely and gets behind the reception. She asks him for personal details — name, occupation, address, the usual. He should have foreseen this dreariness: he couldn't just drop off Sleeping Beauty here anonymously and flee. But a vestige of curiosity is keeping him here too — to find out just what is wrong with this girl, what exactly she was doing walking alone in the middle of the night, in this so-normal city, where she is from. She looks kind of French. But she also has looks similar to the girls in Istanbul. Or Jewish? No, her skin isn't white enough.

The doors are flung open again and the two men carry the sleeper inside, curled up on the stretcher, her hair spread out in appealing disorder.

'So, you don't know the woman,' Judy says, scrutinising his face.

'No.'

'You don't know her name.'

'No, of course I don't!' He mustn't get too defensive.

'Why did she get into your car?'

Is this a criminal investigation? She is alive, after all, and untouched! 'I don't know.' He shrugs his shoulders with guilt.

'Was she speaking to you?'

'Yes. Well, sort of. She said she was cold.'

'Right. Would you like to wait here?' She points to a seat.

There is a slight buzzing in the waiting room and the bright, cheap light makes him nauseous. He paces around the miserable chairs stained with sick humanity. It's a long way from the stylish blue bar where he sipped wine with his friend to the sound of muffled jazz. Stepping out of the bar, he stepped directly into this unlikely story.

A sleek young doctor is standing next to him. 'Hi, I'm Dr White.' He shakes his wrist, getting his expensive watch into place. 'She woke up because we needed to do a blood test. She's fine. It appears that she was sleepwalking at the time when she got into your car. Otherwise, there's nothing wrong with her, no drugs or anything in the blood. We'll just make sure she gets home. Thank you for your assistance.' He shakes his watch again, a kind of substitute for hand-shaking.

'That's all right. Good night.' But it's not all right. He wants to know more. He must be careful not to come across as being dodgy. 'I could take her home — I've got my car outside.'

He instantly hears the idiocy of this statement. Dodgy man brings unconscious girl and when she comes to he wants to take her home, even though he doesn't know her!

'No, that's fine. She'll get a taxi.'

'I want to talk to her when she comes to, just to tell her what happened, so she doesn't worry about it. Will she remember conversations?'

'Most likely not. If she was sleepwalking, she wouldn't have a clear recollection.'

'Well, I'd like to reassure her anyway. If you find out her contact number, maybe I can get it tomorrow.'

And so he does. The drive home is positively surreal. He finds himself watching, from the corner of his eye, for the slender figure to cross the still city like a cursed princess in a petrified forest. But the princess has been imprisoned in a grey castle. A spell has been cast. Of course, he doesn't think in these terms because he is a dealer in Oriental rugs and his mind, although finely attuned to beauty, is even more attuned to evaluating beauty for the purpose of selling it.

In the morning, he calls the hospital. The staff has changed and the receptionist takes a long time to understand his request. They keep him waiting on the line a long time, before he is told, frugally, that her name is Nadejda Taneva and she is staying at a youth hostel in town.

Nadejda wakes up on her bunk and is struck by two things at once: first, that the room is pleasantly flooded with sun; second, she has the unpleasant feeling that someone has been watching her sleep. There's nobody in the room, only backpacks and white towels drying around her like wet dogs after an exhausting swim.

Then she remembers: the awakening in a strange midnight hospital with a needle stuck in her arm, a pudgy nurse on one side and a bearded doctor on the other. She thought she had died and was in some hell or other, or abducted by aliens. They explained to her how she came to be there. A man, they said, smartly dressed, who apparently didn't know her, brought her in a red van. Did she know him? She didn't. They had the number plate, his name and contact address. He was just outside. She was shivering and sick with shock. All she cared about was to be in her warm bed in Christchurch, with her mother asleep next door. She was too tired to care about some man in a red van, smartly dressed or not. They let her go, even called a taxi for her. She climbed in next to the tiny Indian driver and lulled by the smooth speed, fell asleep. She was shyly woken up in broken English outside the hostel. She crawled out and somehow found the way to her bed in the fifth-floor room, in the smelly, cosmopolitan darkness saturated with three sleeping women.

She props herself up on one elbow and inspects the view below. A forest of boat masts signalling water. White clouds stuck on a blue sky. Toy cars in the supermarket car-park. A skateboard ramp with boys plunging down from one end and emerging at the other almost simultaneously. A hill of colourful houses, densely stacked and all turned to the harbour like a pile of presents at the door of the sea. The whiteness of summer after the whiteness of winter. Nadejda remembers her rendezvous with Maria at lunchtime.

The curtain of the night has lifted. Another play begins and the set is superb.

CHAPTER TWENTY-ONE

All day Nadejda puts off calling
her father.

The place that still exists

All day Nadejda puts off calling her father. Lying can be tiresome. One lie a day per maximum — that's all she can manage. Today's lie becomes tonight's lie, as the city buzzes around her, white, insouciant, and gently contracting as if to accommodate all new arrivals. There is room for Nadejda here, she feels — the city loves itself enough to give or not to care.

She goes around the shopping area. Shoplifting in a new place is a particular thrill, but she is not equipped; stupidly, she forgot to take a bag. She has no summer jacket either — all her clothes are winter-oriented; she has only sweaters and a polar jacket. She had to buy shorts in Auckland, upon arrival.

She meets with Maria and her paramour of the moment — a weedy student with a groomed goatee. His trousers sag on his bottom. It's one thing Nadejda can't stand: a man with trousers sagging on his backside, like a pensioner. She tries to be nice, although she doesn't feel like seeing any acquaintances. She'd much rather talk to strangers.

They have lunch in a grungy semi-dark café where Maria, in her long gauze skirt and the philosopher-to-be in his fashionable tight T-shirt ('No To Nuclears') look so natural as to be part of the decor.

'You have to come round for dinner, my parents insist on seeing you,' says Maria, her hand on the philosopher's chicken thigh.

Nadejda wants to flee. The seal of her anonymity has been broken. 'Yeah, that would be nice. Thanks.'

Maria must dash — she's helping some friends set up a show. 'It was very nice to meet you,' says Terry and Nadejda realises he hasn't said a word until now, like her, having been silenced in advance by Maria's incessant chatter.

They are standing in the street, just outside the café. 'Do you want to come round tonight?' asks Maria, switching to Bulgarian. 'I won't be home, I've got to go to my friend's show, but Mum and Dad will be delighted to have you.'

'Oh. Actually, I can't tonight. I've got something else planned.'

'Oh yeah?' Maria nudges her and makes a conniving face. 'Who is it?'

199

'I've got to see some people. A Bulgarian family.' She could do that, in fact — she knows a few people in town. But she won't.

'Who are they?'

Fortunately, at that point a big, white-haired man stops and asks in the unmistakable, harsh Balkan accent:

'Excuse me, I'm sorry, what language are you speaking?' His bushy eyebrows tremble as he lifts them quizzically.

'Bulgarian,' says Nadejda.

Maria is annoyed. Terry is expressionless.

'Ah. It sounds like Serbian, I heard, you know, something.' He laughs uneasily. 'Sorry to bother you. It's nice to hear, you know.'

'Where are you from?' braves Terry.

'Me? I'm from Yugoslavia. The capital, Belgrade.' His imposing physique clashes with his nervous agitation.

'I've been to Belgrade,' says Maria. 'It's a nice city. It's similar to Sofia.'

'Yes, yes, I've been to Sofia,' the man shouts, lighting up but then suddenly sinks into sombreness. 'Anyway. All the best.'

He takes Nadejda's hand in his paws and squeezes it, then does the same with Maria and Terry. 'Don't forget your home country. Despite everything. It's not the same here. It will never be like home.'

They nod, all three of them, serious.

He hesitates for a moment, agitated again, then rushes down the street, his long elegant coat blown behind him.

'Well,' says Maria, lifting her eyebrows.

Out on the wharf, Nadejda is drinking Coke and watching the boats. A hint of fish stink spices up the perfect, postcard tidiness of the view. Dark blue mountains endlessly multiply around the blue harbour. The silence is torn by the shrieks of vicious-looking gulls which brush over her head as they shoot towards the water. 'Shhhit!' A tourist sitting nearby is wiping his bald head with a handkerchief. He and his wife get on their large knees, gather their McDonald's lunch and move a few metres down, for better protection from the offensive birds.

A middle-aged man sits a metre or so away from Nadejda. He is carrying a bag, his hair is wet — or what's left of it; his trousers are too big for him. Nadejda wonders if she has seen him before. She often sees vaguely familiar faces, unable to locate the time and space in which she has previously known them. Sometimes they turn out to be near-doubles, or similar types to old friends and bullies from school. Human similarities know no race or nationality. She glances at the man casually, straining to remember. He too glances at her casually. There is something in his eyes which signals distress, or at least extreme melancholy. He smiles as he takes out a pie:

'How are you?'

'Good.'

'Beautiful day.'

'Yeah.'

'Are you from around here?'

'No, I'm not.'

'May I ask what your country of origin is? Let me guess. Portugal?'

'No,' she laughs, 'why do you think so?'

'Because,' he acquires an air of expertise, screwing up his eyes, 'you remind me very much of a woman I know.'

'Is she Portuguese?'

'No, she's Canadian but her mother is Portuguese.'

'I see.'

'You look *very* similar.' He stares at her unblinkingly, then suddenly smiles. His teeth are yellow. So are his fingers which break off some pastry from the pie and throw it to a gull nearby. A dozen others appear out of the sky and a violent battle ensues.

'She has the same long, beautiful hair, dark reddish-brown, but her eyes are green. I think she wears lenses actually. They are unnaturally green, you know the kind.' He look mysterious.

She does.

'She is amazing. She's the most intelligent woman I know. I met her through a friend. She's a journalist, a bit like me, really, except I do free-lance work and she works for a journal.'

He is staring at the now pacified gulls. He tears off another piece of pastry and throws it to them. Sauce and suspect stuffing ooze out of his mutilated lunch. Nadejda is watching with interest. He looks rather impoverished, except for his new leather bag.

201

Chapter Twenty-one

'I loved her,' he said, staring at the distant mountains, oblivious to his fingers awkwardly holding the pie and to his trousers trembling around his thin calves in the warm breeze as if he had forgotten about his body. His bag falls to one side and a thick bundle of paper spills out with a mellow ruffle. People are so strange.

'She went back to Canada, eventually. She was here for a short time only. I wrote to her. She wrote back.'

'So, what was the problem?'

Nadejda can see that there was a problem, but finds it useful to prompt him.

'What was the problem?' He looks at her, as if waking from a coma. His eyes have no colour, they are made up of specks.

'The problem was she didn't care about me.'

Nadejda doesn't know where to look. His eyes are still fixed on her, accusingly.

'I wasn't rich enough for her, or young enough, or handsome enough. I am only a writer from Wellington.' Irony mixed with pride.

Nadejda can't shake off the feeling that she is in a corny film: 'I was only a writer . . .' the writer says wistfully. 'But she wanted *more*.'

He puts the pie on the concrete ground.

'When was that?'

Practical questions are always helpful in bringing the nostalgic and the troubled back into focus.

'Last year.'

Nadejda decides not to interrupt.

'And you know the strangest thing?' he stares at her maniacally.

'No.'

'I could never bring myself to tell her that I loved her.'

'Maybe that's why she left. Maybe she didn't know.'

'That's what I fear. But I couldn't. I knew she'd reject me. There are things we prefer to pretend not to know. But one way or another, they grow to dominate our lives. They lurk in the attic, like the mother in *Psycho*.'

He stuffs the manuscript back inside the bag.

'What's this?' Nadejda asks.

'Oh, that's a manuscript for a film script. I've just got it back.'

'Is it yours?'

'Yes.'

'Was it rejected?'

'Yep,' he shrugs his shoulders, 'not the first time. But it will be the last.'

'You know,' says Nadejda without thinking, already cringing at what she is about to say, 'I think you should find a woman who loves you.'

He bursts out laughing. He laughs, and laughs. He laughs a little too long, looking at her with a kind of pained hilarity. Then his laughter begins to sound like sobbing, until his face crumples up, emphasising his worn skin. His head sinking into his neck, he cups his hands over his mouth and nose, eyes leaking.

Nadejda feels terrible.

'I'm sorry,' she says quietly.

'No no, don't be,' he smiles, his eyes lost in a flood, 'you are totally right. Totally right. Everybody should find someone who loves them. Because that's the only thing that matters, in the end, isn't it. The only thing that matters.'

Nadejda sits very still. A lucky gull is tugging violently at the now gutted pie. The man gets up and straps the bag across his chest.

'Do you think so?' Nadejda looks up.

'Oh, I have no doubts about it, no doubts at all.'

He smiles a stained, sincere smile, breathing out deeply like after a jog, and adds:

'I hope you find someone to love you.'

Inside the Queen's Wharf shops, the lunch crowd is thinning out. Nadejda wanders around. Across from the bookshop where she is eyeing up the postcards, there is a sale of Oriental rugs in a large room. She is tempted to go over and walk on the silky floor, but she doesn't have the look of a prospective buyer and resents being looked down on by vulgar and snobbish salesmen. She resents being looked at as if she's a thief. A tall, smart man paces around the carpeted hall, touching up a sign here, adjusting a rug there, dialling a number on his cellphone, trying to look busy.

Nadejda walks out with a bunch of postcards and heads back to the hostel. A gull lifts off and flies across the harbour until it blends with the sky. The sky is a puzzle made of gulls perfectly fitting together, like an Escher drawing. That's where the gulls go. When the sky looks imperfect, it is because a gull is missing.

In the supermarket car-park an old man is giving out yellow flyers. He is scruffy; the hand reaching out to Nadejda is covered in black hairs. It reminds her of her uncle. 'Hey girl, miss, excuse me,' he calls as she continues on her way, screwing up the yellow paper. He has a strong foreign accent.

She turns around. He steps forward. 'You're not Greek, are you?'

She smiles. If only her uncle could hear this, with his inveterate hate for the Greeks. 'No,' she says, shading her eyes from the sun.

'Where are you from?'

'Bulgaria.'

'Ah, Bulgaria! Yes. Sister country. That's why you are beautiful like a Greek.'

Her uncle would have a heart attack if he heard this.

'You are Greek yourself, obviously,' she chances.

He fondly takes her by the arm and speaks in her face: 'Of course I'm Greek. Now tell me, how long have you been here?'

'Three, four years?' Her voice rises at the end, in the colloquial New Zealand way.

'Ah. Yes. Not long, not long at all.' He nods pensively. 'Me, I've been here long time. You can't imagine. Forty years I been here, can you imagine? Forty years!'

'Did you come when you were a child?'

Only a road separates her from the privacy of the hostel. He automatically holds out a leaflet to a woman laden with shopping bags.

'Well, I was young. You know,' he lowers his voice, breathing sourly in her face, 'after forty years, I still dream of Greece. I dream, and dream, and dream. The white houses, the olive trees, the heat, the sea. I don't know why I'm still here. But forty years pass just like that.' And he snaps his fingers, then points a grubby finger at her. 'You will see.'

Nadejda nods. People his age take special pleasure in threatening the young with mortality — it's a kind of a perverse affection. 'Nice talking to you.' She smiles genuinely, for she likes him, and heads for the hostel.

He bows to her back in an exaggerated manner and somehow, in the process, drops the leaflets. A sudden sweep of wind scatters them around. He bends down to pick them up, but the wind gets stronger. A queue of impatient cars is forming behind him. One of them blows its horn. He turns around and waves his hands helplessly, then gets out of the way. A couple of people have picked up a few and hand them back to him. He thanks them profusely. He arranges the yellow leaves in a neat pile again and looks at the top one, screwing up his eyes. Nobody knows that he can't read English.

Upstairs, in the empty hostel room, Nadejda takes a Wellington postcard and writes in English: 'This city is populated with people who have lost something. They look at you like they are looking for an affirmation that what they've lost still exists, somewhere. A word they hear, a face they see, reminds them of the place they hope still exists. Is it because I'm called Nadejda, Hope, that they turn to me?'

At the top, she puts 6 February and 'Dear . . .' knowing that the card is not going anywhere.

Chapter Twenty-one

CHAPTER TWENTY-TWO

"*Tatko? It's me!*"

Ocean of damage

'Tatko? It's me!'

'Nade! How are you?'

'I'm fine. I heard about the news! That's amazing. Happy victory!'

'Yes, it's been amazing. Everybody's drunk with happiness. Where are you anyway?'

'I'm back in Christchurch. Everybody's really happy here. We heard it on the news last night. It's a shame I can't be there.'

'Yes, that's true.' There is a silence.

'But the main thing is,' he continues, 'now it's looking up. The communists are dead.'

'Yeah. We're so relieved here.' Her voice has the intonation that signals running out of things to say. But the main thing is, she called. He's been expecting her to call.

'What are you doing?' he says.

'I'm just . . . unpacking, really.'

'You're still unpacking! You've been back a week now,' he laughs. Suddenly everything makes him laugh, although the wine has worn off.

'Yeah, well, I've been putting it off, you know how it is.'

'Yes, I know. So, what's that noise? Is your mother having a party?' He can't suppress the irony in his voice.

'No no, I'm calling from a friend's place. We're having a party here.'

'I see. That's good. I see Anton quite often. He's been like possessed over the last weeks. I've never seen him like that. I think he misses you — yesterday he asked about you, if I've heard from you. I think he was sad that you left in the middle of it all. But that's beside the point. We didn't know how things were going to develop. We had to make sure you were safe.'

'I know. But I wish I'd stayed.'

'Let's not dwell on this. You wouldn't have missed much. Freezing on the barricades, burning tyres, more songs and slogans, and finally — the denouement. You've probably seen it all on the news.'

'Yeah.' Nadejda sounds despondent suddenly. He wonders how she really feels.

'Nade, I'm thinking of you, I love you very much.' He is

207

speaking fast, in order not to falter and let her interrupt him. 'It's all going to come right. Fingers crossed, you can come in a few months, for the summer here, and it'll be much better, we'll go to the seaside, we'll have a ball. Okay?'

'Okay.' Suddenly she sounds like a lost child.

'Now you take care. Write when you can. Okay?'

'Okay.' Perhaps she *is* a lost child.

'Bye, Dad. I'm thinking about you too,' she says and hangs up with urgency.

Mladen puts the receiver down and lights the first cigarette of the day. He realises that he sounded guilty. By promising to her things he knew were not going to happen he was trying to compensate for his omission, for his failing — but he can never make it up to her. He regrets his extreme actions three years ago, his ultimatums to Ana, his bitter words, his silence. Nadejda didn't deserve all that but she was caught in between. Children always are, what can you do? Of course now he can't go back. He will never speak to Ana again, even if he no longer hates her. There is an ocean of damage between them, inhabited by the sharks of violent words they've exchanged. He cannot cross it. Time doesn't heal damage — it immortalises it.

Nadejda sounded mixed-up, odd. He cleans up the kitchen table, puts the heater on, and sits down with pen, paper and cigarettes. Some things are better written than said.

Sofia, 6 Feb. 1997

My dear Nade,

Some things are better written than said. I have just spoken to you. I was waiting for you to call. I'm glad you're well. I'm good too. It is funny that we had three weeks together, and yet I feel there is so much more to be said. I guess we have four years to catch up on.

I have been caught up in the recent events, as you know. People were prepared to put up a fight till the end. There could've been a civil war. Or rather it would've been a massacre. But it's over, we're safe. It's another bloodless revolution. Let's hope it won't be just a velvet one like the one in '89. In any case, we'll be no longer the savages of Europe. Just the paupers. But anyway.

RECONNAISSANCE

I wasn't sure what to make of your phone call just before. At first you sounded very positive and uplifting, but then there was a touch of je ne sais quoi in your voice.

There are things about your mother and me we haven't discussed. I've wanted to discuss them with you. There is also something about me which you should know, if you are to believe that you truly know your father. We ran out of time, somehow. The protests set off a stream of events which swept us along its current, leaving little time to talk.

The phone rings. Mladen hates being interrupted when he is writing or reading, but he answers it.

There is a silence at the other end. 'Mladen? It's Ana here. I'd like to speak to Nadejda, please.'

He must be having a bad dream. Ana's voice is tensely matter-of-fact.

'Ana! What do you mean? She's not here.'

'Look, I don't feel like games. I've had enough games with you. I know she's there.'

'But she's not here! She just called me, as a matter of fact. She said she was back in Christchurch.'

'She's not here! That's nonsense.'

There's another silence, much worse this time. 'I saw her off at the airport a week ago. Why do you think she's here?'

'Because,' Ana groans with frustration, or exhaustion, 'she told her uncle so.'

'Really? When?'

'Yesterday.'

'That doesn't make sense. She must have called from somewhere else. She is in New Zealand, that much I know.'

'Actually, I don't know where she called from. I assumed she called from Sofia.'

'Didn't she say?'

'I don't know.'

'What do you mean you don't know. Didn't Vassil tell you?'

Ana is breathing heavily. 'No,' she says in the sudden ripe voice

209

of contained despair before it becomes full-blown, 'Vassil didn't tell me anything.'

Mladen can't say much to this. To the shock of speaking to Ana after three years of cold war, Nadejda's strange call, her lying, is added the puzzle of Vassil and Ana's crisis. He can't take it all.

'Vassil died yesterday.' Now Ana's despair rushes down the line like a terrible avalanche.

Mladen is swept away, speechless. Two years ago, he would have said: 'Serves him right.'

'I'm sorry,' he says.

Then there's only her silence. Of all the sounds of this woman he once adored, silence is the one he can hear most acutely. Silence is the lid to the bottomless pit of her emotions — the very emotions that attracted him to her. What happened to them?

Ana anticipates the question. 'He died while on the phone with her.'

'Heart attack?' He knows the family history.

'Yes.'

'I'm so sorry.'

'He didn't even smoke.' She has lost everyone, and her voice, free of hysterics, says it. Now he will never make up for his share of the damage. The more he says, the worse it gets. Every word of his has been wounding and always will be. Why is she talking to him at all?

'Look, I wish things had been different for us. I wish I could go back and do things differently. I realise it's been tough for you and Nadejda.' He runs out of fuel. The task of summarising the last years is beyond his capacity.

'I know, I know,' she says, in a dead voice, 'I wish it had been different too.'

When they hang up, Mladen lights a cigarette and imagines Ana lighting one at the same time as him, and like him dragging the smoke deep into her lungs and holding it there, not wanting to let go. His chest feels hollow, as if his heart is suddenly missing. Perhaps he has been living with a hollow chest all these years, but only now realising it. He looks at the half-page letter. 'I'm glad you're well.' What a lie. A lie following her lie.

210

He screws the paper into a ball and leans his back on the window. He tries to systematise his thoughts. To think of all three news items separately, on top of the still fresh news of the government's capitulation.

He is afraid to think of Nadejda, her voice still resounding in his hollow chest, her voice lying.

Ana: Why did she talk to him at all? She called because of Nadejda, yes, but she didn't have to explain anything to him. Prostration causes a reflex of forgiveness. When you are that much in pain, you have no resources to maintain your enemies. She was that much in pain. She only has Nadejda left now. Only Nadejda to lose.

Despite himself, he is afflicted with Nadejda's voice, her laughter, her abrupt goodbye, and is struck by a sudden chill: he was not speaking to his Nadejda, he was speaking to a stranger. A stranger with no pity. Just like him, in fact, when he decided to stay in Sofia four years ago, against everything they'd planned. Knowing she is the cause of her uncle's death, she still stays away, playing sick games. She killed her uncle. He, Mladen, killed his family, metaphorically speaking. Still, he can't suppress a certain macabre satisfaction, a tingling of triumph, a tickle of retributive joy. Vassil, the cause of the family's continuous dismemberment, is dead. After a lifetime of toughness, he dies on the phone. If Vassil had died four years ago, Ana and Nadejda wouldn't have left at all. The irony is bleak, but Mladen is no stranger to bleak ironies.

And now what? Nadejda lied to him, and to her mother. Who knows what she told Vassil? She may not be in New Zealand at all. She could be in Australia, or any other island over there, in the huge desert of the Pacific.

To have the strength to choose what one prefers, and to stick with it, said Albert Camus. Yes, but do we choose only once? And what if each next choice is the negation of the previous one, in these times of cataclysm? He stayed behind, four years ago. Does that mean he chose to stay behind? He chose to wage a cold war with Ana, to isolate himself. Now he has no strength left. His entire strength has been consumed by the act of sticking with that choice which may not have been a choice at all. If he sticks with it, it isn't out of strength, but because he has cut all the bridges.

211

No, Monsieur Camus, this time you are wrong. He stubs out his cigarette and takes a fresh sheet of paper.

Upstairs someone is practising the bass. A truck thunders down the road. Sirens wail in the distance.

CHAPTER TWENTY-THREE

I can hear your heartbeat,
Nadejda, the thump of an organ
suffused with meaning.

The voice: I can hear your heartbeat

I can hear your heartbeat, Nadejda, the thump of an organ suffused with meaning. Hearts break. Hearts ache. Hearts fail. Hearts bleed. Hearts murmur. I should know. Your family should know.

Then I see you. The picture becomes clearer and clearer as your heartbeat fades. You pick up a receiver. That's why your heart is thumping. In your family, phones have a special meaning. The heart of your family has pumped blood out into the arteries of phones, for many years. The phone news is always bad. You have inherited this telephonic terror. You have the genes of pain. Now you are dialling a number. I don't know who you are calling.

I am tired. I must sleep. Go away, Nadejda. I am tired of waiting for you, of hearing your voice in my head, seeing your imperfect, beautiful face so like your mother's face. I have no rest. I both suffered and rested when you were away, for a few weeks. The distance prevented me from locating you. Just like it was before you came to New Zealand, four years ago. I was calm. But it was a calm before the storm, because I knew you would come. I sensed you approaching.

I'm afraid of you coming. Will you be like your mother? Will you shatter my last hope for being part of your family again? Because I belong there. With you. With Ana. Even with Vassil. I owe them the truth about their mother. They owe me recognition. Nobody is free of debt, except you. That's why you are my only hope, my only Nadejda. I don't know how you'll end up here, on this island, in this town, but you will. You have to. You have to come by your own choice. I won't chase you, because I am immovable. The truth is immovable. It does not follow people; it waits to be found.

Ana cut me out of her life. She had a reason. I haven't seen her since 1975. I stopped existing for her. Mladen too, gave in to her pressure. I was alienated from both. Sounds banal, doesn't it, like a soap opera. I fled. I came here, to forget about them, about my Bulgarian life. But it was like trying to flee from myself. There is no escape from your family. I am tied to you, I can't break free any more than I can flee from myself.

But why am I telling you all this? You can't even hear me. And when you finally do, when you materialise outside my door, I don't know what I'll say to you. 'Hello, Nadejda. I'm Bojan. I've been waiting for you. You don't know me, but I know you. I am an ex-spy for the . . . I was your mother's . . . I was your father's . . . My father saved your . . . I saw the death of your . . . I've been here for twenty-one years, exactly your age. I can see you with my mind. And by the way, I am your father. Welcome to my house.'

I'll have to lie not to drive you away. I'll have to feed you spoonfuls of truth not to poison you. I'll have to violate your innocence — the innocence of ignorance. I'll have to tell you what nobody else has the stomach to tell you.

I can't stop the sound of your heartbeat. I can't erase your image. I see you running down some steps. Walking out of a door, tourists swarming around you. It is as if I'm seeing Ana in another life. Long hair glowing in the night like the copper gypsies once made in Old Plovdiv, hunched in the corners of cobbled streets. Ana and I would go to Plovdiv, stay in bright blue, eighteenth-century house-inns, make love under a copper moon. The neighbours, disturbed, banged on the wall.

Outside, in the brightly lit street, a smart man waits for you. The headlights of late traffic stream past like a river of gold. You shake hands, you smile. Your lips move but I can't hear you. He has a dazzling white smile that lights up his olive-skinned face. You linger there for a while, speaking. You walk along together, then turn round the corner. He opens a door for you. You brush past him.

He is keeping you away from me, I can see that, but I've waited twenty-one years, I can wait another week. No I've waited my entire life. For what? To tell someone, to be free of the burden of history — mine, yours, Ana's, everybody's — that has been crushing my heart since I was four. Sometimes, hearts are not allowed to break. Hearts are crushed.

I must sleep.

Chapter Twenty-three

CHAPTER TWENTY-FOUR

Nadejda and Tarik are sitting
opposite each other.

Where Tarik lives tonight

Nadejda and Tarik are sitting opposite each other. The bar is filling up. 'What would you have done if I hadn't returned your call?' She looks at him without blinking, in a most disconcerting way, she hopes.

He looks at his glass, raising his eyebrows. 'I would have come to look for you.'

'Why?'

'Because I wanted to see you, I guess.' He looks up at her, trying to withstand the hazelnut irradiation of her eyes.

'Why?' She is as strange awake as she is sleepwalking.

'Because I was interested. I wanted to talk to you. Last night, we didn't have much of a talk, really. You gave me a fright.'

Nadejda smiles. Tarik's jagged smile lights up his face in response, and a wave of relief washes over it. He must feel awkward, she thinks. She herself feels strange. Here is a man who is dressed like a yuppie with taste and has the face of a thief: tanned skin, full, ravenous mouth, a nose which would be perfect if it wasn't slightly squashed along the ridge, eyes which defy description — a mes-merising dark green, specked with brown-gold. These are not eyes to be trusted, or to be forgotten. His hair, slicked back, is black, with fine threads of silver.

'And why did you call me back?' A glint of mischief appears in the green eyes. He takes a sip from his wine.

'Because I was interested.'

He smiles. He picks up the irony. It's a good sign, thinks Nadejda. 'I was interested to hear what I did last night, since I don't remember. But now I know.'

'Today, I almost wondered if last night was real — it was so bizarre, I just needed to make sure you really existed.'

'I exist. But sometimes there are degrees of existing.'

'Well, you're lucky to experience degrees. Most people just get the one.'

She's not sure if he is being genuine or ironic. They drink in silence. On the opposite wall, there is a painting of a clown screaming. He is wearing a red and yellow striped costume. His hair is standing up. His eyebrows are raised in horror.

'So, Nadejda. Where are you from? I've been dying to ask you.'

217

'Bulgaria.'

'Bulgaria! I would've never guessed that.'

'I know. Nobody does.'

'Actually, I've met one Bulgarian. In Istanbul, a few years back. He was a porter. He helped transport my new stock.'

'What were you doing in Istanbul?'

'I was there on business. I have a rug business. Oriental rugs. Turkish, mainly. It's my father's business, but I'm a partner.'

'And where is that business based?'

'In Auckland. But we travel all over.'

'And you're not Turkish yourself? Your name's not exactly local.'

'No. It's Turkish. My father is from Istanbul, but I was born and bred a Kiwi.'

His soft, narrow vowels confirm this.

'So your mother is a New Zealander?'

'Yes. Dad came over from Turkey when he was about my age, and set up his trade. At the time, the competition wasn't as vicious as now. Now you can't do that any more. He married Mum soon after he arrived. But what about you? What are you doing here? What do you do?' He sips from his glass. He has a tic: shaking his wrist, to adjust his heavy, expensive watch.

'I'm at university. I'm doing psychology.' Where did that come from? Nadejda is sick of lying, and yet she feels she shouldn't be sincere with this man. She doesn't trust green-eyed people as a rule, but she is drawn to them. It must be the rarity factor.

'Psychology! That would be heavy going.'

The truth is she wanted to impress him — computer science isn't going to blow anyone away. Nadejda wants to blow Tarik away, no more, no less. 'Yeah, it's quite hard in the third year. I'll be fourth year this year.'

'That makes you, let's see, twenty-three?'

'No.' For a second she considers the age lie, to go with the subject lie, but decides there is nothing unglamorous about being twenty-one. 'I'm twenty-one, going on twenty-two.'

'Right. You look younger. Especially asleep.'

She stirs uncomfortably and drinks the red wine. He has seen

218

her asleep. The slightest touch of intimacy from him equals full-blown sexual fury with others. He has the power to induce that dull ache in her chest, just with his looks and mannerisms, with his name even. Tarik. Suddenly, she registers that he is a Turk. No, he could have been a Turk. No, he *is* a Turk — his father is a Turk, that's enough. She has never spoken to a Turk, except in kebab takeaways. And here she is, drinking and being seduced by one.

'How old are you?' Again she fixes him with unblinking eyes; being direct is the best way to counteract intimidation.

He smiles and tilts his head to one side. His teeth are dazzling, but irregular, somehow crammed in his jaw, giving him a predatory look. It is as if he has too many teeth for a human jaw. 'Ah. Never ask a man his age. Men are very vain.'

'I know. I've noticed.' She tries to sound like a connoisseur, but instead she feels like an amateur. He makes her feel like a dilettante of the men-experience.

'I'm thirty. The age of reason.'

He has a way of speaking that tickles her in a melancholic way — a soothing, quiet way, but a tickle nonetheless. Everything he says is a tickle. Sometimes what starts off as a tickle becomes irrepressible arousal. Okay, he says, this is what we have: we have you and me, and we're going to make love, and it'll be okay. This is what Nadejda hears in his voice.

They drink up. 'Are you hungry?'

'I've had dinner,' she lies. After she spoke to her father, she couldn't eat. She had coffee, and watched the sunset bathing the sky in its violent colours, like ink running on a silk scarf.

'Okay.' Part one of the introduction rite is over. They need to shift to a next level of intimacy, but neither dares make that breach.

To prevent him from indulging in the latent sensuality of the moment by saying something seedy like 'Would you like to come to my place?', she asks the first question that comes into her head: 'Where are you set up in Wellington?'

'In the Queen's Wharf shopping centre. You can come see it tomorrow. I've got some new stock.'

'Okay. But if I come, it'll be probably to see you, not the carpets.'

Chapter Twenty-four

He laughs. His eyes send wicked flashes. His hand brushes against hers. 'Is that a proposition?'

'No, it's a warning.'

'That's too bad. I was going to suggest we go to my place, because I have some rugs there too, if you'd like to see them. But now that you're not interested in them . . .'

She laughs. She pushes her chair back and gets up. His eyes glance down at her tightly jeaned thighs.

'Did I offend you?'

A cheap way of demonstrating misplaced sensitivity, Nadejda thinks. She's suddenly annoyed with him, rebelling against this unforeseen seduction by a tradesman Turk, determined not to give in. And yet she feels unable to go away from him, to tear her eyes off this irregular, haunting face, this body she already imagines stripped and moving against her. 'No, not at all. I just want to go and have a rest.'

'Okay.' The multi-purpose, reconciling 'okay'. An agreement, a concession, a frustrated resignation? 'Can I walk you to the hostel?'

'Sure.'

He holds the door open for her again. They walk: not too close, not too far apart.

'How long are you staying for?'

'I don't know. It depends on how long I feel like staying.'

He laughs. 'That's fair enough. How long do you think you might feel like staying?'

'I don't know. Depends.' She looks at him. In the street light his eyes are unnaturally, luminously green. 'What about you?'

'I don't know. Depends,' he shrugs.

'Oh, come on.'

'No, really, it's true. I only tell the truth.' His eyes grow deeper in colour. The outline of his mouth and nose is pure like the outline of desire. Nadejda feels a wetness between her legs. 'Depends how the sale goes. I was thinking of staying till the weekend.'

She nods, disappointed.

'Would you like to do something tomorrow?'

'I *will* do something tomorrow, yes, thank you.'

He laughs. 'You're a smartarse, aren't you. I like that.'

'And I like your laughter.'

'Well, then we're equal. Would you like to do something *with me* then? You could come and see me at the Queen's Wharf, if you like. I'll be there pretty much all day.'

'Yeah, I could.'

'And I've already been warned, so I'll tell my rugs not to get their hopes too high. Because you'll be coming to see *me*, not them.'

She sits in a small waiting area separated from the kitchen by a window, and wonders. Is he a normal rug dealer? She'd like him to be untypical of his trade, not because she has any prejudice against the trade (except that it's a shady business), but because typicality is pitiable. Anton is typical of the philosophy faculty in Sofia, and of his generation of post-communist, intelligent youth — cynical beyond their age and agitated beyond safety. Tony is a typical child of a middle-class Christchurch family gone astray in the mild way such offspring go astray: smoking dope, voting Alliance, a typical arts student with a baffling ignorance of the world north of the South Island. And Nadejda? What is she typical of? Of the chronically sick at heart. Of sleepwalkers. Of shoplifters. Of those who don't believe that being loved is the most important thing — because they have too much of it.

She goes upstairs; the room is empty. She turns the lights off, climbs up into her bed and masturbates frantically to the thought of Tarik burying his face in her neck, Tarik travelling down her body with painful slowness, his hands pressing her thighs around him, the blinding novelty of Tarik's body. Tarik's body is the place where she has always wanted to go, but which hasn't been on the map until now.

She turns the light back on and scribbles on a postcard of Wellington: 'This city is where Tarik lives tonight.'

Then, alarmed by the stupidity of this gesture, she tears the card in half, then in half again, opens the window and lets the pieces go in the wind. They fly towards the sea and soon disappear into the sky puzzle.

Chapter Twenty-four

CHAPTER TWENTY-FIVE

"We are gathered here today"...

Sisyphus

'We are gathered here today . . .'

We are gathered here today to stare at the coffin of Vassil and watch it slide mercilessly between the small curtains, towards the blazing fire of the crematorium. Ana is gathered here today — because she feels as if she must gather the dispersed parts of herself — to think of how Vassil's body burns until it crumbles to ashes and is contained in a small urn.

Ana dispensed with the church service: Vassil couldn't stand priests. But even this is bad enough. Vassil would have hated this. He hated the cliché of formalities. But isn't death the ultimate cliché, the ultimate formality? Death is abstraction. Death doesn't exist. Ana stares at the coffin, numb, emotionless. People in different shades of black sit behind her, filling the small building. It smells of flowers and ash.

Death is the negation of everything that can be defined. Death is a subtraction — that of Vassil, of her mother, of her father — whereby the equation of her life tips over and falls on its back, like a stunned beetle, waving its legs in the air. One morning, she wouldn't be surprised to wake up and find that she has turned into a giant beetle. At least that would be an expression of how things really are: nonsensical. Ana is sick of things carrying on the way they always do, even after the worst happens. People disappear, but everybody else is here. They may be wearing black, Vassil's colleagues may be sniffing and pale, but they are here. They will go back to their families and continue as they always have. The damage always has to be internal. The world is too egotistical to crumble when someone dies. She wants the world to crumble, in tribute to her brother. She wants this town with tidy roofs to crumble as if it were made of old cheese, the stink of death to emanate from these streets where cars are parked neatly as always. Why should the world outlive Vassil? Ah, the humiliating equation of things: the world is everything to us, but we are not everything to the world.

Vassil was her last link with a life nobody else knew and shared. Between them, they flicked through the album of the fractured years, they bowed their heads over its faded snapshots of parents, partings, reunions, lapses, hopes, nightmares of guilt, and, above all, the vicarious cure of New Zealand reality. They held each other up like two frail matches propped against one another at an awkward angle. To stay alive, you have to stand up, somehow. But how?

Peter, Vassil's colleague and friend, clears his throat and puts on his glasses. He is reading from a typed page: 'When Vassil and I first met, fifteen years ago, we were young and innocent.'

A muffled noise rises from the audience — it is appropriate on such occasions to come up with something jovially mellow. Vassil was neither young, nor innocent fifteen years ago. Not that she knew him then. Ana dreads her own speech. She can't really say anything normal or meaningful. She wants to speak about the senseless loss, the absurdity of his death, the fact that nobody knows what he heard before he died, that his niece has gone missing, that he had so much more to do and enjoy. She wants to say things which won't require treating him like a nonentity. 'He was, he loved, he helped, he achieved, he was an extraordinary . . .'

What about 'He hated'? Because Vassil hated a lot of things. He hated priests, for instance. So did their father, according to Vassil. Her mother kept icons at home and prayed, every now and then. When Ana asked her why, her mother said, 'Because I need there to be someone who knows that there is a reason for everything that happens.' Ana had shrugged. She needed to believe that too, but she couldn't. Besides, it was below her dignity to pray, even if she could believe. Bojan, whose mother was also religious, used to joke about that: 'You and I, my dear, are a product of the system; it's been beaten into us that religion is opium for the masses.' Ana protested: it wasn't the system, they chose to be that way. No, said Bojan in his fatalistic voice, we don't choose anything, things choose us. She had laughed and embraced him. At that time, unknown to her, he was already an informer. She was embracing a traitor. Hadn't he *chosen* to denounce people?

Ana tries to look away from the coffin. It is as though her eyes are nails in the coffin — impossible to pull them out. This coffin encloses her loneliness. Loneliness has caught up with her. When she lost Mladen, she felt lonely, but at least she had the comfort of knowing it was his fault. She had Vassil, and of course Nadejda.

Once, when she lost her mother, and had a near-fictitious brother and father, there was Mladen. And of course Nadejda.

Once, further back into the dingy corridor of things past, there was Bojan. She loved, and was loved. She was the least lonely then. She felt she was saved from everything that had happened to the family, from everything that could yet happen — because Bojan knew everything about her, and lived it with her. They were carrying the same burden. But she doesn't want to think about Bojan. Is he still here? Has he gone back to Sofia? When he called, three years ago, she went into shock. She didn't believe it was really him. She hung up. She never told Vassil about him.

Suddenly Ana feels the weight of the coffin crushing her chest: Vassil's unlived life. No, it's not that. It is the weight of the unsaid. She ran out of time to tell Vassil about what happened to the man who saved him and their father, what happened to his son, the irony of events. She would tell herself that she was gathering strength, but she had never gathered enough. She was afraid for Vassil, that he wouldn't take it well. She had thought she was sparing him, when in fact she was depriving him of the truth he had a right to. The truth is expensive, she would tell herself, it shouldn't be administered with a light hand. But now she is paying for her thriftiness. Like Sisyphus she will spend the rest of her days carrying the rock of the unsaid up some foreign hill, only to watch it tumble down from the top. And she will walk back down.

She ran out of time to tell her mother too: who Bojan was, the boy she grew up with, the man she loved for years. She hasn't told anyone. Mladen knows, of course. But Mladen is the outsider, he came too late into the family to be part of it. Mladen has always been out of the picture, but that only became obvious in the last few years, when finally they came apart. And yet they loved each other. From her time with Bojan, through to her life with Mladen, love was the thread with which Ana tried to sow up the torn pieces of her life. Love is not enough. The thread rots away and breaks.

Now it is her turn to speak. She walks up, the piece of paper in her hand, and turns around to face the strangers who are Vassil's friends and colleagues. In the dim light of the white room, everybody looks deathly. The coffin is behind her. For a moment, she is not quite sure why she is here, why this assembly stares at her, expecting her to deliver the goods. She opens her mouth, then glances at the piece of paper.

'I am very aware of the paradox whereby, despite being Vassil's sister, I have known him for a shorter time than most of you. In my adult life anyway.'

What is the point of saying this to strangers? This is for Vassil, not for them. He knows this. She abandons the text and looks above the heads. 'When someone dies, we realise how many things we haven't had time to say to them. Vassil's death was sudden. We had too little time together. We had four years to catch up for forty-four years. We ran out of time. I don't know if we ever would've had the time.'

A vision of Vassil inert in his coffin takes her voice away. She clears her throat.

'Vassil never went back to Bulgaria. After Nadejda and I came out here, he said he had no reason to. But it is my belief that there *was* a reason. I know he would've gone back. If he had a last wish, perhaps it would've been that. But then, he once said that Stewart Island is the home of his mind, and the Pirin mountains in Bulgaria are the home of his heart.'

She is afraid she may run out of voice, of things to say; but she is also afraid she may not be able to stop. Say it all, now when he can't hear. What futile sincerity.

'It is strangely fortunate that, before he died, Vassil was in the process of recording himself on tape.' There is a stir of curiosity. The tape was for Nadejda, yes, but she is not here to hear it — in fact she interrupted that recording forever.

'I can only hope that he died lighter for having said some of what was on his mind and heart for many years. It is my hope that if he had known he would die, at least he would be happy, through his profession, to have made others lighter, too, from their personal burdens.'

Would Sisyphus be happier if he was to run up and down the hill, clutching at somebody else's rock?

Ana returns to her seat, drained. Sweat trickles down the side of her face, although it's cool in the crematorium. But it is the presence of the furnace, only a few metres away, that suffocates her.

The immaculate coffin slides into the opening of the curtains. She can hear the devouring yawn of flames inside the furnace. The coffin is now in their embrace. Vassil is burning. But she can't think of that now, not now.

The congregation rises and walks out, slowly, so slowly. She must make it through the wake.

The undertaker hands her a small, nicely shaped urn. His thick eyebrows are twisted in a single compassionate arch. He looks like a sad puppy. Ana takes the urn and thanks him. In this country, you must thank everyone for everything. The checkout girls in the supermarket for serving you. The stranger for holding a door open for you. The undertaker for handing you your brother's ashes.

Ana drives to Vassil's house, where she has set up a couple of tables. The mourners follow. They have all arrived in couples. They are all people who knew Patricia, when she and Vassil were together.

When she arrives at the house, she realises it was a mistake to have the wake here. She can't face the empty rooms. She can't open her mouth to talk to anyone. But the people follow, cars pull over outside, doors slam, a church bell strikes four times, a dog wails somewhere in the neighbourhood, there is a giant fracture in the quiet afternoon, and as Ana steps into the living room where Vassil was lying, powerful even in his death, she knows the fracture will only keep growing, until it swallows her. There is no one to hold her from falling.

She offers drinks on a tray. People accept them with sad, contained semi-smiles. Ana talks to them or rather she listens to herself talk. She listens to others talk. She has to concentrate very hard to hear and make sense of what they are saying.

'If you need anything, anything at all, please don't hesitate.'

'Do you need any help with the . . .?'

'Yes, what's going to happen with the house?'

'Where is Nadejda? We've been wondering why . . .'

Ana listens to herself lie. Nadejda is still in Bulgaria, with her father. Why didn't she come back for the funeral? Oh, because she couldn't fly out, the airport was shut during the barricades (which are now long gone, but thankfully nobody is up to date with the events there).

Chapter Twenty-five

'That's just terrible. She must be so distraught.'

'Poor kid.'

'She was very fond of him, wasn't she?'

'And he often talked about her.'

'They must have had a special relationship.'

Ana is now breaking out into a cold sweat and shivering. Very special. Nadejda kills uncle dear. Nadejda doesn't bother to call back. Nadejda disappears without a trace, sending her disembodied voice over the Cook Strait, and over the Pacific, like a poisoned arrow. If she doesn't know what happened, she is running on some beach, over some dunes, light with ignorance. She is the opposite of Sisyphus. But if she knows, and is staying away deliberately, she must be standing at the top of a hill, looking down at the fallen boulder, terrified of descending.

The guests gradually disperse. Ana lights a cigarette and closes the curtains again, as they were when she first found him. She puts Vassil's tape in the big stereo. 'Today, the fifth of February, is my New Zealand anniversary. Your grandfather and I arrived in Lyttelton precisely forty-two years ago. Long time ago, huh? I was twenty-one, your age. I am not celebrating.'

She pushes 'stop'. He was twenty-one when he and their father arrived. Nadejda is twenty-one now, when he died. Exactly twenty-one years ago, after Nadejda was born, their mother flew over the Pacific — twenty-one, no, twenty-two years after the two men left Sofia. When Ana was twenty, the Prague spring was happening somewhere far from Sofia. Mladen and Bojan, also twenty, were young recruits in the army, sent over together with the Russian troops to protect the people of Czechoslovakia against criminal elements. When Nadejda was born, Bojan left the country to go to Munich, on a research programme. He ended up here. She never saw him again. He called her. Why didn't he call Vassil, all this time? Only Kaikoura separated them.

But it's all history now. The present presses on. Ana must gather the pieces of herself, like putting on a ragged cloak, and go in search of Nadejda.

She looks out the window. Houses light up as the sky is torn by an inexplicable pink drama, and nothing is a reflection of anything. Her entire life suddenly resonates in a single note — the chiming of the last ray of sun on a window on a house on an island. The glass tinkles with that drop of sun: the note has resounded only once, unknowable, untraceable, and she imagines herself running past houses where families have never known hunger, cold and terror, running after the echo of that single note of the dying sun, chasing it down the row of windows, as if hearing it again will illuminate her, explain everything.

She cups her hand over the small urn; it is pleasantly cold. Inside, her brother's body is a handful of ash. Soon she must climb the highest hill, take this handful and scatter it in the wind that travels over the blue ranges, the wind that knows the reason for everything but never stops to tell.

Chapter Twenty-five

"*Which one do you like best?*"

Punching the canvas

'Which one do you like best?'

Nadejda looks around. Her senses are drenched in reds, blues and greens.

'I don't like so much red. I prefer the blue ones. That one over there is my favourite.' She points to a medium-size turquoise rug, with green and red patterns.

'That one's from south-eastern Turkey. Kurdish. Very beautiful. It describes a scene from an eighteenth-century poem.'

It costs $4700, half-price.

'What's the scene?' The picture is enclosed in a frame of leaves and flowers. There are women with noticeable breasts holding some twigs, and men waving their hands about in the direction of the breasts. It looks like a typical Middle Eastern picture — general merriment with erotic overtones, but nothing really is happening.

Tarik follows her and stands beside her. 'It describes the sexual initiation of a young girl by her husband. She is being watched by older women.'

'What about the other men?'

'I'm not sure, really. I suppose they're making sure he's doing the job properly. Not cheating or anything.'

He raises his eyebrows with a semi-curious, semi-amused tilt of the head. He studies the picture. Nadejda is not sure how to react. At least he's not dropping a hint — that would have been very tasteless. But Tarik has taste.

'So, are you interested?'

'No.'

He smiles. They are standing on the edge of the rug, each firmly planted on a different rug, their arms crossed, as if ready for defence. 'Actually,' he says, 'this is a funny one, because normally in Muslim art they're not supposed to depict human faces.'

'And why is this one an exception?'

'I don't know, to tell you the truth. I don't know. It was delivered from Turkey but it's very unusual. That's why it's so expensive, because it's a bit of a freak.'

He laughs. His laughter gives Nadejda goose-pimples.

'Don't you like it any more?'

'I don't like poetry.'

Chapter Twenty-six

'Okay.' He moves over to another rug, in brownish reds, hanging on the wall. 'How about this one?'

It has the disturbed colours of menstruation, but Nadejda keeps this to herself.

A young couple are looking at a rug in the far corner. 'Excuse me,' says Tarik, 'I'd better tend to the customers.'

He slides off in their direction. Nadejda watches him. His body is perfect. He approaches the couple with seriousness and ease. His hair is carefully slicked back, but a lock of black hair overshadows his eye. She can see the two bays of slightly receding hair. Maybe he will be bald in a few years' time. She is afflicted with desire. Maybe he is a despicable sleaze. Her body tingles. Maybe he is a shady pawn in a shady business. She can feel the throbbing vein in her throat. Tarik is so beautiful that she wants to contemplate him before she can touch him. But she knows she will want to touch him — it is in the nature of female desire to always want to touch, Anton said (but he couldn't keep his hands off her). And what is in the nature of male desire, she would like to know?

Tarik returns after the couple have signed some papers.

'I'm going to go now,' she says.

'Already? But you didn't buy anything!' He looks at her with pretend disappointment. They are standing by his desk. Nadejda feels the weight of her hair on her back. She longs for him to lift it up, drape it over his arm. His mobile rings. He picks it up: 'Excuse me.' He exchanges a few uninteresting words with the caller and ends with, 'Yep. Sure thing. Ciao.' And to her, 'Sorry about this. A call from Auckland.'

'Okay,' she says, 'I'll leave you to it.'

'I'd rather you didn't, but tell you what. How about dinner tonight?' He sits on top of his desk, his thigh muscles visible through the linen of his trousers.

'Tonight,' Nadejda says, looking away from his thigh, as if deliberating.

'I hope you haven't got something planned already.'

'Well I do, but it's okay. I can do that some other time. I was supposed to be at some friends' place for dinner.'

'That's funny, because I'm supposed to be at my mother's place for dinner tonight as well.'

'I thought your parents were in Auckland.'

'My mother's here. They're separated, like yours.' He grins, without a trace of sadness. Perhaps he's used to it. Perhaps he doesn't love his parents as much as she does.

'How about I pick you up at six-thirty?'

'Okay. See you tonight then.'

'See you tonight, Nadejda. Bye.'

Ah, Nadejda, so well pronounced, Nadejda in his mouth. The last thing she sees of him is his forearm, tanned and wiry under the rolled-up linen sleeve, his large veined hand leaning on the desk surface.

She flees out into the wider Wharf shopping centre. She feels Tarik's eyes burning greenly on her back, down her jeaned legs, and back up again, messing up her hair. She walks out into a bath of sun with a spinning head. She doesn't know where she is. On one side, the harbour; on the other, the city. She inhabits a thin strip in between. She can reach out and touch either, but she doesn't need to. She only wants to touch Tarik.

Nadejda dials the number of Maria's parents. She realises that it's impossible to visit them. She couldn't bear to lie all evening to them while eating their food and smiling to them. Maria's parents are both civil engineers, and although they are generous and full of good intentions, their materialism and candid racism irritate Nadejda.

'In Zimbabwe, you could live like a white man,' said Maria's father once, at a party. 'If you don't have a swimming pool, your neighbours don't speak to you. The standards are different. It's a life. Here, there's bloody equality everywhere. I'm sick of equality. We've had enough equality in Bulgaria, forty-five years of it. All equally poor. Thanks very much.'

'Why don't you go back to Zimbabwe then, to live like a white man?' Nadejda said rudely.

'Because I wanted a proper education for my kids. And things weren't exactly peaceful there.'

'Why don't you go back to Bulgaria then?' Nadejda interrupted.

Chapter Twenty-six

'Ah, my dear girl.' He stroked her arm with an ironic smirk. 'That's the trick, you put your finger on it. We can't go back. Once you leave that place, there's no going back. You miss it, you cry your eyes out, but you can't go back.'

'Why not? If you're not happy anywhere else . . .' Nadejda was only eighteen at the time and things seemed simpler . . .

'Well, if you're not happy, then . . .' His smirk had died. He rattled the ice in his whisky. 'Then you've got to move on. But you can't go back. They have driven us all out. The blossom of the nation. The best minds. Do you know that in the last few years, five percent of the population of Bulgaria have left the country? And eighty percent *want* to leave. That tells you something.'

'Hello, it's Nadejda here.'

'Hi Nadejda! Nice to hear from you. You're coming tonight?'

'Well, that's why I'm calling. I'm leaving tonight. I can't come. I'm sorry, I know I told Maria I'd come, but . . .'

'You're leaving so soon! Are you going straight to Christchurch?'

'No, actually, I'm thinking of going to . . . Nelson. For a couple of days.'

'Nelson? It's a lovely place. Not very exciting, but beautiful. Who are you staying with?'

'I don't know anyone, I'll stay in a hostel.'

'You should've stayed with us here, you should've called us earlier, it's just such a shame. How are your mum and uncle?'

'They're good, yeah.'

'Give them my love. Tell your mum I'll write to her. It's been ages. Now, in Nelson, you should go and see Bojan Dimov, this guy we know. He's been here for aeons. He's quite interesting, so if you've got nowhere to stay, or nothing to do . . . I think he lives in town. I'll go find the address.'

Nadejda sighs with boredom. She's not going to visit any Bojan — why should she. He's probably an old bore with grown-up Kiwi kids who have professions like mechanics and forestry. Anyway, she had no intention of going to Nelson at all.

'Does he live with his family?' she asks when Maria's mother returns.

'No, he's alone. He doesn't have a family.'

That's even worse — he's even more certain to be a bore.

'He works in an antiques shop. He's got a lot of junk but some really quite exotic things.'

Nadejda says thanks, goodbye and hangs up. She has no intention of going to Nelson. She intends to have sex with Tarik, and she can see no further than his imperfect face and perfect body. He is the wall that separates her from the days to come, but she has no desire to climb over that wall; she wants only to lean her naked body on it.

Nadejda is wearing green mascara and lip gloss — make-up she wears only on special occasions. In the candlelight, the long, green lashes emphasise the amber of her eyes. She has a loosely cut, thin angora top a size too big (a present from her aunt in Plovdiv), which allows for a bit of cleavage — also a rare indulgence. She catches Tarik glancing at her cleavage absent-mindedly whenever he bares his superb teeth in laughter. His hair is particularly sleek tonight — it looks as though it has Brilliantine in it, which Nadejda finds hilarious after two glasses of wine. She wants to feel his hair, to find out what makes it so shiny and black.

'How's your lamb?' He leans over and looks into her plate. She enjoys the proximity of his face to her plate. The lamb steak is a temporary substitute for her body. He looks at it with the hunger with which he would look at her naked body. 'It's quite rare, isn't it?'

'How did it go today after I left?' she asks. 'Did you sell any more?'

'No no, but one's enough. One's good.'

'Really?'

'Yeah. I had another potential customer, but she didn't like anything.'

'Then how do you know she was a potential customer?'

'Because she looked at the rugs. She looked at one in   235 particular, a really beautiful one, Kurdish, depicting a scene from a poem. But she didn't like poetry, so that was a disappointment.'

Nadejda smiles impishly. She is struggling with a forkful of rebellious salad. She chews before she can reply. 'Why? Do you like poetry?'

'I don't read much of it, but I like some old love poems.'

She stares at him. 'Kurdish ones?'

'Oh, any, really. And why don't you like poetry?'

'I find it, what's the word, precious. It's precious, over the top. Poetry doesn't allow for things to appear in their true light. Poetry kills meaning, it's gratuitous.'

'Well! You obviously know what you like and what you don't.' He takes a bite from the tender pink salmon, and chews. His jaws protrude slightly. The top buttons of his shirt are undone, but there's no hair. Nadejda is puzzled by this. She wants to check why he has no hair up to his neck. Suddenly, her throat contracts and she can't swallow. She can feel his knee against hers. It might be accidental — but it's not. He puts his fork and knife down and dabs his lips with the white napkin. Nadejda becomes acutely aware of the large surrealist paintings on the restaurant walls: distressed Cyclops and three-armed, sharp-breasted women with hyena faces. She doesn't move her leg. But he moves his. 'Sorry,' he says, with no repentance in his eyes, but no playfulness either.

'Any time.'

He smiles and this time his jagged white teeth and the tilt of his head make Nadejda go limp from the waist down, but she chews on. Having dinner before a desire has been consummated is a commonplace cannibalism. Food and sex. The first can symbolise the second. But the second can't symbolise the first. What does sex symbolise? Nothing. It's the only human endeavour which is simply itself. Does that give it the special status of immutable things, such as death? Nadejda would like to discuss this with Tarik, but not now.

'Do you have a girlfriend?' Nadejda wants to give their conversation some edge.

He is taken by surprise. But he remembers to smile. 'No.'

It is the simplicity of his reactions in sexy tandem with the self-control of his secretiveness that Nadejda finds so beguiling. She expects a similar question, but it doesn't come. He doesn't care about her availability. He already assumes she's available.

'Do you have a wife?'

'No.'

He is no longer surprised — he's entering the spirit of the game.

'That's a shame. I find taken men attractive.'

She has never considered a taken man. Obviously, this is going to be the Year of the Lie. Why, why does she do this? Because she thrives on provocation. Because nobody else will say this. Because she is afraid of the truth, any truth.

'That *is* a shame. But for you, I'll be married. And with a girlfriend. If that's all it takes.' He is amused, but there's a reconciling air about him. He is decisively mellow. Perhaps it isn't lust after all. Perhaps he's a genuinely mellow man. Is that because he's a New Zealander, or because he's Turkish? What is he? She'd like to ask him this.

'It takes much more than that,' she says.

'I can see that. I can see you have high standards. Because you're perceptive.' His expression is fake. His voice is fake. He is screwing his eyes with fake acumen. He raises his glass, with casual elegance.

'To Bulgaria.'

It's his way of saying, 'To Nadejda.'

'To Wellington,' she replies, clinking his glass, but then realises he's an Aucklander and this is not an equivalent toast. But it is a toast for them meeting here.

'Actually, there is a reason to toast,' she says. 'The other day the communist government in Bulgaria resigned.'

'Didn't you have a democratic government?'

'For a while we did, then the communists came into power again. Except they called themselves socialists, to fool the enemy.'

'You mean the West?'

'No, the people.'

'Okay.'

'What about Turkey? Do you follow the political situation there?'

237

'Not really. I keep up with the business side of things, mainly.'

'We have a large Turkish minority in Bulgaria.'

'Do you?' His interest is polite.

'We were a Turkish province for five centuries.'

'No kidding! The whole country? You probably don't like the Turks very much then. I mean, think of what happened in Yugoslavia. It was all based on ancient hatred. Are Bulgarians Christians?'

'Yes. Eastern Orthodox.'

'So is there still tension between Muslims and Christians, I mean Orthodox — whatever?'

'Yeah, sort of. It's too complicated to explain. There was a nasty policy a few years back, when the government made all people with Turkish names change them to Bulgarian ones. We thought it was done peacefully at the time, but recently government archives have revealed that it was done by violence. There was desecration of graves too.'

'That's nasty.'

'Oh yes. But otherwise the people get on fine. Although, I don't know, there's always a fear that the Turks have aspirations towards us, like once before. People have a secret fear of them.'

For a moment, they fiddle with their napkins. Nadejda feels depressed. 'But the whole drama is, you see, that many of the Turks in Bulgaria aren't actually Turkish.'

'What are they?'

Tarik is getting tired of this, she can tell. He sighs and leans his elbows on the edge of the table, like a conscientious student.

'They're actually Bulgarian.' Nadejda enjoys knowing things. He nods blankly.

'They used to be Bulgarian, but under the Turkish occupation they were forced to convert to Islam. Now they're, well, they don't know what they are. They're called Pomaks. They are Muslims but speak Bulgarian.'

'That *is* complicated,' Tarik says, hoping to put a timely end to the explanation.

'Anyway.'

'So, there's ancient hatred there as well,' he tries to recapitulate.

'Yes, of course.'

So he pays the bill and they walk out. Nadejda feels that all this time she's been oppressed by the surrealist paintings. They live in the restaurant, those desolate mutants; the diners are mere shadows passing in and out.

Outside, in the light breeze, she is faced with the blank canvas of the night. She must fall right through it, with Tarik; that will be their joint artwork — a punch in the canvas. Abstract, yet concrete. On the other side, there will be some revelation. There must be.

It is in the nature of sexual desire to expect the resolution of all life's torments and questions to lie in the moment of its consummation. Two slender, tall figures walking along the waterfront hand in hand have discovered the fallacy of this expectation, time after time. But only one of them thinks that tonight might be an exception.

239

*From Tarik's apartment, Nadejda
sees a blotch of spilt ink nesting
among the dark swellings of the
mountains.*

The moment's blood

From Tarik's apartment, Nadejda sees a blotch of spilt ink nesting among the dark swellings of the mountains. It seems to grow, pushing the hills outwards. The city twinkles under the dome of the sky like a caveful of glow-worms.

Nadejda is holding a thick glass of Scotch. Every time she lifts the glass, not so much drinking as bathing her tongue and lips in the burning gold, the ice cubes rattle heavily and pleasantly. Tarik stands behind her, with a matching rattling drink. She can hear him breathe. She is weak from the proximity of his mouth to her nape.

'I stay here whenever I come down. It's actually my brother's place — he's overseas for a few weeks.'

'Is he in the rug business too?'

'Yes. Sort of.'

Tarik is succinct in his replies. She doesn't mind. She ought to be looking around the lounge, inspecting all the small trinkets that give a home its character, but she doesn't care. The place is large, spacious and rather empty. There is nothing indigenous about it, it is wealthy and modern in a dispassionately tasteful way. Only the carpet — must be Turkish — injects colour and vibrancy into the room.

'Where is that from?' She points to a large charcoal and water-colour drawing of a stunning, dark-nippled nude in a provocative pose: she is sitting on a bed, leaning back on her arms, her small breasts pointing up aggressively, her world-weary face immobile, a corner of her mouth creased in contempt. One long, fleshy leg is stretched out, the other propped up on the bed's edge. Her elegant foot resting against her thigh conceals her genitals.

'That's my brother's girlfriend, Leah.'

'Who's the artist?'

'My brother.'

'He's a brilliant artist.'

'You think so? Yes, I guess he is. He sells work too. He's particularly good with nudes.'

Tarik seems absent-minded about his brother. Nadejda stares at the drawing, fascinated, while he puts some music on. Her heart can't stop its senseless race. Normally, two glasses of wine and a Scotch would make her head spin a little, but she feels unnaturally

241

lucid. Everything is precise and clear. Tarik's features are tattooed on her retina, his movements around the room are relaxed and well-measured, like the Miles Davis blues emanating from the expensive stereo.

Tarik walks towards her. He puts his glass on the coffee table; she does the same with hers. He kisses her lips without touching her. It feels odd. She doesn't touch him either. Then his hand slides under the shiny falls of her hair and strokes her neck and nape. His other hand does the same. Then he stabs her hair with his fingers and combs it down, flipping it over her shoulders like a cloak. 'You have the most amazing hair,' he whispers.

Nadejda stands very still. The warmth of his agile hands sends shivers down her back. She feels her body dissipating into a wet heap. He bends slightly and places his lips on her collar-bone. Then, very slowly, his face brushing against her fluffy top, he kneels. Her hands find themselves on the sides of his face, digging into the collar of his shirt, feeling his smooth back. One button comes undone. She slides her hands down his chest as she descends onto her knees. Another button goes. These are intelligent buttons. He pulls her to him, sitting on his heels, so that she bestrides him with her knees and envelops his neck with her arms. He is her love-chair. Her hair casts a shadow over their faces. His eyes are very dark, the green almost eclipsed by the spilling ink of his dilated pupils; the ridge of his nose seems more acute in this light. They kiss. His hands press her back, slip under the soft material and feel her skin, up to her bra. She can feel the lump in his trousers beneath her. His kisses move down her neck and semi-uncovered shoulders. His hands skilfully undo her bra. His shirt is undone, almost by itself, the buttons surrendering to a mere thought on Nadejda's part. She presses feverish lips to his chest, like a desert wanderer dying of thirst who finally stumbles into a spring. He has little chest hair, and she is charmed to find it is silver-grey, with only a few remaining black ones. His nipples are dark and hard. He has more flesh than she expected. She pulls the shirt from his shoulder and glues her face to the warm skin. He is cupping her breasts under the top. He lowers his face down her front and pulls her top down together with the bra-straps, revealing her tanned, sharp shoulders, her full, round breasts with erect nipples, her ribs. She peels his shirt from his arms and discards it like an old skin. They freeze for a moment, contemplating each other with tremulous disbelief, their senses saturated to the point of bursting. Nadejda senses that this is a moment not unlike the one before an important operation, when the surgeon stands, scalpel in hand, and contemplates the body before the first incision is made. Or it is like the moment before the sun sets on a summer night, round and serene before it dives out of sight? What is it they are about to perform: an act of sex or an act of violence?

They kiss again. He buries his skilled hands into the back of her trousers. She holds his waist. A slight bulge of skin folds over his tight belt — it isn't fat, she quickly establishes, just skin. She tries to undo his belt, but it's a complicated belt with a tricky buckle. She struggles. He undoes it with one deft flick of the hand. His face has taken on the urgent grimace of desire. If she were to resist now, he would take her anyway. Not that she'd dream of resisting. But the thought of him taking her anyway, regardless of her desires, suddenly chills her. She searches his face. He has another face now — the face whereby yearning merges into action, desire into determination, the charmer into the beast of sex, the man who is in control into the man who loses himself, who can only go one way — forward. But she notes this in just a fraction of a second, because she is swamped by the profound sense of having found the lover she has missed all this time. She looks at his face twisted with desire, his body breathing and living against hers, and all the others vanish. They are all thin dust that she blows from the canvas to reveal his picture.

He scoops her up and carries her to the bedroom. She has always wanted to be carried.

There is a soft glow in one corner, some kind of red lava-lamp. The sheets are exotic but stylised — dark blue elephants stomping on ivory ground. He throws her on the bed and bends over her, burying his face in her neck, between her breasts, licking a small path down to her navel, pulling her pants down, kissing her hips, the inside of her thighs, the wetness between her legs. Nadejda still feels inordinately lucid — these elephants, the dark blue of the curtains, the ugly print on the wall, the built-in wardrobes with mirrors, she is registering everything. And yet she is completely immersed in his fragrant warmth, in the precise hallucination of skin against skin,

243

mouth against mouth, mouth against skin, mouth on nipple, hand on hip, hand between legs, fingers in mouth, tongue inside her, the look, touch, smell, sound of a dazzlingly foreign body, each little detail crying for exploration, the total flooding of the senses to the point where they begin to hurt and whimper, the unendurable pleasure, the tense, savage joy of imminent possession, the world spinning around their two knotted bodies with its galloping elephants, red flowing lava, distant guttural saxophones, amber flashing in crystal caves, pools of ink, no, lava, spilling towards them, catching them up, lapping at their feet, though it's not ink, nor lava, it's something else, it rushes upon her, it's an incandescent body, heavy like lead, quick like light, melting inside her and she melts with it, she spills with it, she's a scream spreading over the tops of high glaciers where nobody can hear, or the whole world can hear, she's a ball of pleasure rolled in the hands of love, water stirred by the perfect finger, she is hit by something so hard it is soft, so close it is not here, so absolute it is violent, so perfect it is falling apart, so fleeting she wants to kill it, and then it's over.

They kiss. Their kiss has the bitter breath of post-rapture. Tarik suddenly becomes too heavy. They roll over. She lies on top of him, staring at his face. His eyes close; he is out of breath. She feels that they can never say another word to each other. They exist only in silence. The saxophone dies. The elephants on the creased sheets look crooked. The red of the lava-lamp hurts her eyes.

'You are terrific,' he says, opening his eyes which are once again green.

There is such cold melancholy in his voice, such distance in the green, murky glow of his beautiful eyes, as though he is a bad actor rehearsing a line. Nadejda is pierced by a sense of déja-vu. She stares at him, trying to identify it, trying to remember that other man, in that other time, those green eyes. Bridges. The thunder of a river below. She remembers. She is stunned. The vicious green eyes, the girl flying off the cliff, her face staring up at the viewer as the current carries her away. 'Kalinna, you faithless bitch,' says the voice, and the green eyes laugh.

'Are you okay?' he asks, brushing away some hairs stuck to her damp cheek.

244

She flinches like a scared animal. She stares at him, unable to shake off that momentary impression. It's absurd. It's a mistake. It's a film she saw years ago. It was filmed on location in the Wondrous Bridges area, Turks converting Christians. Rape, torture. She licks her dry lips — there is a sour taste in her mouth. She nods and falls back on the heap of pillows. It's nonsense to see things in this dramatic light — the victim, the oppressor. This is an atavistic echo, the halter of history tugging at her neck. Wake up, Nadejda, snap out of it! This is the late twentieth century.

Gathering her strength, she turns to look at him. His eyes are tender. She enlaces his neck with one arm and kisses him on the ear, ordering her body to stay calm.

'It was wonderful,' she whispers into his fragrant ear. It's the first sincere thing she has said in days, it seems. He presses her against him and kisses her hair. He pulls the covers over them — a herd of elephants rush towards her. They lie in each other's arms, very quietly.

Tarik is sleeping peacefully; the grace of his waking self hasn't abandoned him. His face seems innocent in sleep, like all faces.

Nadeja feels that nothing bad can happen now. The world takes on a new simplicity, a harmony of forms, colours and meaning, which fills her with euphoria. Everything has to be the way it is. She wants to cry this out, her words to travel across the bay outside. She wants to run along the waterfront, go back to her mother and reassure her that everything has to be the way it is, everything is fine. Shake her uncle, shake the gloom out of him, the guilt. Pull her father's beard and sing to him, in the juicy voice of Edith Piaf, 'Non, je ne regrette rien.' Dance with Anton in the moonlight, and with all the other students, take off their T-shirts in the cold and wave them about. Slap Tony on his unshaven face: 'Wake up, there's so much more to life than dope.' Make her grandfather's broken jaw rattle with laughter. And the gulls will screech in accompaniment, pies dropping out of their beaks.

She flips the covers and gets out of bed. She needs to move, to expand, to fill the night, to burst out of this apartment. She wants to call everyone. She looks at the time. Doesn't matter it's five in the

245

morning. She'll call her mother to say she's okay, she's here, she's happy. And her uncle. And her father. Tell them where she is, no more lies, she doesn't need to lie any more.

She pulls her pants on, her top, and her shoes, leaving her bra behind. She can't be constrained by such things now. She checks the bedroom once more — Tarik hasn't moved. She opens and closes the front door very carefully. She runs down the four flights of stairs, to the ground floor, pushes the red button on the wall and exits.

Nadejda walks along the water — it has the faded colour of dried ink. It has stopped expanding. The sky begins to breathe light in. Boat masts sway although there is no breeze — the ink too, is coming back to life. At five in the morning, the city flickers its eyelashes in the grips of REM sleep.

She recognises the painted blue bird with a red beak and flippers — she has arrived at the hostel. The door is locked. There's a sign saying they open at eight in the morning. It's dark inside, with no sign of life. She should have known.

She sits on the step and looks up. The moon is nowhere to be seen. Suddenly, she is tired. She must be the only one awake in this ghost city. She can't remember what day it is. She locks her arms around her legs and leans her chin on her knees. She is too tired to go and look for a street telephone. She'll call her mother in the morning. She'll go back to Tarik in the morning. He'll be waiting for her with coffee and breakfast. They'll make love, they'll go to the rug sale where she'll be his assistant, they'll make love again, and again. Then he'll invite her to go and live with him in Auckland, in his luxury apartment.

But she wants to stay here. She can't admit this to herself, but she wants to stay here, in the space of this weekend and this bay, because this is the only space where she and Tarik can exist. The student with the rug dealer. The Bulgarian with the Turk. The Bulgarian with the New Zealander. The outsider with the local. Tarik. What a strange name. What does it mean? Nadejda means Hope. Every name must mean something.

246

*

RECONNAISSANCE

'We were outsiders in Deli Orman,' her mother told her once, 'and the Turks were the locals. In our country, we were the outsiders. But they were kind.'

When the name-changing policy was implemented among the Turkish population, Nadejda's mother was distraught. 'How can they do that? It's humiliating to those people. You've been called Mahmud all your life, and suddenly you have to be called Mikhail.'

Her father chewed thoughtfully.

'All governments have stupid policies. It's unnecessary, but what's it to you?'

'What's it to me? Do you know that when Mum and I were deported to Deli Orman, these people saved us? They put us up, they fed us, they found Mum a job. They didn't have to do it, but they had good hearts. The Turks were human to us when our own had abandoned us. Now who will stand up for these people? They have no rights in this country. The Turks never have any rights.'

Mladen sighed, dabbing his mouth with a napkin. 'You're right. What they did to you and your mother, they're doing to the Turks now. Taking your house away amounts to taking your name. It's the same thing all over again. And they're getting away with it again.'

Her mother collected the dinner plates, rattling them angrily, and turned off the TV news. 'Bastards,' she said.

Nadejda sat in her chair, eating her vanilla dessert, trying to understand. She was ten. She'd never heard that word in her mother's mouth. Were some names worse than others, to be changed like that? What if a person didn't want to change their name? Did they force him to? She imagined being forced to change her name. What would she be if she wasn't Nadejda? Nothing. She would be nothing because she could only be Nadejda.

A red van pulls over on the road. Nadejda snaps out of her reverie. Tarik gets out and comes over. He is wearing a white sweatshirt over his creased trousers. His beauty hurts Nadejda like a slap in the face.

'Are you all right? What are you doing here?'

247

'I'm, I'm waiting for the door to open.'

She sounds mad. He must think she's mad. He crouches in front of her. 'I thought you'd gone sleepwalking. I was worried. You're not asleep right now are you?'

'No.'

'Why did you leave?'

'I was, I went for a walk and, I, I couldn't go back because the doors are locked.'

'Well of course they're locked at night.' He shakes his head disapprovingly and gets up, not understanding.

'Okay. Come with me. We'll go back to bed.'

She gets up, feeling heavy. They get in the van, and she falls asleep immediately.

And it's that first night all over. Tarik watches the copper-haired stranger asleep in the seat next to him, and wonders what this means. It is as though he has never known her wakeful self, as though this is a repeat. She has talked to him, but she has talked as if through her sleep. He has no time for such complications. It's already bad enough that he is involved with Leah. His brother comes back in two weeks. He has no time for this girl — she is too weird, and he's leaving town soon anyway.

He carries her to the lifts and then inside the apartment. He puts her to bed, carefully undressing her. She has a real gift for sleeping. When he removes her clothes, he remembers why he took the trouble of going out into the night to look for her. He lies beside her, tortured by lust, feeling her smooth body with one hand: the curve of the small hip, the flat belly, the round, perfectly full breasts — an exciting surprise in such a pure-faced girl, the exact opposite of the girlish chest and provocative face of Leah. He places his lips on the outer curve of her breast. Her faint musk smell adds to his arousal. She stirs. He touches her hair, rubs it in his fingers, buries his face in it. The texture is silky. He puts his hand on her throat and slowly moves it down, between her breasts, over her stomach, his thumb touching the left hipbone, his little finger — the right one. She stirs again, with a distant moan. He kisses her neck, gently stroking her. She semi-opens her eyes and stretches pleasurably. Her hands search his body. He gets a condom. He lifts her towards him

248

while getting up on his knees. Sit on this prickly chair. She descends on his lap and a veil falls over his eyes.

Nadejda wakes up in a naked body, next to another naked body. She looks at the time: twenty past nine. She looks at the man's face. A bright stain of blood blossoms on the pillow among the elephants. His breathing nostrils are thinly coated in dried blood.

Nadejda strains to remember last night. They made love, but how many times? She walked along the bay, but why? He came looking for her and brought her back here, but what did he feel for her? Something extraordinary has happened, and nothing has been a dream.

Looking at this man, his tanned arms, chest, face, his black hair sprinkled with silver, she understands that violence occurs when you are making love, not when you have sex — violence is the desperation of the future loss, the desperation to create eternity out of flesh that spends itself too soon, flesh that cannot be replaced. Violence is wanting this weekend to stretch beyond all the weeks to come. Holding the moment of beauty, when life beyond the body doesn't exist, when the body is asleep, so that it doesn't vanish. That is the function of sleep — to keep us from vanishing.

Nadejda lies still, contemplating Tarik's face which is enduring its own quiet violence. Only the face can perform beauty's trick par excellence: the savage coercion of the viewer into love. She can't stop looking at him, she can't stop the ebbing tide of her heart. If this moment was a heart, and if time could swell to the point of rupture, Nadejda would want to be spattered with the moment's blood.

Chapter Twenty-seven

CHAPTER TWENTY-EIGHT

Ana dials a Wellington number.
For a while now she hasn't been in
contact with the Toshevs.

The burnt colours of summer

Ana dials a Wellington number. For a while now she hasn't been in contact with the Toshevs. She hasn't missed them since they left for the North Island. She'd rather not call them now, but she has to. If anyone knows anything, it would be them. Nadejda has no other friends her age in Wellington except Maria.

'Hello. Eli, it's Ana, from Christchurch.'

'Ana! My God! It's providence! I've just been talking about getting in touch with you, and there you are.'

'How's things?'

'Good, I guess. Shouldn't complain, really. And how about you? I talked to Nadejda yesterday, she seems to be having a good time by herself. She was going to come round for dinner last night, but she changed her mind. I guess we're boring for her. Maria saw her though. She's just come back from Sofia, right?'

'Yeah. So, what did she say?'

'Well, not much. She left last night, for Nelson.'

'For Nelson? What is she going to do there?'

'I don't know. I mean, she really didn't say much.'

'What was she doing in Wellington?'

'Ana! Haven't you talked to her recently?'

'Actually, no. She talked to her uncle, but he didn't live to tell me what she said.'

'What?'

'Look, Eli, I need to know where Nadejda is. Vassil died three days ago. Nadejda hasn't called for over two weeks. I don't know what's happening.'

'Jesus! Ana, my dear, that's, that's just horrific.'

Yes it is, it is. Ana needs a shoulder to cry on, but she has only a phone with the voice of a friend who is no longer a friend. Friendship is not measured by the degree of shock and pity in the face of horrific events — you don't have to be a friend to be shocked or feel pity. Ana's friends in Bulgaria have faded away — by not writing, only sending the occasional Christmas card. Her friends here often turn out to be circumstantial, like Eli — as soon as they leave for the North Island or Australia, it is as though they never leaned together over full ashtrays and confessional cups of bitter coffee, bemoaning the loss of home, friends and family, the

251

plight of their country, the shortcomings of the adoptive one.

'Hold on, does Nadejda know about Vassil?'

'I don't know. I don't know what she knows.'

'My God! That's unbelievable! She didn't say anything, but she did sound a bit weird, as though she was unsure of something. She sounded strange, like she was in a hurry to leave.'

'Did she say where she was going to stay in Nelson?'

'Well, I suggested she contact this guy we know, Bojan Dimov. He lives in Nelson, and might be able to put her up so that she doesn't have to pay for accommodation. He's a nice man.'

'Bojan!'

'Yes. Do you know him?'

Bojan! Of course, he lives there. He still lives there. Impossible to keep him away from Nadejda in this tiny country. It had to happen. She was naïve to ignore the chances of them meeting, one way or another. 'A land like the palm of a hand,' the communist poet sang once, 'but I don't need you to be any bigger.' But she does. She listens to herself ask for Bojan's address. The street number, the phone number, a surreal enquiry after a lifetime of — what? Confusion. Grudges. Regrets. Torments of silence.

Eli suggests that Ana come up to stay with them, to get away from it all. Ana declines politely. She has nothing left to get away from.

She throws some basic things into a bag, along with Vassil's mobile. She hasn't cancelled his number yet. She hasn't touched his things because sorting them would be like putting a seal on Vassil's life. She gets into her car and drives out to the motorway. She has no clear plan of action. In fact, she suspects she may be making a mistake, but if she doesn't do something she will go insane. Driving up to Nelson is the only thing she can think of doing.

The last time she called Bojan was in 1974 to tell him she was pregnant but wasn't going to keep the child, because she didn't want to have a child that could be his — the child of a communist pawn, even if there was only a speck of a chance. She meant it. She hung up. Stupid revenge — for what? She too was a pawn of communism's stupid ironies. He kept calling, writing, imploring her to keep the child. Then he disappeared. Ana had Mladen's child. She had no choice anyway. Has she ever had a choice? Has any one of them ever had a choice? Vassil, Bojan, her mother and father, those washed up on this island, and those who didn't make it. And Nadejda? What are her choices?

Chapter Twenty-eight

CHAPTER TWENTY-NINE

*At the central Sofia Post Office a
bored, shivering employee is
browsing through large piles of
mail waiting to be picked up by
the courier van and taken to the
airport.*

Lunch break

At the central Sofia Post Office a bored, shivering employee is browsing through large piles of mail waiting to be picked up by the courier van and taken to the airport. It's far more interesting to look at the incoming mail — exotic envelopes and stamps, pretty cards and hilarious photographs — but today she is stuck at this desk, so she makes the best of it. Let's see, what do our fellow countrymen send and where? She flicks through the motley collection. It gives her a special thrill to handle strangers' mail, the outpourings of their hearts, their secrets, their photos, lovingly sealed and addressed, stamped and kissed goodbye. White birds of hope flying to Italy, France, Australia, Portugal, Sweden, South Africa, Morocco, America, America, America, Japan, Turkey, Germany, New York (country missing), Canada, Austria, Czech Republic, Hungary, Botswana, America, America, New Zealand. New Zealand? That's rare. She's never seen a letter to New Zealand. She has seen one from there, but not in that direction.

> *Nadejda Taneva*
> *52 Pacific Street*
> *Christchurch 1*
> *New Zealand.*

Okay, and the sender is another Tanev. Brother? Husband? Distant cousin? Son? What would anyone do in New Zealand, she wonders. All that way — she wouldn't do it, personally. She'd rather stay here, in this hole, than have to leave everyone behind and land on that island in the middle of nowhere. Then again, it must be so exotic there. She saw a film recently, she can't remember the title, which was shot in New Zealand. Stunning, definitely impressive. She unseals the envelope. A hasty nail makes an ugly tear. Never mind, she'll Sellotape it afterwards. She picks up a forgotten cigarette still shedding its ashes in a coffee saucer. She opens the thin rustling paper and reads:

> *My dear Nade,*
> *I have just heard the news about your uncle. I am so sorry.*
> *I don't know where you are, but I tell myself that you're safe, and that furthermore you have your reasons. Please call me when you get this letter.*
> *I spoke to your mother today. She called, asking for you. At first,*

I thought she was playing some game. But this time she wasn't. I don't know what happened between you and Vassil on the phone. This family is cursed by weak hearts. I want you to make sure your mother gives up smoking. She is far too stressed now. It must seem strange to you that I am concerned for your mother, after such a long cold war, after everything that happened. I've been thinking recently, after you left. Not that I didn't think before, of course, but now there is something I'd like you to know. Perhaps it will help you understand why I acted the way I did, three, four years ago.

In 1967, I was in the army. There I met a guy who was to become my best friend. We were nineteen. In 1968, we were sent to Prague, to join the Soviet Army in their endeavour to 'watch over the peace' in our sister nation. We didn't know what exactly was expected from us. We waited around in the outskirts of Prague for a few days. Nobody told us anything. We knew there was some kind of unrest, but you just didn't ask questions. We played cards and got drunk. Then one sunny spring morning we were in tanks, right in the centre of the city. There were crowds of people running about, photographers, and more tanks. I was in a tank with two others. I don't know if I understood the significance of the event at the time. I sensed it was important, because I couldn't remember anything like that happening in my lifetime. Was it the end of communism? No, that just couldn't be — communism was too big and powerful, too many people believed in it. I had already accepted it as something immutable, bigger than me, bigger than my country — perhaps an immutable evil, like serving in the army. A year later, at university, I found my route of escape to an alternative world.

The reader yawns and shivers. She's had only one coffee today. She contemplates going to the snack bar across the road, but she dreads the thought of getting outside in the cold. Not that inside is much warmer, with the heaters not working and all. She turns the page over (this letter is getting a bit boring) and reads randomly:

I was never a very good shot, but this one time, the only time I applied my military skills to a real-life situation, it was ironically successful. I didn't even aim at him, I just shot into the crowd, without thinking, trying to aim at the gaps so as not to hit anyone. But I didn't try hard enough. At first I thought somebody else had hit the young guy. But it was me. I don't know if he died or was only wounded. He

256

was hit in the stomach. Then he sank out of my sight. I shouted, 'I've killed him! My God I've killed him!' but my voice was drowned in the thunder of Russian tanks, the shooting, the shouting, the chaos. We had to roll on. My instant reaction was to get off and help him, take him to hospital, do something. But that was absurd. The tanks rolled on. There were tanks in front and behind us, we were trapped. I felt sick. I was shaking, I thought I was going mad. But I didn't go mad. What happened . . .

This is heavy stuff. She wasn't even born in '68. Digging up the past is a favourite pastime of post-communist confession-lovers. She's tired of it. All the criminals coming out and saying they were forced into doing things; that they were innocent deep down. She can't be bothered with it. The letter is long, and it's probably all in the same vein. She stuffs it back into the envelope and goes in search of coffee.

Five minutes later, a large man sways in, carrying a pie and a cup of steaming coffee. The jacket buttons of his regular Post Office navy suit are bursting. He sits at the table strewn with letters and parcels, and bites into the hot pastry. On top of one pile he spots a torn envelope and picks it up. With his other hand he balances the coffee cup. In the complicated manoeuvre of pulling out the letter with one hand and taking a sip from the coffee with the other, he spills some hot liquid on his letter-opening hand and the letter itself. He wipes it with a soiled handkerchief and unfolds the top page — page three. He reads at random:

He was about my age, probably a student. Perhaps he lived. For years I dreamed of that moment. There were hundreds of variations on that shot: I shoot but miss him. I shoot and kill a little girl. I shoot, the gun bounces off and the bullet hits me straight in the heart. I shoot and wake up, sitting up in bed and praying for it all to have been a dream. I shoot, and kill Ana.

After Prague we were discharged from the army and given automatic entry into university — for our contribution to peace in the sister nation. I would've got in anyway. But my friend from the army wouldn't have — he had a family history which tainted his personal record. In the '50s his father had helped some fugitives from Sofia cross the border with Yugoslavia. They were the family of his . . .

257

The pie finished, he discards the greasy paper and gets up. He needs another one. At the door, he runs into his colleague who is carrying a paper coffee cup and a lit cigarette. 'All right?' he says.

'Yeah,' she moans. 'It's fucking cold in here.'

'I know, I'm freezing my balls off. I'm off to get a pie. Want some?'

'Nah, I'm on a diet.'

'You're on a what?' He shakes his head in disapproval and sails on.

She sits in the still-warm chair and wraps herself in her coat. Absent-mindedly, she picks up the opened letter.

Later, I saw with painful clarity that I, like everyone else, had been a pawn in a game I hadn't yet understood. I saw, and felt to the marrow, how it was possible to do something evil without being evil. When, later, my friend became an informer for the secret police, Ana couldn't forgive him. But I could because, if you like, I'd already been there. I'd had an insight into the paradox of it. Gradually our friendship deteriorated, but it wasn't only because of his spying activity; that's only what I wanted to believe at the time.

Anyway, soon after Prague, I made a vow: never to do anything without deciding it myself; never to do anything random, never to be led. That's why I stayed behind when you and your mother left. It was my vow. This time, if you like, I was a belated conscientious objector. Maybe I made a mistake again. Maybe I can never get away from that mistake, whatever vows I take.

The door is flung open. 'Hello, my beautiful!'

The courier driver is here with his giant leather bags. She folds the letter anyhow and stuffs it in the coffee-stained envelope. She sweeps the mail into a gaping bag he is holding at the table edge. He strokes her behind, she slaps his hand, the plane takes off, and six days later Mladen's letter is in a letterbox at 52 Pacific Street, torn and stained, safely resting between a Telecom bill and condolence cards.

CHAPTER THIRTY

Bugger!

Fire for everyone

'Bugger!'

There is a soft buzz in the lounge. Tarik throws the covers off with annoyance and pulls out his arm from under Nadejda's back. They are still breathless and sticky from making love. A couple of large strides, and his naked body disappears into the lounge. Nadejda sits up and listens.

'Shit! You're joking! But he said . . . Where are you now?'

'No, I mean, hold on, you can't come over, I'm on my way to the Wharf Centre. I'm about to walk out the door. Yeah, I'll be there. Okay. See you there. Ciao.'

Click.

Nadejda tries to think. She stares at the dark patch on Tarik's pillow. It's the colour of that carpet he pointed out to her yesterday. Why that particular carpet? Tarik is taking a long time coming back.

She pulls her knickers on, then her top. He is standing in the window, naked, cellphone in hand, looking out to the harbour. His face is tense, unwelcoming. 'I've got to go to the centre,' he says. 'I've got an important meeting there. It looks like I'll be going back to Auckland as early as tonight.'

The nude on the wall screws her beautiful mouth in contempt. Nadejda feels lost, standing here in this semi-empty apartment on the fifth floor, the city at her feet and this naked man bending before her to pick up her bra and hand it to her.

One day, she would lean out of a window to look at the Pacific, while someone fetches her clothes . . . She is suddenly stung by a bitter regret for the innocent times in Nessebur, when Anton brought her clothes in the high ruins and they looked at the young sea at dawn; for the innocent times in Sofia, only days ago, when once again Anton handed over her clothes, not to drive her away but to keep her warm. Recent or distant, the past is just as lost. She crumples her bra in her fist like a detestable message found on the kitchen table the morning after. And the lover is nowhere to be found.

Tarik is getting dressed. His clothes are strewn all over the floor. Their golden drinks on the glass table are less golden now that the ice has thawed. She doesn't even care about the reason for his hasty departure. She remembers all those bad films in which the man walks out the door, fully dressed, and the woman weeps in bed, flabby

260

and abandoned. The post-coital flatness of such farewells, the banality of the pain — she never thought she'd be on the receiving end. She never thought she'd gaze over the Pacific with such disgust and sadness.

'Nadejda,' says Tarik tenderly and her heart shrinks, 'I'm sorry I'm in such a rush. Something has come up and I have to pack up and leave.'

She smiles and knows. Brave Nadejda is smiling with understanding. But she mustn't let him explain, she mustn't allow even a minute for further humiliation.

'How can I contact you?' he says and his eyes are absent. Again, she looks instinctively at the sneering nude. 'I don't know. I'm going home.'

Home. Perhaps she is, after all. She feels as if she's going to a funeral — 'home' has the same resonance. She makes for the door.

'Wait!' He grabs her, presses her hard in his arms. 'I hope we meet again,' he says.

She doesn't speak, from fear of suddenly losing her voice. Besides, what can she say? She tears herself out of his embrace and almost crashes into the door, then opens it with a hand that isn't hers, and walks out on legs that aren't hers. The door doesn't slam behind her. That's a shame.

Down the stairs. Sweaty hand clutches crumpled bra. Out into the blue weekend. Locks of sweaty hair stick to neck. Where to now? Wet knickers are cold.

Nadejda is browsing through magazines, just like two days ago. The tall handsome man across the hall is pacing up and down among his rugs, talking into a cellphone, just like two days ago. Except that now she has knowledge of him. Of his body, at least. Did it really happen, or is it still the same day, Thursday? Except that now she has no desire to steal anything. She feels robbed herself. Her loss is too huge to be comforted by small treats. The postcards, the glossy magazines, the trashy novels lie forlorn, undesirable. Nadejda is like them.

She came here despite herself. She had to make sure he had an important meeting. She has nothing else to do. But above all, she can't bear the thought of not looking at him any more. She never wanted to stop looking at him. She stands behind the postcard stall, in case he looks her way — but he doesn't look her way. His distant white shirt flashes through the scarce forest of strollers like a flag of distress: her distress.

And here comes his business partner: sunglasses, dark ponytail, slightly heavy hips, immaculate trousers and slim from the waist up. A charming impression, overall. She takes off her dark glasses. They kiss on the lips, then he hugs her, as if to comfort her. Nadejda thinks back to this morning when he bent over her and kissed the hollow of her collarbone with such tenderness and sincerity as if she were his first lover. Her head spins. She feels as if she is going to vomit. It's the lamb from last night, *his* lamb. She hesitates between sorrow and disgust, but is unable to make a choice. They are talking now, in an intimate fashion. A giant dark rug in greens and blues cushions their fall, should they fall. The meeting is evidently terribly important.

Prostration or revenge? The only thing she feels is robbed, devastatingly robbed.

She makes for the exit of the mall. Outside, the sun is shamelessly bright, it is summer as yesterday, and the sea is still here, every single drop of it. Nadejda sits on the concrete bench by the water, blinded. Her body is as limp as a rag-doll. Gulls shriek, brushing her head, wanting to scalp her.

I hope you find someone to love you, said the sad man as the gulls devoured his pie. Poor wretch, she had thought.

I will always love you, said Anton. Yeah, yeah, she had thought, it's only Anton. He's always sentimental.

Christchurch will be a desert without you, said Tony. Oh don't be pathetic, she had said.

Can Tarik ever utter these words to her, to anyone? Or even just one of them? This is what it is to be heartbroken then. This is how Tony will feel when she leaves him. This is how Anton felt ten years ago, when she went off kissing Moni in the boat. This is how everyone feels.

Except Nadejda. She tosses her hair back in a sudden rush of anger. Not her, the limp doll; not her, the broken heart; not her, the silent lovesick puppy. She stares at the water hard, then looks towards the centre's entry. As if on order, the dark-haired beauty appears. She walks down the steps on her elegant heels. Her sunglasses are tucked in her tight top. Does she look familiar? She is about thirty, or late twenties. The lips, the body proportions, something odd about the expression. It's her, the dark-nippled sneering watercolour nude! She's her. Nadejda stares, unbelieving. The brother's girlfriend. Their eyes meet. Nadejda shifts her gaze. The nude unlocks a shiny, dark-blue Nissan and grabs something from inside. It's a child — an exquisite, olive-skinned little girl in denim overalls. The door slams. The nude goes back inside the mall, holding the long-haired elf by the hand.

Nadejda tries to put the story together. Tarik has an affair with his brother's girlfriend. Unless he lied about her being his brother's girlfriend. Maybe he has no brother, and the apartment is his. And so is the child. Maybe she is his girlfriend, and his brother is having an affair with her, after he painted her. Maybe he *is* his brother, and this is their legitimate child. Maybe he is the author of that drawing. Why was the child waiting in the car? Lies, lies. She is sick of lies. Her own, others', all the lies that make up this fucked-up puzzle in which we try to fit but fail, fail miserably. The gulls fail too — screeching, shaken, tumbling in the hourglass of sea and sky . . .

Except Nadejda. She quickly walks over to the Wharf Centre. The two are still talking business, only now he is talking into brother's girlfriend's face and brushing away locks of brother's girlfriend's hair. The little girl is not with them. Nadejda buys a box of matches from a fast-food counter and a lighter from the bookshop opposite the rugs. The handsome couple are absorbed in their business exchange, she's in no danger of being spotted. Outside, on the concrete bench, a few people squint against the sun. She sneaks over to the blue Nissan and looks inside. Casually, she looks around. If someone sees, they'll think it's her car. Casually, she tries the driver's door. It opens! She slams it shut. Now a large stone or brick. Here's one. Nadejda crouches between the Nissan and another vehicle. Stone in hand, lighter on the ground, Nadejda is smashing the plastic tube. It's harder than she thought. She has to hold the lighter as she smashes it, so it doesn't skid under a car, while

263

also watching her fingers. She is preparing a fire: lighter fluid spilt and a match struck and dropped in the driver's seat. The nude won't go very far today. Tarik will just have to come and extinguish the mess with his rugs; how about the Kurdish one? Pity about the little dark fairy though. Nadejda had the same denim overalls when she was little.

Hammering away to no avail, Nadejda has the sudden weird sensation of being in a comedy. It's the saddest comedy — with no audience. She pauses. Her knees are sore from crouching. Her thumb hurts, more susceptible to the blows than the stubborn lighter. The fires outside Sofia University were smoky from the tyres students used. Burnt tyres made people cry. Fire is not so easy to make. Besides, there is something wrong with this method. The realisation makes her sit on the ground: lighters are filled with gas! She can't make a fire with a lighter, even if she manages to break it open before she breaks her thumbs. Great. What's the point of revenge anyway? But the protests in Bulgaria were a revenge, a retribution for the evil done to the country, surely. No, they weren't. They were the extreme spasms of desperation's bravery claiming what was long overdue. The protesters were the ones who took the blows anyway, they were the ones freezing outside for days, they got beaten and shot down. And yet they won at the end.

She slips the lighter in her back pocket, still holding the useless stone. She leans against a tyre. Now she's wallowing. Pick yourself up, Nadejda, she orders herself and doesn't budge. The tyre is large and smells of rubber. Instinctively, Nadejda fingers a valve; a teat from which the tyres can be milked. She unscrews it. It's hard at first, but she uses the bottom of her T-shirt to cushion the abrasion of the metal on her fingers. It comes undone. She leaves the cap on the ground. No fire, no mess. She learned this from Batko Dimo; she would stand by and watch as he took revenge on the cars of obnoxious neighbours, cigarette in his mouth. She gets up and moves to the rear tyre.

If the nude comes out now, she'll run. Nausea comes over her, the hand that unscrewed the valve is shaking, more from the strain than anything else, she notes. The nude doesn't come out. Too bad. Nadejda gets up and assumes an air of normality, straightening her shoulders, clearing her throat, flicking her hair back. A few metres away, ice-cream in hand, is the girl, observing with contained, adult-like curiosity. For a moment they look at each other. The ice-cream is dripping down the little hand and onto a little shoe. The little dark head looks down. Nadejda takes a tissue out of her pocket and hands it over.

'Here,' she says, 'wipe your shoe.'

The diminutive creature doesn't take the offering but responds by licking the yellow cone assiduously, her serious black eyes on Nadejda's face, as if sealing a pact of silence. Nadejda knows she won't give her away.

'What flavour is it?'

The girl continues to slurp her ice-cream with competitive determination, as if proving the excellent quality of the flavour.

Nadejda walks away. She is just a passer-by. Behind her the hiss of deflating tyres, no, of feeding fire. Before her the blades of the city. She turns round. The girl is standing in the same spot, oddly perched on one leg — a cross between Andersen's one-legged lead soldier and the paper ballerina. Nadejda waves. The ballerina waves with her free hand. The little soldier is motionless.

Her legs casually cross the big road. Her head turns left, her head turns right. Any second now someone will shout, 'It's that girl over there!' Right now someone is running up behind her, grabbing her by the back of her top: 'Hey you, come back here! You're not getting away!' The mortification, Tarik's shock, the cruel green stare (he knew she was mad), the brother's girlfriend's confusion and anger (it's probably the brother's Nissan), the police, calls to the family, mother's hysteria, uncle's disgust, father's sadness, the fucked-up puzzle is blown to pieces once and for all . . . Nadejda is falling through circles of blue. She runs.

She runs through traffic and suits, green lights and red lights, swinging doors, oceans of white steps, small armies of columns, faces, legs, eyes, bags, ties, glasses, smells, sun-spots and shadows. Behind her, the fire; before her . . . She runs and the further away she gets, the larger the fire grows, all-engulfing, joyous fire, sunshine of surprise, golden bouquet at the weekend's doorstep, fire for everyone: for thin Anton in the snow, for ageing father in the unheated flat, for mother in her shivers, for uncle in his big empty house, for Tony in his chemical desert, for the dead who are cold, for Tarik who doesn't love her, for his brother, for the nude who sneers, for the writer who lost his pie, for the Greek who dreams of Greece, fire for all. Except for the ballerina in denim overalls. She will just stand on her watch, loyal to the end, ice-cream in hand.

It is dusk again. Nadejda is still running, though she stands still. She leans over the metal railing. The hard body of the vessel is making a deep incision into the water. Its darkening ink is blood in a black and white sequence. The horn of the ferry sounds across the harbour, long and mournful: the last call of a dying elephant. She looks back at the city. It is lighting up its thousand fires; it is shrinking fast. It seems far away now. Both islands seem far away.

Is there nothing more to be desired, or everything to be desired from now on? The legs on which she sat. The hands that covered her from head to toe. The face that was so tender. Hot tears burn her cheeks and drop into the darkness below.

The ferry, a drifting lit-up Christmas tree, emerges from the darkness, and plunges into another darkness. A tiny figure hangs on to the top railing, hair flapping in the wind like a flag.

RECONNAISSANCE

PART THREE

CHAPTER THIRTY-ONE

And here you are.

The voice

And here you are. You get off the ferry. You jump across the small gap between the bridge and the shore. Now you're on the same piece of land as me. It is so irreversible I shudder. You look around. You sink into the darkness. I hear you breathing. You are so close. You have found your way. Will you find your way? Will I find the words? Will I find Ana in you? Will I find myself? Will you hear me?

RECONNAISSANCE

CHAPTER THIRTY-TWO

Nadejda takes the last bus to Nelson.

Let me tell you

Nadejda takes the last bus to Nelson. It is filled with the passengers from the ferry. From a back pocket she extracts a piece of paper with an address scribbled on it. She has cold shivers though her face feels feverish. The unfamiliar darkness creeps up from all directions. She wants to find a clear, shaded spot in the high grass of a parallel time, curl up, lay her overheated head on her pack and sleep until it is safe to wake up. But there is no parallel time. And all the lawns are mowed.

The sea runs alongside the bus, rustling with its scales, its leaves, its feathers, its hair, still bleeding from the iron plough of a ferry. At any one time there is a ferry harvesting the Pacific current between the two islands, bringing that much closer the head and the tail of the cut-up fish that is New Zealand. Even so, the head watches, the tail twitches. One night, without warning, they will finally lock together in one mighty spasm, a ferry will be crushed flat, and there will be no trace of the passengers. Just like once, somewhere in the wild Ottoman provinces in the Balkans, when an important building was under construction, masons would build in a live person, usually a woman, for her spirit to inhabit happily the house.

They arrive. The passengers pour out of the bus and she stumbles to a phone box. What if that Bojan guy isn't there? She'd have to find a hostel for the night. Who said she should contact him anyway? It's as though she's obliged to call him. She doesn't actually need to see him at all, she never intended to. Never — as if it's been a long time, when in fact she only learned about his existence yesterday, before it all happened with Tarik. Things are happening so fast, yet she feels as if she's been travelling for years with this pack, in these jeans, with a feverish forehead and no idea where she's going next.

Suddenly she is in the grip of panic. Alone in the lit-up phone booth, she is an insect trapped in a piece of amber. She hasn't spoken to her mother for years, days, a lifetime. She has been an idiot, a headless chicken, a monster of egotism. All this time, she has stubbornly refused to call her mother. Now it is urgent that she call her. Tell her everything, tell her where, why, when and how much. Whether . . . Her mother always listens. Nobody else does. Her father was always absent, even when he was paying attention. Everybody forgets Nadejda, except her mother. She feels as if she is shrinking, regressing, belittled and diminutive in this benighted town, in the gaping pit of this trip where there are no hands to catch her.

She calls home. The dialling tone echoes for long minutes. Her mother must be at some friend's place or at Vassil's. She could ring there. She dials her uncle's number. The same tone offends her ear. Where is everybody? 'Hello, you have reached the home of Vassil Naumov. Leave a message and I'll get back to you as soon as I can. Thank you.' Beep.

'Hi Uncle, it's Nadejda. Sorry I wasn't in touch for a while. I'm in Nelson at the moment, I'm well. I wasn't actually in Sofia that last time I called. I was in Wellington. I lied. I'm sorry. I hope I didn't get you worried. Can you tell Mum I'll be coming down in the next couple of days? I miss you. See you soon. Ciao.'

Why is it that whenever she wants to talk to them, they aren't there, and when they *are* there, she tries to escape by lying? She is getting tired of this hide-and-seek game. It's time she faced everyone there is to face, and explained, and asked for explanations. Nothing good comes out of dialling numbers.

She dials Bojan's number. It's a weird name. Bojan means 'of God': how presumptuous, how stupid.

'Hello?'

'Hi. Can I speak with Bojan Dimov, please?'

'Speaking.' The voice is gentle. Gentle bachelor sipping gin and tonic in front of the fire, stroking the dog.

'Dobur vecher. Good evening,' says Nadejda and continues in Bulgarian. 'My name is Nadejda Taneva, I was given your number by some friends in Wellington. Actually I can't remember their family name, but they have a daughter Maria.'

'Ah, yes, I know who you mean. I know them. So, are you here just for the night or staying?'

'I'm not staying, I mean, I'm spending the night here. I just arrived on the ferry. I thought I could pop in, if that's not too inconvenient.'

She is mad, calling strangers at night like some kind of brainless puppet, without wanting to, without meaning to, without knowing why.

271

Chapter Thirty-two

'By all means, it'll be nice to meet you. I think I knew your mother vaguely. And your grandmother.'

'Really?'

'Well, it's been a long time, she might not remember me any more. But do you have my address? Where are you at the moment?'

What a hospitable guy. But he doesn't know that her grandmother couldn't possibly remember him. 'I'm in a phone booth, but I don't know where. I don't know the town. It's near some square.'

'I know where you are. I'm just around the corner. Now, turn left, you go past a petrol station and a bakery, then you turn left again, and you're in Sunset Avenue. That's where I live, number 26. Do you think you'll find it all right? I could come and pick you up.'

'No, no, I'll be fine.'

'I'll wait for you outside. It's well lit, you'll have no problems. There are still people around.'

'That's right. I'll see you soon.'

'See you soon, Nadejda.'

Nadejda follows the instructions as if she cares. Laughter and cans of coke and beer litter the streets. Burnt foreign faces shine in the dark, creating the illusion of a healthy tan. A swarm of surfers flutters past her, black and glowing in their suits like beetles. Her pack is getting heavier by each step. It is depressing being in a strange town and following a stranger's instructions to get to a stranger's house and then lie in a stranger's bed and use a stranger's toilet. Like a tramp. But she doesn't know how to get to a hostel, and the information bureau is closed at this time, and the hostels will be packed because this is the peak season. Why did she leave in such a rush, without thinking? She just had to get on that ferry, run from the fire, from Tarik, from the sneering nude, from what she didn't understand, from what she did. Tarik's face descends towards her in slow motion. His green eyes are serious. His hand grips her hip.

Sunset Avenue, there it is. How tacky. It's not really an avenue, it's an ordinary street. Small things are called big names in this country. Streets are avenues, towns are cities, villages are towns. But here shines the most scorching sun over the most immense ocean, here runs the steepest street, here every person has the greatest number of sheep and boats . . . The country of deficiencies and excesses.

'Nadejda.' She is startled by a short figure that hatches from the darkness. The man holds out a hand.

'Hi, I'm Bojan.'

She shakes the hand. It's warm and hard. 'Hi, I'm Nadejda,' she says and feels stupid.

A passing car throws a circle of light on his face. Nadejda is startled. She imagined a musty, bearded hermit; Bojan is a shaved, middle-aged man with deep-set black eyes and thick wavy hair brushed back to reveal a large, regular forehead that could be described as noble. He is smiling, but his face twitches strangely, as if he is nervous or has some muscle problem. His clothes could be described as old-fashioned: a sleeveless cardigan over a short-sleeved summer shirt, beige trousers with a slight bulge over the belt — age taking its toll. Overall, he is a bit old-worldly.

'How did you recognise me?' she asks as they walk on, just to make conversation.

'It wasn't very difficult.' He glances at her with an odd expression.

She smiles. Strange night, strange day, strange encounters. Here she is, following a strange Bulgarian man home. The last time she did this was only last night. But there is no danger with Bojan, he is wholesome, he is 'of God'.

They walk up a short driveway past a small rose garden. 'That's my house,' he says and a wave of sadness washes over Nadejda.

She can't say what has brought it on. The rose garden, the voice, the concept of this house, Bojan's house in Nelson. She steps in with the eerie feeling that she is stepping into a time machine.

'You are most welcome to stay the night, if you like,' he says, leaning her pack on the wall under a large mounted deer head. She wonders if the eyes are real or glass. They stare at her.

'Thank you. I don't have anywhere to stay yet.' She feels uncomfortable taking charity, but then again, how many Bulgarians are there in Nelson? Her mother would do the same.

Chapter Thirty-two

'Well, you do now.' He smiles and points to a door which must be the lounge. 'I'll show you around, shall I?' He looks at her quizzically and his smile is genuinely warm. There is an odd mixture of formality and instant familiarity, as if she is visiting an old friend at a new house, or in another life. She nods and smiles.

'Lounge.' A room full of rugs and wall-hangings, innumerable knick-knacks, and several lampstands in different styles.

'That's the spare room. You can sleep here.' A small, frugal room with a made-up bed, table, and pictures of owls and other birds on the walls. She is in a dream in which she follows this stranger around his cluttered house. There is something unsettling about him, but as in all dreams she can't put her finger on it. 'My bedroom.' A double bed, table, mirror, armchairs. A prodigious clutter of framed photos, statuettes, figures, candlesticks, dry flowers, bowls, and an intricately baroque lustre.

'You have a lot of things,' she says, realising the inanity of this comment but unable to come up with something more original.

'I have an antiques shop just down the road. I do have a lot of junk, but you know, it's personal stuff, I've collected it over the years.'

'Yeah, of course.'

Of course what? Why did she have to come to this museum of memories, this junkshop, a giant heart into which she is gazing, lifting the valves, strolling down the arteries, listening to it live . . .

'Bathroom.' It's a bathroom like any other, except for the glass-covered picture on the wall above the bath. It looks like a blurry photo of a long-haired nymph holding her foot. Bachelor nurturing quiet masturbatory fantasies. But she doesn't have time to take a good look; he quickly switches off the light and they go back to the lounge.

'Please make yourself at home,' he shows her to an armchair. 'I'll take your pack into your room. Excuse me a second.' And he vanishes so suddenly that Nadejda is startled. She is clearly exhausted: there is a delay in the signals her eyes send to her brain. Or the other way round. Stuffed owl above the fireplace, a trayful of shells and stones, rugs, woollen fluffy rugs, ashtrays, shell-trays, glass trolley with unusual looking bottles, photos in frames, free-floating photos tucked into other photos. She is about to get up to inspect the photos,

274

but he is back in a flash, startling her again. 'Can I get you something to drink?'

This time Nadejda feels anxious and suddenly, she knows what it is: Bojan is too *prepared* for her visit; an absurd observation, yes, but it's a fact. He seems too unsurprised, as if he has spur-of-the-moment visitors like her every evening. And in the fuzzy reasoning of her exhaustion, Nadejda says: 'Did you expect someone tonight?'

He stares at her. He rubs his chin which is round and noble, if chins could be noble. He seems taken aback. 'Why are you asking?'

'I don't know, I just got that impression. I don't want to get in the way, if you had some plans already.'

'You're not getting in my way.' He sits in an armchair opposite her very carefully, as if he is sitting on top of a sleeping cat. 'I live alone. I've got a whole house — you're a most welcome guest.'

He stares at her. 'You've been travelling?'

'Yes. I went to Bulgaria.'

'Did you see some family and friends?'

'My father. He lives there.'

He springs up. 'I forgot to get you something. What would you like? Are you hungry?'

'No, thank you,' she lies. She hasn't eaten since that lamb last night . . . That lamb — she was the lamb.

'An orange juice then? A grape juice? Or a hot chocolate, coffee, tea?'

'Coffee, thank you.'

'Okay. I'll be right back.' And he is. He seems to take literally no time doing things. He is carrying a small tray with a coffee plunger, a couple of small pots, a plate of chocolate biscuits and a large glass of dark violet liquid. Nadejda has the absurd thought that it looks like poison. If she died here, nobody would know. No, that's wrong — Maria's parents would know. She sips from the tasty poison. Coffee aroma fills the room. She crunches up a biscuit. Everything tastes good here.

'So,' she says, her mouth full of biscuit crumbs, 'how long have you been here in New Zealand?'

'I came in 1975.'

Chapter Thirty-two

'That's when I was born! It's a while ago.'

'I know.'

She reaches for another biscuit. It's also the year my grand-mother died she wants to add, but thinks better of it. That's too personal. It's about time they plunged the plunger, she thinks, but it's impolite to take such initiatives. 'Did you come by yourself?'

'Yes.'

'You must've been about my age?' she guesses innocently.

'It's nice of you to say that.' He smiles and locks his hands on his stomach, which is now flatter because he is leaning back. 'I was a bit older, I was twenty-seven.'

Soft-voiced, soft-moving, soft-eyed, Bojan has something very likeable about him. She feels that whatever she might say, he will nod and understand. None of the brooding heaviness of her uncle, none of the subdued bitterness of her father. But there is something else about him . . .

'I first went to Germany, actually, then I boarded a plane to New Zealand. It wasn't exactly legal. I mean, I basically deserted. I was supposed to stay in Munich for six months.'

'Were you working there?'

'Sort of. I was on a research grant. But I left straight away. I only stayed a week.'

'Why did you leave?'

'I was, I wasn't happy there. It's a long story. You see,' he fidgets, uncrossing and crossing his legs, 'I was working for the government.'

'Were you a diplomat?'

Bojan's laughter is brief and raucous. 'No. I was an informer.' His voice is the vocal equivalent of brushing away an obnoxious fly.

Nadejda isn't sure what being an informer involved twenty-one years ago, but it can't have been anything good.

'I was sent to Germany to keep an eye on compatriots, to see what they got up to.'

He was an informer on people like her uncle and grandfather! She puts back the third biscuit she was about to bite into. Fortunately, Bojan is already set up to provide answers to the questions she doesn't know how to ask. 'That's why I got the grant in Munich.'

'But why didn't you stay? You weren't happy being an informer? Didn't they pay you well?'

Nadejda senses she's being an ungrateful guest. He offers her a room, chocolate biscuits and coffee (probably cold by now), and she condemns his actions of twenty years ago. But Bojan understands. 'They did. But that wasn't the point. The point was, I had started working for the secret police *in order* to leave the country and never have to do it again.'

'It's a bit of a vicious cycle though.' Nadejda is proud of thinking straight, at least.

'Of course. In a sense. That's why I had to leave. I took a plane to Hong Kong.'

'So did my grandmother. The same year too!'

'I know. We were on the same plane.' He looks at her unflinchingly.

'What do you mean? Did you know her?'

'Well, yes.' He reaches over to the plunger and presses the handle down. His hand is shaking. He leans forward, elbows on his knees, tensely focused on the plunger as if consulting it on what to say next.

'She died on that flight,' says Nadejda. It's no longer too personal. Nothing is too personal any more, it seems. The valves are opening by themselves.

'I know.'

'How do you know?' Nadejda feels defiant in the face of such knowledge.

'Because I was there.'

He hasn't unglued his eyes from the plunger, which is still mute. Finally he looks up at her. His eyes are no longer soft. They are restless, wandering towards her, then retreating, shrinking back into their deep, shadowy sockets. His face is twitchy again.

'You were there when she died?' Nadejda can't believe she is uttering these words so carelessly, as if she's saying 'So you saw the puppy drown?'

'Yes, I was there. On the plane.' He leans back again, arms on the chair-arms, as if surrendering. 'I was on the plane,' he opens his mouth with an effort, 'and I was next to her.'

277

Chapter Thirty-two

They look at each other for a long moment, vacantly. Nadejda's lap is covered in crumbs she notices. She desperately wants to brush them away but her hands are frozen. She is aware that in the far corner of the lounge there is a stuffed bird which stares at her with its yellow glass eyes. Or are they real? Do they preserve the eyes when they stuff the bird, or do they stick in glass buttons? Nobody knows how her grandmother died. She was hospitalised immediately after landing, though it was obvious that she was gone. Then her uncle and grandfather were called, then her mother was called by her uncle. Heart attack — it was as simple as that. Then she was flown on to New Zealand where she was buried.

'Why, how?' Nadejda begins to put some words together, but there are too many words.

'You mean how come I was sitting next to her?'

'No, I mean — Yes, that's right.'

'Because we already knew each other and there was a free seat in my aisle, so we asked somebody to move, and she took the free seat.'

'That was in Munich?'

'Yes. I didn't know she was going to New Zealand until I saw her. I hadn't seen her for a while.'

They are talking normally now. The main thing is to make sense of it all, gradually. 'So you knew her?'

He nods, obviously anticipating the question. He rubs his chin, the side of his face, as if checking that they are still there. His small, fine hand is shaking. 'Yes. She knew me too but, how can I put this, she didn't know exactly who I was.' He crosses his legs again. His trousers are worn out at the knees.

'Who are you?' she says and is afraid and appalled. Afraid of the radical nature of this question, and appalled at the cliché.

His lack of immediate response is the unequivocal proof that there is more than meets Nadejda's eye. They look at each other. Nadejda is now more afraid than concerned about appearances. His eyes are completely black, so black he has no pupils. But his hands, his hands are good, with their pointed sensitive fingertips, the type that give Nadejda the impression that whatever they touch hurts them. They are on his thighs now, inert and helpless. A man with

278

hands like this can only be good. But an informer? But someone who saw her grandmother die and didn't tell anyone? Unless he did, but they too kept it to themselves. Nadejda's head hurts. She leans it back on the furry couch and glances at the ceiling. She wants to concentrate on the idea of him; the face can be so distracting.

'I want to tell you a story. Please bear with me.' If faces can shake, his face is shaking. He clears his throat; he is still looking at Nadejda, or rather through her. She dreads what he might see.

'In the early '60s, I was living in the remote countryside known as Ludogorie, Mad Forest, or Deli Orman in Turkish. Do you know about this province?'

'Yes. That's where my mother and her mother were deported after . . . That's where they were living anyway.'

'I was living there with my mother. I had no father. I spent a lot of time hanging around in the fields by myself or with my best friend, a girl my age, Ina. I hated school, and she did even more — we weren't allowed any creativity, the teachers were brutes, we felt we were too good to be there, among all those retards. One spring afternoon — I was thirteen — I sneaked into a neighbour's yard and got hold of his donkey. We often played with that donkey, he didn't mind at all, but that day I took Mario without permission. He was a very large, quiet, submissive animal, with eyes that just melted your heart. Ina and I drove Mario down the gravel road and out into the fields, where we often rode him and fooled around. The cherry trees were blossoming, there were bees and flowers everywhere, and high grass. Naturally, we were in love. We got on top of Mario and spurred him, and the poor animal, struggling with our weight, stumbled across the field. We gripped each other, for safety, of course! No, we wanted to feel with our damp hands each other's warm skin through the clothes.'

There is something unseemly about a middle-aged man recounting teenage lust, Nadejda feels. But that's unfair — he is only reminiscing.

'We went far out that day. We "galloped" through the prairie in a cloud of blossoms and insects, until real clouds began to gather above us. Soon the sun disappeared behind a thick grey curtain. The sky descended very low, as if inspecting us with its disapproving eye.

279

Chapter Thirty-two

Everything went very still, very warm, as if we were caught under a lid. Mario was braying and shaking his head, as if saying "No, no." We headed back at full speed, though Mario was tired. We knew the kind of storm that was about to be unleashed. Those spring storms were frightful. But we'd gone far into the country and the storm hit us at once with all its might. A warm torrent poured down, and huge slashes of lightning split the watermelon sky. We were soaked in a second, Mario was miserable, virtually impossible to control, so we got down and walked. It was a deluge; the thunderbolts hurt our ears. We ran. At one point, Mario strayed. He just walked away. I went after him. He was heading towards a large tree. Ina yelled behind me but of course you couldn't hear anything. The next moment, a giant lightning crossed the sky from one end to the other. I had reached the tree where Mario had stopped in a daze and reached out to grab him. For a fraction of a second the electric arc flashed in front of me. Then it hit me.

'The electric current ran through me. It was the touch of death. I couldn't describe it, there's nothing to compare it to. It is like having your life run through you at the speed of light: before it's begun, it's over. It hurts, and it's exhilarating, and you are all-powerful, and you are nothing, nought. I thought I was dead. Then came the thunder, bursting my eardrums, or so it felt. Next thing, Ina grabbed me and shook me. She was in a panic. I couldn't say if I was okay, I still didn't know what had happened. My body was tingling, and I felt as if I was sprouting wings, about to take off. I was breathless, and as thirsty as if I hadn't drank for a lifetime. She screamed "Look!" and pointed to the tree. It was black. Coal. Twisted in a grimace of pain, a skeleton where there had been a green, breathing body just a minute ago. Mario was galloping in a circle like crazy. She yelled that she thought I was going to die. She cried, and gripped me. I was on a high. I gripped her and I drank her tears, I drank the tears streaming down her face and neck. I drank all the water from her body. The rain stopped at once as if by an order. It vanished like a dream from which we had woken up. In the high rain-beaten grasses, Ina and I lost our virginity, awkwardly, feverishly, and swore to love each other until we died.'

*

Bojan hasn't been looking at Nadejda for a long time now. He is looking at the damned plunger. His fingertips aren't touching anything but they look as if they're feeling an invisible surface, as if they're in pain. Nadejda's throat is dry. She doesn't dare swallow for fear of disrupting the story.

He lifts his round cherry eyes and smiles, though his eyes remain buried in the cave of another time. Now Nadejda knows where the piercing sadness comes from. From that rain-drenched field, from the kids in love, from the donkey. From the runaway youth in Munich prostituting himself for freedom. From this middle-aged antiquary in Nelson. Everybody is an infinitely slow time machine. Every time machine runs with the fuel of sadness.

The phone rings. Bojan doesn't budge. It rings three times.

'Hello? Hello? Anyone there?'

He looks at the mute receiver and hangs up. His hair is wavy. He is stooped. He turns to Nadejda and attempts a smile but instead, his round, noble chin trembles.

'Malicious call?'

'I don't know anyone malicious here,' he says, standing in the middle of the room like a punished child.

'Yes, but maybe they know you.'

He nods vaguely and thoughtfully, either bothered by the call, or still preoccupied with his story.

'What happened next?' she asks.

'Next? Everything happened next. We got back, we were told off, I handed Mario back to his owner who said that was the last time he would give him to me. He turned out to be right, because Mario died the next day. I think we rode the life out of him. I was constantly thirsty, I drank litres of water. But above all, I was thirsty for Ina. We had several haunts. The barn of the Turkish house where she and her mother lived as tenants. Of course, we all lived with Turkish families. A derelict shed at the outskirts of the village, which was said to be haunted, and that was right — it was haunted by us. We were mad for each other, made for each other.'

'But what happened later with you and Ina?'

'It's a long story, or rather it's the same story. Years later, we

281

had a bitter falling out. She met someone else. Actually, she met my best friend. I haven't seen her since then.'

'Did you meet someone else?'

'No. I mean, sure, I met a lot of women, but nobody like Ina. I never loved anybody like I loved Ina.'

'Where is she now?'

He doesn't respond. He is travelling.

'Why are you telling me this story?' Not that she isn't liking it, but Bojan is someone who wouldn't tell a story to someone on a Saturday night just for the hell of it. She wants him to know that she is aware of that.

He clears his throat and locks his fingers together. 'Because it's part of a big story.'

'What about my grandmother?'

'She's in the story too. I want to tell you another story. It's all the same story of course, but this is another chunk of . . .'

'But I don't want another chunk. I want to hear about my grandmother first. I have the right to know! I wonder why my uncle hasn't told me anything.' Again, she has to remind herself that this is her host she's talking to. But they have quickly ventured beyond host-guest pleasantries, that's clear.

'About?'

'About you. I mean, he knows you were there when she died, right?'

'No, he doesn't.'

'Why? Surely you told him!'

'No.'

'I don't understand. I don't understand.' Nadejda crushes half a biscuit in her saucer. This man is uncommon. He knows. He is someone she should've met long ago.

'I know you don't. Sometimes I don't either.'

'You said you knew my mother, didn't you? My grandmother *and* my mother! When, how did you know her, them, I mean?' Nadejda senses some unsavoury truth, she is on the brink of making a connection.

'Let me tell you this story. Just bear with me, I have to tell you, so that you can make sense of the rest.' His eyes are so beseeching. He leans forward. She wants to and she doesn't want to. Some things, once we know them, we wish we didn't. But we spend our lives wanting to know them.

'Yes,' says Nadejda.

Chapter Thirty-two

CHAPTER THIRTY-THREE

*A couple of hours into the drive,
the front of Ana's car begins to
give out a strident, intermittent
noise.*

Intermission

A couple of hours into the drive, the front of Ana's car begins to give out a strident, intermittent noise. She tries to locate it. It seems to come from the tyres, though it's hard to tell. Then she notices that the noise is triggered by the use of the brakes. It gets worse, as if something is about to tear or break. She pulls over. The screeching is intolerable. She looks at the map: she has a couple of hours to go. She extracts Vassil's cellphone from the bag and dials breakdown services. They are on their way.

She waits for half an hour, watching the blue ranges on the left and the blue ocean on the right. She leaves the radio on. Obsessively, she tunes it to different stations; she flicks through songs, voices, ads, laughter. Vassil's new BMW has a new CD-player. He couldn't stand the radio and wanted his new car to have a CD-player, so he could listen to his favourite operas and concertos. He played them for a couple of weeks, for as long as he drove his new car. Now the car is sitting in his garage. What is she going to do with it? She turns the radio off and opens a new packet of cigarettes.

Sea of whales and dolphins, land of fine wines, empty roads of high quality, life is a shallow song, neither happy, nor sad, whose refrain is separation. The lyrics change, but the refrain is always the same. For so long, Ana has been the one who doesn't die but carries on after everybody else's death. And the separations? Mladen chose to stay behind, she didn't leave him. Bojan chose to go abroad. No, first he chose to become an informer, to spit on the suffering of their two families — he chose, in other words, to break away from Ana. Her mother chose to leave. What have Ana's choices been? To keep the child? She didn't have a choice. But she would have had her regardless of the abortion laws.

She is going on a mad mission. She can't possibly face Bojan. It is unlikely that Nadejda will stay at his house at all — she wouldn't visit him in the first place, she is too independent. Instead of Nadejda, she is about to discover Bojan — ghastly error. She can't conceive of this encounter. It is already bad enough thinking of what to say to Nadejda, how to ask her whether she knows what she has done, why she has done it.

Breakdown services arrive, smiling and efficient. She needs to get the belt changed at the earliest opportunity. They fix it

285

temporarily. She nods and thanks, and thinks what a bloody waste of time, she could have just carried on without any danger. But she has a fixation on safety. Overcompensation for what can't be recovered. She presses on.

For hours, she has been psyching herself up to call Bojan. Just make sure that he is there. She can't imagine what she is going to say. But at least call him, she must.

Two hours later, she is in Nelson. She still hasn't called him. It's dark. Soon, she'll have to wake him up. She stops at a petrol station to fill up. She holds the cellphone in one hand and a forgotten cigarette in the other. The town itself won't be sleeping for a while — it's pumping with music, footsteps, voices and alcohol. Is this a monumental mistake she is about to make? She has to find out. She dials the number from the yellow piece of paper in her notebook.

'Hello?'

There is no question of speaking. She can't. She doesn't have the words.

'Hello? Anyone there?'

The voice of her youth — it hasn't changed. Voices don't change. The same gentleness, which became perfidy; the same sensual attentiveness, which became calculation. And then vanished. The voice of her life, answering some incidental phone number in Nelson.

No, there's no one. She pushes 'Over'. But it's not over. It's not over between them. She consults her map of Nelson and drives to Bojan's house.

CHAPTER THIRTY-FOUR

"What's your earliest memory?"

Let me tell you more

'What's your earliest memory?'

Normally, Nadejda would say 'Why?' to a question like this. But with Bojan, questions have a reason. She thinks. 'Probably my mother and father having a fight. You know, screaming at each other. It used to traumatise me a lot, in my childhood. Soon after that my best friend told me that her father hit her mother when they fought and I felt better.'

'Your parents fought often?'

'Yes. But that's normal. It wasn't because they didn't love each other.'

'No, of course not.'

Nadejda isn't sure if Bojan is being genuine or ironic. Her parents' fights are none of his business, she wants to say, but instead says: 'What's your earliest memory?'

'My earliest memory is the story I wanted to tell you.'

Nadejda is aware that this mock-confession session is in fact a strategy for getting at something other than earliest memories.

'I was with my father in the forest. He was a forester. He sometimes took me with him, in the donkey cart. We had a donkey called Toshko. I liked to ride Toshko. I would speak to him and he would nod his long head and chew. My father talked to him too. My mother made hot bread in the morning that made my mouth water. One morning, I woke up and there was no bread smell. I went into the kitchen, there was nobody around, no smells, no talk. I went into my parents' room, to wake them up. There, sitting in a corner on the floor, was my mother. She wasn't doing anything, just sitting and staring into space. I ran up to her. She gripped me and squeezed me very hard, hurting me, pressing my head into her bosom, and she made a sound I hadn't heard before. I thought she was singing some strange tune. But she was wailing.'

Bojan locks and unlocks his fingers. His face is calm, his eyes fixed on a time loophole. Nadejda is reminded of her mother's memories of the time when Vassil and their father disappeared — how her grandmother cried in the early morning, and little Ana was suffocated, soaked in her grief. 'What happened? Did your father leave you?'

'Yes. He was taken by the militia.'

288

Nadejda waits for an explanation. But Bojan is having a block — deliberate, perhaps. He smiles. His smiles unnerve Nadejda; they are the concessions of an extreme, self-conscious sadness towards those who can't even conceive of this sadness. Nadejda can't conceive of it perhaps, but she too, has her own sadnesses. Does Bojan realise that?

'He was an enemy of the people, of the same type as your uncle and grandfather. Except they didn't save anyone other than their own skins.'

'What do you mean? How do you know about that?'

'Through what happened to my father, through my mother's story. He was murdered. Executed, to be more precise. Or rather, it was a murder, because it was unofficial. It took place in a local militia station. They strangled him, though nobody knows what exactly happened. I think he died from torture.'

'What did he do?'

'He saved some people, some runaways. You see, he knew the border zone very well. The funny thing is, I was there with him on the day of their escape, but I don't remember a thing. In fact, nobody knows how he helped them, because he didn't have time to tell my mother before they took him.'

'Surely those people know. Are they alive?'

'One of them is.'

'But he was murdered just for that?'

'Yes.'

Nadejda leans back. Her throat is dry but she can't swallow. She is disgusted. Life is disgusting. People are disgusting. So much suffering for nothing. Rivers of blood, mountains of bodies, for nothing. Before she was born, and after she dies, there will be suffering for nothing, and she will have made no difference. Here they are, forty years on, having coffee and a nice conversation as if all is well.

Bojan leans forward and says very slowly and articulately, as if speaking to a foreigner: 'The people he helped cross the border were your uncle and grandfather.'

Nadejda looks at him and tilts her head, as if saying, 'Come on, stop pulling my leg' — but of course he isn't. They sit there for what could be only seconds — he waiting for Nadejda to accept what he has just said, and she ... she is not accepting it. She needs to swallow but can't. She needs to cry, but needing to swallow stops her. She wants to laugh at this lie, at this impossibility, at this irony, at this mockery. But she needs to cry too much to be able to laugh.

She wishes he would stop. But Bojan can't afford the luxury of stopping. 'I haven't finished my story,' he says, and there is a note of menace in his voice. It is as though he is saying, 'I haven't finished with you.'

Nadejda takes a breath and finally swallows. The need to cry and laugh has passed. Now she just prays to get out of here sane; she prays to wake up and for everything to be like before.

'Remember? We were talking about your grandmother.'

She remembers. All her life she has remembered her grandmother who she never met. Her shadow floats in the Pacific sky, never to rest. She can't forget her — and yet she can't remember her. Grandmother is a troubled dream of a storm.

'Yes.' Her voice is small. She hears it as if from the other end of a funnel. No, her voice is a funnel, and she falls inside. Falling, falling ...

'Your grandmother didn't know about my father, although she did know me for many years. When I found myself next to her on that plane to New Zealand, totally by chance, I felt I owed it to her to tell her. Of course she knew about Vassil and your grandfather crossing the border, she knew that Kosta, my father, helped them, but after she and your mother were deported to Deli Orman, she lost touch with everyone there. Or at least she thought she did. I was around all the time of course, but she never knew I was the son.'

'Why? Did you hide it from her on purpose?'

'I didn't. Ana ... But we'll come to this. The point is that when I told your grandmother what had happened, that my father was subsequently killed, she ... At first she didn't react badly. Then she got up to go to the toilet. I was surprised how well she was coping with the news. If I'd had time to think about it, I would've been nervous about her reaction. But it was all very spontaneous. After all, she'd known me for what, maybe twenty years, only to find out then. In any case, I wanted to make contact with Vassil and his father,

290

meet them at least, and tell them. It was fair that your grandmother knew first. She would be my connection with them when we arrived. I didn't expect anything from them, just to know that my mother was a widow and I was an orphan because of them. This sounds spiteful, I realise, but it wasn't like that. I had no grudges, or at least I thought so. Because it was more complicated still. There was something between me and . . . But anyway, she collapsed on her way to the toilet. Her face had gone white. The flight attendants must have thought she was afraid of flying. In any case, nothing could've been done; it turned out she had a heart attack, or rather a series of quick heart attacks. She was gone within minutes.'

The silence is complete. Nadejda desperately needs to empty her bladder. But she feels that she's never going to leave this couch. In moments like this, one just doesn't go to the toilet. Above her simmers a lampstand, an eye watching her from under its blue silk tassles. She is a growth on Bojan's couch, a bladder full of pain, a balloon-head full of hot air and tied to some lamp-post in the endless avenue of sunsets that is history. She has gone through life knowing nothing. Pissing, laughing, crying, climaxing, watching the waves, watching the calm ocean, dreaming and walking, waking and sleeping, she has sleep-stumbled through life.

'You can imagine how many times I've asked myself if she would have had that heart attack regardless of me. I went through stages when I told myself that whatever was meant to happen, happened; that nobody could be blamed. Then there were phases when I was sick with guilt and anxiety, sure I had caused her death. But then came the moments when I saw the entire picture: I could be blamed for what happened to Maria no more than the Naumovs could be blamed for what happened to my father. It's the death-lock of greater history and smaller destiny. You might ask how I feel about it now, twenty-one years later . . .'

'No,' says Nadejda. This is her first no. 'I'm not asking. I know how you feel.'

Bojan props his chin on his hand, still leaning forward, elbows on his knees. From the ever-deepening caves of his eyes, he blinks like an owl — once in a night.

'You feel relieved that you can tell me all this. And that relief   291 is the first step towards reconciliation.' She is defiant. She understands him. But why this irony? She hasn't even had time to decide whether she dislikes him now. Bojan looks down at the carpet like a reprimanded child. It's a nondescript carpet, nothing like Tarik's.

'What happened to the donkey?' It is as if all this time she's been missing the main point which is precisely this. Something always happens with the donkey.

'Toshko? He didn't speak, he understood. But he might as well have spoken. He stayed behind. We gave him to the neighbours when we left. I didn't cry for my father, but I cried for Toshko when I waved goodbye to him from the cattle wagons that took us away. I waved, and he waved his long ears. I think the whole sadness of parting is in the act of waving, you know . . . I would've cried for my father had I waved to him, had he waved and smiled at me, never to see me again. But he vanished without ritual, without a sign. I don't know what became of Toshko. Perhaps he died — he was like the shadow of my father.'

'Unless shadows have a life of their own,' says Nadejda. When her uncle and her mother had their regular discussion about him going back to visit, he said, 'I will only find a place full of shadows,' and her mother said, 'Shadows too have a life of their own.'

Bojan smiles, for the first time in hours, it seems. 'You are one smart devil.'

'I must go to the toilet, excuse me,' says Nadejda, and heads for the door. She has known him for a lifetime, somebody else's lifetime. Like an object that has always been lying around but that she never took the time to inspect. Now, finally, she has walked into him, and bruised herself. She turns the light-switch on.

The doorbell rings. So she was right about that late visit he was expecting. Interesting to see — maybe he has a girlfriend. She notices that drawing again, above the bath. No, it's a photograph. It's both. She flushes the toilet and gets up to study the picture. A nude behind pale blue glass. She is reaching for her foot, or something like that. Her hair is long and wavy, like the hair of all nudes should be (except Tarik's sneering nude who had a boyish haircut). She is looking at the viewer, mischievously, disarmingly, from under her fringe. Her face is pretty, her face is . . . No, that's not right. Nadejda's heart stops. It's Nadejda's face. Nadejda looking at Nadejda. No, impossible. Feverishly, she inspects the body. It isn't her body. The breasts are too small, the hips are too wide, the hair is too wavy. It's not her. It's not her. But it's her.

What if this is some sort of trap? What if Bojan is a psychopath, making up this story. But what for? Now he is with someone. Maybe she should stay here, lock herself in, before it's too late, barricade herself and think of getting away. No, she's tired. Her imagination is working overtime. She looks at the picture again. It's her face. It's not her body. What is he hiding? This series of coincidences is too unlikely. She leaves the light on and steps out. In the house there is silence. A wave of cool air laps at her from the room where she is supposed to sleep. Needles in her feet. Lightning in her head.

In the lounge, there is a strange composition: her mother and Bojan, standing a few metres away from each other. They look at Nadejda with faraway eyes, without a movement, as if they are both under water and she is bending over the surface, to see if they are drowned yet.

Chapter Thirty-four

*The three figures form an
equilateral triangle.*

Reconnaissance

The three figures form an equilateral triangle. It is as if they are standing on three islands, gazing over across to the other.

Ana steps off her island and sinks. 'Nadejda,' she says and it sounds like an echo.

She takes a step towards Nadejda, but then retreats and leans on the old-fashioned papered wall. She crosses her arms, to stop herself from reaching out.

'Mum,' says Nadejda's echo and her chin trembles. She feels pathetic. She feels like that time at the pioneer camp when she called her mother, and she and her father drove over and saved her.

'She looks like you,' says Bojan and his face shakes so badly as if his tidy features are about to collapse back into some original chaos — a handful of eyebrows and nostrils, lips and round eyes.

'There is a photo of me in the bathroom,' says Nadejda feebly and looks at her mother, then at Bojan.

Ana is looking at Bojan. Bojan is looking at Ana. As if trying to remember something, as if trying to remember each other.

'She looks like me too,' says Bojan.

'You see what you want to see,' says Ana softly.

'There is a photo of me in the bathroom,' says Nadejda in the same flat voice. The other two are crashed and lost in the desert. They are looking at the invisible remnants of a smouldering aircraft.

'I see more than you see,' says Bojan.

'I have seen enough not to want to see more,' says Ana. 'What have you told her?'

'What she needs to know.' He glances over to Nadejda warily.

'She needs to know the truth,' says Ana and uncrosses her arms.

'What truth?' asks Nadejda.

'About me and Bojan.'

'Ana,' says Bojan and steps off his mount, 'why didn't you want to talk to me when I called you?'

'Because I was afraid. I was afraid Vassil would find out about you, about what happened to your father.'

'You mean you haven't told him yet?'

'No.'

'Why, Ana?' He seems to take special pleasure in saying   295 her name. 'Don't you think he should know what happened?'

Ana turns away abruptly, like a grumpy child. 'It's too late now,' she says in a subdued voice.

'Can someone explain?'

They turn to her at once. 'Well, Nadejda, among other things, your uncle has died,' says Ana.

Now Bojan and Nadejda turn to Ana, and they look as if they are under water, moving their lips silently, trying to say something. Ana leans her head on the monstrous paper-wall (huge carnivorous flowers on a blurry background) and fixes Nadejda with her green eyes, which are darkening by the second. Nadejda asks the obvious question asked in such situations, as if the details would tone down the news. 'How?'

'Heart attack.'

'That's dreadful,' says Bojan and steps towards Ana, lifting his arm as if to stroke her. But she doesn't notice him. He freezes.

'How?' says Nadejda again.

'I'd like to know that myself. He was on the phone.'

'To who?'

'To you.'

Suddenly Bojan lets out an unnatural laugh. It is the dry, unamused laughter that accompanies the discovery of some gruesome coincidence. It is a chilling, indecent, ironic laugh which stops as abruptly as it started, like a rotten trunk cut off with an electric saw. Nadejda dashes between them, pushes the front door open and is gone.

Ana rushes after her. Bojan rushes after her, because he has been waiting for this for twenty-one years.

'Nadejda!' cries Ana into the summer darkness. 'It wasn't your fault! It wasn't your fault!'

'Ana!' cries Bojan. 'She's my child! I've known it for years. Now I see it with my own eyes! Listen to me!'

Slumped against a tree, Nadejda is wailing the way all the women before her wailed.

CHAPTER THIRTY-SIX

I've been silent for so many years,
Ana.

The voices

I've been silent for so many years, Ana. Listen to me for once. I'm sorry about Vassil.

I didn't tell Vassil because I was afraid he couldn't live with the guilt.

How do you think I live with the guilt?

He was a child when it happened. He was not responsible, he and father couldn't have known.

I too couldn't have known.

What? You knew exactly what it meant to be an informer, to betray people like your own father, like my . . .

Yes, I know. I'm not talking about that. It's something else, it's what happened when . . .

You've changed a lot, Bojo.

And you haven't. The same face, the same hair. Age has been kind to you.

That's about the only thing that's been kind. I have to find Nadejda — she mustn't think it was her fault.

What, Vassil's death?

Yes. It was the same way Mum died, heart attack.

You didn't have that abortion in the end, did you?

No. But that doesn't mean that you are the father.

How do you know I'm not?

A mother knows these things.

Did you tell Mladen?

No, never.

So he's always believed that she is his daughter?

Yes.

And you never bothered to correct him. I know she is mine. I can tell you how I know. Remember that lightning? Mario, the storm, the tree. Remember?

Of course I remember.

Remember how I was thirsty for weeks after that? That wasn't all. Something else happened, but only years later I started seeing things, things that had already happened, and were happening. I swear, I saw my father, how he was tortured and died, I saw my mother, after she died, she talked to me. And listen to this, I knew how Nadejda looked before I saw her tonight. Before I saw her! I saw her in my mind, I saw

298

her for the first time when I went back, in 1990, after the changes. I went to my parents' graves. I went to the Ludogorie, to see the family we lived with, and your family. Remember Feride? She was called Marina, after the name-changes. Now she's Feride again. She's got three kids. You know what happened to them? She was raped by the militia, in front of her husband, and so was her teenage daughter. Then they left for Turkey. Can you imagine, Ani. It's monstrous. While I was there, in Ludogorie, I felt Nadejda. She was in Sofia then, no doubt, or maybe in Plovdiv? I fled, I was terrified. I came back here sooner than I had planned. I didn't want to be part of your lives, I was still full of bitterness. I was frightened too. Then you two came over. And it started again. I feel her. There's no getting away, we end up together, we end up the way we belong, the way we deserve. She is my blood, do you understand?

I don't believe you.

Why? Why don't you believe me? The past is gone, no more lies, I'm telling you.

Nadeeeeee! Nadeeeee!

For so long, I tried to stay out of your way, to forget you, your bloody family which brought me nothing but horror and sadness. You know, I could've told Vassil everything, I could've done it in spite of you. But he wouldn't listen. Do you know that I called him, before you and Nadejda came? I wanted to explain about your mother, about us, about my father, the whole story, but he hung up on me. He hung up on me! Your brother didn't want to know me! And you didn't bother to tell him. You didn't care.

I did care. But I cared about him too. He has suffered so much. He too had a weak heart. What was that about my mother?

I saw her die, Ina. I was on the plane with her.

Chapter Thirty-six

CHAPTER THIRTY-SEVEN

This is the space in which
Nadejda's grandmother would
have spoken, if she could.

The dead

This is the space in which Nadejda's grandmother would have spoken, if she could. Or even her grandfather, though he wasn't very articulate. But the dead have no voice. The dead have no rights. Their story is always told by someone else.

Chapter Thirty-seven

Epilogue

We returned to Bojan's house. They were arguing the whole way. Mum wanted to leave immediately. She was afraid he might do something, I don't know what. But we went back inside and they sat carefully, the way Bojan had sat a few hours earlier, as if the armchairs were alive and they didn't want to hurt them. I was so exhausted I slumped on the couch and didn't move until the morning. Just sat there. Maybe I slept.

Much was said. No blood was shed, except verbally. For hours they went on, accusing each other, then blaming themselves, then asking for forgiveness, then trying to explain what had already been explained. It was hard to tell whether they were explaining to me, to each other, or to themselves. At first, Mum was censoring her words, but she soon realised it was useless — I already knew enough to deduce the rest. That night I realised that my mother had never been fully honest with anyone; that for her to love meant to hide as much as possible. She loved her mother, so she didn't tell her who Bojan was. Likewise, she loved Vassil. She loved Dad, and so she never told him that she'd slept with Bojan when Dad was away for a week. She loved me and so she never told me anything except about her life in the Mad Forest — naturally leaving Bojan out. She spared everyone; she hurt everyone. And most of all, of course, Bojan. She loved him the most. He loved her the most. He did the same to her.

I didn't even have time to ask any questions. The explanations came out by themselves: bizarre, discrepant explanations. Why was Mum so inflexible when she found out about Bojan's activities, after Prague '68? Because it was the ultimate betrayal of what his own father had died for; it was like spitting not only on his father's grave, but on both families' suffering. He went over to the enemy's camp — he became what he and Mum had hated all their lives, a pawn of the system. But perhaps she wouldn't have been so inflexible if she hadn't met Dad. And why wasn't she just as inflexible about Dad killing the student in Prague? He did it by mistake, but does that make it any less hateful? I think it was just that Mum fell out of love with Bojan. When you're not in love with someone, they can never do right. Besides, Dad didn't do it by mistake. He did it because he didn't question enough.

Why did Bojan become an informer to start with? Because he

303

desperately wanted to leave the country and knew that was the only way; he wanted to leave the country because, among other things, he was heartbroken by Mum. But by the time she and Dad got together, he was already a party valet.

Why did Mum sleep with Bojan that last time, despite the fact that she had cut all bridges with him and made Dad do the same — with his best friend of six years? Because she still loved him. She loved both of them. I can understand that. Then she called Bojan in the middle of the night, two months later, to tell him that she was pregnant but wasn't having the child because it could be his. Why? Because she was full of guilt towards Dad and so took revenge on Bojan who apparently had cajoled her that night into something she didn't intend to do. But she knew she couldn't have an abortion; Bojan knew it too.

Why did Bojan go to her that night? In the hope of talking to her, explaining why he was doing what he was doing, try to win her back. But he ended up sleeping with her only. He won back only her despair and accusations. He was as faithful a best friend as Dad was to him. Of course, Dad had already set up a precedent. Sometimes I wonder if Dad doesn't suspect that something happened then while he was away. Sometimes I wonder whether they could have done things differently, in a less ugly way. But I don't blame them. They lived in an ugly time when every choice was a bad choice.

That night I lay on the couch, concentrating on several things: not thinking of Bojan as my father, remaining vaguely sane, and not sinking into the huge, stinking stir-up of bones. The main theme of the lively exchange between Mum and Bojan was, 'Who is more guilty, who has suffered more?' The eternal Balkan question, accusingly thrown at the enemy who was your best friend only yesterday.

But I didn't say or unsay anything. I listened.

I have one question: What is worse — having everything or having nothing? Am I unhappy because I have everything, or because I have nothing?

I have two fathers, for example. Mum denies that Bojan could be my father. At the time, she probably couldn't have had tests. And abortions were banned back then. Bojan considers me his only family, which means that he either knows the truth or wants to believe his own truth, like everyone. He has the same blood group as Dad. I look at myself in the mirror, trying to decide which father I resemble more. But the truth is, I can see only some resemblance to Uncle. I've never looked much like Dad. I take after Mum's family. As to Bojan, he is unique. I can't imagine anyone looking like him.

Every time I take the ferry down from Wellington to see Bojan, I feel guilty towards Dad. I have written to him, a reply to his letter which arrived all torn up and open, but I didn't tell him about Bojan. I will soon, when I gather enough guts. He told me about Bojan in his letter; I owe him the same. I love him more than anyone and that will never change. I don't care about the dumb biology of it. Bojan is touchingly happy to see me every time, and he doesn't insist on his fatherhood any more. But I sense a calm certainty in him. He is a strange man. I don't think I'll ever understand him.

Mum is tense whenever I go to see him, but she has accepted that there is some connection between us. We have become the closest strangers. She never comes with me. They speak on the phone, sometimes, and Mum always cries afterwards. I feel ill at the thought of them having a child. I am not that child. Mum and Dad never speak on the phone. They spoke only that one time before Mum drove up to Nelson. Now I know Dad will never come as long as Bojan is here, as long as Mum is here, as long as I am here. Dad won't go anywhere.

Sometimes I look after Bojan's shop. It's a fascinating place. I dust the quirky objects, the guns, the stuffed animals, the crystals, the nineteenth-century footrests. He says I can have the shop one day, if I want it. He says I can have everything. I never know how to take what he says. At least I know he's telling the truth. That's a rare commodity in this family.

Today, Mum and I are standing on a hill overlooking the wilderness of Stewart Island, the southernmost inhabited island in the Pacific, or so I'd like to think. I take a tiny handful of ash and offer it to the

305

wind, like crumbs to a giant bird. Uncle was a big man, but his ashes are so little. I follow the fine dust. It has its own course above the ocean. Uncle is flying towards Antarctica. He is moving, only he doesn't know it. I wish he knew it.

I don't think I'll ever be rid of the guilt, even if Mum has forgiven me. Even when the whole world forgives me, officially, I'll still wake up in the middle of the night, outside in the garden, or in the kitchen, or in my own bed, from the excruciating effort of saying, 'Uncle, I'm here, I'm coming, I'm back!' And I shout it night after night, I replay countless times the tape that he recorded for me, and I imagine the follow-up, I erase the desolate dialling tone, the thump of his body on the carpet, I fill the tape with more of his voice, alive and precious. We play chess. We drive his new car. I am sorry. I am sorry.

Now half of his ashes are gone. Mum is silent. The island is silent. Half are still in the urn. They will fly over the Pirin mountains, the home of his heart. I ask Bojan, every time, if he can see Uncle. But he can't. He says he only sees me, but less and less, probably because he sees me for real. I have tried to 'see' Uncle too. Mum says it's better not to see. Bojan says he sees the truth. They are both wrong, as usual. We are all wrong.

I wish I could freeze the Pacific of time into an iceberg, then break it up into millions of icicles with an axe, melt them down and start again in the new ocean. Like Noah's ship, I would put everybody aboard and get afloat, in a different direction this time. Everybody would say what should have been said, do what should have been done. Everybody would be there, not their ghosts.

But the ocean doesn't freeze. The lake, yes; the river, yes; the sea, yes; the earth freezes. But not the Pacific. And so we can't stop moving, we can't stop dying, we can't stop living.

For as long as someone is here to see it, the puzzle of the Pacific is complete. Nothing is a dream although I never wake up. Nothing is healed although there are stitches of light on the torn water.

having words with you

having words with you

stories that stalk you from the moment you turn your back

Sarah Quigley

You crunch out of your row to let him sit beside your best friend. His entrance, your exit. You feel a jab somewhere near the heart.

Meet the fabulous gourmand whose meal is ruined by the carping of his one-time lover; the teenager who errs in introducing her new girlfriend to her father; the stand-up comic whose words fail at a mystery woman's invitation. These stories are in-your-face and unrepentant, showing sides of human nature which may make us uneasy but which we all share.

Rich with the incredible strangeness of daily life, this first collection is a twilight tour of the things that drive us to distraction: lovers and solitude, fears and fantasies — our private obsessions.